EXODUS

ONE SMALL STEP ᴼᵁᵀ ᴼᶠ THE GARDEN OF EDEN ™

Series

Part One: Call of Destiny

Part Two: Chasing Tyranny

Part Three: Exodus

EXODUS

Being the third part of

ONE SMALL STEP OUT OF THE GARDEN OF EDEN

Robert Wagoner

Beechstreet Publishing
Vermont

Exodus

A Beechstreet Publishing Publication

ISBN: 978-0-9826285-2-2

Printed in the United States of America

First edition, printed April, 2011

To my wife and children.

i. Another Mission

"So, have you heard the rumors?" Michael Gillen inquired.

"What rumors?"

"About the Weightless?*"*

Tom nodded no.

"Sounds pretty bad," Michael sighed. "Death counts into the hundreds of thousands—maybe millions; women and children rounded up with the men—whole cities eradicated in some cases."

*   *   *   *   *   *   *

... Michael beheld the unusual ship sitting on its moorings. ... The vessel was a long-range mission ship. "She's beautiful. Where did she come from?"

"The Europans—at least the design. ... The Europans discovered Slipstream propulsion. ... They constructed a massive generation ship with Slipstream capabilities. Aurelian Galerius used the ship to escape to 18 Scorpii. ... The Weightless *want Galerius brought to justice. Mos Thieren will fund the post-war rebuilding—but only if we bring Aurelian Galerius back for trial." Cyril looked him in the eye. "We need* you *to bring Galerius back."*

Michael turned inconsolable.

"If we don't secure Thieren's funds," Cyril pleaded, "Terrae Solaris will collapse. Your country needs you. The President is personally asking for you."

"I'm not sure I can help the likes of Mos Thieren ... too much history ... too much bad blood."

Cyril's gaze pleaded that much more. "Mike, I need your help."

ii. A Hero

... President James Mitchell emerged from the group. Michael saw that the man's larger-than-life persona was no fabrication of television. No, Mitchell was stately in appearance, having a natural grace and charisma that beckoned respect. He radiated an assuring confidence and swagger beyond that of a mere man, while in his blue eyes lay a sense of deep conscience and conviction. In the presence of such a great man, the young captain was tempted to bow.

... President Mitchell moved in closer and put his hand on his shoulder. "Michael, do you understand why you're here?"

"Not really, Sir."

"18 Scorpii is the key to securing Mos Thieren's funding of our postwar rebuilding efforts. Without rebuilding, the whole system will collapse." He looked Michael squarely in the eyes. "I desperately need your help once again."

iii. A Cretin

... Mos Thieren's face waxed over dejectedly; President Mitchell had backed him into a corner. The odd-looking Weightless *had nowhere to go ... until he glanced at Michael—and with such a gleam in his eyes.*

"We Weightless *are no longer viewed as humans. Because of gravity, we are despised. Gravity gave Aurelian Galerius his platform. Now, millions of my people are dead—all because of ... the man who betrayed his own people: Jonathan Gillen.*

"... My grandfather warned him ... but Jonathan Gillen didn't listen. Before he submitted to genetic reengineering, he was a Weightless. *He thought weightlessness was a curse! He betrayed his own people ... and he is to blame for the atrocities as much as Galerius. So, what are you going to do to make amends?"*

iv. An Old Friend

... Michael had not seen Tom Andrews since that fateful day on the Comanche *three years earlier. After waking up in an Europan medivac hospital, the young captain found Tom and the rest of the surviving crew gone. His captors told him nothing, except he was alive only because of a stubborn, loud-mouthed, and impatient first officer. So Michael owed Tom for saving his life.*

* * * * * * *

... Tom—a slightly perplexed look coming over him—said, "Kate is why I can't understand your eagerness to jump back into exploration. You barely had a honeymoon. Just stay home and make babies. That's what I would do—well, if I were you, of course."

v. A Reluctant Wife

"... Michael, you've got to tell them no," Kate Gillen pleaded.

"If we don't agree to the mission, things are going to get worse."

"... I'm not the same person that I was five years ago. Things change."

"You can't mean that," he pleaded.

"You of all people shouldn't be surprised," she chided him. "You're the one who cloistered me away for five years, while you put yourself in danger on the front lines. I stayed back here like the good little newlywed housewife, worrying about you—waiting for your return so my life could start. I want a normal life now ... to be a wife ... to have children."

... She flashed him a reproving grimace. "At least this time you're not planning on leaving me behind."

vi. A Man Possessed

"... That was my family—my pride and joy," Emir Kern said, losing himself in the picture. "My wife, Maddison, and our children, Nicholas and Anna."

"You were married?" Kara Ricci asked, surprised.

"All the Coverts had families. We were stationed at Ceres Fleet Base long before the war. We were like one big, happy family." The warmth drained from his face. "But then the Europans attacked. While my men and I were out defending the base, the goons firebombed our residences. Everyone burned to death. It should have been us."

"... Is that why you're here? For revenge against Galerius?"

"You have to admit," Emir quipped self-consciously, "It's the second chance of a lifetime."

vii. A Mission Gone Awry

"... Kara," Michael shot back. "What's going on?"

"Fine," Kara huffed. "We weren't in stasis twenty-three years. It was more like ten years. ... And we only have enough fuel for one or two light-years at the most."

"We're stranded?" Kate gasped.

* * * * * * * *

... Mark Armstrong's vitals declined rapidly—far faster than Kara could intervene. ... His sinus rhythm flat-lined altogether. Despite her best efforts, nothing changed the grim patterns displaying on his monitors. Reluctantly, the young physician relented her fevered pace until stopping altogether. She threw down the instruments in defeat.

Mark Armstrong was dead.

* * * * * * * *

"... Someone tampered with the engines," Kate said. "That's why we arrived early."

"Kern," Michael seethed, staring at the irrefutable and troubling evidence.

"... We have a conspirator aboard. Someone's trying to scuttle the ship."

... Finally, he looked her squarely in the eyes. "If the Coverts want to destroy the ship ... we'll let them."

* * * * * * * *

... Kate sounded out the demise of the Endurance: *hull temperatures rising, radiation breaching the shielding, critical support systems disabling, and the like. The transmission grew more garbled as the disaster played out. Eventually, the transmission stopped altogether.*

The Endurance *was gone.*

... When everyone else had left, Kate gave Michael a rather serious sigh. "I hope you made the right decision."

"Me too."

viii. A New Threat

... The odd-looking creature stared down at Brent Tasker and Glen Volk menacingly. The creature towered almost four meters tall. Its mass was four to five times that of the sizeable Tasker, who easily fell into its hulking shadow. Its massive frame lay covered in thick, dark, creviced skin with matted hair all over. Thick muscles layered down its overly large arms and legs; the same with its torso garbed in rags. The creature's mostly bald head was of smaller proportion to its body, boasting a prominent forehead, sunken in eyes that brooded, and an oversized, rock-like jaw. The only sign of civility in the beast was a metal collar around its thick neck. The collar glowed as if it were some sort of restraining device.

* * * * * * *

"... We have a serious problem," Glen Volk announced.

... Three thousand warships sat packed together in long rows. A partially constructed fueling tower sat in the center. *"... These ships have retractable Slipstream nodes built into their hulls. ... That puts this fleet within two to three years of Solaris."*

"... Aurelian Galerius came here to regroup," Michael declared. *"To strike while Terrae Solaris remains bogged down in rebuilding efforts. The Allies are sitting ducks."*

"This fleet will be operational within two months."

"Before leaving 18 Scorpii," Michael looked at them, *"We will destroy that fleet."*

ix. An Untimely Attraction

"... Promise me you'll take Galerius back for trial," Kara pleaded.

Emir's face sobered. *"Kara, don't ask me to do that."*

"... But Michael will try to stop you. We could all end up dead."

"I'm okay with that."

The terrible truth hit her. *"You want to die!"*

"... I know you want more from me," Emir offered. *"I'm sorry. I can't give you more."* He watched her tears trail down her cheek and over his fingers. *"We still have tonight ... before everything changes."*

Kara gazed at him—pitying him. Nervously, her fingers played with the heart-shaped locket hanging from her neck. Finally, she shook her head sadly. *"That's not enough. That's never enough."*

With one last pleading look, the young woman stole away.

x. An Ambush

"... Stop this!" Kara cried out, hurrying around the perimeter of the standoff between the Coverts and Centauries. *"Emir, put down your gun! Michael, you too!"* When neither man relented, she pleaded once more, *"We're all on the same side!"*

... *Kara drew her pistol and seized Aurelian Galerius in a chokehold. "Put down your weapons, or I'll kill him myself."*

"Kara, don't do this," Michael warned.

... *Emir Kern raised the remote detonator in his grip. "This ends here, Gillen. Since you won't see things my way, we'll all go up in flames."*

... *The shriek of an energy blast ripped the tense silence! Aurelian Galerius slumped over onto the ground and died.*

Kara Ricci had executed him.

xi. A Trap

... *Amidst the chaos surrounding the moment—weapons fire suddenly broke the air! Europan troops appeared from the west. At the same time, other troops rushed over the bluff in the direction of the Coverts to the north. Weapons fire echoing from just over the bluff soon followed.*

The Centauries looked at each other desperately: They were in grave danger!

* * * * * * * *

... *A massive concussion rocked the entire area, and Kate looked on in horror! The high wall towering over Michael exploded! Massive rocks fell headlong, crushing the transport and burying the entire area! ... Mortified, Kate rushed to Michael. However, not too many steps out, Kate slumped to the ground unconscious. She had been hit from behind.*

* * * * * * * *

... *Kara watched Tom disappear over the hillside with the two Europans.*

... *A solitary gun blast pierced the silence! ... Another shot broke the air from the same direction!*

... *The Europan commander appeared at the top of the hillside. A guard followed him. Both men proceeded along, unfazed by whatever had happened above.*

Kara conceded that Tom and Kate were dead.

* * * * * * * *

... *Aurelian Galerius—very much alive and well—emerged from the transport.*

Kara looked over at the dead body lying at the ambush point. She had not killed Aurelian Galerius—she had murdered an innocent man!

"... If you were hoping to die today, that won't happen," Galerius exclaimed. "... You will *(eventually) be executed. But until then, you will be treated like the murderer you are."*

* * * * * * * *

... The escorts stepped aside, directing Phil Marcotte and David Tashjian through the entryway. The lavish suite bordered on the extravagant. Marcotte and Tashjian nervously paced, waiting for the dignitary that owned the residence to appear.

"Here are your quarters," the lead guard stated, "—compliments of Aurelian Galerius."

The two men looked at each other quizzically.

... When the guards left, Marcotte turned to his companion, "Shouldn't we be dead?"

* * * * * * * *

... The Coverts rushed into the base camp cavern—and came to a sudden halt!

The Aurora, loaded with most of their munitions and supplies, was gone.

"... We'll take the land craft and go into the mountains," Emir Kern declared.

... The Coverts rushed out of the cave and jumped into the land craft for a quick escape. But Emir stopped and put his ear squarely to the air. ... All of them heard the sounds of approaching troops and vehicles in the distance.

* * * * * * * *

... Kate Gillen opened her eyes ... she recognized her position: the notch carved into the top of the bluff. Tom Andrews lay unconscious well behind her—a gaping wound in his upper right chest caught her eye.

... When Andrews stirred, she gently slapped his face. "Tom, wake up! Where is everyone?"

"... Gone. Two squads showed up and flanked Kara, Phil, and David. Kern and his team surrendered. That's when the Europans executed everyone."

Four Europan soldiers appeared directly behind them. "Drop your weapons, or you're dead!"

* * * * * * * *

... Tom sat down beside her in the shadows against the wall of their prison cell. Ignoring the pain in his chest, he wrapped his good arm around her and watched the first few tears trail down her cheek.

"I miss Michael," she sobbed. "I miss our friends. I can't believe they're gone."

"Me too, Sunshine ... me too."

Kate leaned in toward Tom and hid her face in the crook of his neck. Nestled safely within his reassuring embrace, the young woman fell to pieces.

While he prepared himself to keep a long vigil with Kate, Tom's thoughts returned to the hillside overlook, just after the Europans had captured Kara, Phil, David, and him. He stung from his deception ... and he found himself at a loss over how to undo its impact. ... But Tom eventually realized he found no allure in undoing the deception—at least not right then. No, the deception was necessary. And as he looked down at Kate nestled against him and crying on his shoulder, he knew it was for her own good.

A LOOK BACK

CHAPTER ONE

Trajan

The beautiful woman followed the servant down the main hall of the lavish residence, keeping a reassuring arm around her seven-year-old son walking at her side. With ice-blue eyes that churned uneasily, she took in the extravagant dwelling in awe, and her anxious thoughts returned to that fateful day eight years earlier when she had fled Europa.

Her journey through the capitol city had not assuaged her concerns. Nothing had really changed in Tyre since her escape. Of course, some things *had* changed. The rioters were long gone, as were the many problems that had fueled the unrest of that era. A tenuous peace blanketed the city instead, and its citizens went about their business as if those turbulent days had never occurred. She even sensed an emerging pride among the people, a nationalism the Jovian moon had not seen for some time. The dark times that were coming upon Europa—and all of Terrae Solaris—were still far into the future.

But for her, everything had already changed for the worse.

The servant led them to a beautiful mahogany door and opened it.

"Sir," the man called into the room behind the door, "The visitors you were expecting are here."

"Send them in," came a familiar voice from inside, causing the servant to step aside and gesture for her and the boy to enter.

With her arm still draped over the young lad, she took a deep, anxious breath and escorted him inside. At first sight of the man garbed in his ranking senators' regalia, she forced a warm smile. Not that she was unhappy to see him again. No, not at all. Just the sight of him brought to mind fond memories and deep emotions.

But what lay ahead troubled her so.

"Livia!" he greeted as she crossed the large room. Taking in her countenance, her striking features, and pleasing form, he smiled a familiar smile. "I never thought I would see you again." But his eyes looked immediately to the seven-year-old, and his face beamed.

The senator's relishing smile did not assuage her trepidation. Coming to stand in front of her husband, she saw the nervousness building in her son's eyes; the boy had such an intuition about him. So she offered an assuring smile. "Trajan, I'd like you to meet your father"—when the boy looked up at her in defiance—"... your *real* father."

"Hello Trajan," the senator greeted him, kneeling and taking in the sight of the lad with such pride. "I've waited *so long* to meet you. I've seen your pictures, but they don't do you justice. You're a handsome, young man—and very capable, I've heard."

However, young Trajan simply stared back at the stranger.

"*Trajan*," Livia goaded the boy, "Greet your father."

Trajan remained nervous but defiant as he stood eye to eye with the strange man. Finally, he said, "Hello, Sir."

"Hello, *Father*," she corrected him.

The senator shook his head at her and smiled back at the boy. "*Sir* is good enough for now. I'm sure this is a lot for you to take in all at once." He gestured to the expensive toys heaped atop a table at the far end of the room. "Those are for you." Though young Trajan looked at the toys with a gleam in his eyes, he stayed beside his mother. "*Go ahead.*"

Trajan hesitated, until curiosity got the best of him. Mustering his courage, he set off for the table and indulged himself in play.

Watching the lad fall under the spell of the many trinkets, the senator offered a contented sigh, stood, and gestured for Livia to join him at the observation window. When they came to stand there together, he beamed with pride once more. "What do you think of the view?"

Livia looked out at the city of Tyre stretching all the way to the horizon, particularly taking in the sight of the Parliament building in the distance. Jupiter hung prominently in the pitch-black sky, as if keeping watch over the city. "It reminds me of the view from our old apartment— though this place is a far cry from that broken down efficiency." She fixed her gaze upon him once more, the warmth growing in her eyes— though her trepidation remained. "I read the announcement of your appointment to ranking senator. Now, no one can question your status as a noble."

"Certainly not the outcome I was expecting when we parted so long ago."

They traded sentimental gazes in silence, taking in the years of separation and the subtle changes in each other's appearance.

"Did you ever remarry?" she asked after a nervous hesitation.

"No, I always had too much work to do—and no one could match your memory." He let his words linger. When sadness crept into her gaze, he pressed, "What about you? Was your Terran husband good to you?"

"Yes ... but he wasn't you."

"Was he a good father to Trajan?"

Livia turned and watched the boy playing on the far side of the room. She rather smiled. "Yes. He never knew Trajan wasn't his child, and so he focused all his attention on him." The uneasiness returned to her face once again, and she looked him straight in the eyes. "That's the problem ... and that's why I had to bring him here."

But the senator's face sobered. "You shouldn't have—*not right now at least.* The Prime Minister still holds power, despite all my attempts to expel him from office. If he figures out how to disgrace me, I become a fugitive again. You've put Trajan in danger by bringing him here."

"I had no choice. *Look at him.* Life on Earth and his surrogate father is all he knows." She paused, her face filling with regret. "He's a *Terran.* If something isn't done soon, there will be no turning back for him."

3

The senator fixed his gaze upon the boy, who remained preoccupied and at play at the table out of earshot. The man kept that way for some time. "Yes, I noticed that vile accent in his voice—and that weak, Terran demeanor."

"He *has* a softer side. That's my fault." After watching Trajan through an awkward silence, she turned back to her husband. "How could he ever exercise his right of succession? Europan law forbids such a transfer of nobility to him. No, he must *become* Europan."

"But why didn't you send him here with someone else? Why did you put yourself in danger? And me in such a difficult position?"

Livia dropped her head and fell silent for the longest time. She leaned in close to him too, even taking hold of his arm while fighting the strong emotions washing over her. Finally, she lifted her eyes, which swam in the first of her tears. "He doesn't need me anymore. He needs *you.*" She looked at him with such longing, and her mouth twisted into a sentimental smile. But her countenance fell. "And this matter between you and me ... it needs to be settled the Europan way—a way that will assure Trajan's right of succession."

The senator's face filled with dread. *"No."*

"You have no choice, my love. That's why I came here myself."

Withering under her resolve, the senator waxed pensive and joined his wife in watching their son play in blissful ignorance. "I'll protect him. I'll keep him out of the public eye—isolated from my wait staff too. No one will even know he's my son until the time comes for him to take his place. He'll be *Europan.* I promise."

Livia, the tears trailing down her cheeks, took him in her arms and kissed him with such passion. Even after parting, she held him in a long embrace and whispered, *"I never stopped loving you."*

"I can't do this," the man shook his head, keeping her in his arms. When she tried to pull away, he only tightened his grasp.

Nevertheless, she pushed away from him. "Delaying won't help."

From where he stood off to himself at the table, young Trajan remained deeply engrossed in the many toys holding his attention. Some of the toys sparked a familiar enthusiasm: His father—not the man across the room—had already given them to him as gifts. Other toys—strange toys, the likes of which he had never seen—lay among the more familiar ones. Those toys struck his curiosity, so he could play for hours. He almost forgot where he was.

"Trajan," he heard his mother calling from behind him. He didn't want to turn. No, he was too preoccupied. And that name—he hated it. *Trajan* was an unfamiliar name—an odd name—that she only started using the day she took him from Earth.

"*Trajan.*"

Reluctantly, he turned. Young Trajan beheld his mother wiping tears from her eyes. With the sight cutting him to the quick, he rushed over to where she knelt, paying no attention to the strange man walking over to the desk behind him.

"I have to leave you now," Livia said haltingly, taking Trajan into a tight embrace.

"Take me with you."

She patted him on the back when he locked his arms around her. "It's okay. I'm leaving you here with your father. He's a good man, and he'll teach you so much about who you really are." Withdrawing from young Trajan's defiant grip, she took his hands in hers and looked him straight in the eyes. "Promise me you'll listen to him."

"*I want to go with you. I want to go home.*"

"This is your home now."

The seven-year-old, tears running down his cheeks, looked up as the strange man came to stand over him. Trajan noticed just how unsettled he appeared, despite the reassuring smile shooting down at him.

"Promise me you'll do whatever your father tells you," Livia pressed. When Trajan offered a reluctant nod, she waxed over in a warm smile. "I'm so proud of you." She took his small hand and placed it into the senator's free hand. "I love you *so* much; never forget that."

When Trajan looked up, he spied the pistol in the man's left hand. The young boy assumed it was another toy for him to play with.

He didn't know the pistol was real.

Neither did the boy know his mother would die just minutes later— when young Trajan intentionally fired the fatal shot that would kill her.

CHAPTER TWO

Fallen Rock, Fallen Hero

A distressed Michael Gillen awoke from unconsciousness into unrelenting darkness. He heard the muffled sounds of someone groaning in pain—eventually recognizing the tortured voice as his own. However, the notion barely registered. Instead, he lay in a half-conscious stupor, and a surreal fog covered him as if deep waters. Suffering under a maddening disorientation, he considered that perhaps he was dreaming—maybe he was dead. He really didn't know.

Incredible pain!

He gasped in agony!—but excruciating pain from his broken ribs stopped him mid-gasp! A wave of intense pain, made more unbearable by the darkness, overwhelmed him. Desperate for consolation and terribly uncomfortable lying down, he shot up to sit—but his face smashed against unseen rock just a hand's length away! The painful concussion bounced his head backward. Once more, Michael lay flat on his back and in terrible pain.

Where am I? he thought, the darkness imposing a surreal trepidation upon him.

The young man came back to himself that very second—as did the urgency of his predicament. "*Kate!*"

The injured twenty-nine-year-old reached with his left hand to his side—

The thick of the arm immediately burned white-hot with pain!

"*Ahhhhhh!*" he screamed through gnashed teeth, his whole body rigid against the agony.

Images of the high wall explosion flooded his thoughts, mocking him. Falling rock had snapped the bone in his left arm cleanly in two. Painful bruises from a hailstorm of stones that had knocked him to the ground covered him. All the exposed skin on his face and arms—scoured by a sandstorm of dust particles—felt like sunburn.

But the pain in his arm took prominence right then. Specks of bright light appeared in his field of vision, dancing before him. Tears welled up in his eyes, and his head spun as if unconsciousness were imminent.

But the sensation faded, and he mustered his courage once more. Cautiously reaching with his right arm to his left side, he felt around in the darkness at his utility belt. The narrow gap between him and the rock above challenged his resolve. Straining, he grasped a familiar object, brought it to his chest, and activated it.

The flashlight washed his face in a narrow but blinding stream of light. He pointed the device up and examined the rock ceiling just a hand's length away. Its close proximity and the odd angle of the flashlight made seeing its edges difficult. Memories of the immense boulder falling toward him from far up on the high wall filled his mind. The images repeated, for he had blacked out while the rock was still falling.

Why wasn't I crushed? he thought.

Following the rock's surface outward to his right with the stream of light, he spotted the dusty remains of a crushed land craft under the boulder. Its metal frame bent inward on itself like an accordion, and the entire frame—reduced to a half-meter tall—lay crushed on the ground. He turned the flashlight to his left. Stacks of fallen rock held up the other end of the boulder, thus creating a protective space around him slightly larger than the inside of a coffin. Rather than crushing him, the boulder had instead saved his life.

Of course, he was still trapped.

Ignoring his pain, Michael brought his field watch to his eyes. The time was already early evening. He had been trapped under the rocks for hours.

"*No,*" he gasped against a parched throat, his face twisting in urgent concern.

With a terrible dread shuddering through him, he sucked the blunt end of the flashlight into his mouth to free his good hand. Fiddling with his utility belt once more, he brought his scanner to his chest and examined it in the unsteady light.

The device provided two functions. The bottom interface controlled a vital signs dampening field emitter within the unit. Every *Endurance* crewmember had worn such a device to mask his or her presence from Europan scanners. Michael, seeing the display indicating a strong dampening field enveloping him—hiding him—deactivated the emitter.

The device's top interface housed a small scanning display showing the immediate area. The smashed, top-right quadrant of the screen hung loosely, the unfortunate victim of falling rocks. The display flickered in and out because of the damage. However, by turning the crude scanner in various directions, he saw what he needed to know. His shoulders dropped tellingly, and he let the device fall to his side.

The area around the high wall rubble was deserted.

Letting the flashlight drop from his mouth and falling into the resulting shadows, the young man withered in the darkness. His face twisted, and tears flooded his eyes. Buried alone deep within the mound of fallen rock, Michael Gillen sobbed uncontrollably.

"*I'm so sorry, Katey,*" he cried out a hapless confession, his eyes burning as tears mixed with the dirt and blood on his face. The pain radiating throughout his broken body faded for the moment, replaced instead by the horror of what had certainly become of his bride—Kara, Tom, and the others too. His unmanly weeping only worsened at conjured images of Katey's summary execution. So many tears would rightly turn him to dust.

And his heroics back at the ambush site? Rushing back to the excavator amidst the oncoming Europan horde? Escorting his team with the excavator to protect them? Dashing for the land craft under a firestorm of artillery to effect the Centauries' escape? They weren't heroics at all.

No, the second he had spotted the Europans rushing them after the failed ambush, Michael realized his mistake. From that point on, he struggled to right an incredible wrong. Nothing worked. No, his obsession over taking Aurelian Galerius back to the *Weightless* had cost him everything, and fate dealt its justice upon him. Sco-II, an alien planet that had captured his explorers' imagination for so long, had swallowed him up.

So he sobbed for the longest time.

The longer he mourned, the more his predicament brought to mind the *Comanche* destruction long ago. He was waiting to die, just as he had waited while lying in the rubble of the *Comanche* bridge. This time, however, he had no opportunity to die an honorable death. No, he had acted despicably at the failed ambush—perhaps the whole mission. And what would David, his long-gone brother, have thought of his actions? Just the thought shamed him. But worse than anything, shivers ran up and down his spine at the thought of that cold blackness imposing itself on him again, stripping him of his humanity.

Given the fresh air penetrating the rock pile, his nonfatal injuries, and lack of food and water, he would suffer a prolonged, painful, *unabsolved* death.

"Please, let me out of here!" he whispered a cry to no one in particular. He didn't really know why he had mouthed the words in such a quiet voice. Thoughts of him mocking his brother's notions of God long ago came to mind, and nothing had changed in that regard. Nevertheless, *"Please, help me!"*

However, the rocks remained still and his coffin-like dwelling eerily silent—save his continuous sobbing.

Panicking, he once again picked up the scanner. After changing the settings to show a representation of the surrounding rock pile, he studied the display. Three to five meters of rock lay heaped overhead. Yet the rock pile had settled mostly behind the crushed land craft. He even detected the mangled left-front edge of the land craft jutting out from the pile. The rubble was shallowest just at his head.

Setting down the scanner and taking an anxious breath, he lifted his right arm over his head and scraped at the smaller rocks. When they dislodged and fell to the side, he wedged his hand into the new space before rocks from above fell and replaced them. After a trepid pause, he pulled himself upward into the open space—his body wrenched by excruciating pain!

More reluctant to repeat his actions, the broken, young man once again scraped at the exposed rocks above his head. His raw fingers protested the scraping, and his panting made him choke on the dusty air. Tears welled up in his eyes as the agony fought against him pulling himself up again. However, he had two options: stay there and die, or suffer the pain of digging himself out—perhaps dying anyway.

Evening began falling over the desolate construction site. Shadows grew thick and full across the ground, draping coldly over the entire landscape. There were no heroes to be found, no clandestine duty to fulfill. There were no sounds of gunfire, no cries of desperation. No, the place once again sat barren and silent.

In the darkness lay a large pile of rocks against the high wall, burying all but one mangled corner of what had been a land craft. The rubble sat arrayed as if a memorial to the ill-fated mission of the *Endurance* crew.

Their mission was over. Aurelian Galerius still sat in power over Sco-II, more emboldened than ever. Emir Kern and his men had scattered to the wind, soon to be hunted down like common animals. The Centauries were no more, whether kept in an extravagant suite or in misery awaiting a death sentence. The darkness that fell over the land had fallen over the *Endurance* crew as well.

Two of the most hideous creatures—rags draping the leathery skin covering their thick, muscular frames—appeared at the top of the bluff. Casting long shadows upon the rocky ground, the massive creatures plodded along down the pathway to the bottom of the channel. Their undersized heads turned back and forth warily, and their brooding eyes anxiously searched the terrain.

Coming to stand before the rocky debris piled in front of the high wall, one of the creatures spotted the corner of the crushed land craft jutting out. He pointed a gigantic hand at the mangled metal, and the two conversed in indiscernible, hushed tones. All the while, they looked around nervously.

Drawn by the arrival of the small band of humans earlier that day, the creatures had witnessed such an odd thing: humans fighting humans.

11

That was why they had waited before coming out into the open; they needed to see it for themselves—find out who these humans were.

However, the remnants of the conflict left little clues.

Just as the beasts turned to leave, a subtle noise caught their attention. Near the base of the rockslide, close to where the mangled corner of the land craft jutted out of the pile, a single stone toppled from its place. The small stone fell away, tumbling erratically and harmlessly over its companions to the bottom of the pile. The cause for the unnoticeable disturbance remained aloof, for the massive pile sat firm and still.

The creatures looked at one another curiously.

Another stone on the pile moved. This stone didn't topple to the bottom like the first. Rather, it merely shifted aside. Soon, all of the smaller stones filling in around a larger rock there began churning; some shifted, while others toppled off the pile.

Finally—unexpectedly—the small stones shot into the air! A fist erupted out of the pile, until the greater part of an arm protruded into the air. The filthy limb was bruised and bloody—and it belonged to Michael Gillen.

ONWARD

CHAPTER THREE

Tropical Sunset

The young family of four sat huddled in somber resignation on the sandy beach of the tropical paradise, spellbound at the magnificent sunset before them. The warm evening sun sat low in the sky over endless waters, its soft glow nestled in the cottony reddish-orange light draping the horizon. The sky directly overhead had waxed purple, and the contrast reflected in the shimmering water. A soft breeze pushed delicate waves up onto the shore and rustled the broad leaves of the surrounding palm trees. Only the smell of salt in the air was missing.

However, the spectacular sunset and sky weren't real.

No, the tropical paradise of Ceres Beach, just one isolated part of Ceres Fleet Base, was a masterful accomplishment of Earth States engineers thirty years earlier. The entire settlement, including fleet operations for hundreds of warships in other habitat bays, lay buried within the rocky core of Ceres, a dwarf planet in the asteroid belt between Mars and Jupiter. The sky was merely a projected distortion field hiding the bay's ceiling hundreds of meters above; the sunset, a similar projection. In fact, Ceres Beach was the only place where one could witness both a sunrise and sunset over the same horizon.

Yet neither did it matter. The virtual paradise, a popular destination for Earth States newlyweds, hosted so many visitors. Every now and then, a couple passed by hand-in-hand and walking almost in each other's footsteps, temporarily obscuring the romantic view that Ceres Beach offered.

However, romantic notions weren't prevalent between the husband and wife, who sat barefoot in the sand, keeping vigil over their two small children. Instead, they had surrendered to their own fatigue. Sunset gazing—even a virtual sunset—afforded them a chance to unwind from an enjoyable but exhausting day.

The young man, his suit jacket and tie heaped next to him and his boyish charm subdued, sat lazily in the sand with legs crossed and his arms propping him up from behind. He watched his eleven-month-old daughter, adorned in the prettiest white dress, lay stretched out haphazardly across his legs, fast asleep. His wife, wearing a matching dress made elegant by her curving form and flowing auburn hair, reclined against him with her legs curled up to one side. A toe-headed three-year-old lay draped over her legs. The lad lay motionless with his head resting on her protruding hip. Facing toward the water, he clutched a toy fighter jet under one arm while nursing his thumb in his mouth. His discarded suit jacket and top hat sat off to the side.

Taking pause from the beautiful sunset, the young husband took in the sight of his family heaped against him. The sensation was all too familiar: His life had become a chaotic mess of long hours of work, followed by even longer hours of dirty diapers, fighting, noise, confusion, and chaos—certainly not the life the aspiring serviceman had envisioned. The long holiday weekend and wedding festivities that day had only complicated his week. This singular, peaceful moment was a rare event in his world.

And Emir Kern was completely at home.

"*Is he asleep?*" Emir whispered to his wife, gesturing with his eyes toward little Nicholas.

Maddison Kern leaned over and crooked her head just enough to spy the boy's face. Her face washed over in the warmest smile. "*Not yet. His eyes are pretty heavy though.*" Savoring the child's countenance like any doting mother, she stroked Nicholas' short, blond hair. "He's had a big day with all that running around at the reception."

"We *all* had a big day. Playing father of the bride was harder than I thought."

Maddison gestured discreetly with her head toward little Anna asleep on his lap, and her mouth twisted impishly. "Maybe it was good practice."

"Don't even go there."

Maddison laughed while fawning over Nicholas lying on her hip. "But wasn't the wedding just *wonderful?* Jaden looked so *radiant* ... and such a pretty dress too." She looked up at Emir and fixed her shimmering gaze on him. "You can tell she really loves Glen. I think they'll be so happy together."

"You'd better hope so,"—nodding in acknowledgement when she mouthed the words '*he's asleep*'—"Otherwise, all that conspiring and match-making you and Bailey did will be all for naught."

"Don't worry," she cracked a coy but confident smile. "They will—and Jaden really deserves it after all she's been through."

After trading mutual smiles, the young couple fell into a contented silence before the magnificent sunset. They remained that way for some time. Emir—ever the proud father—once more fell mesmerized at the sight of little Anna asleep on his lap. Maddison caught the gleam in his eyes and waxed over in a relishing smile. "Do you want me to take her?"

"That's okay. I won't get to do this much longer; she's getting so big."

"That reminds me: What did you do with the picture?"

As if laboring to take his eyes off Anna sleeping, he reached into his shirt pocket and retrieved a photograph. He held it out for both of them to see.

The still-frame image, taken earlier at the wedding reception in the park behind them, glistened with newness. In the picture, a gazebo lined with tropical flora stood in the background. Maddison knelt in the center of the frame, protecting her white dress from the grass while holding Nicholas in one arm. The lad stood smartly dressed in his suit and top hat; he smiled from ear to ear and clutched his lapels proudly. Little Anna barely stood on Maddison's other side, leaning away from her mother with one leg out ahead of her. Maddison's hand chased the infant from behind, and the woman looked wide-eyed at the unsteady infant.

"Can you believe we actually got a picture of her taking her first step?" Emir beamed while taking in the image. "How rare is that?"

"I thought you were crazy when you called that beach-leech photographer over to us. They're expensive"—cracking a coy smile—"and you're so cheap."

"You three looked so happy, I just had to get a picture."

"What are you going to do with it?"

Emir studied the photograph for a long moment, eventually tucking it back into his chest pocket. "It's staying right here. I can take it with me on missions." He returned his gaze back to a sleeping Anna, though catching quick glimpses of the sunset now and then.

Maddison watched him doting over the child for the longest time, her brown eyes shimmering that much more. "Fatherhood *really* becomes you." When he looked up with a sheepish grin, the young woman added, "You've changed so much over the past several years. ... *And to think I had to beg you to have children.*"

"I think the word is *harangued*."

They rather wagged their heads at each other.

"But look at how it all worked out. The children just adore you too."

Emir waxed sentimental while watching the children. "I can't even remember what life was like before Nicholas came along. ... And Anna"—turning a broad smile—"... *she's the apple of my eye.*"

"And what about *me*?"

He returned her expectant gaze, his boyish charm uncontainable. "You're the whole *fruit basket*, Darling."

"You're such a poet," she laughed before falling under his spell. An endearing sigh followed. She wrapped her arms around him, rested her head in the curve of his neck, and took in the beautiful sunset. "This is wonderful."

"The day's almost over though."

"Maybe, but the best part of it is still ahead of us."

"Oh, *really?* And how do you know that?"

"*I know* ..."—lifting her head from his shoulder and looking at him—"... and so do you."

Emir took in the playful gleam in her eyes and laughed—perking up too. "Okay, *Mrs. Clairvoyant*, what's going to happen?"

The young woman, brushing her long, auburn hair from her face, flashed him a coy half-smile. "Well ... we'll sit here awhile and reminisce about how good life is. I'll be *real* playful."

"*Oh, really?*"

"And you'll get that *look* in your eyes … kinda like right now."

"That's predictable."

She took the fabric of his shirt into her fingers and played with it, her eyes intentionally trained on the task. When he wrapped his closest arm around her, she continued, "Then Bailey will happen upon us. She'll *insist* on taking the children and putting them to bed for us. And when she's gone, you'll suggest how to spend the rest of our evening."

"Will this be my idea … or *yours?*"

"… *That's* when you'll realize you've been set up … that Bailey conspired with me and is keeping the kids at her house all night." She trained her eyes upon him with much intent. "You're in for a very romantic evening, Lieutenant Kern."

Emir took in her amorousness, his gaze growing increasingly eager. "Then why are you ruining the surprise?"

Maddison's face suddenly fell sober, even sad. "Emir, you already know all this."

> *As the dreadful truth hit him, his countenance fell. His breath grew cold in his chest too. All the warmth and beauty of the tropical paradise drained away—becoming sterile—causing his insides to churn terribly. The crowded beach was suddenly deserted, save his family. Yet even the sight of Maddison, Nicholas, and Anna gave him no comfort. Falling victim to the despair overwhelming him, the young man turned his eyes onto the tropical sunset.*
>
> *"Emir."*
>
> *The man simply stared at the sunset, brooding.*
>
> *Maddison searched his expression—though he never looked at her. Everything that defined him faded away. His brown eyes grew haunted and weary, and a cynical sneer crept in and laid siege to his boyish charm, the more affable demeanor never standing a chance. Occasional scars from the coming war appeared over his face and arms, giving him an unnatural ruggedness. His whole disposition grew calloused. So she kissed his cheek, rested her head on his shoulder, and held him with abandon.*
>
> *"None of this is real … is it?" he finally lamented while shaking his head. "I'm dreaming again, aren't I?"*
>
> *"Yes, you're on Sco-II with Curran, Eric, Glen, and*

Brent. *You fell asleep. Curran's coming back from his scouting mission. You need to wake up and leave.*"

He didn't move. Instead, he kept staring at the sunset.

"You're giving up, aren't you?"

"It wasn't supposed to turn out this way."

She lifted her head from his shoulder. "You can't keep doing this to yourself." When his vacant staring at the sunset persisted, she took his face in her fingers and searched his eyes. She watched him fighting his vulnerability behind a calloused expression. "You need to move on."

"I can't, Maddison."

"You must. *Your destiny lies elsewhere. It's time for you to become the man you were meant to be.*"

But his face churned all the more. Finally, he choked out, "And who was I meant to be?"

They traded gazes through a long silence.

"You rescue people," she smiled. "*Just as you've always done.*"

He fell speechless.

The specter of his wife took in his tortured expression. "You've been running away for a long time, Emir—because of the secret you're still keeping. But it's time to stop running." Maddison took in his pleading look—how he searched her and the children as if fighting the inevitable. "You're not a dreamer, Emir. Your team is in trouble. Rescue them. Take them into the mountains before the Europans show up." The sky darkened, and her face sobered. "But whatever you do ... do not *approach the heart of the settlement.*"

"Why?"

"Because that's not why you're here."

Emir Kern suddenly found himself sitting alone on a deserted beach.

"Maddison!" he cried out, jumping up and searching the beach horizon to horizon. But she and the children had vanished. Noticing how dark the sky had grown, he turned around—

The entire Ceres Beach Village in the distance was on fire! Choking black smoke rose into the air. Two Europan FW-190s swarmed about in the sky, pummeling the *settlement with deadly firebombs. One of the fighters dove toward the Covert bungalows just off the beach. Emir looked on in horror!*

"No!"

He ran toward his home with abandon, his face ripe with a terrible dread. Yet the bungalows—with Maddison, Nicholas, and Anna inside one of them—burst into flames.

With each desperate step, he watched the flames grow until they engulfed the entire bungalow structure. His despair mocked him, causing him to fall headlong into the sand and bury his face from the horrible sight.

Inconsolable, the young man wailed terribly.

"They're gone!" an all too familiar voice chided him from behind.

Emir, taken back, rolled over and looked toward the water—his eyes squinted at the bright light. Standing in the dimming light of Ceres' virtual sun, the familiar silhouette of a man looked down at him.

"You weren't here when this happened sixteen years ago," the man scoffed. "Why torture yourself with these images?"

Emir, frozen in terror on the sand, fell speechless.

"It's time you stop blaming Aurelian Galerius for what happened to your family. You know I'm the one you're looking for." A goading pause followed. "I'll be waiting for you."

Emir Kern opened his eyes and took in the darkened Sco-II forest around him. Curran Zeidler stood over him.

The dream was over.

"The Europans moved off to the east," Zeidler said, looking down at him. "They won't stay there long. What do you want to do?"

Emir Kern made his way through the darkened undergrowth to where Brent Tasker, Eric Gunn, and Glen Volk lay fast asleep. He paid no mind to two of Sco-II's three small moons hanging low in the night sky, both quickly retreating toward the horizon. Neither did he ponder how he and his team were marooned forty-six light-years from Earth. No, all of Sco-II was hunting for him and his men. Not having any time to waste, the Covert leader gently swiped each man with the side of his foot. "Get up."

The Coverts stirred and looked around with blank stares at the hushed thicket draped in darkness. Quickly coming to, they began packing up their things.

"What's going on?" Brent Tasker inquired, wiping his face with his hand while yawning.

"Zeidler thinks the way out of here is clear. The goons have given up for now."

"They're probably regrouping," Volk quipped. "When do the Europans give up after just one evening of searching?"

"That's why we're leaving."

By then, the three men had broken camp—not that it was much of a camp in the first place. Gathering themselves and readying their rifles, they followed Emir toward the lookout point where Zeidler waited for them.

"Where are we going?" Gunn asked.

Kern pointed to the mountain range in the distance, its highlands barely visible against the night sky. The three tired subordinates groaned in protest.

"Haven't we been going in the opposite direction all this time?" Tasker asked.

"You never heard of doubling back?"

"But the farther we move away from the settlement," Gunn protested, "the newer the terraforming. We won't have much cover."

"There are lots of caves and other cover—and they won't expect us to go that way."

"Making the trip would be easier if we still had our land craft," Tasker grimaced at his leader.

"I needed a diversion."

Upon reaching the place where Curran Zeidler waited, Zeidler slung his pack over his shoulder and started toward the mountains. Looking at his scanner, he said, "We'd better leave now. I think our escape window is already closing."

CHAPTER FOUR

The Next Day

General Aulus Taun stood waiting to enter the inner courtyard atop the Europan Royal Palace in the New Tyre settlement on Sco-II. Of course, to the Europans occupying Sco-II—a planet orbiting the 18 Scorpii sun forty-six light-years from Earth—the planet bore the name *New Europa*.

The inner courtyard, awash in morning sunlight, was actually part of a larger, rather opulent garden courtyard adorning the roof of the towering palace. Outside the inner courtyard, a small Greek-style marble edifice, serving as a gateway to the courtyard from below, rose up from one corner of the palace roof. A stone wall, just short of two meters in height, enclosed the perimeter of the roof and a lush, green lawn. A stone walkway looped around the courtyard just inside the wall, adorned with statues and meticulously groomed shrubs, gardens, and small trees.

However, Taun did not have the luxury of enjoying his surroundings. No, the aging, heavyset Europan fidgeted in place. His eyes fixed on Aurelian Galerius, who stood at a distance before a marble fountain at the center of the inner courtyard. The frail, grey-haired dictator paid

Taun no mind. Instead, Galerius gazed up at the statue of an angel fixed in the center of the fountain. The angelic image, arrayed in flight over an effervescent, waist-high cloud of rolling water, looked down upon the old man likewise.

"*Aulus*," a voice greeted the general from the side, causing Taun to look. A thin, older man, garbed in a meticulously neat prosecutors' uniform, sidled up next to him.

"Malach. Can't say I'm surprised to see you here."

"How long have you been waiting for him to wave you inside?"

"Ten minutes, maybe more. He seems rather preoccupied today."

The two watched Aurelian Galerius for the longest time. When the dictator never wavered from his mesmerized gaze upon the statue, Taun leaned in toward his long-time acquaintance. In a hushed but sarcastic tone, he asked, "Do you think the statue talks to him?"

The prosecutor took in his mocking sneer. "Be careful, Aulus. I hear he's been up here since last night, just after returning from the Terran assassination attempt."

Taun waxed grim, and he turned his wary gaze back to Galerius. "How does this happen? One moment, I'm about to reap my reward for years of dedication and hard work. The next—I'm lucky if he doesn't execute me on the spot." Laboring through a long moment, his voice hushed even more. "We could end this madness if the old man just up and died."

"You're not planning on ensuring that happens, are you?"

"*Of course not*," Taun grimaced. "I'm as loyal to him as you are. He's just not the same leader without Carus at his side. If only we had known just how mad—and how weak—he really was." Falling silent, he watched for any sign that Galerius had overheard the hushed conversation. Satisfied, he leaned in once more toward his friend. "Did the commander in charge of the capture yesterday speak to you?"

"Yes, he conveyed everything—including your intentions."

"*And?*"

"I think we have an agreement, Aulus—not that I like what must be done."

"What choice do we have?"

"Indeed. For the first time in a long time, we have a common goal—and a common enemy."

"*General Taun*," Galerius called from his place in front of the statue, waving both men toward him. Taun and the prosecutor traded an uneasy glance before entering the inner court. As the two men approached him, the brutal dictator's weak, blue eyes sharpened. "Do you realize just how much you ruined what should have been a joyous day for me?"

"I'm sorry, my Lord, the Terran ambush caught me off guard. The communication came in at the last minute. We barely had a chance to send your double ahead, while our troops organized."

"Why didn't you inform me when the communication came in?"

"Our troops had technical problems too. I'm sorry."

"Sorry isn't good enough this time," Galerius huffed. "Because of your lack of vigilance, one of my most loyal subjects is dead."

Taun fell under the leader's recrimination while fighting his own indignation. Unable to contain himself, he shook his head and glanced to his friend beside him for support. "But how were we to know the Terrans had infiltrated 18 Scorpii?" An impassioned pause followed. "*Aurelian, we're forty-six light-years from Terrae Solaris!*"

"*I knew* they might come here," Galerius declared. After relishing Taun's dumbfounded expression, he pressed, "And I would have told you as much if you had informed me about your smuggling activities investigation." He let the general bristle through an awkward moment. "Aulus, there was a time when you told me everything."

Silence fell over the courtyard, save the sound of water effervescing in the fountain. Galerius crossed his arms and rather paced back and forth while brooding. His thin, gangly frame kept rigid the whole time, and he glanced now and then at the general with much impatience. Eventually halting, he looked Taun in the eyes. "Your soldiers have grown soft on this planet, as soft and as pliable as your ever-increasing midriff." Looking conspicuously at Taun's rotund waistline, he added, "I didn't bring you here to get *fat* and *lazy*—or careless."

"*My Lord*, I assure you that he was *never* in danger! When we moved against the Terrans at the construction site yesterday, I followed his orders to the letter—despite our problems."

Galerius only waxed more indignant. "I'm talking about your *technical* problems. This is *not* the crack military that played havoc with Terrae Solaris once. How can we launch our offensive against the Allies in such a sad state?"

"We should slow down and reorganize."

Aurelian Galerius steeled. "No, we have *one chance* to move against the Allies. Our communications drone is due to arrive from Solaris any day. I expect Carus will confirm everything is ready for us to deploy." The dictator paced once more, deep in thought. Once more he stopped, and his face grew flint-like. "My seventieth birthday is in forty days. After the celebration, we leave for Terrae Solaris. You have until *then* to fix the problems. Don't let me down on my birthday." A foreboding pause followed. "Dismissed."

Taun, suffering under Galerius' piercing gaze, turned and left.

"You wanted to see me too?" the prosecutor asked when Taun was gone.

"Yes, Malach, what do you know about the failed Terran assassination attempt yesterday?"

"Only what's in the official reports," the prosecutor shrugged. Of course, the statement was a necessary lie, as far as he was concerned.

"Then you know how *disturbed* I was when I arrived and learned what was going on." When the prosecutor nodded, he shook his head in disbelief. "Too many conflicting reports—one of which hits far too close to home." He paused in thought, but also sizing up the prosecutor's poker-faced reaction. "Something else is afoot that no one is telling me … and I think Taun knows what it is. I need you to find the truth."

The prosecutor bowed his head in obeisance. "I will start to work immediately."

Galerius watched the man turn to leave. "And Malach"—after the man stopped in mid-stride and turned toward him once again—"Remember: the fate of the Europan Empire may very well be at stake here."

The prosecutor took in the comment, bowing his head in obeisance once more. "Yes, my Lord. Rest assured that I will uncover the truth." Regarding the dictator one last time, the man left.

Aurelian Galerius, his face full of concern, turned and fell once more under the spell of the angelic statue looking down at him.

The door creaked opened, and a very cautious Phil Marcotte peered out into the narrow hallway. Looking both ways, the Centauri navigator took in his unfamiliar surroundings. Everything remained tranquil and bathed in the light of a new morning—a virtual light, for the dwelling had no real windows.

Nevertheless, the man's ready stance and intent gaze betrayed his wariness.

Less than confident, he crept down the hall until reaching the open door to David Tashjian's room. The quarters were deserted. Plush covers on the oversized bed lay folded open to one side, suggesting that David had left on his own accord.

Metal clanging somewhere in the apartment broke the silence, causing Marcotte to turn. However, when the sounds persisted, he realized the source posed no immediate danger. The most tempting aroma of food cooking hung in the air too, the reason for his sudden awakening.

He sighed in relief and relaxed his whole frame. With the pleasing aroma tugging at the gaping cavern inside his stomach, the bed-headed man turned and walked back up the hallway toward the sounds.

The hallway opened into the lavish suite that was his new home.

Marcotte took in the sight of the living area before him, almost gasping at its overwhelming luxury. He wasn't used to the place yet. Such extravagance fell beyond anything the thirty-something navigator had ever dreamed of obtaining for himself. Of course, he hadn't forgotten that the residence lay well protected within the Europan Royal Palace on Sco-II.

"You want breakfast?" came David Tashjian's voice from the kitchen.

Walking the few steps to the kitchen entryway on his right, Phil spied the eager propulsion engineer working an oversized skillet on an old fashion stove. Waves of steam billowed into the air above the skillet, and the sounds of bubbling and searing filled the whole room. "What are you doing?"

"Making breakfast. You want some?"

Marcotte shook his head and gestured toward the apartment door. "How can you think about food right now? Any moment, those Europan goons will barge in and execute us."

Tashjian grimaced. "That won't happen."

"And what makes you so confident?"

"Who do you think delivered all this food this morning? The Europans came in today bearing groceries—not guns. They were more than hospitable too."

"*Hospitable?*" Marcotte rather mocked. "That should have been your first red flag. Those goons aren't hospitable unless they want something."

"Maybe they don't consider us a threat," David mused, working the skillet in front of him. Lowering his voice, he added, "And I suggest you refrain from using the word *goons*. I suspect we're under surveillance."

"Have you forgotten where you are?"

"No, but I can't do anything about it. I'm starving too. ... And *Phil*..."—tilting the skillet and displaying the heaping mounds of eggs cooking inside—"these are *real* eggs!"

Marcotte fell silent. A wanton gaze replaced his concern. "Not synthetic?"

"Do you see a food processor unit anywhere in this kitchen?" He relished his companion savoring the sight of the rare food. "And guess what I'm cooking them in ... *butter!*"

Marcotte surrendered. He grabbed one of the empty plates sitting to the side of the stove. Holding the plate out with such a ravenous stare, he chided his companion, "You're over-cooking them."

Moments later, the two men sat at the kitchen table, devouring the heaping portions of eggs on their plates.

"This is incredible!" Marcotte sighed, shoveling more eggs into his mouth. Swooning under the power of the rare taste, he added, "I haven't eaten like this since before we left Mid-Earth Station. We should have raided the kitchen last night."

"Yesterday was a nightmare; food was the least of our concerns."

Marcotte abruptly stopped. Memories of the previous day flooded his mind: Aurelian Galerius' ambush going awry when the Coverts and Centauries stood off against each other, Kara Ricci unexpectedly killing the brutal dictator, Michael Gillen crushed to death by the rockslide at the high wall, the sounds of Tom Andrews and Kate Gillen's executions echoing over the hillside, and watching Kara's mortified look when the Europans escorted him and David away. He put down his fork and looked around at the lavish apartment. "What are we doing here?"

Tashjian also paused from eating, and his face sobered. Taking in the sight of the comfortable dwelling with his friend, he eventually shrugged. "I don't know."

"*We shouldn't be here.* We should be locked in a cell … or *dead*—just like Michael, Tom, and Kate."

"The door's locked from the outside, so this *is* a prison—just a nice one."

"And if Aurelian Galerius is dead, how can we be his guest?" Marcotte looked to Tashjian, who once again shrugged. "And if the Europans are so happy we're here, why isn't Kara with us?"

Kara Ricci, her hands bound by restraining cuffs and all the life gone from her blue eyes, followed the lead guard down the bustling corridor of the New Europa Imperial Strategic Command complex on Sco-II. She kept as close to the man as was humanly possible, while the sound of the other guard's footsteps chased her from behind. In a morbid way, the young woman found comfort in their presence: Their close proximity buffered her from the many Europans gawking at her. Taking in the crowd's hostility—self-conscious of the shame inhabiting her—she couldn't move along fast enough. Yet exhaustion and pain radiating through every muscle made her labor at the modest pace.

She was a mess. Her *Endurance* mission uniform, filthy and torn here and there, smelled of must from the cold, damp floor of her cell. Painful bruises covered her arms, legs, and torso, and she assumed the bruise throbbing in her left cheek must have looked ugly. Her dreadful condition betrayed the abuse she had received from her captors the previous day: they had frequently rifle-butted her to the ground during the forced march from the ambush site. She was terribly hungry too.

Yet she expected no hospitality from her captors.

Kara took no comfort in the soldiers whisking her from her cell deep in the bowels of the complex. Nor did she take comfort that the nightmare of the previous day was over. No, everything had ended tragically. Michael was dead, crushed by a mountain of falling rock. Tom Andrews and Kate Gillen were dead too, and the sounds of the gunshots that had killed them still rang in her ears. And what had become of Phil Marcotte and David Tashjian? Were they suffering like her?

But more than anything, her thoughts ran vivid with the memories of Emir standing off on the bluff, looking at her with such a dejected gaze—because she had betrayed him.

And the new morning would certainly bring new miseries.

Several levels higher into the complex and many corridors later, the soldiers led her into a large, elaborate office. A solitary desk with a sprawling white top sat away from the curving wall behind it. An older man sitting behind the desk kept working as the three entered. Even when the guards brought her to stand directly in front of the desk in shackles, his eyes remained fixed on the reader holograph screen hovering in front of him.

Immediately, the two soldiers withdrew to the doorway and snapped to attention.

Trembling ever so slightly, she watched the grey-haired man behind the desk—a noble, no doubt. His neatly fitting uniform denoted his high rank, and the insignias on his chest indicated he was some sort of judicial official, probably a prosecutor. Taking in her bound hands and disheveled appearance, Kara realized just how out of place she appeared.

Finally, the man lifted his eyes.

"You don't *look* like an assassin," he said in a thick Europan accent. When she didn't respond, he added, "Of course, looks can be deceiving."

Her expression withered.

"My name is Malach Severus, Chief Prosecutor to Lord Galerius. My job has been rather ceremonial since leaving Terrae Solaris. I rather liked the solitude." Studying her with much curiosity, he put a closed hand to his chin. "But now I have much work ahead of me."

Fear welled in her eyes during the silence.

"Aren't you going to say anything in your defense?"

"There's nothing to say," Kara choked out.

The man laughed a singular, cynical laugh. "You have *a lot* to say. Perhaps you can explain why you came forty-six light-years to assassinate Lord Galerius—shed some light on your insanity." He leaned forward. "Tell me about your mission, about the men who escaped to the north."

Images of Emir flooded her thoughts again, and she lingered over the memories for as long as she could afford. Of course, Emir's dejected gaze lingered longest of all. "So they're still alive?"

"Only for the moment. What can you tell me about them?" When Kara said nothing, his eyes narrowed. "Stubbornness will not help you."

"I'm going to die anyway."

"True. But many paths exist between right now and that finality—and many degrees of unpleasantness too. Don't make things worse for yourself." He paused with dreaded effect. "What was your role in this operation?"

Still, she said nothing.

"Several witnesses claim you were the leader of your group." When her face waxed quizzical, he added, "That's the opinion of six construction workers found bound and gagged in a ditch near the crime scene. They claim the whole team was following your orders."

Once again, she said nothing, though her trepidation grew.

Severus studied her unsettled reaction for the longest time. His eyes caught sight of part of a gold chain edging out from behind her collar. "What are you wearing around your neck?"

"Just a piece of jewelry."

The prosecutor nodded to one of the guards, who approached her from behind, unlatched the locket chain, and handed the jewelry to him. As the soldier stepped back into place standing guard at the door, Severus studied the locket and medal at the end of the chain. Opening the locket and examining the picture inside through a long silence, he looked back up at her. "Who's the child?"

"My niece. Her name is Mia."

After searching her reaction, he took the medal hanging next to the locket into his fingers and studied it carefully. "What did you do to earn this medal?"

"Nothing. It's a good luck charm."

"Do you expect me to believe that," Severus shook his head. "Such a medal is a rare thing to have. You must have killed many Europans to earn it."

"It's not mine."

Severus leaned back, his face filling with a sad empathy. "Yes, that I can believe. I think the construction workers were wrong about you being the leader of your group. I doubt your team would even listen to you. Am I right?" He paused while setting the jewelry on his desk, his face boasting an omniscient intuition. "Can't you at least tell me your role in this mission?"

"I was a doctor on the flight crew."

"*A doctor? Hmmm.* An Europan corporal from the recon team claims you executed Lord Galerius' body double. Tell me he's wrong."

Kara remembered the solider from the previous day, the one with oversized binoculars slung around his neck. She could still see him coming forward, wagging his finger accusingly at her as he told his tale. Tom Andrews came to her defense right then. She hadn't seen either man from when the Europan commander took them up over the hillside overlooking the capture point. "If one of your soldiers testified against me, what could I say to convince you otherwise?"

Severus grimaced. "Unfortunately, the corporal in question is missing in action. I'm sure he'll show up soon." Pausing for effect, he looked her straight in the eyes. "Did you kill Lord Galerius' body double?"

Kara, the angst welling within her, fell speechless.

"If you don't confess, we'll question the two men we arrested with you. They'll find our techniques *very* unpleasant, Kara Ricci—that's right, I know who you are." Through another strategic pause, his face waxed flint-like. "For the last time … did you kill Lord Galerius' body double?"

She suffered under the man's probing gaze, her face awash in so many conflicting emotions. Her eyes welled up too. "Yes."

Severus' probing stare turned bitter.

"It was an accident. My finger slipped on the trigger."

"An *accident?*"

"*Yes.*" Though she fought to maintain her composure, her eyes swam with tears. Her face twisted painfully too. "*I never meant to kill him! I swear!*"

Severus took in her tortured expression with much indifference. "Who are you trying to convince? Me—or *yourself?*"

Kara fell silent.

Taking a moment's pause while she labored over her confession, Severus waved the two guards out of the room. When the door shut behind the soldiers, he stood, navigated his thin frame around to her side of the desk, and sat on the corner. Folding his arms in front of him, he offered a reassuring nod. "I believe you."

Kara momentarily forgot her despair. "What?"

"*I believe you.* I know about the infighting within your team at the ambush. The two men: the one buried under the rockslide … *Michael Gillen* … and *Emir Kern*, the Covert leader—yes, I know who they are too. Gillen wanted to take Galerius alive; Kern wanted Galerius dead." He shrugged his shoulders. "The next thing you know, everyone's pointing guns at each other. Gillen, trying to take Galerius to safety, puts you in charge of the body double. Kern, unable to carry out his threats, manipulated you to kill the man."

"But that's not—"

"You're a doctor, someone not use to such deadly standoffs—and vulnerable to persuasion. Kern used your own sense of compassion for your team against you."

"But that's not—"

"Just when you think Kern is about to kill everyone … *the pistol in your hand goes off*"—nodding—"and Kern got what he wanted."

She fell silent under his sympathetic but intentional gaze. To break the mounting tension, she wiped the tears from her face with her cuffed hands.

Severus stood and paced a casual circle around her. "I'm about to offer you a once-in-a-lifetime opportunity: Testify that Emir Kern murdered the body double, and all charges against you will be dropped."

Kara looked at him, slack-jawed.

"You probably don't believe me. But then again … what do you have to lose?"

"Why would you do that?"

His face waxed cold, and his eyes narrowed. "*Personally*, I wouldn't. Both of us know you murdered that man—accidentally or otherwise. You deserve everything our interrogators can inflict on you." He let his words linger in the air through a tense moment, and he kept his eyes fixed on her as she stood before him in shackles.

"Then why are you offering?"

Once more, his expression grew affable. "Things have grown very complicated since your team's arrival. I received a very special appeal on your behalf, one I am more than happy to entertain. All—"

"You would lie to Aurelian Galerius?"

"I told you it was complicated. It could be worse for me if I *don't* lie." A pause. "Do we have an agreement?" When she remained silent, he gestured to the door. "All you have to do is tell me what I want to hear in front of the guards—nothing as ceremonial as a testifying at a trial."

Kara remained silent, her face betraying her desperate ambivalence. Finally, she shook her head. "Emir Kern didn't kill the body double. I did."

"It doesn't matter. Kern will die anyway—he could already be dead."

Kara, her eyes heavy with the fear of what awaited her, shook her head *no*.

Severus rather huffed.

However, after watching her in silence, he sighed and walked over to where a large potted plant sat against the wall. He fawned over the tall plant, even taking one of its delicate leaves between his fingers and gazing at it awhile. "I didn't want to come to this planet. But I had a choice: come here or face war crimes trials"—glancing back at her— "and I would have certainly received the death penalty." Once more, he fixed his attention on the delicate plant. "So I accepted Lord Galerius' gracious invitation to board that dreaded generation ship. I dare not think about what would have become of me otherwise."

Plucking a withered leaf from the plant, he turned around toward her. His face sobered. "But never in my wildest dreams can I imagine being in *your* position. I prosecuted too many would-be assassins. I know how undesirable we make any form of dissent ... and you know that too. You must be terrified over what is about to happen to you."

Her resolve began to wither.

Seizing his opportunity, the old man drew close to her. "Tell me what I want to hear. Tell me Emir Kern murdered the body double."

Kara, her eyes betraying the terrible fear accosting her, shook her head again. "I—I can't."

"*Don't be a fool!* You know the nightmare that awaits you." When her eyes welled up again, he pressed that much more. "Give me the answer I want to hear, and all this will be over for you." Though he waited her out—watching her eyes churning something terrible—she refused him. "Why you are protecting someone you know is going to die anyway?"

She stood trembling before him, feeling the shackles bounding her hands and fighting the dread of what would become of her, should she not betray Emir. She wanted to comply—her mouth wanted to speak the words that would end her suffering.

Reluctantly, she looked him straight in the eyes. "No."

Severus gazed at her sadly for a long moment. Then he sighed. "Fine." He activated a call button on the desk, and the guards entered the room once more. "Take her to the interrogators." When the soldiers seized her—the terror ripe in her eyes—he added, "The interrogators' jobs have been rather ceremonial since leaving Terrae Solaris too. … But now, they have much work ahead of them."

Michael Gillen opened his eyes, only to find himself staring up at a blurry and indiscernible brown enveloping him. A surreal fog covered him as if deep waters.

Incredible pain once again!

He gasped in agony—and once again, his broken ribs stopped him mid-gasp! So he froze in place and stared up at the blurry brown, suffering under the terrible sensations. The images of the high wall explosion and his failure at the ambush mocked him. Katey's angelic face still lingered prominently in his mind's eye, and his despair over whatever had happened to her returned.

The fog covering his mind dissipated, as did the intensity of the pain—though the shame of his actions at the ambush never relented. The blurriness faded from his vision at the same pace, and the subtle details of the brown haze sharpened into an uneven, adobe wall. The wall towered over him at an angle five meters high. At the top, rough-hewn timbers held up a thatched roof. Light from outside streamed in through the gaps in the thatch.

Where am I? he thought, for he had blacked out under the intense pain of digging himself out of the rock pile.

The unfamiliar surroundings brought him completely to himself. He crooked his head and looked down. He lay on a padded mat on a dirt floor, undressed but covered with a loosely woven blanket. A makeshift pillow sat tucked under his head. He was freshly bathed. Bandages wrapped his ribs and right hand, while a brace fitted his left arm. A medical device enclosed the arm's fracture point, emanating a low hum as it did its work. Salve dotted all the lesions on his arms and head.

The hospitality confused him: Europans were not hospitable.

A tremendous shadow moved over him from behind. Turning his head in the direction of the movement—

Michael gasped in terror! He recoiled against the wall, keeping the blanket fast around him! Not even the excruciating pain of his movements caught his attention. No, his fear-struck, blue eyes fixed on the hideous beast standing over him.

Though inhabiting a basic humanoid form, the odd-looking creature's resemblance ended there. It towered almost four meters tall, its mass four to five times that of the largest human. Its enormous frame lay covered in thick, dark, creviced skin with matted hair all over. Thick muscles layered down its overly large arms and legs, as did its torso garbed in rags. It smelled bad too. The creature's head, which was smaller in proportion to its body and mostly bald, boasted a prominent forehead, sunken in eyes that brooded, and an oversized, rock-like jaw. The only sign of civility in the beast was a metal collar around its thick neck.

Four other creatures, all flashing the same brooding gaze at him, mulled around a fire pit at the far end of the large room.

The beast standing over him looked down with posturing eyes. The air moved around Michael as the creature drew breath in and out of its lungs. The arms of the massive creature, hanging menacingly before him, appeared as if ready to swat him like a fly. Whatever the beast intended, Michael was at its mercy.

CHAPTER FIVE

The Dulos

Phil Marcotte and David Tashjian walked the luxurious corridor, following their Europan escorts through the Europan Royal Palace in the New Tyre settlement.

"Do you still think our captors are happy we're here?" Marcotte whispered to Tashjian, gesturing with his eyes toward the rifles in the soldiers' hands.

Tashjian studied the guards walking ahead of them through a few silent steps. *"They're not aiming at us. Haven't rifle-butted us around or insulted us either."*

"But they also didn't tell us where they're taking us. That's a bad sign."

"Europans always keep things close to the vest."

"And how do you know so much about Europans?"

"My father was a propulsion engineer like me. He spent a lot of time in the Outer Rim before I was born, working on projects for the Callistan government. He had a lot of dealings with the Europans too."

Marcotte rather grimaced. *"Did he ever face down one of their firing squads?"* When Tashjian rolled his eyes at him, he added, *"I'm not convinced we're as safe as you think. I hope you enjoyed your breakfast this morning ... it may have been your last meal."*

The two men traded contending gazes.

The soldiers led them up several levels and through a labyrinth of secured corridors. Reaching a large, elaborately decorated door guarded by two soldiers and one menacing guardbot, one of the escorts handed a reader to the lead guard.

"Did you search them for weapons?" the lead guard quizzed the two escorts.

"Yes, everything's in order."

"He's expecting them," the soldier announced, studying the reader in his hand. Opening the secured door, he waved Marcotte and Tashjian through the entryway.

Trading awkward and nervous looks, the two Centauries reluctantly entered the foyer of a grandiose personal residence. When the door closed behind them, they rather gulped and proceeded through the foyer, until the wall at their left gave way to the primary living area. Upon catching sight of the old man approaching with a broad smile across his face, Marcotte and Tashjian's jaws dropped in unison.

"Gentleman, welcome to New Europa," Aurelian Galerius brimmed with an uncontainable excitement, reaching out to shake their hands. "I've waited so long for you. Come in and make yourselves at home. Lunch is almost ready."

Michael Gillen, still cowering against the adobe wall and holding the loosely woven blanket fast around himself—the only thing he was wearing—stared up in fear at the hideous beast standing dressed in rags over him. The intense pain from his abrupt movements had fled from concern. Instead, the young man recoiled at the leviathan's obvious intent to do him harm, for the creature glared down at him. The air moved around him as the creature drew breath in and out of its lungs. Every muscle layering down the gigantic arm hanging before him was rigid, as if the beast intended to swat him through the wall at his back. In fact, every muscle on the creature's body stood tense. Its massive foot, planted on the ground beside him, could easily rise up and crush Michael's head.

"Lie still," the creature said in deep tones as it came to lean on its long arms. "You safe."

Michael's mouth dropped, and his brow crumpled. He stared up at the creature while keeping flush against the wall with his good arm grasping the blanket. The pain of his movements returned to his thoughts. Out of the corner of his eye, he saw the other four creatures watching him from where they mulled around a fire pit across the oddly shaped dwelling. "Where am I?"

"Dulos village," the creature assured haltingly, its deep voice resonating in waves through Michael's chest. Much to his surprise, the creature sat down next to him and crossed its gigantic legs. "Rescue from rocks, we did."

He stared up at the beast, clearly dumbfounded at its gentle manner. As he felt his whole frame relaxing, his concern for Kate, Kara, and the rest of the *Endurance* crew returned. "Am I the only one you found near the rocks?"

"Yes."

"I was with other people. Do you know what happened to them?"

"Not good. Master's guards take. Some run north; not found yet."

"Are they alive?"

"Alive ... for now."

Michael sighed in relief. Even his broken ribs failed to diminish the moment. Though trepidation filled his thoughts, a glimmer of hope sparked within him.

Celebrating the unexpected news, the young man struggled to make sense of everything. He took in the beast's brooding gaze, remembering the Coverts' reconnaissance report of seeing these creatures. However, Tasker and Volk's descriptions didn't do the creatures any justice. No, the beasts watching him were certainly larger, stronger, and far more menacing than he had pictured—smellier too. He also remembered reports of a crude, isolated settlement well outside the main Europan settlement. "Is this a prison?"

Three of the creatures mulling about the fire pit across the room spoke at once. When the beast sitting next to him turned and replied, a rather animated discussion arose. However, Michael didn't understand a word: The primitive utterances resembled no language he had ever heard. Neither could he understand their tone, for the beasts radiated a subdued disposition. Eventually, the one closest to him huffed at the other three, as if warning them off. Michael reckoned the one sitting next to him was the dominant male.

"Masters not know you here," the leader replied, turning back toward him. "Safer with us, not masters."

Michael's face twisted quizzically. "*Masters?*" A long pause followed. "*The Europans?*"

The beasts shook his sizeable head in the affirmative.

Michael, feeling his frame softening even more and his grip on the blanket relenting, caught sight of his gear heaped with an Europan uniform against a near wall. "So you're hiding me?"

"Already said. You safe here."

"When the Europans don't find me under those rocks at the high wall, they'll start looking for me."

"Found dead master too," the leader turned his head side to side. "Give him you cloths." He cracked a relishing smile and slammed his fists together, making a thud that reverberated through the whole room. "Crunch dead master bad! Like rocks crunch him. Bury master under rocks in you place. Masters won't know he not you. You safe. You stay here. Get better. Help us."

Once again, Michael fell slack-jawed. As he looked up at the creature from his bed mat, his many injuries goaded him. "How can *I* help *you?*"

Just then, the fourth creature mulling around the fire pit—the smallest of them—came over and handed him a plate of what he assumed was some sort of food. "Eat. Get strong."

Michael studied the strange substance—and its pungent smell—through an awkward pause. Deciding that offending the beast was not in his best interest, he took a handful of the saucy meat into his mouth. An odd taste followed. Nevertheless, he nodded in appreciation as the strange sauce dripped from his fingers.

Grunting in acknowledgement, the creature returned to the fire pit, retrieved another plate holding much larger portions, and handed it to the dominant male sitting beside him. The dominant male cracked what Michael interpreted as an endearing, even deeply affectionate smile at the smaller creature, who returned the sentiment and returned to the fire pit.

That's a female? he thought, his face betraying his astonishment. Even more surprised, he realized the smaller creature was the dominate male's mate. *Where am I?*

"Why here?" the dominant male probed.

Michael, feeling a little self-conscious and vulnerable from wearing only the blanket over him, paused at the question. Despite the creatures' odd but gracious hospitality, he knew nothing about their intent. So feigning ignorance, he replied, "In your house?"

"*On planet.*"

"I live here."

The creature huffed, and his brooding eyes under its prominent forehead narrowed. "You speak masters' words different. Not from here. *You lie.*" When Michael persisted in offering a blank stare, he said, "Think we dumb?" He huffed again and pointed a large finger at him. "I see face; same look from masters. Why see us that way? Hope you different. You not ... but we *human*—you human too. Answer question!"

Michael hesitated under the creatures imploring stare. A nervous gulp followed. "You have me at a disadvantage. If you know the Europans as you claim, then you know why I'm cautious."

The dominant male huffed and glanced at the others. "I Raathe." He gestured to each of his three companions near the fire pit, save his mate. "This Haanai ... Miiseal ... and Aazarii. We *Dulos*; Dulos *chiefs*. Come see Dulos."

Raathe stood up and towered over him. Gesturing for him to stand, the creature leaned over and extended an arm to help him.

"Are you native to this planet?" Michael asked as he came to his feet, holding on to Raathe's great hand while keeping the blanket fast around himself.

"Masters say make us in lab; here for them; we owned to them. But proud, we are. Serve, we must. Dulos hope not always."

With the large creature's formidable help, Michael struggled over to a large window—just a gaping hole in the adobe wall. His chin barely cleared the bottom of the opening, and the young man suffered under his diminutive status among the creatures. Next to the four meter tall Raathe, he felt like a small child standing on tiptoes to see.

Peering out the window, he beheld a large courtyard. Beyond the courtyard, adobe homes ran all the way to the bluffs in the distance, where a thick forest bordered the village. A network of dirt streets ran through the village, separating the adobe structures and organizing them into rows. Hundreds of Dulos going about their business inhabited the view. Despite their immense size, the creatures were a poor lot.

After letting him survey his surroundings, Raathe looked down at him. "Brought you here. Helped you; hide you. Master may punish Dulos; Dulos may die. Have told enough. Now *you* tell."

Michael took in Raathe's insistent gaze before relenting. "I'm Michael Gillen. My team came here from a star system called Terrae Solaris, the same place the Europans came from."

The three Dulos near the fire pit started speaking again. Once more, a rather intense discussion in the primitive language filled the room. However, Raathe waved them off and turned to him. "Know of place. Far away. Why here?"

"I came to take Aurelian Galerius back to Terrae Solaris." The creatures suddenly traded intentional looks with each other. Bewildered at their reaction, he shrugged. "Of course, I guess that won't happen now."

"Why say?"

"Because someone on my team killed him yesterday."

Raathe once again traded odd looks with his three companions— his mate too—before turning back. "Master not dead." Upon watching Michael's brow crumple, he turned his sizeable head side to side. "Master send other; look like Master. Master safe. Fool Gillen."

"You mean a *double?*"

Raathe nodded.

Michael, his countenance falling, turned and looked out upon the Dulos village outside the window—though he really didn't see it. Laboring over the revelation while furrowing a hand through his brown hair, he shook his head in disbelief. He didn't hear the Dulos, availing themselves of the moment, conversing once more in their primitive language behind him.

"Gillen friend of Master?" Raathe eventually asked, causing him to look up with a quizzical brow.

"Aurelian Galerius?"

"Yes."

"Why would you think that?"

"Masters very happy Gillen people arrive. News spread quick. Master not kill Gillen people either. Dulos not know why." He paused and searched his face. "So Master's friend?"

Michael, grimacing, fought to suppress his indignation over such a thought. "Aurelian Galerius is a war criminal. My government sent me here to arrest him and take him back for trial."

Commotion erupted at the fire pit behind him.

He turned at the unexpected noise. Haanai, Miiseal, Aazarii, all brimming with enthusiasm, jumped up and began waving their massive arms over their heads while yelling. The ground shook at the ruckus, and the sounds of their deep, booming voices shuddered through his chest. The creatures continuously repeated the same phase in their native tongue as if chanting. However, Raathe, watching the other three at Michael's side by the window, remained unnervingly calm.

He looked up at Raathe. "What are they saying?"

"Means *Master has master too!*"

"What's that mean?"

"Dulos slaves to Master. Solaris people to undo everything—free Dulos. Dulos wait long time. Gillen come. Dulos want free."

Michael, his face sobering, fell speechless.

"Why look that way?"

Michael hesitated, and his face betrayed his nervousness. "I can't free you." The Dulos chiefs' celebration came to an abrupt end. Silence fell over the room, and the Dulos fixed their shocked gazes upon him. "—even if I wanted to."

Another awkward moment followed.

"Master Gillen has power to free Dulos," Raathe declared. "Must *end* Dulos suffering. *Say words to free Dulos.*"

Michael's skin crawled at the urgent attention lavished on him. He pulled the loosely woven blanket around himself even tighter. Falling under their pleading gazes, the young man pondered how such large and powerful creatures expressed dissatisfaction. So he broke the tension with a rather feeble laugh. "I'm just one man—*I'm marooned. I don't even have my team anymore.*"

"Not just man," Raathe pressed. "Master's master now! Dulos master too!"

"And I'm hurt."

Raathe put his massive hand on his shoulder. "Rest up. Get better. Then help us!"

Michael shrank under their angst—but more at a loss over their undue expectations. Taking in Raathe's expectant gaze, he shook his head. "I can't help you. I can't even help myself." Another cautious hesitation. "And if I could do just one thing, I would find my people and leave this planet—but do whatever you want."

The Dulos chiefs fell eerily quiet, and all Dulos eyes fixed upon him.

Raathe looked down at him with those brooding eyes for the longest time. "Many Dulos suffer. ... Stay. Rest. Get strong. Then Raathe show Gillen how Dulos suffer."

A barely conscious Kara Ricci hung limp between the two Europan guards carrying her back to her cell deep within the Europan military stronghold. Her bare feet dragged along the cold floor. She paid no mind that she was completely undressed, with one of the guards carrying her clothes tucked under one arm. She cared less that her body boasted so many bruises and injuries, mostly from the previous day—but some new ones too. The soldiers' jeers and insults echoed indiscernibly in her head, and the gawking onlookers appeared as mere shadows in her skewed field of vision.

Her thoughts ran wild with the horror imposed upon her. The pain and humiliation inflicted by the Europan interrogators mocked her. Her entire body cried out in agony even then—but the images of her humiliation stung most of all.

Reaching her open cell, the two soldiers unexpectedly dropped her just inside the entrance. She crashed hard onto the rocky floor, her auburn hair falling over her face. Kara came to in pain, but also feeling the familiar sensation of the damp, cold floor soaking into her withered frame. The musty cell wept for her. Lying there in torment while one guard cuffed her right wrist to the cot frame, she hid her face with her left arm and fought the urge to break into tears.

The guard carrying her clothes threw them into a heap onto her, and the two men left. Listening to the sound of their footsteps fading away, she realized they had left the door open.

"I gave you the chance to avoid all this," a morbidly familiar voice said. "After all, the murder *was* an accident … right?"

Still rather disoriented, Kara lifted her head and brushed her hair from her eyes. Malach Severus stood over her.

"Do you see why I pleaded with you?" the old man pressed. "Such needless suffering."

However, Kara remained lying on the floor in silence.

"I'm giving you one last chance to name Emir Kern as the murderer." Yet she said nothing.

"This won't get any easier for you."

He waited through a long silence. When Kara simply laid her head onto the cell floor and ignored him, Severus rather huffed. "Have it your way." He threw her locket with the medal also hanging off the chain onto the floor next to her. "I suggest you get off the floor, dress yourself, and rest up. Tomorrow, the interrogators will not be as lenient as they were today."

Shaking his head in disbelief, he stepped over her and left the cell.

Lying lifeless and naked on the cold floor, Kara waited in terrible anticipation as the cell door closed shut. She was alone again. When the sound of footsteps faded, her face twisted painfully, and she broke into a desperate and inconsolable cry.

She muffled her wailing with her left hand, for she refused to give her captors the satisfaction of seeing or hearing her distress. But realizing that one hand was insufficient for the task, she swung her right hand to her mouth—

Clang! And the cot frame shuddered when the cuff chain stopped her hand in mid-swing.

Plink-plink!

The strange sound subdued her travail for the moment. Curiously, she turned and looked underneath the cot in search of the source. Straining to see through her tears and the dim light, she spotted a metallic object lying in the shadows against the wall.

She looked around warily—wiping away her tears in the process—and pulled herself closer to the cot. Straining at the end of the restraining chain holding her to the cot frame, she reached in and pulled out the cold metal.

She pushed the heap of clothing aside and struggled into a sitting position, facing away from the cell door. With her left knee up and her leg against her torso to hide the object from unexpected visitors, she studied the metal shard in her hand.

The object was long and thin, perhaps a broken part of the cot frame that had fallen off. One long edge was smooth to the touch. The other edge was just as smooth, though the far end where the metal had snapped off was uneven and sharp. Curious, she gently brushed a fingertip across the uneven surface—a twinge of pain and a few drops of blood followed. Wincing, she brought the finger to her mouth.

Kara studied the shard, relishing the finding. The crude metal could certainly cut, though the edge was far too rough for any precision. But as she looked around her cell in search of some use for the object, the rock walls caught her attention. Remembering all her scientific training as a Centauri long ago—a gleam came to her blue eyes.

So the tormented, young woman hid the shard under her mattress.

"*Sorry*," a nervous Kate Gillen winced, letting go of the bandage covering Tom Andrews' chest wound. Tom, sitting on his bunk against the rock wall with his shirt off, sighed in relief at her pause. Mustering her courage once more, she pulled the rest of the dressing away from his skin ever so gingerly.

Despite her caution, his gangly frame snapped rigid against the pain.

"*That's okay*," he assured through gnashed teeth—but his eyes also radiating sympathy toward her. "You're doing fine."

Comforted by his gaze, Kate tended to the wound as if singularly focused on the task. Aside from keeping her unsettled thoughts over his condition at bay, the task also provided a much-needed diversion from her dire situation: Just like Tom, she was hungry, dirty, and cold. Neither had the gloomy prison cell lost any of its morbid charm since the previous day (at least she assumed only a day had passed, for the cell contained no natural light). No, the chamber deep beneath the Europan Royal Palace seemed darker … filthier … mustier—and even more terrifying than before. The Europans were bound to show up anytime.

Then the real nightmare would begin.

"How does it look?" Tom asked, having averted his eyes in an attempt to block out the pain. Yet every time she touched the wound with the damp cloth in her hand, he winced terribly.

She strained against the dim light to study the injury. The uneasiness in her expression mounted. Nevertheless, she resolved to return the encouragement he afforded her. "It's hard to say … but it *does* look a little better." She looked at the filthy bandage. "We need to make sure the wound doesn't get infected."

Kate stood up, crossed over to the sink, and rinsed the cloth under cold water. Returning to his side, she tenderly applied the wet cloth to the injury again. Tom shuddered each time, and Kate cringed at his reaction.

"You know what puzzles me?" she asked in a vain attempt to distract him. He returned a quizzical shrug. "I can't understand how I came out of the ambush unscathed. I was hit too, but I don't even have a burn mark on my clothing."

"Maybe you were hit by a deflected round. It must *have*"—cringing when she moved the cloth over a particularly sensitive part of his injury—"… lost most of its charge by the time it hit you. You were lucky."

Kate looked around at the foreboding sight of their prison cell, her face waxing grave. "This isn't luck. We may have been better off suffering the same fate *as*—" she fell silent, her gaze growing distant and her motions robotic. Tears welled up in her brown eyes. "… well, *you know.*"

Tom, offering sympathy, placed his hand over hers.

"Thanks for bearing with me last night, Tom. I was a complete wreck."

"We helped each other. I was as distraught as you."

"I'm sure it won't be the last time for me," she sobbed a laugh. After an awkward moment of choking down the strong emotions, a sentimental smile came to her face. "After I fell asleep last night, I dreamed we were all together back on Mid-Earth Station—just like the old days: you, me … *Michael* … *Kara* … everyone—even Ben

Morris." As she relished the memory of the dream, the gleam in her eyes lingered. But once more, her face waxed grave. "What will I do without Michael?"

Kate averted her eyes, and silence fell over the dimly lit cell.

"I've asked myself the same question."

"I can't get the image of him dying under that rockslide out of my head." A heavy pause followed before she looked at him. "It must have been terrible for you—having to watch the Europans execute everyone else."

Tom reflected such a troubled gaze for the longest time. "I *will* get you out of here, Kate. I promise."

She took in his reassurance, savoring his noble efforts amidst such dire circumstances. She grew sentimental once more. "The *two musketeers?*"

He let out a quaint laugh. "Something like that."

Taking in his familiar smile—and tiring of the heavy discussion—she quietly finished redressing the wound. Since the Europans had confiscated their replacement supplies, she turned the bandage around and re-taped it as best as she could. "We'll have to recycle until we find out if they'll take care of you."

"I'm not holding my breath."

"Do you think they're—"

The abrupt, heavy clang of metal felled them silent. The guards barreled in with weapons drawn.

"Don't move unless instructed," the lead guard barked.

The soldiers wasted no time. One of them stood over Tom, while the other wrenched Kate by the arm toward the door. Dragging behind the soldier, she looked back at Tom in sheer terror!

"*Where are you taking her?*" Tom pleaded, laboring to stand.

The guard over him rifle-butted him in the chest. Tom collapsed onto the floor in agony.

"*Tom!*" Kate yelled, wrestling out of the soldier's grip and rushing to kneel over him. Just as she took him into her grasp, the soldier seized her in a chokehold. Despite her resistance, the irritated guard once more dragged her toward the open door.

"*Where are you taking her?*" Tom pressed, fighting against his injuries and attempting to right himself on the floor.

"The interrogators have some questions for her," barked the second guard.

"But she doesn't know anything!"

"That's for the interrogators to decide."

From where he lay on the floor, Tom watched the other soldier drag Kate from the cell. Terror filled her face. The guard standing over him joined his comrade, grabbed Kate's other arm, and helped pull her from the cell. So moving in a deliberate and unthreatening manner, Tom stood. "She was just the medic. I was second in command of the entire mission. You'll get what you want from me."

Both guards stopped and traded curious looks. Shrugging in unison, they threw Kate in the direction of her bunk. She tumbled onto the floor, her knee striking hard against the stone.

"Then let's go," the lead guard mocked Tom.

Lying on the floor against her bunk, Kate watched them drag him out of the cell. As quickly as they had arrived, the soldiers were gone—and with Tom too. The door slammed shut behind them.

Kate, her heart still in her throat, looked around at the solitary cell.

CHAPTER SIX

Tom Andrews

NEWSFLASH: Phrynia, Titania (May 10, 2501A.D.) — *In a stunning turn of events, the socialist government of Titania has pledged allegiance and support to the Europan Empire, forming an alliance of trade and mutual protection with the Jovian power. Leaders from both sovereigns announced the alliance to their peoples in a joint news conference held in the capitol city of Phrynia today.*

Neither of the two Mars republics offered an opinion or statement on the alliance, though officials in charge of overseeing the Pallas Treaty charged that Europa and Ganymede are still in violation of the terms of that treaty.

In the boldest move yet of any nation in the Outer Rim, Titanian socialist party leaders cited interference of trade by the Mars Federation as the key reason for entering into the alliance. They also charged the two republics with engaging in covert support of antisocialist factions, in an attempt to seat a pro-Mars government on the Uranus moon. The Mars Federation offered no response.

The Europan Empire pledged all necessary resources to expel Inner Rim interests from Titania.

---

*T*he heavy wooden door opened, and Doctor Abner Caffry appeared through the entryway to his office at Earth States Military Academy on Earth. Being a rather tall man, the aging university president bowed his head to avoid grazing himself on the top of the old, wooden doorframe—

The well-dressed man sitting in the visitors' chair at his desk stopped him in his tracks. Caffry paused uneasily, glancing at his secretary's empty chair in the adjacent room. The businessman, a lawyer and self-proclaimed friend of the family he represented, never turned around at his arrival. Instead, the barrel-chested man in the expensive suit remained facing away as Caffry studied him from the doorway.

Letting out an inconspicuous sigh while rubbing his neck, Caffry shut the door and negotiated his slender frame around to the opposite side of the desk. He forced a smile. "Mr. Voigt, this is a pleasant surprise. Can I offer you a cup of coffee?"

"Black, please."

Turning to the refreshment stand beside the desk, Caffry set up two empty cups and poured the steaming drink into them from a carafe. His anxiousness was readily apparent. "My assistant didn't tell me you were coming."

"She didn't know. I waited on the bench outside the building until she left for her morning break."

"I could have made arrangements if I had known you wanted to meet me."

"That's okay," Voigt smiled a serious smile, extending a large hand to receive the beverage from Caffry. Though the drink was obviously very hot, the man didn't flinch while cradling the cup within his thick fingers. "It's a beautiful day, and I can rarely spend time outside lately."

Silence fell as the two men sipped their drinks. Caffry cleared his throat against his mounting awkwardness.

"*Your surprise visit is very timely, Mr. Voigt,*" *Caffry offered, though certain the man already knew what he would say.* "*Just this morning, the placement committee officially approved Cadet Andrews into the Deep Space Exploration Program next year.*"

"*That is very good news indeed.*"

"*Feel free to pass the news along to your client—though quietly please: We won't publicly announce the candidates until we fill all the slots for the program.*" *When Voigt nodded, he added with much hesitation,* "*I guess that concludes our business.*"

"*What do you plan to do with my client's generous but anonymous contribution?*"

"*That's up to the university's Board of Regents,*" *Caffry rather sighed while swiveling in his chair.* "*They have a backlog of urgent projects. I'm sure it will be spent this year.*"

"*I meant the anonymous contribution you personally received—or do you prefer the word* bribe?"

Silence fell over the room.

"*There's no need for that,*" *Caffry rather winced.* "*I haven't forgotten your warnings not to draw attention to myself.*" *Fighting his nervousness, he leaned back in his chair.* "*Money aside, I was more than happy to help Tom. The young man has had a lot to deal with in his short life ... what with all that mess with his mother and all.*"

"*Indeed. He doesn't talk about it though—and I suggest you refrain from asking him.*"

Caffry shook his head. "*I would never do such a thing.*" *He paused, returning the lawyer's gaze.* "*But why does Tom insist on such secrecy about who he really is? This university is full of affluent and well-known families. Is it embarrassment over everything that happened?*"

"*Not at all. Tom lives in the shadow of a larger-than-life father. Most in his position would avail themselves of all the luxury that comes with such a reputation—but not Tom. No, he always struggled to find himself— and his demanding father was not easy on him. Tom wants to make his own way; he wants to be an astronaut, and he wants to accomplish this dream on his own. That's why he can never know that I helped him along.*"

"*You have my assurance on that,*" *Caffry nodded.* "*But I can't assure you he'll make the cut at NSEA in two years. His performance to-date didn't merit him a slot in our program—save my overwhelming support. I'm not sure his performance and skills are enough for NSEA."*

Voigt looked him straight in the eyes. "That's why you'll make sure Michael Gillen also receives a slot in next year's program."

"You've got to be kidding."

"Tom is confident that his friend will *become an astronaut. Michael Gillen will enable him to make the cut in two years. What's the saying ... ride his coattails?"*

"You need to straighten the young man out. Cadet Gillen is a trouble-maker. I already voiced my objections over him to Cyril Davidson and the rest of the DSEP selection committee." He mustered his resolve against Voigt's mounting impatience. "No, you'll have to bribe one of them if you want Gillen in the program."

Voigt fought back the irritation clearly visible in his expression. "Tom has an uncanny ability to read people. He has great faith in Michael Gillen. I suggest you take heed." His eyes steeled. "Bribes aren't the only thing I'm capable of."

The two men traded looks across the desk through a tense silence.

"You're not the family lawyer, are you?" Caffry said, taking in the man's unflinching gaze. "Fine. I'll make the necessary arrangements."

"You have the family's appreciation."

Caffry watched Voigt set down his empty cup, stand up, and head for the door. "Did the authorities ever find out who was responsible for what happened to Tom's father?" When the man turned around with a bothered expression, he added, "The story just disappeared from the headlines one day."

"The family prizes their privacy," Voigt warned. "But since you've been so good to them, I'll let you into their confidence. Tom's father was murdered by an Europan named Trajan."

Caffry, sobered by the revelation, mused over the thought. "I guess all those business ventures outside Earth States caught up with the man. That's why I never leave Earth."

"A wise decision on your part," Voigt said as he opened the door. "The last thing you want to do is involve yourself in interplanetary affairs."

"*Are you nervous?*" *Tom Andrews asked over the din of noise, hurrying with Michael Gillen down the bustling corridor on Mid-Earth Station. Both men were garbed in their military dress blues.*

"*A little,*" *Michael replied with a dismissive glance, though his eyes betrayed his anxiety. He kept running his hand through his brown hair too.* "*I'm just grateful that Kate said yes.*"

"*I had no doubt about her answer.*"

"*You—*" *Michael accidentally bumped into a female passerby going in the opposite direction, much to the amusement of his companion. After apologizing to the accosted woman, he resumed his pace.* "*You should have seen the look in her eyes when I told her she wasn't shipping out with me. I wasn't sure what she'd say after that.*"

"*Yeah, you could have handled that a little better.*"

Michael, the most preoccupied look covering his face, ignored the comment. Instead, the nervous, young man rushed along, waving for his companion to keep pace. "*Hurry up! We're going to be late.*"

Tom laughed while complying. "*Then I suggest you pay attention and stop running into everyone.*"

"*Tom!*" *a man's voice called from somewhere in the crowd.*

Tom paused—causing Michael to relent his pace too—and looked in the direction of the voice. His eyes widened in surprise. "*Hold on, Mike.*" *He broke through the crowd toward a large, well-dressed man standing off to the side of the corridor.*

"*Hello, Tom,*" *the man greeted him as Michael sidled up next to his friend.*

Tom studied the man before coming to himself. "*I'm sorry*"—*gesturing toward the man while looking at his companion.* "*Mike, this is Mr. Voigt, an old family friend.*" *Then he turned toward the visitor.* "*Mr. Voigt, this is Mike Gillen.*"

Voigt, waxing over in a warm smile, extended a large hand toward Michael. "*I've heard good things about you, Captain Gillen.*"

Michael nodded while shaking his hand, though his mind was elsewhere.

"*Please excuse my friend,*" *Tom smiled.* "*He's getting married in twenty minutes.*"

"*I should have recognized that familiar terror on your face. I assume the waiting bride is the woman who was at your side during the Alpha Centauri Mission announcement?*"

"Yes."

"You're a very lucky man."

"Mike," Tom interjected, "Go on ahead. I'll only be a couple minutes."

Michael nodded appreciatively and turned toward Voigt. "Nice meeting you—and I apologize for leaving so abruptly."

"I understand."

However, Michael was already rushing down the corridor.

"This is a pleasant surprise," Tom said when Michael disappeared from view. "What brings you here?"

"I wanted to see you before you left—a herculean effort, I might add."
Lowering his voice and looking around with much caution, Voigt added, "The whole country is in an uproar in the wake of the surprise attack on Ceres."

"Yes, I imagine you had much difficulty getting here."

"The authorities are looking for saboteurs and spies under every rock and behind every tree. They screened me at every point in my voyage. I never saw anything like it ... and it's only going to get worse."

The two men fell silent and watched the crowd pass around them.

"Did you receive my message?" Tom asked, changing the subject. "I transfer to Intelligence in a week."

Voigt nodded. "Yes, that's why I wanted to see you personally." He took in Tom as he stood before him in his dress blues, and a smile came to his face. "You look very respectable in that uniform—a natural born leader."

"I don't know about that."

"You're putting the needs of others ahead of yourself. That's what a leader does. You should be very proud."

Tom nodded sheepishly.

"And what you're about to do ... going off during such difficult times and putting yourself in jeopardy." He took the thick of the young man's arms into his large hands and offered an assuring smile. "I sense a great destiny waiting for you." But his gaze sobered. "Of course, I can no longer protect you."

"I know."

The two men remained silent through a long moment.

Voigt looked him in the eyes. "You don't know how much your father would have wanted to see you like this ... to tell you how proud he was of you."

Tom bowed his head, and his eyes churned over the words.

"Go catch up with your friend," Voigt said, breaking the moment. "I'll see you before you ship out."

"I look forward to it," Tom shook his hand. Reluctantly, he turned and hurried down the corridor where Michael had disappeared minutes before.

Tom Andrews stood shoulder to shoulder with Kara Ricci outside the small chapel on Mid-Earth Station, watching among the small crowd gathered to send off Michael and Kate Gillen on an abbreviated honeymoon. The entire group that had witnessed the wedding ceremony stood by, giving best wishes to the newlyweds, throwing rice, and even clapping while the couple made their way to the awaiting transport. A clear-blue, virtual sky overhead boasted a magnificent sun that warmed his face. He didn't care that just the slightest discoloring betrayed the image as a fake. No, the day was a beautiful day indeed!

As the newlyweds exchanged goodbyes while pushing toward the awaiting transport, a broad smile washed over Tom's face. The unexpected nuptials, the result of Michael receiving orders to ship out for his tour of duty sooner than expected, were a bright spot in the chaos overshadowing Earth States since the Ceres Fleet Base attack. He relished his friends' blissful expressions as their new life awaited them.

More than anything, he watched Kate keeping arm-in-arm with Michael. He lingered over her contented smile, how her shimmering eyes took in Michael's countenance even when his friend was unaware of it; how her flowing brown hair swayed as she moved about; the gracefulness of her form and the radiance of her face. The images would stay with him forever, kept alongside thousands of images he hoarded in his thoughts from his time with her and Michael at the university and NSEA—the three musketeers.

Things would never be the same again.

Standing there and throwing an occasional, comical quip at the newlyweds, Tom consoled himself with thoughts of his upcoming assignment in Intelligence. In the shadow of the coming war, the opportunity—afforded him by Cyril Davidson—was his chance to begin a new life.

"You okay, Kara?" Cyril Davidson, who stood shoulder to shoulder on the other side of her, asked, interrupting Tom's thoughts and bringing him back to the moment.

She paused for a long moment, a little tearful. "Yeah … I'm very happy for them."

Tom looked on as Kara tried to brush off Cyril's concern. Her sentimental smile fought back the sadness inhabiting her face, and she rather squirmed about uncomfortably while watching Michael and Kate reach the transport. Her eyes fixed mostly on Michael, causing Tom to remember everything that had happened: how Kara's gaze always lingered on Michael when she thought no one was looking, how Maura Enzler had revealed Kara and Michael's indiscretion at the university, how she always seemed to carry the weight of distant thoughts.

He realized just how much she had in common with him.

So he waxed comical and looked her in the eyes. "What do you think, Kara? Maybe you and I should tie the knot before this war gets too crazy."

She looked at him with a quizzical brow. A grateful smile followed. Kissing him on the cheek, she returned a comical grimace. "I'll have to think about that one awhile."

Tom smiled back at her, and the two shared the mutual sentiment.

"Don't wait too long," he quipped. "Before you know it, we'll both be deployed. I'm only weeks away from flying a desk at Intelligence."

Davidson smiled while listening to the banter. Just as the transport pulled away down the street with the newlyweds, he interjected, "You're shipping out sooner than you think, Tom."

"What do you mean?"

"Michael didn't want me to tell you before he left," Davidson began, smiling once more. "But he requested you to be his first officer on the Comanche. *In two days, you ship out with him."*

Tom's face fell deadpan as he watched the transport disappear down the street.

Commander Tom Andrews, standing beside Michael Gillen in the command center of the Allied refueling station somewhere in the asteroid belt, stared into the tactical display in stunned silence. Captain Argall, his subordinates standing with Tom's replacement nearby, had just shown Michael and him the dire predicament President James Mitchell faced under an Europan ambush. Comanche, *docked for respite and repairs at the remote space station, was the only ship close enough to lend aid to the President. Seeing the trepidation building in his best friend's eyes, he realized what a dire cup fate was handing him. Yet he could also see his determination mounting.*

"Signal my ship," Michael exclaimed, continuing to peer into the display. "Tell the OOD to order an emergency departure."

As Tom watched the back-and-forth discussion between Michael and Argall, he felt his own trepidation mounting. He wasn't boarding the ship this time. Instead, he had finally won his transfer to Earth States Intelligence. Watching Commander Ivers, his replacement, leave like a shot to the Comanche *bridge, he felt his stomach twisting in knots. He didn't realize that he would change his mind and board* Comanche *a short time later. Nor did he know that* Comanche *and crew would not return from the defensive (though that fate seemed rather certain). Nor did he realize that, years later, he would watch Michael die under a mountain of falling rock. All he knew was the conflict raging within him right then. "I hate to leave you like this, Mike."*

"Don't worry," Michael assured with a rather optimistic, albeit false expression. He smiled. "Just do the type of work at Intelligence you did on the Comanche, *and I'm sure the war will be over in no time."*

"I hope so."

The two men went silent through a long, awkward moment. Finally, Michael said, "Goodbye, Tom."

Michael extended his hand and smiled warmly once more. Tom reciprocated, and the two men shook hands awkwardly, with Tom barely able to say anything. Much too quickly, Tom stood alone, watching his friend walk away.

Before Michael walked out of earshot, Tom called, "Hey, Mike!"

Michael stopped and turned around. Once more, Tom remained dumbfounded over what to say, prolonging another awkward moment. So Michael just nodded his head and smiled one last time. "I know." He paused for another long moment and then added as he turned, "Take care of Kate for me."

"I will."

With one last esteeming glance, Michael Gillen turned around and disappeared, leaving Tom wondering whether he had seen his best friend alive for the last time.

Tom Andrews struggled through the darkened thicket with abandon, stumbling over every rock and fallen branch lying hidden in the heavy undergrowth. Every breath came haltingly, for the young man pushed against his exhaustion. A muddy blend of dirt, blood, and sweat covered his face, and his brownish-black hair lay drenched in a similar fashion. His Earth States commanders' uniform he had worn since his capture was just as dirty from the abrupt escape; the fabric was torn here and there too. His whole body ached from the harsh treatment he had received.

He glanced up through the darkness at the cavern's ceiling far overhead, just waiting for those barbarians to override the nighttime programming in the area. A look down at the detection dampener in his hand followed. The stolen device showed a strong, balanced masking signal enveloping him. He found little comfort: The forested habitat was located deep below the surface of the alien moon. The remote location and dampening field provided little protection from the swarm of soldiers in pursuit. If only he could reach the lights in the distance, perhaps he could still escape.

But the sounds echoing from far behind him grew closer each minute.

The young man's thoughts had turned into a jumble of dreaded emotions. Concerns over Michael Gillen, a prisoner of war held somewhere in the Outer Rim, had fled far from him for the moment. Memories of everything that had transpired on the Comanche, *particularly images of the terrible condition Michael was in when Tom had left him, were gone too. Instead, his mind raced to figure out how to escape his terrible predicament—and what would happen to him once those barbarians captured him again.*

Tom kept running, knowing that his captors would surely kill him.

A petrified Kate Gillen sat on her cot in the dimly lit prison cell on Sco-II, her back flat against the cold, rock wall and her legs drawn up close to her chest. The sound of unnerving silence filled the cell. With her arms wrapping her knees to make herself as small as possible, she stared at the metal door across the room. Had her face not betrayed her anxiousness so capably, the thumb held to her mouth would have. The fingernail, formerly long and perfectly manicured, was rough and chewed to the nub. In fact, all fingernails on both hands had suffered the same fate during the unbearable wait.

Though terribly hungry, she paid the empty knot in her stomach no mind. Neither did she care about her deplorable surroundings for the moment, nor her desire for fresh clothes and a hot shower. Thoughts over the tragic events of the previous day had fled from her too. Even the terrible despair over Michael's death had faded for the time. Instead, one thought held her captive: She was desperate for Tom to return—but feared of what would happen when the cell door finally opened.

The sound of the door's locking mechanism turning broke the awful silence. Kate sat up straight. When the door swung open, she gasped at the sight! Two guards, carrying a bloody and beaten Tom Andrews between them, appeared through the entryway. Another guard holding his rifle at the ready followed behind them.

"Don't move," the soldier brandishing the weapon barked at her.

Keeping flush against the wall behind her cot and careful not to move, Kate watched the two guards carry Tom into the cell and let go. Tom, all his strength withered, fell to the rocky floor with a hard thud.

The guards left as quickly as they had come, the door shutting behind them.

Kate rushed over to where Tom groaned and moved about inconsolably on the floor. Taking him into her arms—recoiling when he gasped in pain—she welled up. "*What'd they do to you?*"

"… Hi—*Sunshine*," he tried to assure through gritted teeth. "Our new neighbors … *th—threw* me a surprise *welcome to the neigh—neighborhood* party."

"Let me help you to the cot."

"I'*m*—*m* … fine. Just let me lay here for a while."

Kate relented. When his gaze grew distant and vapid as he suffered, she held him in her arms in anxious silence. Eventually, he looked up at her and forced an unconvincing smile. Yet she withered inside. The Europans had beaten him badly. His face was bloody and bruised, as was every part of him she could see. His mission uniform was filthier and torn in more places, each new place boasting its own fresh wound. Blood seeped out from the bandage covering his chest injury from the previous day, as if the Europan's harsh treatment had aggravated it.

As she held fast to him and watched him suffer, only one other thought came to her tortured mind: When would be her turn for interrogation?

CHAPTER SEVEN

Raathe

Raathe, squeezing his hulking frame through the entrance to the inner courtyard atop the Europan Royal Palace, beheld Aurelian Galerius and General Aulus Taun. Standing before the statue fountain at the center of the courtyard, the two men carried on a rather tense discussion. Taun cowered under the frail dictator's stern gaze. Upon seeing him arrive, the two Europans stopped talking and turned their attention toward him.

"Master call?" Raathe said, bringing himself low before Galerius.

Galerius took in the sight of the Dulos with repugnance. "Yes, Raathe. A team of Terran infiltrators are loose in the mountains surrounding the settlement. General Taun here has yet to find them, despite all his manpower and equipment. Show General Taun whose soldiers are better: Dispatch a team of Dulos into the mountains. When you find the infiltrators—and I'm sure you will—bring them to me."

"What of city?"

"Not every Dulos, *you simpleton*. Just enough to find the renegades." An intentional pause followed. "Raathe, this is *your* chance to show your prowess—perhaps even win some much-needed relief for your people. I can be quite generous. Are you up to the challenge?"

Raathe nodded his large head.

"Good," Galerius said, his gaze steeling when he looked at Taun. "Keep your men out there too. Let's make this a contest."

Emir Kern lay facedown at the mouth of the narrow cave, surveying Sco-II's topography with his binoculars. Curran Zeidler, studying the scanning device in his hand, lay beside him. Brent Tasker, Glen Volk, and Eric Gunn lay huddled within the tiny cave out of view.

The cave was a cave only in the most technical sense of the word. Rather, the crack in the rock connected to the water table underneath the mountain. Foliage had overgrown the narrow entrance, making it barely noticeable. With a scant two feet of clearance, the small band had to lie side by side and covered in mud.

"Everyone down!" Zeidler said in a hushed voice, waving his hand likewise and shutting off his scanner.

Everyone, conforming to the shape of the ground, froze. The air fell eerily silent, except for the sound of water droplets falling from the low ceiling above.

Moments later, an Europan gunship, hovering just meters off the slope of the mountain, flew by at a slow and deliberate pace. The portside gunner surveyed the terrain as the ship moved along. Fortunately, the cave's entrance remained well hidden behind the thick undergrowth, while the cold water and mud masked their presence from the gunship's scanners. The Coverts still wore their life sign suppression gear too.

As quickly as it had arrived, the gunship was gone.

"Did they see us?" Kern whispered after Zeidler gave the *all clear* sign. The other Coverts moved from their uncomfortable positions.

Zeidler reactivated his scanner and studied the small screen. "I don't know."

"This is crazy!" Tasker protested, receiving approving looks from Volk and Gunn. "They're gonna find us—and soon. Let's go out with guns blazing and take a few of them with us."

"Yeah, I'm tired of all this running," Gunn heaped on.

Emir shook his head. "We can't give up. If we can lose them long enough to sneak out of the immediate area, they'll tire. We've done it before."

"But they're eating, drinking, and sleeping in warm beds during their breaks," Volk huffed. "We're out here fighting the elements."

"Your field bed not warm enough for you?"

"You know what I mean. We're gonna die before ever getting the chance to lose them."

"The terraforming watch station is less than six kilometers away," Zeidler interjected. "We'll have everything we need after the raid."

"But the Europans know we're in the area," Tasker grimaced.

"Not completely—and we've successfully raided expected targets before."

Everyone looked to Emir, who had fallen deep in thought.

After a long moment of obvious deliberation with himself, the Covert leader shook his head—as if convincing himself. "We're going back to the settlement. The goons aren't expecting that." When the rest of the team, save Curran Zeidler, nodded in agreement, he added, "We'll hide in the undeveloped areas. There's lots of animal life to hunt too." A familiar gleam came to his eyes. "And maybe we can do what we came here to do."

"*What about your dream?*" an unconvinced Curran Zeidler whispered to him.

"That's all it was. It's time to be more practical."

"Are you sure it's safe for me to be out in the open like this?" Michael Gillen asked, walking with Raathe down the dusty road in the Dulos village. The young man, his left arm hanging in a sling, walked as close as he dared to the mammoth Raathe. The ground shuddered at each step the Dulos leader took. Seeing his massive size and muscles rolling in waves underneath his thick, creviced skin covered in matted hair, Michael wondered how the Europans kept such tight control of the Dulos.

Raathe, walking slowly enough to afford Michael a casual stroll in his injured state, shook his sizeable head. "Masters leave Dulos alone here. Know reconbots' schedule. Safe for Gillen. Gillen need fresh air. Exercise. Clear head."

Taking in the creature's brooding smile, Michael eased out from under Raathe's formidable shadow into the 18 Scorpii sunlight. Immediately, the muscles in his neck relaxed: Looking up at the towering Dulos at such close proximity was a formidable task. The sun warming his face felt good too.

Keeping pace with his host, the young man took in his surroundings. The primitive Dulos village stood in stark contrast to the cosmopolitan Europan settlement far away. Single-story adobe structures, boasting various shops and trades, lined the dusty street on both sides. Commerce operated on an archaic level, and technology of any sort was nonexistent. He could taste the dust from the street hanging in the air, and an unpleasant smell wafted before him. Despite the Dulos not lacking food or water supplies, they lived in such deplorable conditions. Like Raathe, the few inhabitants he saw went about their business garbed in rags. "How do you live like this?"

"Dulos *home* in village," the gargantuan replied, his face grimacing. "Simple better. Enjoy land; hunt in woods; enjoy peace of fire at night; Dulos bonds strong." He pointed toward the Europan settlement over the horizon. "Masters have many machines; Masters not have what Dulos have. Gillen have what Dulos have?"

Michael fell silent under his probing gaze. Choosing to avert his eyes, he took in the mostly deserted street once more. "Where is everyone?"

"Master's construction place. Build city for Master. Dulos slave all day, night too. Take Gillen there soon. See Dulos suffer. Then Gillen free Dulos."

The young man rather laughed—though to himself. After all, the Dulos leader was serious. Raathe had worked his '*Gillen free Dulos*' line into every conversation since his arrival. Brushing off the comment, he said, "Is that why the Europans created you? To build cities?"

"No. Master make Dulos to crush. Dulos mighty army. Soon, Master take Dulos on ships to Terrae Solaris." He paused, taking in Michael's sober reaction. "Master invade Gillen's home. Use Dulos to crush Master's enemies."

"When are you leaving?"

"Soon. Master birthday. Then leave."

With his thoughts laboring over the Europan's imminent invasion of Earth States, Michael waxed pensive. Thoughts of his failure at the ambush site mocked him once again. "Have you heard anything more about my crew?"

"No. But alive. That good." Taking in his churning expression, Raathe added, "Gillen rescue friends soon. Gillen free Dulos; Dulos help Gillen."

"I already told you," Michael rather bristled this time. He gestured with his left arm hanging in the sling. "I can't help you—I can't even help *myself* right now. I don't know why you keep asking. Do what you have to, but don't put me in the middle."

Raathe, letting out a heavy sigh, bowed his sizeable head in frustration. His mammoth shoulders fell too. "Gillen not understand. How make understand?" He walked a few steps while brooding. "Only Gillen free Dulos. Then Dulos crush masters. Masters gone. Take planet for selves."

"What about the Europan civilians?"

"Dulos suffer harm. Dulos demand justice—or forever harmed. Dulos crush all masters!"

"You can't be serious. Besides, you'll need the Europans if you intend to survive on this planet."

"Wipe planet clean of all masters!"

"Two and a half million people? Seventy percent of them are children!"

Raathe huffed. "Master take Raathe's child! Saw never again. Son would be man now. Master take many Dulos young."

Michael stopped in mid-stride—causing Raathe to stop—and looked up slack-jawed at the towering Dulos. What little he knew of Europan genetic reengineering came to mind. He also knew The Europans had only arrived nine years earlier. "*How old are you?*"

"Only know came on Master ship," Raathe shrugged, his eyes betraying his angst over the simple question. The leviathan's eyes brooded even more. "Masters twist Raathe's mind—all Dulos suffer same when masters make us Dulos." An awkward pause followed. "Sometimes, see self different in dreams; float in sky; see faces Raathe should know—but don't. ... But only dream."

"So you weren't always a Dulos?"

Once more, Raathe offered a hapless shrug. "Just dream suppose. ... *Am Raathe.*"

Michael, wide-eyed at the startling revelation, took in the creature's gaze for the longest time. His breath grew strangely cold in his chest.

A spec of light high in the sky caught his eye.

He looked up, squinting against the 18 Scorpii sun and shielding his eyes with one hand. A small ship, appearing out of the yellow glow, passed over the Dulos village. Then, it turned and executed a landing pattern toward the Europan settlement over the bluffs. His brow crumpled at the sight. Transports coming and going over the settlement were commonplace. However, Michael immediately spotted an array of Slipstream nodes dotting its small, compact hull. The vessel bore all the marks of a long-range ship. He directed Raathe's attention to the craft. "What's that?"

"Communication drone from Solaris. Come every year. Bring Master news.

Michael's jaw dropped. "You mean Galerius is getting intelligence reports from Solaris?"

Raathe shook his head. "Send back orders too."

"*How'd they do that?*" Michael mused while watching the ship fly through the air. "It took my ship ten years at full speed to get here."

"No matter," Raathe shook his sizeable head, watching Michael's eyes follow the ship, until it disappeared over the bluff. "Master need news to go home. Gillen friends still in danger. Dulos time to help running out. Masters leave soon. Gillen hurry. Tell Raathe where men to north are; Raathe bring to Gillen to help."

Looking up at the towering Dulos leader, Michael nodded a hapless nod while taking in Raathe's insistent gaze. A newfound respect for—and caution of—the simple-looking creature washed over him. He realized Raathe had known of the ship's pending arrival; Raathe had purposely brought him outside to see it—to force his hand.

Kara Ricci knelt on the mattress of her cot, facing the rock wall of the dimly lit prison cell deep within the Europan military stronghold. With her feet tucked underneath her, her knees apart for balance, and the curve of her back well pronounced, she leaned in toward the formidable, rough-hewn surface with much intent.

The metal shard she had found—and kept hidden through an eternity of suffering—rested comfortably in both hands. With the deftness of an experienced surgeon, she drew the shard's jagged edge across the coarse rock before her, causing a low *scraping* sound throughout the lonely cell. Her eyes trained keenly on the metal as it moved along. Upon finishing the pass, she turned the edge of the shard toward her and examined it thoroughly. Satisfied, the young woman drew the shard across the rock in the same meticulous fashion.

She remained singularly focused on the task. She paid no attention to her sore back crying out for rest, despite the pain from so many injuries compounding her discomfort. Hunger pangs went unanswered too—as if she had a choice. Ignoring the gaping hole in her stomach was easiest of all, for she had grown used to its presence. In fact, had her filthy mission uniform not been tattered and torn from abuse, she would have realized just how loosely her clothes fit as of late.

But her haunted eyes radiated the oddest, most unnerving energy, and her heavy expression kept sober and businesslike. Only quick, infrequent glances toward the door diverted her attention, for she labored at a hurried pace. After all, she had little time.

The faint sound of footsteps far down the corridor outside broke the quiet!

Wide-eyed, Kara gasped! Rolling off the cot onto the floor, she concealed the metal shard back into its hiding place on the underside of the frame. Just as the locking mechanism within the heavy door began turning, she pulled herself up onto the cot, sat back against the wall, drew her knees to her chest, and wrapped her arms around herself. At the sound of the lock disengaging, her face drained of the last remnants of warmth.

Malach Severus, carrying a saucer holding a cup of tea, appeared through the opening door.

Kara kept to herself and her eyes to the floor as the prosecutor stood waiting. A guard following the noble carried a folding chair. Navigating around Severus, he opened the chair onto the floor so that it faced her. He bowed his head in obeisance, receiving the cup and saucer from his superior. Severus took his time sitting down and settling into the chair before taking the cup of tea from the underling. The soldier bowed once more and left, closing the door behind him.

"How are you today, Kara Ricci?" Severus asked while crossing one leg over the other and taking a sip of tea. When she kept staring at the floor, he added, "Not in a talkative mood?"

"It took you long enough to show up this time," she rather scoffed, glancing at him briefly.

"What made you think I was coming for a visit?"

Kara gestured with haunted eyes at the restraints hanging empty throughout the small cell. Her muscles ached just at the sight of them. "Because I'm not rotting away in any of those chains."

"I see you're learning my habits," he said with a smug grin. "Yes, I want you looking forward to our time together." When she looked away in disgust, he pressed, "It must be terrible for you ... being restrained all alone for hours at a time between interrogation sessions ... unable to do even the most basic things for yourself—"

"*Stop it.*"

"... Having to yell and plead to the guards for help but never knowing if they heard you ... or if they'll come to help—and fearing that they *will.*"

"I *know* what you're doing."

The two traded contenting looks.

Severus let out a wry chuckle. "Very well." He took another sip of tea, his face once more waxing hospitable. "How are you getting along with the interrogators?"

"You mean those *barbarians*?"

The old man chuckled once more. "They'd consider your remark a compliment." He sized her up through an intentional pause. "A most unusual profession, don't you think? The perfect blend of twenty-sixth century technology and medieval justice." He fell silent through a long moment, his face betraying his satisfaction when her eyes welled up. "Do you even feel human anymore?"

Kara, fighting to maintain her composure, suffered under his piercing gaze. She hated him! He didn't deserve the satisfaction of seeing her broken by the torment imposed on her, whether through the interrogators or through his diabolical manipulation. Yet she knew her expression betrayed her despair, increasingly so as her face twisted under his relishing gaze.

"I used to be an interrogator," Severus said matter-of-factly, as if carrying on the most genteel conversation. "I excelled at it."

"Then that makes you a barbarian too."

Severus laughed again. "Should I feel moved to remorse by a cold-blooded murderer under a death sentence?" He let the statement linger in the air. Then feigning regret, he shook his head at himself. "I'm sorry, I keep forgetting ... the murder was an *accident*."

Kara simply looked away in wavering defiance.

"I have a present for you," he offered, pulling a reader from the inside of his uniform jacket—but then his face waxed quizzical. Hesitating, he tucked the reader into the pocket again. "But I'm curious about something: I keep going over in my mind the scenario at the ambush. For the life of me, I can't understand what motive caused you to kill someone—*accidentally*, of course."

She glared at him.

"It's a personal curiosity. Murder—even accidentally—is not a normal character flaw for someone such as you." Though he waited her out, she remained silent. "My brother-in-law was a surgeon: an arrogant man, deluded by his own sense of self-importance ... hiding behind the *respectability* of his profession ... always thinking he could solve everyone's problems. I hated him for that." Watching her wither under his boastful, omniscient gaze, his eyes narrowed. "You *meant* to kill that man."

"That's not true."

"Yes it is. You're a manipulator. When things went wrong at the ambush, you inserted yourself right into the middle of conflict. A man is dead because of your interference."

"No!"

"And not only at the ambush site. No, you were manipulating the entire mission since your arrival on the planet." An intentional pause. "Your face betrays your guilt. What happened to Aurelian Galerius' body double *and* your friends is *your* fault." Another pause. "I just can't figure out why you did it."

Kara, sitting with her knees still drawn up and her arms wrapped protectively around herself, looked away. Severus noticed her clutching the heart-shaped locket and medal hanging from the gold chain around her neck. Her preoccupation with the jewelry piqued his interest.

Standing and setting the teacup and saucer on the chair, he reached in and opened her hand to examine the items. Oddly, Kara didn't resist—nor realize she hadn't resisted. After opening the locket and examining the picture inside through a long silence, he took the medal lying next to the locket into his fingers and studied it carefully. "Do you still think this brings you good luck?" When she said nothing, he laughed dryly. "In all the time you spent with our interrogators, they've yet to force you to confess what you did to earn this medal."

Kara once more withered under his probing gaze—and a gleam came to Severus' eyes.

"*You didn't earn this,*" he exclaimed with a relishing grin. "Emir Kern *gave* you this medal, didn't he?" When Kara's expression betrayed her, his face waxed over in a broad smile. "Everything makes sense now. You're romantically involved with Kern. That's why you won't implicate him as the murderer to save yourself. That's why you killed Galerius' body double: You killed him to save Emir Kern. You traded one innocent life for another."

"*It was an accident.*"

"No, it wasn't. You're a surgeon; *Surgeons cut.*" His eyes steeled. "When the man you love was going to die in the standoff, you did what any surgeon would do: You cut out the offending organ. You killed Galerius' body double to save Emir Kern." When her eyes welled up, he added, "So much for your altruistic views on the value of life."

Silence fell over the room.

As Kara labored under the accusation, Severus pulled the reader from his pocket again. Setting the device on the floor and activating it, he smiled. "I almost forgot your present."

The reader, coming to life, projected a broad holograph viewing screen into the air. Kara, still wrapped in a ball on the cot, watched the unfamiliar video pictures rolling before her. They were family videos: clips of a young husband and wife playing with four small children in their home. The clips continued one after the other in silence. Her gaze waxed perplexed.

"You don't recognize the man, do you?" Severus pressed.

"No."

"The man's much older now … he just became a grandfather. These pictures are from long ago—before he underwent cosmetic surgery for his job. Happy times for a man who loved his family, don't you think?" He paused, letting her linger over the happy images and his obvious intent.

Abruptly, a still frame of a dead man's face flashed onto the screen—and Kara's countenance fell. Another family video clip quickly replaced it, though the picture of the dead man flashed intermittently among the happy scenes. "His name was Sigmund Pollux … loved by his family … adored by friends and neighbors alike … a pillar of the community. He was Aurelian Galerius' body double—the man *you* killed."

Kara fell speechless, and tears flooded her eyes.

Severus, delighting in her despair, stepped toward the door and knocked twice. As the door opened from the outside, he looked at her. "Pollux's widow wanted you to know the man you killed—*accidentally killed*, I mean." An intentional pause. "Maybe you won't resent your next session with the interrogators so much."

Flashing her one last reproving glare, he left. The door slammed shut behind him.

Kara, frozen in place on the cot with tears streaming down her face, stared at the family videos playing before her.

———

Michael Gillen, jostling about inside the transport's cargo bay with Raathe and seven other Dulos, held on to his safety grip for dear life. Every bump and shake made him cringe in pain, for he was still tender from the injuries sustained during the high wall collapse. However, his broken left arm had healed enough that he no longer wore a sling.

"Almost here," Raathe said in deep tones to him from across the narrow aisle. "Few masters. Stay back. Guard transport."

Michael, nodding in acknowledgement, looked down at his stolen Europan corporals' uniform. As Raathe had promised, he and the Dulos were en route to the New Tyre Capital Center construction site.

The thought of leaving the safety of the Dulos village formed a lump in his throat.

The transport slowed to a stop, and the Dulos stood and exited the bay. Michael followed closely behind, keeping hidden behind several of them. When he took up position beside the transport as if guarding the vehicle, the creatures fanned out and turned toward the construction pit below.

With the morning sun warming his face, Michael surveyed his surroundings. The immediate construction site stretched a kilometer in the distance. Though mostly rocky and barren, the area boasted the foundations and beginnings of opulent pyramid-like structures, obelisks, and other Egyptian-style buildings—but contemporary in function. Sprawling courtyards with fountains and other water features would surround the structures. To the northwest, the Europan Royal Palace towered into the sky, causing his mind to fill with thoughts of Katey somewhere in that palace. He lingered over the sight for some time.

Looking to the northeast, he spotted the top of the fueling tower kilometers away. The tower marked the place where three thousand warships sat waiting to set off for Terrae Solaris. Stretching from horizon to horizon and trailing the construction site perimeter on the northern side, a row of spiny transmission towers stood. The towers generated an invisible but deadly perimeter shield, preventing the Dulos from crossing into the northern parts of the Europan settlement.

Raathe, taking a sweeping look around, turned to him. "Raathe go down. If trouble, will come."

Michael nodded as discretely as possible.

When Raathe and the other Dulos approached the construction pit, the metal collars around their necks lit up.

Michael, portraying his best impression of an Europan corporal standing guard at the transport, looked on in stunned silence at the thousands of Dulos working the construction site below.

Raathe had not exaggerated the Dulos suffering.

Europan taskmasters, armed with whips and clubs, had spread out into the sea of Dulos slaves lifting, pulling, and dragging heavy construction materials into place. Though heavy robotic machinery did similar work, the taskmasters pressed the Dulos into hard labor to accelerate construction. The cracking of whips and the sounds of verbal abuse rose above the din of construction noises. And no matter how cruel the taskmasters acted, the Dulos—those metal collars around their necks lit up—merely cowered under the treatment.

Just then, Michael spotted a group of Dulos carrying large, decorative stones toward a half-finished fountain. One of the creatures stumbled, and the two stones he carried fell out of his hands. One stone fell upon the other and broke.

Without pause, the supervising taskmaster drew his club and beat the Dulos, slinging a round of obscenities at him—but the cowering Dulos erred by putting his arm out to protect himself. The ruckus drew the attention of other taskmasters nearby, who rushed in with clubs and whips. The taskmasters beat the Dulos likewise, until the creature eventually fell to the ground unconscious.

Yet the beating persisted. After several failed attempts to force the wounded Dulos to his feet, one of the taskmasters drew his pistol and shot the creature at point blank-range, killing it instantly.

The taskmasters walked away, leaving the corpse as a warning to the other Dulos.

Just after midday, a small land craft pulled up and came to stop near the transport. When an Europan officer stepped out of the vehicle and approached him, Michael's heart leapt into his throat. A small boy, about six or seven years old, appeared out of the craft behind the man and began playing in the dirt.

"Corporal," the officer greeted him, "Can you watch my son, while I go down to the site?"

Michael felt his whole frame relax. Mustering his best attempt at an Europan accent, he replied, "Sure."

"Thanks. I promised to show him where I work, but I don't want to take him down to the main construction area."

"No problem," Michael replied, hoping the man would go away.

But the officer looked at him oddly. "You've got a lot of scars ... from recent injuries it looks like."

Michael fell speechless under the Europan's probing gaze, and his breath grew cold in his chest.

"Do you always work with the Dulos?" the officer asked.

The young man sighed inwardly. "They're clumsy creatures. I got a little too close—but you should see the one that hurt me."

"I see," the Europan laughed. Turning and heading toward the site, he waved instructions to his son to remain there.

After watching his father walk away, the boy proceeded to do what boys do: run around, play in the dirt, and the like. The lad was rather entertaining to watch, and Michael fell victim to the frivolity.

"Hi, mister," the toe-headed boy eventually greeted him while playing in the dirt. "I'm Ethan. What's your name?"

"I'm a guard here," Michael replied, avoiding the question. "Your father asked me to keep an eye on you."

Ethan pointed to where his father had disappeared. "Yeah, he's down there. My dad's *really* important! He's in charge of this whole place!"

"He must have a very important job."

"He's the best! He says if I work hard at school, someday I can work here too!"

The child ran off to another pile of dirt. Michael, watching the child playing with such enthusiasm, caught sight of Raathe approaching from the construction pit.

When two other Dulos happened by the transport, Ethan ran up to the one nearer to him and kicked the creature several times. The mammoth creature looked down at the boy, unfazed. Hurling childish insults and following the Dulos, the lad continued kicking the creature until it moved far enough away. Ethan gave up and returned to playing in the dirt as if nothing had happened.

Michael looked at the boy, flabbergasted!

"What think?" Raathe asked as he sidled up to him.

Michael, trading glances between young Ethan and Raathe, fell speechless.

"Father teach child," the Dulos leader said, his brooding eyes fixed on him. "Child teach his child. Never end." He gestured to the construction site below and then to where the Dulos corpse still lay nearby. "Just another day for Dulos."

CHAPTER EIGHT

Emir Kern's Troubles

"How can we be lost *again*?" Emir Kern fumed in a hushed voice at Curran Zeidler, who walked beside him through the darkened, rain-drenched woods somewhere close to the New Tyre settlement.

Zeidler waited as he and Emir negotiated through some stubborn undergrowth and low-hanging branches. After clearing the obstacles, he looked down at the scanner in his hand, and then to where Brent Tasker, Glen Volk, and Eric Gunn trudged well ahead of them. Ensuring the other Coverts remained out of earshot, he grimaced. "Maybe the scanner is succumbing to the elements."

"Our gear is tougher than we are. That's not the explanation."

"Have you taken a good look at us lately?"

Emir looked around at his haggard team and nodded a concession. "Maybe the goons are sending out some sort of interference field."

"I would detect that," Zeidler replied. After taking a few step, a sober gaze waxed over him. "Maybe you should have listened to your dream and kept us in the mountains. None of these problems started until we arrived into the settlement."

"You're not getting superstitious, are you?"

"No, but maybe your sub-conscience knows something you haven't figured out yet."

This time, Emir brooded through several steps, finally turning his head side to side as if dismissing the notion. "I had another one of those dreams last night. This time, Maddison told me to go back to the base camp."

"The cavern?"

"Yeah, how much sense does that make?"

When Zeidler shrugged, the two men fell silent and pushed their way through the darkened undergrowth and the rain. Emir stared down at the ground with a distant gaze. His recurring dream of Maddison and the children at Ceres Beach filled his thoughts—as did the familiar silhouette of the man who always infiltrated the dream. Just seeing that silhouette against the sunset—and repeating the specter's accusations in his mind—made him shudder. After a long pause, he looked up and made sure Tasker, Volk, and Gunn were still well ahead of them. "Curran, do you think we've been chasing the wrong person all these years?"

His subordinate's face turned tellingly, and a few awkward steps followed before he looked him straight in the eyes. "That's the fifth time you asked me that question. We're not going to discuss—"

Ahead of them, Tasker suddenly turned around and waved everyone down!

An unsteady beam of light appeared in the distance, cutting through the dense forest.

Immediately, the small team crouched into the undergrowth. After a moment's pause to assess the danger, Emir and Zeidler skulked ahead to where Tasker, Gunn, and Volk hid behind thick vegetation.

As the source of the narrow beam of light neared, the five soldiers huddled in the darkness with their guns ready. The sounds of footsteps on a makeshift path ahead of them soon broke the quiet, and they strained to see through the brush obscuring the view. When the narrow light moved off from where the Coverts hunkered down, a small party traveling through the dark woods appeared on the path: an Europan lieutenant wielding a flashlight and carrying a firearm at his side, a woman with her arms bound behind her following him, and an Europan guard with his rifle at the ready following the woman.

The Coverts, still straining too see, watched in stunned silence as the trio disappeared over the hillside.

"We've got to save her," Tasker urged, suddenly jumping up and gesturing for everyone to follow.

"Don't," Zeidler warned—his mouth dropping when everyone sprang up in pursuit. Shaking his head in disbelief, he reluctantly followed.

The Coverts, in pursuit with their guns at the ready, followed the makeshift path to the edge of the hillside.

"*Let them keep ahead of us,*" Kern whispered, stopping where the path descended the hillside.

"We should get out of here," Zeidler urged as he met up with the rest of the Coverts.

However, none of the soldiers listened to him. No, all of them stood at the edge of the hillside, looking down at where the light moved back and forth in the darkness well below. After holding the eager team back with a raised arm for several moments, Kern started down the path and waved for them to follow.

The Coverts cautiously descended the hill, keeping watch on the beam of light far below while pushing through the foliage. The rain tapered off to a drizzle during the descent.

Eventually reaching the bottom of the path, the Coverts took in the sprawling roadway before them. Manicured trees lined the grassy sidings bordering the road in both directions. However, the light from the mysterious trio's flashlight had vanished.

"*Where'd they go?*" Emir whispered, searching the darkness with the rest of his team. When he looked at Zeidler, the man simply held up his scanner to him. "*Why aren't they showing up on your scanner?*"

"*They were never on the scanner to begin with. Why do you think I was warning you not to follow?*"

"*It's probably your scanner malfunctioning again.*"

Tasker, who had ventured ahead of the team, returned once more. "*I hear voices coming from the east.*"

Waving his men to follow, Emir darted behind the trees lining that side of the roadway. The five Coverts hurried along in the dark down a drainage ditch, which ran the base of the hillside parallel to the road and the tree line. Eventually, voices echoing from the unseen road grew audible.

So hurrying his men even faster, Emir once again spotted the narrow beam of the flashlight, and then the two Europans escorting the woman prisoner. Keeping his eyes trained on them through the scattering of branches and foliage, he signaled his men to prepare to strike. But unexpectedly, the Europans escorted the woman off the road, and the trio disappeared behind the trees ahead.

"*Go!*" Emir whispered, waving for his men to strike—

A tremendous fireball erupted on the opposite side of the trees!

The five Coverts, feeling the searing heat, sprang from their cover onto the road with weapons drawn—but abruptly stopped and looked slack-jawed at each other. The place where the Europans and woman had disappeared—where the fireball had erupted but had also vanished—was a ten-meter-high rock wall carved out of the hillside. The whole area was dark, save the roadway's navigation lights towering well overhead.

"*What's going on?*" a dumbfounded Brent Tasker eked out, looking around at the other Coverts with such a perplexed gaze. "And did anyone else see a fireball?"

Everyone fell silent and looked around wide-eyed in anticipation of an ambush.

However, the sprawling roadway lay abandoned.

"They couldn't have scaled that wall," Gunn mused, staring up at the top of the chiseled rock.

"They were *right here*," Tasker insisted.

Once more, everyone traded odd looks.

"Did you see how much the woman looked like Jaden?" Volk hesitated— quickly recoiling at the incredulous stares reflecting back at him. "That's why I followed without thinking. She looked like her twin— blonde hair and all."

"*She had brown hair,*" Gunn shook his head. When Tasker nodded in agreement, he added, "She was much shorter than Jaden—about Alexis' height."

"She was *tall,*" Tasker grimaced at Gunn. "Your eyes going bad? She was taller than both men." Upon trading contending glances with Gunn and Volk, all three of them looked to Zeidler. "What did you see?"

"A woman with red hair—just like Vicky had."

After a round of quizzical looks, Tasker, Gunn, and Volk fell into a rather heated debate about the woman's appearance. Zeidler, quickly tiring of the discussion, took in Emir's silence and troubled expression. Rather than rallying everyone to leave, Kern simply stared at the rock wall with a bewildered gaze.

Suddenly, Zeidler caught sight of the off-ramp ahead—and his eyes shot wide. "Look where we are!" When everyone returned dumbfounded gawks, he declared, "This is where we ambushed Aurelian Galerius!"

The others, their faces waxing tellingly, fell silent.

"The road's finished now, but this is *definitely* the place."

"How could we be south of the palace without seeing it?" Gunn gasped. He looked around at his teammates, who returned hapless stares.

"What does all this mean?" Gunn asked.

Emir remained silent while staring at the rock wall, his face boasting the most troubled expression. But falling under the concern of his unsettled team, he bristled. "*It means we're all going crazy.*" Another preoccupied glance toward the rock wall followed, before he waved everyone in the direction they had come. "Let's head northwest to the outer regions of the settlement."

While his team resigned themselves to another long march, Emir took one last long look at the rock wall.

"What did the woman look like to you?" Volk asked Emir as everyone set out to find the path leading up the hillside. When his superior kept silent and to himself, he repeated, "Kern, what did the woman look like?"

Emir flashed him an irritated scowl. "*Let's just get out of here.*"

Tom Andrews lay on his cot in the gloomy prison cell deep beneath the Europan Royal Palace, his head and chest propped up as much as he could bear. Kate Gillen, sitting close to him, fed him cold soup delivered earlier by the guards.

"Are you getting enough to eat?" she asked, the concern in her voice readily apparent. She dipped the spoon into the weak broth and lifted it to his mouth again.

"I think so," Tom eked out—cringing in pain as he readjusted himself on his bed. "But I'm realizing just how awful this soup is."

She rather laughed. "I guess that's a good sign."

Though leaning in over him and spoon-feeding him his meal, she desperately wanted to avert her eyes. Thanks to repeated interrogations, Tom looked terrible. His face boasted some notable bruises and cuts, as did his arms. His mission uniform, tattered and torn here and there, betrayed the beatings he had received. She assumed he suffered from internal injuries as well, including the psychological torment that made Europan torture infamous. Of course, he never talked about the interrogation sessions—she didn't want him to either. But his condition grew worse each day. She didn't know how long she could maintain her facade. The veneered expression would eventually break, and then he would know just how anxious she really was.

And what if Tom died and left her all alone?

"How many days do you think we've been here?" she asked, trying to keep her mind off her concerns.

"I figure over three weeks."

"It feels like forever."

After feeding him the last of the soup, she set the bowl on the floor, took the water glass sitting at her feet, and attended him through a long drink. Not that Tom was unable to perform these tasks himself. In fact, he insisted on doing as much as possible—to no avail. No, Kate held her ground, reaffirming her orders for him to rest.

After setting down the glass, she carefully opened his shirt and examined his chest wound. For the first time, he didn't wince when she tended to the injury. "Looks mostly healed."

"See, there's always a silver lining to be found."

"We should get you cleaned up."

She unfastened the rest of his shirt, pulled him up into a half-sitting position, and removed the garment. Despite her best efforts, he winced in terrible pain as she did all this. She went over and dampened the cloth hanging from the sink, as she had ritualistically done for the last three or more weeks. Returning to him, she carefully wiped the dirt and clotted blood from his face, arms, and chest. Though she possessed the warmest of bedside manners while doting over him, her countenance fell. "I can't stand it when they take you. You come back worse each time."

Tom took in her anxiousness and forced a smile. "I'm okay, Sunshine. And I couldn't be in better hands."

Kate paused and took in his reassurance. Her face warmed, and her eyes shimmered for the first time since before her capture. "You're bravery surprises me sometimes."

"I never had to be brave. Michael was always the brave one. I was just the guy who told jokes."

For the first time since the ambush, the warmth didn't drain from her face at the mention of Michael's name. Rather, her eyes remained bright and warm.

"The *Three Musketeers*," she said with a sentimental nod. When he waxed sentimental too, she added, "Those were good times. I never appreciated them until now."

"Me too, Sunshine."

A heavy silence fell over the prison cell.

"Michael would want us to move on though," he nodded, watching her respond in kind. With his gaze growing distant, he added, "*I need to move on*. As much as I cherish all those adventures with Michael, I never got a chance for a normal life. I just followed him from one dream to the next." His face grew increasingly pensive. "I want a chance to enjoy the simple pleasures of life ... evenings at home ... the company of family—all those things I never got to experience."

She bowed her head and averted her eyes, her face waxing grave. "I don't even dare hope for such things anymore." After falling silent through a sad moment, she shook her head. "Every time I got close to having those things ... they just *slipped* through my fingers—and this *stupid* mission. What was Michael thinking?"

He took in her sadness for the longest time. "I'll make sure this nightmare ends soon."

She dismissed his hopeful comment with a subtle smile.

"No, *really*. I'm earning their trust. Europans want cooperation; that's what they think I'm giving them."

"They'll never let us go," she replied, surveying his deplorable condition. "Once they finish extracting information from you, they'll come for me."

"Don't say that."

She fell silent and took in his insistent gaze amidst her own doubts. To break the awkwardness, she grabbed his discarded shirt and began dressing him again.

Footsteps echoed from outside the cell!

Wide-eyed, she quickly redressed him.

The guards burst into the cell. They approached the bunk, pushing Kate to the floor. Without any regard for Tom's condition, the two soldiers picked him up and began dragging him toward the door—Tom writhing in pain the whole time.

"Please! Don't do this!" she pleaded, jumping up and pulling at one of the guards. "You're hurting him!"

The guard in her grasp abruptly let go of Tom, who fell into the other guard still carrying him. Despite her pleas and Tom moaning in agony, the soldier dragged him out of the cell and down the corridor.

"I warned you!" The guard in her grasp barked, pummeling her backward against the wall.

Kate winced in pain from the blow—but fell terror-struck at the soldier's foreboding glare shooting down at her. She recoiled flush against the wall.

"Am I not paying enough *attention* to you?" he snarled.

"*Please don't take him. He told you everything he knows!*"

"The interrogators will decide when they're done with him."

"*What good will it do you if you kill him?*"

The guard pressed against her with his whole body, wedging her against the rock wall. He stared her down with a mocking sneer. When she bowed her head to avert her eyes, he wrenched her hair back, forcing her to look at him. "You look healthy. Would you rather we take you instead?" A sinister paused followed. "I can make that happen."

Kate, desperate to disappear deep into the formidable rock behind her, fell captive to his ravenous gaze.

"Since your friend told us you were a medic," he began, reveling in the terror leeching into her eyes, "You haven't been of interest. But you don't seem to be caring for him very well. Maybe you're not a medic. Maybe he's protecting you for some reason. Maybe we should take *you* to the interrogators instead."

Kate withered all the more. Images of unspeakable torments flooded her mind. Yet she could also hear Tom moaning in agony far down the corridor outside. His suffering cut her to the quick. In defeat, the young woman bowed her head. "Okay … take me instead."

The guard, still pressing against her, took in her surrender—relishing her fear.

Unexpectedly, he laughed and stepped back toward the door. "Unfortunately, I can't do that. We canceled your interrogation sessions a long time ago." When Kate mustered her courage and looked up, he waxed smug. "When we threatened to interrogate you, your friend spilled his guts. In fact, he volunteered to take your interrogation sessions too. The interrogators are pleased with his cooperation." Seeing her face twisting in dread, he let his words linger. "Your friend is in such bad shape because of *you.*"

He flashed one last foreboding look at her before turning toward the door.

Kate stood there, stunned at the revelation.

Reaching the door, the guard turned to her once more. "Of course, we'll revisit your offer soon. I look forward to it." Then he left.

The door slammed shut, leaving Kate alone again in the gloomy cell with only her troubled thoughts.

Emir Kern, crouching with his team in the darkness in the thick undergrowth somewhere on the remote edges of the Europan settlement on Sco-II, studied the four Europans mulling around the campfire in the clearing below.

"What are we waiting for?" an impatient Brent Tasker pleaded in subdued tones behind him. "Let's jump 'em. The smell of whatever they're cooking is driving me crazy."

"Just let Zeidler do his thing," Emir reassured, trying to put out of mind the pleasing aroma of cooking food wafting in the air. He watched the rest of his team fighting the same primitive calling that had drawn them from far away. For that simple reason, Kern was suspicious. He waited through a long moment before turning to Curran Zeidler. "What do you think?"

The subordinate, keeping his eyes fixed on the scanner in his hand, shrugged. "The only life signs I'm picking up are those four campers— and all the wildlife, of course, which is playing havoc with the scanner."

"You certain? I don't want to have to escape into those mountains again."

"At least the Europans kept our minds off how hungry we were," Tasker interjected. When Glen Volk and Eric Gunn grimaced at him, he returned an indignant look. "Hey, I'm bigger than the rest of you. I need more food."

"I'm getting tired of hearing you complain about your stomach," Gunn said.

"Guys! Keep it down!" Emir barked in a hushed tone. "Curran, is it safe?"

"You know how limited these field scanners are." Still keeping his eyes on the small screen, he pointed in the general direction of the opposing bluffs. "I can't be sure of anything too far up those hills. But according to the readings, the whole region is deserted: no sign of other troops or vehicles, no reconbots, no *strikebots* ... not even a hint of a dampening field playing with my scanners. So—"

"So let's get this over with!" Tasker motioned for everyone to move out. "I'm starving."

Irritated, Emir flashed a reproving stare at the underling. "Tasker, I'll shoot you *myself* if you don't shut up!"

"... Everything looks clear," Zeidler continued again, ignoring the banter. He shared a mutual gaze with Kern when the man looked back. "That can only mean one thing."

"It's a trap."

However, Glen Volk shook his head as he stared into his binoculars at the campers below. "I don't think so. Those rifles sitting near the fire are hunting rifles, not military grade. They're just a bunch of hunters out for game."

"How can you be so certain from this distance?" Eric Gunn asked, bearing an incredulous look.

"I grew up on Earth in a family of hunters. It's not too hard to figure out: That's wild game on the fire spit, and—"

"*So that's* what *smells so good*," Tasker mused, his eyes fixed wantonly toward the clearing below.

Volk ignored the comment. "—And watching a bunch of fat men with rifles getting drunk around a campfire in the middle of the woods ..."—briefly glancing out from behind the binoculars and nodding—"... it's like *old* times."

"Europans on vacation," Gunn mused. "Who would have thought?"

"Let's hope you're right, Glen," Emir nodded while studying the clearing below. "We won't survive long without taking their provisions." He studied the Europans for another moment before looking back at Tasker. "Since you're so eager, take Eric and work your way around their flank. Glen, Curran, and I will go straight away down to the edge of the clearing. Hurry up: We jump them in two minutes." As the two men started out, he called just a little louder. "And put your weapons on stun."

Tasker and Gunn stopped and glanced back, with the sizeable Tasker looking disappointed. "So we don't get to kill Europans today?"

"If Glen's right, they're most likely civilians."

"That never stopped us before. You getting a conscience?"

"It'll save energy," Zeidler interjected.

Emir scowled at Tasker. "Just do what I tell you."

With the quick flashes of energy rounds against the night—the sounds of gunfire breaking the quiet subduing the clearing—the four Europan campers slumped unconscious onto the ground, never realizing what had happened. Emir Kern and team stepped out of the undergrowth into the firelight of the camp.

Curran Zeidler brought his field scanner up once more and studied the small screen, letting the others pilfer the camp of its many supplies. "No sign of hostiles."

"Hurry up," Emir urged as his team scoured the unconscious campers and their supplies. "Grab as many provisions as you can carry in your packs—and as much as you can carry otherwise. We can't linger here." When Brent Tasker made a beeline toward the fire spit holding wild game, he barked, "Tasker! First things first."

The dejected Covert reluctantly returned to pilfering the supplies.

"This is *definitely* a hunting party," Glen Volk announced, searching one of the Europans.

"You sure?" Eric Gunn asked from just across the fire where the main supply stash sat.

Volk, his face close to the unconscious man, waved the air around him to disburse the strong stench of alcohol. "*Definitely*. We could have

87

used a lower stun setting: The alcohol had them halfway unconscious already."

"Let's take the alcohol too," Tasker said while stuffing his pack. Upon receiving a round of grimaces from his teammates, he added, "for medicinal purposes."

Volk and Gunn looked at each other, grinned cynically, and shook their heads at one another. The moment quickly passed at Kern's urging, and the Coverts hurried their pace of stripping the camp of anything of value.

Zeidler suddenly looked up from his scanner, his face sobering. "What's the *one* thing my scanner can't pick up?"

Everyone stopped and surveyed the air. A spec of light rose from the wooded bluffs in the distance. Though appearing as if hovering erratically low in the sky, the spec grew larger as it neared the camp. Each moment, the anomaly's speed increased.

"You mean it was just *sitting on that bluff watching the camp?*" Volk asked, the dumbfounded trepidation apparent in his voice.

"These strikebots are getting smarter," Kern shook his head.

Snatching their field packs and rifles from the ground, everyone scrambled away from the light of the fire.

Artillery rained down onto the clearing from the darkened sky, sending the Coverts in several directions. The spec of light, quickly morphing into the all too familiar shape of a strikebot, soared overhead. When the Coverts fired back in defense—one of the rounds catching an artillery armature—the machine flew into cover behind a canopy of trees.

The strikebot would not hide there long.

The Coverts, coalescing into a small band once again, fled the clearing. Glen Volk's voice echoed into the night, "I guess they know where we are again!"

Back at the clearing, Brent Tasker suddenly jumped out of the darkness toward the campfire. Grabbing the handle of the fire spit holding the succulent wild game, the man disappeared once more in the direction of his teammates.

CHAPTER NINE

Understanding and Reflection

Kara Ricci stood affixed in the center of the lonely and dimly lit prison cell deep beneath the Europan military stronghold. Chains hanging from the ceiling bound her arms high over her head, and her ankles were fastened to the floor likewise. Having been bound that way far too long—and for just how long she did not know—she contorted her posture in a futile attempt to minimize the agony and exhaustion screaming from every muscle and joint.

Her empty bunk sat near the door, its paper-thin mattress, musty sheets, and tattered pillow calling to her. However, the dream of indulging in such luxury was just that: a dream. When the guards finally did come and unshackle her, they would drag her straight to the interrogators—just as always.

She looked down at herself, mortified over what she had become. With her filthy clothes tattered and torn from abuse, the exposed skin bore so many bruises and cuts. One side of her face was swollen and tender. She smelled bad too. Yet the physical injuries paled in comparison to the emotional abuse. With the memories of being humiliated day after day tormenting her weary mind, her cheeks lay covered in the salt of dried tears.

The cell door unlocking broke the quiet.

Her heart leapt into her throat!

Two guards, appearing through the entry in an urgent fashion, came over to her. One knelt and unshackled her feet, while the other worked the locking mechanism securing her wrists overhead. Just as the guard who was kneeling stood again—the sound of empty foot shackles hitting the rocky floor—Kara's wrists fell free from the chains overhead. The soldiers caught her in their arms, for she was too weak to balance herself.

Suspended between the two men as they carried her toward the door, she trembled at the thought of another interrogation session—

But ever so gingerly, the guards eased her down onto the empty cot. With every muscle and joint celebrating the unexpected reprieve, Kara melted onto the musty mattress.

The soldiers promptly left, shutting the door behind them—

But her countenance suddenly fell.

Malach Severus must want to see me again, she thought, lamenting the realization.

The locking mechanism within the door turned once again. She propped herself up and stared in fear as the door once more swung open—

Tom Andrews, wearing a filthy, tattered mission uniform and covered with notable bruises and cuts, appeared through the entryway. The cell door closed behind him.

"*Tom?*" she barely eked out, her eyes wide.

When his eyes adjusted to the dim light—his face waxed over in dread at the sight of her. The assuring greeting on his lips evaporated, and he even recoiled away at first.

Kara stared up at the specter, convinced she had finally gone mad.

Swallowing his pity, he choked out, "Hello, Sis."

"*Tom!*"

With her face twisting in surrender, tears streamed down both cheeks. Tom rushed to her cot and pulled her into a reassuring embrace. Kara, clutching onto him with abandon, erupted into uncontrollable weeping.

"It's all right, Sis, I'm here now."

"*I thought you were dead,*" she said through her sobbing.

Letting her cry, Tom simply held her in his arms, repeating, "It's all right, Sis," and "I'm here now," every so often while stroking her disheveled, auburn hair. Kara barely heard the encouragement, for a stream of rambling laments spilled out of her as she wept.

Kara eventually cried herself out. Still holding on to him with her head buried in the curve of his neck, she could feel the holes in his tattered uniform with her fingers—the swollen flesh of his bruises and welts underneath too. Grime covering the fabric stuck to her fingers, and the familiar scent of must from his clothing wafted before her. Her countenance fell all the more.

Yet she relished his embrace and his hand stroking her hair. Thoughts of seeing him disappear over the hillside at the ambush site long ago filled her mind. "How can you be alive? I heard gunfire."

"Yes, there was definitely gunfire."

The Europan private, his rifle at the ready, walked to the edge of the fort-like impression at the top of the bluff. The 18 Scorpi sun warmed him uncomfortably within his combat gear. As unobtrusively as possible, he peered down into the construction site at where Kara Ricci, Phil Marcotte, and David Tashjian stood to the west, surrounded by his many comrades at the bottom of the bluff. Farther to the west, a stalled transport sat in the middle of the road, and three dead Europans lay near the craft. One of the dead men resembled Aurelian Galerius. Of course, the private knew that the sovereign was alive and well protected. Directly below him, a giant excavator sat abandoned against the bluff. Just slightly to the east, an impressive pile of rocky debris from the high wall explosion lay heaped against what remained of the towering rock wall.

Satisfied, he turned and looked at Kate Gillen lying facedown and unconscious near the center of the notch. She hadn't moved at all since his arrival with the Europan commander, the corporal, and Tom Andrews (the soldier didn't know Tom's name, Kate's name—or any of the Centauries' names). Tom stood off on the far side of the notch with the ranking commander. The two engaged each other in a rather intense discussion.

"They've been over there forever," the private whispered, coming to stand where the Europan corporal guarded the unconscious woman. "What do you think they're talking about?"

The corporal, boasting a large set of binoculars slung around his neck, looked over at Tom Andrews with a sneer. "That Terran's trying to talk his way out of a death sentence. I hope the commander lets me kill him."

"You itchin' for a kill?"

"He challenged my honor! He knows the woman at the bottom of the bluff killed Galerius' body double. The commander does too." He gestured with the end of his rifle barrel at Kate's lifeless form on the ground. "That's why he hasn't bothered reviving this one."

"Maybe the Terran's trying to bribe him. I overheard him say something about rewarding the commander's cooperation 'generously'."

The corporal shook his head. "A futile effort. The commander's letting him wallow in all the lies he told. But no amount of fast-talking will prevent what's going to happen to him." Shaking his head with much resolve, he nodded. "Prepare to dig a grave or two."

"If that's true … then why is our commander the one with the petrified look on his face?"

The two fell silent and traded concerned looks. The corporal, whose face waxed quizzical, turned his attention to where Kate Gillen lay facedown and unconscious before him. "What happened to her?"

The two men studied her lifeless form, until the private shrugged. "I don't see any burn marks."

The more-experienced corporal, holding his binoculars to his chest with one hand, leaned over and lifted up the very bottom of her shirt with the end of his rifle barrel, briefly exposing a small patch of reddened skin on her back. "Look at the discoloration … and how fast it's fading away. She was hit directly from behind with a stun charge—that's odd."

"Yeah. Who puts their gun on stun for a raid?"

However, the corporal didn't hear him. Instead, the man stared at Kate's lifeless form heaped into a lump on the ground. "She's beautiful." His mesmerized gaze grew in prominence, until he smiled at his companion. "After I kill the Terran, maybe the commander will put us in charge of her. Why should the interrogators have all the fun?"

"Come here!" the commander waved to them from the other side of the notch.

The two soldiers complied, meeting the commander at the mouth of the fort-like impression.

"Give me your gun," the commander ordered the corporal.

Perplexed, the corporal complied—but he recoiled when the officer handed the rifle to Tom Andrews. "What's going on?"

"Never contradict me!" Tom declared, shooting the corporal in the chest! The binoculars hanging from the man's neck exploded into shards of debris, and the corporal slumped over onto the ground and died.

In disgust, Tom threw the dead man's rifle onto the ground beside him.

The Europan private, frozen in place, looked down in horror at his dead companion.

Tom, not even batting an eye, took the private's rifle. After adjusting the settings on the weapon, he handed it back to the private, walked to where he had knelt with Kate earlier, and turned around. Looking at the private, he said, "Shoot me."

"What?"

"You heard me … shoot!"

The terrified private looked to his commander.

"If you don't," Tom warned, gesturing to the dead corporal, "Your fate will be the same as his."

"Do what he says," the commander assured. "—and no one can know what happened here. If anyone finds out, I'll kill you myself."

Trembling, the private looked down at the dead man and then up at Tom—and then to his commander again. With much reluctance, the soldier lifted his rifle to the ready, aimed it at Tom, and pulled the trigger.

"Is Kate alive too?" Kara asked, withdrawing from Tom just enough to look at him in the dim light of her prison cell.

"Lay down," he urged, gently easing her onto her pillow. Sitting beside her on the cot, Tom took in her disheveled appearance and expectant gaze, his face betraying his dismay over her deplorable condition. He mustered his courage. "Kara, I need you to do something."

"What?"

"Tell Malach Severus that Emir Kern killed Aurelian Galerius' body double."

Looking up at him from her pillow, she searched his face with a grave expression. "Tom, what have they done to you?"

"It's the only way to get you out of here. Tell Severus what he wants to hear."

Once more, she searched his face for the longest time. Her eyes welled up once more, and she shook her head. "I can't do that to Emir."

"No one can help him anymore, Kara." Taking in her churning eyes and the bruise on the side of her face, he began stroking her hair. "I know Emir would save you from this place if he could. ... But he can't. He would insist you do what Severus demands."

Kara, her eyes churning all the more, eventually shook her head and sobbed a despairing laugh. "Nothing will change." As she wiped the tears from her eyes, her face filled with dread. "I made a terrible mistake, Tom ... *a terrible mistake.*"

"What happened at the ambush *wasn't* your fault."

She choked out her despair once more. "Not that. I did something terrible *long ago*, Tom. Everything from then on has happened to punish me for what I did."

Silence fell over the room, and his expression radiated an awkward pity.

So Kara lifted the locket chain out from under the remnants of her torn collar, opened it, and held up the picture of the eight-year-old girl. She watched him take in the familiar image amidst her odd gaze. "Mia's not my niece, Tom. ... She's my daughter."

Tom looked at her in stunned silence.

"You're the only one on the team I ever told—aside from Michael. I told him just before he died." Looking at the picture through tear-filled eyes, she rather smiled. "Isn't she beautiful?"

He took in the girl's picture with her, though glancing curiously at her now and then. His face eventually sobered. "Michael was the father, wasn't he?"

Kara nodded.

He fell silent as she gazed at the picture of Mia. When her eyes filled with longing, his resolve returned. "You can't blame everything on one mistake."

She closed her fingers around the locket and brought the hand to her chest. Mustering her courage, she shook her head. "Mia *wasn't* a mistake."

Tom fell speechless.

Her eyes filled with regret. "Michael was inconsolable—*and so helpless*—when Caffry told him his brother was dead. I saw my chance to win him over ... and I took it." A laboring pause followed. "I just *knew* he would do the right thing when he found out I was pregnant. The next morning, I realized how foolishly I had acted. But it was too late. ... *I tried to make amends* ... but everything I did from then on only made matters worse."

Tom said nothing. Instead, he looked down at her with such empathy and stroked her hair once more.

Kara remained distant through the awkward silence, until she shook her head at herself. "I seduced my grieving best friend to trap him into *my* fantasy." With a singular, self-deprecating laugh, she looked him in the eyes. "Have you ever wanted something so badly, you'd do anything to get it?"

Though he continued his vigil over her, he grew distant and unsettled.

"I did. That's why I'm being punished."

The awkward silence persisted—unnervingly too. Tom scooped her up into his arms and held her. "I'm sorry, Sis." He looked over her shoulder, his face churning and his gaze still distant. "It's my fault you're here, not yours—I made a mess of things since we arrived." Hesitating, he struggled with his words. "I have secrets too. I'm not who you think I am. My name is *Trajan* ... I'm a very powerful Europan"—unable to see her cringe—"... and I *will* get you out of here."

Kara's eyes welled up again as she held on to her friend even tighter. With much caution, she withdrew from his embrace just enough to take in his insistent gaze—and the sight of his tattered uniform, his bruises, and the smell of must too. Her face filled with such sadness. *"Tom, what have they done to you?"*

"I'm telling you the truth."

"Okay ... okay. ... I believe you." Though she didn't.

"No, really." His eyes pleaded with her. "I'm sorry for what's happening to you. I couldn't stop them from arresting you at the ambush. But I will get you out of here eventually."

Kara searched his face for the madness that plagued him. He seemed so sincere—and that scared her. Ironically, she saw subtle traces of the typical Europan build amongst Tom's Terran features. Of course, the resemblance meant nothing. No, she had known him far too long to believe such nonsense. "Why are you telling me all this now?"

Tom took in her concern, and his face waxed sad. "I know you don't believe me. I understand." After kissing her on the forehead, he stood and knocked on the cell door. "But I *will* get you out of here. Believe me."

The door opened, and a guard stepped aside to let him through.

"Tom," Kara pleaded just before he stepped out of the cell. When he turned around, she sat up and gestured with her eyes toward his tattered uniform and injuries. "If you really are who you *say*, why don't you look any better than I?"

"Did you ever want something so badly, you'd do anything to have it?"

Offering one last sober look, he turned and left.

Kara eased back down onto her pillow and listened to the footsteps fade away. The mattress no longer brought her comfort, and she shifted about on it nervously. With Tom's words and outrageous claims repeating in her mind, she filled with dread over what had become of him. She hated Malach Severus and the Europans that much more. But an even worse dread crept into her thoughts.

What if everything Tom said was true?

Michael Gillen sat against a large rock outside Raathe's adobe home, finishing his evening meal alone. The night chill had set in over the Dulos village, and so he relished the rock's proximity to the warm fire. The pleasing smell of smoke lingered in the air.

He sat lazily against the rock, thankful he no longer suffered over the pain of his injuries for the first time in a month, the span of time he had stayed with the Dulos.

Yet the thoughts haunting him would smart for some time.

Looking toward the wooded bluffs on the horizon, he gazed at the soft glow of lights from the Europan settlement illuminating the night sky. Katey was out there somewhere—and he was helpless to go to her. His thoughts labored under so many uncomfortable emotions.

He dared not ponder the terrible things she may have endured since her capture. But holding on to the hope that she was still alive, the young man longed for the fleeting chance to snatch her—and the others—away from the dangerous planet.

But what if she was already dead?

He winced at the thought.

Raathe appeared from the adobe structure and sidled his hulking frame up beside him. Michael looked up at the leviathan. Though he had spent over a month as a guest in the village, the leader's size and muscular appendages still intimidated him. He felt the knot in his neck too—from looking up all the time.

"Word of Gillen men to north," Raathe exclaimed, sitting down next to him. When Michael perked up, he continued, "Masters find trail. Find soon. Not end good."

The young man sighed and melted back onto the rock behind him. "I was hoping for good news." After a sober pause, he looked back up at the Dulos. "Can you help them?"

"Much risk for few of Gillen's. If Master learn, kill many Dulos." Watching his reaction, the Dulos' gaze grew intentional. "Raathe offer trade: Dulos help Gillen, Gillen help Dulos. Free Dulos."

Inwardly, Michael laughed at the familiar proposal. "Maybe we can work something out."

Both fell silent and turned to watch the fire. After quite a while, Raathe turned to him. "Gillen quiet all day. Thoughts?"

"Too many."

"No, think Gillen think *one* thought."

Michael looked up and smiled back at him, amazed at the leader's intuition. He regretted his preconceptions of the Dulos upon his arrival into the village. Despite their strange appearance, the Dulos were human to the core. Raathe, in particular, was as capable a leader as any man he had met, President Mitchell of Earth States included. He turned his gaze upon the flames once more. "My wife."

"Come with Gillen?"

He nodded. "She didn't want to—but I forced her to come with me."

"Sorry. Part of trade? Free mate when Dulos free."

Michael shrugged. "One thing is certain: I'm running out of time—maybe I already have."

Raathe bowed his head. "Yes. Do soon. Master unrelenting. Raathe miss son. Still regret day Master take."

"I'm sorry."

"Gillen not know *many things* when come. Now, not see Dulos like masters; know Dulos human; give respect. Dulos grateful; Dulos respect back. Gillen know Dulos suffer; know it wrong. Want to help Dulos, but not able alone. Dulos help Gillen: Share risks, we will; share rewards, we will. Dulos get freedom; Gillen get mate, friends. Help Dulos. *Do now.*"

Michael hesitated. "I don't know *how* to help you. Why do you need me anyway?"

Raathe looked down at shook his massive head at him. "Gillen still not know; need learn. Yes, Dulos strong"—putting a massive finger to Michael's chest—"Gillen twig. You no think we know?" He grabbed the metal proximity collar around his thick neck. "Collars not hurt. Just remind Dulos." He pressed his fist over his heart. "Dulos made deep inside to obey; *Dulos have no will.* Master make that way; must obey *Master.*"

Michael's mouth dropped, and he searched Raathe's serious expression. "How can that be?"

"Just is."

Raathe, letting his words linger, watched him take in the startling revelation. "Gillen say Master Galerius outlaw..."—pointing to the stars—"... means Master Galerius has Solaris masters. Master no longer chief master of Dulos. Solaris Masters send Gillen; give Gillen power to take Master Galerius; Gillen *now* Galerius' master. *Gillen now Dulos Master;* Dulos now obey Master Gillen; Master Gillen must command Dulos to rebel. Only way. Else Dulos slaves."

Michael sat there looking up at the leviathan, astonished. "You can only fight the Europans if I order you to?"

"Gillen head not so thick now," Raathe replied with a gleam in his eye and a smile. "Gillen command Dulos to rebel. Then, Dulos crush Masters!"

Michael let out a nervous sigh. "They'll annihilate your people if you fail."

"Nothing worth reward that not worth risk. Dulos give lives for chance. Will Gillen help?"

Michael gazed up at the leviathan, unsure how to reply.

"*I'm telling you,*" Brent Tasker urged, looking at his teammates while walking a few steps backward up the rocky trail, "We're not where we think we are. We're going the wrong way."

"Tasker, I'm really getting tired of your complaining," Eric Gunn said. He received a supporting nod from Glen Volk, who labored beside him up the narrow, barren mountain passage. Upon hearing the comment, the sizeable Tasker turned around and kept walking.

"The real question is *when can we stop for the evening?*" Volk rather whined—something atypical of the youngest Covert. "We've been constantly running for over a week now."

"Would you have rather surrendered to the goons we ran into this morning?"

"No, but all this traipsing through these mountains is really getting unbearable."

"Just a little farther, I promise," came Emir Kern's voice behind them.

Emir, looking as haggard as the rest of his team, kept a slow pace several meters behind the subordinates. Curran Zeidler walked beside him. Every muscle in the Covert leader's legs and back cried out to him for relief, and the hole in his stomach begged for a much-needed meal. Of course, he kept all this to himself, just as he kept his concern over their dire situation. But seeing his team trading incredulous looks ahead, he said, "On the other side of this mountain, the passage splits in four directions. There's no way those goons can follow us. Then we can find somewhere to lay low for the night."

"I hope you're right," Tasker lamented, looking unconvinced. "These bluffs look an awful lot like the ones near our old base camp. And you know there was no place to hide there—save the caverns."

Kern nodded, deciding that ignoring the comment was his best course of action—and he was beginning to doubt himself too. He turned to Zeidler, who once more brandished his field scanner in one hand. The man bore a rather perplexed demeanor. After a few more steps up the rocky passage—slowing to fall farther behind Tasker, Volk, and Gunn—he said, "What's it look like, Curran? Any hostiles in the area?"

"Nothin's on the scanner."

"Then what's wrong?"

"It's the metallic deposits in these rocks: Their magnetic field is throwing off the scanning mechanism. Who knows what's out there."

"That means they can't scan us either—passively, at least."

However, Zeidler returned a sober look. "I had the same problem at the old base camp. It's the only region where I had to deal with such a problem."

"The scanner hasn't worked right since we first entered the Europan settlement."

Zeidler shook his head. "I think Tasker might be right about us being lost again."

Emir walked several steps in pensive silence, letting the three other Coverts gain more ground well ahead of them. "Don't tell Tasker. He'll never let me live it—"

Artillery fire broke the evening quiet, accompanied by quick flashes of bright light ahead where Tasker, Volk, and Gunn were.

Both Emir and Zeidler rushed toward the other three with guns drawn. Ahead on the trail, Volk and Gunn stood ready with guns drawn toward something behind the rock face. Tasker lay on the ground, grasping one leg and writhing in pain. When Emir and Zeidler reached them, they saw four Europan soldiers lying lifeless on the ground in an impression carved into the hillside.

"You okay, Brent?" Emir asked as he came to kneel over the injured Covert.

"Don't call me *Brent*," Tasker chided though gnashed teeth. "It's not that serious."

Glen Volk knelt too. Opening his pack, he pulled out his first aid kit and began tending to Tasker's wound. Zeidler, keeping his gun drawn, moved in on the lifeless Europan soldiers. A thorough examination yielded a confirmation: They were all dead.

"What happened?"

"We came around the corner," Eric Gunn pointed, letting his rifle droop. "And there these goons were. They saw Tasker first. The one closest to him got off a shot—but they didn't see Glen and me right behind him. They didn't have a chance to fire another round."

"Good work."

"He just happened to have his gun in his hand. The other three looked as if they were setting up camp for the evening. I don't think they were expecting us."

Emir, standing up and examining the dead Europans, spotted a communicator lying on the ground near one of them. His face fell. "Did this one get a chance to use his communicator?"

"Yes," Zeidler announced, shaking his head while looking at his field scanner. He pointed down the bluff in the direction they had come. "Airborne craft coming this way. We've got about ten minutes before we have company. And I see ground troops deploying from several different locations toward us."

"Can you walk?" Emir asked Tasker, returning to where the Covert leaned against the rock in pain.

"Just go. Leave me enough ammo for a good fight."

"Don't be a hero."

Emir waved Gunn over, and the two men helped Tasker to his feet. With one under each arm of the sizeable Tasker—and both straining under his weight—they helped the injured man up the narrow passage. Everyone followed.

But upon reaching the top of the barren rise—

Every mouth dropped at the familiar sight of the abandoned base camp below them.

"I was right," Tasker beamed amidst gritting his teeth in pain. "We *are* in the wrong place."

"I see they didn't wound your pride," Gunn quipped while holding him up.

"But what do we do?" Volk asked, the urgency in his voice readily apparent.

Emir, falling silent, studied the canyon and cavern entrance below. Then he looked around at his team. "Let's head for the cavern. Perhaps the Europans left our supplies intact."

Zeidler shook his head. "We'll be trapped."

"I think we already are. But I'm not going without a fight."

CHAPTER TEN

Convergence

Kate Gillen sat on the edge of the cot in the gloomy Europan prison cell, keeping an anxious gaze on Tom Andrews lying covered and with his head propped up. With the meager portions of a recently delivered meal sitting before them—pieces of unrecognizable meat portions, dried-out vegetables, coarse bread, and water—she tended to him, just as she had done for what had seemed like an eternity. When he struggled to chew and swallow the stale bread in his mouth, she lifted his water glass to his lips. "Drink."

After receiving the drink, he chewed a few more times and finally swallowed the stubborn food. "Thanks." He looked down at the piece of bread still in her hand. "Aren't you going to eat too?"

"*I'm eating.*"

Of course, the statement was a lie, and she held the piece of bread in front of him intentionally: As long as Tom saw her with food remaining, he wouldn't realize how much of her portions she was actually giving him.

He flashed her an incredulous look, and his face waxed coy. "I don't think you appreciate the fine cooking in this first-class hotel."

Kate smiled.

But the contentment quickly evaporated from the young woman's thoughts. Tom was growing quite ill. Recent interrogation sessions had made him that much more immobile, more lethargic, and even a little distant. She hated watching her long-time friend waste away before her eyes. So she kept close to him, filling the time with chitchat while fighting the urge to break into tears.

But during the small talk, his expression waxed odd. She ignored the change at first, assuming the pain from his injuries had flared again. Yet the odd look persisted, despite his attempts to conceal whatever was bothering him. "You okay?"

"Yeah."

However, his demeanor didn't change. Instead, he grew self-conscious. "What's wrong?"

Tom waved off her obvious and overly concerned reaction. "I'm okay ... *really*."

"Don't con me—I know you too well. *What's wrong?*"

He fell silent under her insistent gaze. Looking up from his pillow with much hesitation, he finally eked out, "I've been feeling guilty lately."

"Why?" she asked, a quirky half-smile leaching into her concerned expression. "Do you think you're undeserving of so much attention of late?"

"Nothing like that—*though it is true*," he strained a laughed. His face fell sober again. "I've kept something from you."

"What?"

Despite her expectant gaze, he hesitated again. "Promise me you won't be mad."

"I promise."

As he labored over whatever disturbed him, Kate felt her stomach tying into knots: She dreaded the thought of hearing a deathbed confession.

"Kara told me something in confidence a long time ago."

"*Okay?*"

With his expression growing heavier, he hesitated again. "Kara's niece ... *Mia* ..."—when she nodded—"... Mia is actually Kara's daughter."

Kate felt the breath go cold in her chest, and she sat there in stunned silence. She couldn't speak. No, the words fled from her lips.

Taking in her troubled reaction, Tom urged, "She told me not to tell anyone. But I couldn't keep it from you any longer. *I'm sorry.*"

She kept silent and wide-eyed, and she held his nervous gaze against her own. For the longest time, she struggled to mouth the obvious conclusion. But the angst welled within her. "Michael was Mia's father, wasn't he?"

Tom offered a telling look.

She fell silent, and her face twisted uneasily. A thousand thoughts raced through her mind, as did the images of Michael, Kara, and what she remembered of the child's face from the pictures in Kara's locket—the pictures Kara had shown her so many times. Kate's desire to have children and her discussions with Michael on the topic flooded her thoughts, how she had put off those plans for the sake of the mission, how any hope of having children with him had died when the rockslide killed him.

"Michael didn't know—if that's what you're wondering," he offered upon seeing her strong reaction. "No one knew but me."

Kate shook her head in disbelief.

"Are you mad at me?"

"No," she replied, though not immediately and more of a deflection. Her gaze grew increasingly distant as the revelation about Michael, Kara, and Mia mocked her. She knew her reaction to the revelation seemed silly. After all, Michael was dead—Kara too. She and Tom faced dire circumstances and an uncertain future.

Yet the revelation nagged at her nonetheless.

Finally, she shook her head again—and with such cynicism. "Life can be so cruel some times."

The sound of footsteps echoed from outside the cell, pushing the nagging thoughts from her mind—for the moment: The guards were coming for Tom again!

"Zeidler!" Emir Kern yelled impatiently, ducking back inside the cavern just before an artillery round pummeled the canyon wall outside. The flash of the explosion lit up the night sky just outside the cave, and the ground shook. *"Where's that escape route?"*

Curran Zeidler shook his head back and forth. "I've got nothing—just like we knew when we arrived!"

"I don't accept that answer!"

Emir, still smarting over leading his men straight into the Europan search parties earlier, looked around the dark cavern. All the equipment left from the time the place had served as a base camp remained. Remnants of the torn blackout netting still hung from hooks drilled into the rock nearby, while the command center equipment sat farther back in the cave. He couldn't see the command center, for the cavern was pitch-black. But everything was still there. A stash of weapon supplies sat near the cavern entrance, bathed in moonlight. His men had heaped the supplies there in preparation for the standoff. However, the ordinances would do little to repel the horde of Europans dug in across the canyon.

Another artillery round exploded near the mouth of the cave, and the whole team cringed. Dust and pebbles rained down on them as the cave shook.

Brent Tasker sat against the wall of the cave, listening to the exchange between Kern and Zeidler while nursing his injured leg. He shook his head back and forth.

"Lieutenant," he called, picking up the rifle at his side and straining to stand. He gritted his teeth against the pain of his injured leg. "They're going to bury us here."

"I'll figure something out. Just rest your leg."

Another artillery round shook the cave.

"No, you won't. We're surrounded—and out of tricks." He paused, looking around at his teammates. "I'm tired of running. If we're going to die, let's take a few of them with us."

Gunn and Volk nodded in agreement.

Emir traded looks with Zeidler through a long silence. Then, he took in the sight of his haggard team for just as long. With much reluctance, he surrendered with a heartfelt shrug. "Okay. Zeidler, where are the goons most vulnerable?"

A wave of morbid excitement washed over the Coverts as they readied themselves.

Zeidler looked into the scanner in his hand. "The goons are positioned in two groups across the canyon." He rather laughed while taking in the overwhelming Europan forces occupying both positions. "I guess the flank to the right is the weakest."

"Volk, get the last of the smoke bombs," Emir ordered. When the subordinate hurried over to the stash of supplies, he looked around at the rest of the team. "We'll lay down a smoke screen over the whole canyon and then rush the goons on that side. Hopefully, our detection dampeners will keep them confused. Don't fire until we run out of smoke or make it up the hill. The rest is up to fate. Brent, do you need help getting around?"

"I'll tough it out and limp along. The pain will keep my mind off this crazy idea."

"Good."

As his team readied themselves for the charge up the hill, Emir looked around once more. His face waxed increasingly awkward. "I need to tell everyone something before we go out there."

Tasker, Gunn, and Volk waited for him to speak. However, Zeidler shot a reproving look at the Covert leader. So they instead watched the two men trading contending gazes.

"What is it?" Tasker insisted.

The odd, silent exchange between Kern and Zeidler persisted amidst the sound of artillery fire outside the cavern.

Emir hesitated. "Back at Cer—"

"The scanner hasn't worked for a while," Zeidler spoke over him, giving Emir another chiding glance. "Kern didn't want you to know— but it's my fault for dropping it against a rock."

"So that's why we kept getting lost," Glen Volk mused.

Zeidler nodded.

"And you don't really know which position out there is the weaker," Gunn pressed.

"Right."

Tasker grimaced. "*Who cares?* We have Europans to kill!" He waved for Volk and Gunn to follow him.

When they broke the huddle and turned toward the cavern entrance, Emir whispered to Zeidler, "*Why'd you do that?*"

"*You should have already told them,*" Zeidler replied in the same hushed voice. His gaze steeled. "*I'm not letting you clear your conscience just because we're about to die. You want to tell them? Wait until we're safe.*"

"*But we're not going to survive this.*"

"*Then I guess you're off the hook.*"

Volk, carrying the remaining smoke bombs, ran to the mouth of the cave amidst incoming artillery. He threw the bombs across the canyon as far as his strength allowed—and dove back behind the rock, barely missing an incoming round.

Thick smoke quickly engulfed the small canyon, obscuring the moonlight from Sco-II's three small moons high in the night sky. Artillery fire rained down near the cavern entrance in response.

Amidst the thick haze, the Coverts emerged from the cavern in random fashion into the cold night air. With Emir in the lead, the men rushed across the canyon, dodging artillery and sidling up behind a series of boulders that had been *Lookout Two* long ago. The concentration of energy strikes pummeled the canyon behind them.

"I can't believe we made it this far," Tasker said in a hushed voice, nursing his injured leg.

"You okay?" Emir asked. When Tasker nodded, he led the team up the steep, smoke-covered embankment onto the hillside above. Tasker limped along at the end of the makeshift line, which coalesced as they progressed up the hill. They noticed that the Europan artillery rounds began originating from over the rise of the hill. Emir looked toward the other Europan position. Through the haze, he saw the same phenomena of flashes: The Europans were charging the canyon; he and his men would engage them soon.

The incoming energy rounds suddenly ceased.

Flashes of artillery lit up the night sky over the hillside—as if the Europans had turned the firestorm in on themselves! Chaotic noises pierced the night air!

Immediately, Emir stopped in mid-stride, stopping his men too.

"What's going on?" Volk asked, looking at the perplexed stares reflecting back at him.

Everyone froze in the thick haze of smoke.

From both Europan positions over the hillside, ear curdling cries and desperate pleas echoed. Flashes of energy rounds lit up the night. The longer the haunting sounds and flashes persisted, the more nervous the Coverts' expressions grew. Chills ran up their spines as the wailing persisted.

"*Everyone, back down the hill!*" Emir whispered with the most disoriented gaze.

The team backed toward the canyon wide-eyed, keeping their guns at the ready. As they retreated down the hill, the echo of the wailing cries diminished—but only because the Europans over the hillsides were dying en masse from some unknown terror.

An Europan soldier suddenly sprang from the smoky darkness. The terrified Coverts trained all weapons on him. However, the man, covered in blood from head to toe and boasting such gruesome injuries, wore the most terrified expression. Paying no heed to the threat of the Coverts' guns, the horrified Europan fled into the night.

The Coverts' cautious retreat turned into an all-out race back to the cavern. Even Tasker hobbled a sprint across the canyon into the protection of the cavern.

"Home sweet home," Tasker said with a wavering voice. No one paid him any mind. Instead, everyone huddled together and fixed their gazes out onto dark, smoky landscape just outside the cave.

"Zeidler," Emir said, "What are you seeing on your scanner?"

"I thought the scanner was broken?" Volk interjected.

Zeidler, ignoring the question, studied the device in his hand. "I see a whole lot of new life forms interspersed within the Europan positions—*and a lot less Europans.* But the new life signs don't appear human."

Emir glanced out into the night, his expression grave. "Are they some sort of carnivores—like the ones we came across near the settlement?"

"Nothing like that. These things are *huge!*"

Everyone traded unsettled stares.

Eventually, the terrifying cries in the distance ceased altogether, while the smoke bombs exhausted their charge. Yet the grey haze lingered in the air.

An eerie quiet fell over the canyon.

"What should we do?" Tasker said, breaking the nervous silence.

Once again, no one paid him any mind. Instead, all eyes gazed out into the dissolving fog.

"The strange life forms are approaching," Zeidler announced, glancing at the scanner.

Moonlight pierced through to the valley floor against the dissipating smoke. Indiscernible shadows in the distance began moving within the remaining haze. The nervous Coverts trained their guns on the movements, and the shadows grew larger.

Out of the remnants of the smoke, the beasts appeared.

The humanoid creatures, garbed in rags, were three to four meters tall. Their enormous frames lay covered in thick, dark, creviced skin with matted hair all over. Muscles layered down overly large arms and legs. Sunken in eyes brooded underneath their prominent foreheads.

Emir Kern had never seen a Dulos before.

"Those are the creatures we saw in the Europan settlement," Tasker said to him as the horde of creatures coalesced toward the cave.

"You weren't exaggerating."

"But what do we do?" an anxious Glen Volk urged.

The towering Dulos came to stand several meters from the cave entrance. Kern and his men stood at the entrance, gawking out at them with weapons drawn and their faces like flint—a futile attempt to appear threatening.

"What do we do?" Volk repeated.

"The *real* question is," Tasker began, looking with his teammates at the horde of Dulos sizing them up, "Do they eat their victims dead or alive?"

Kara Ricci once again knelt on her cot, facing the wall of the dimly lit prison cell deep within the Europan military stronghold on Sco-II. Once again, with her feet tucked underneath her and her knees apart for balance, she drew the jagged edge of the metal shard across the coarse rock repeatedly.

Nothing regarding her deplorable condition had changed, save the increasingly twisted expression on her face, save her whimpering against the pain of brand new injuries from that morning. Each time she moved, the agony and humiliation pooled in her haunted eyes. Nevertheless, she remained missile-locked on the shard in her hands.

The faint sound of footsteps far down the corridor outside broke the quiet.

Wide-eyed, Kara gasped!

But this time, she didn't stop working.

Instead, she worked faster. Each successive pass of the metal against the rock quickened. Against the footsteps drawing closer and her labored breaths, she beamed with pride at the shard's honed edge—

The locking mechanism within the heavy door turned!

Panicking, she spun around on the cot and rolled into a ball against the wall. All the hurriedness drained from her posture. Just as the door cracked open, she tucked the shard underneath her.

Malach Severus, carrying his tea with him as always, appeared through the opening door.

Kara ignored the man's practiced ritual of settling in on the folding chair carried in by the attending guard. Instead, she discreetly adjusted the torn pieces of fabric hanging off her uniform. The filthy outfit had suffered so much abuse from the interrogators and guards, it barely covered her anymore. Severus, smartly dressed in his prosecutors' uniform, only made her feel that much more self-conscious.

"How are you doing today, Kara Ricci?" he asked as the guard left and locked the cell door behind him. Predictably, he crossed one leg over the other and took a sip of tea.

"Don't you think that question's getting a little old?"

"I'm concerned with your welfare."

Kara glared at him.

"Fine. I'll change the subject." Pausing long enough to take another sip of tea, he rather sighed. "I see Trajan hasn't called on you since his first visit. You must be terribly disappointed."

"Are you *really* going to persist with this charade?" she huffed. "What you did to Tom Andrews is despicable."

Severus' gaze steeled. "You say that … yet I think you know what he said was true." He took another sip of tea. When her defiant gaze cracked tellingly, he sighed. "Personally, I'm sorry he insisted on visiting you. No one deserves false hopes—not even you. He might be confident about your future, but I can assure you that Lord Galerius does not feel the same way."

Kara rebuffed his false compassion.

"It must have been difficult learning the truth about your friend … knowing that the man you thought was Tom Andrews was a lie … knowing that everything he ever told you was a lie."

"Stop it!"

The old man took in her revile as if feasting on it. A savoring chuckle followed. "Have you ever played the *lying game?*" When she didn't answer, he persisted. "Here are two statements, one is true and the other is a lie. Statement number one: *We captured Emir Kern today.*" Her defiant stare cracked. "Statement number two: *Trajan is overseeing your punishment.*" A paused followed. "Which one is true?"

Kara, realizing she had fallen under his powerful gaze, looked away.

"*Come now*, don't you Terrans play games? Where's that infamous Inner Rim intellect I've heard so much about?"

She pulled herself tighter into a ball on the cot, still looking away and brooding. She could feel the metal shard tucked underneath her, and her thoughts fixated on the object. A few halting breaths later, she looked him straight in the eyes. "Both are lies. You're incapable of telling the truth."

Severus laughed, and his eyes narrowed with the most relishing gleam. "Haven't you learned by now? It's always easier tormenting someone with the truth."

Kara's eyes welled up ever so slightly, and she fell silent. Severus took in her troubled gaze while sipping his tea.

She hated his manipulation.

"So Doctor Ricci, did you enjoy returning to an operating room this morning?" When she averted her eyes, he pressed, "Of course, I'm sure it's a lot different when you're the patient—and when the surgeons are those clumsy medical interns practicing their skills."

Kara, her whole body still so tender from the nightmare, fought back her tears. Images of the exploratory surgery that morning raced through her head. She could see herself lying on that cold operating table all those hours—*completely conscious! Paralyzed! Feeling the blade of the scalpel! And the interns' hands rooting around inside her! Unable to stop them! Unable to scream!*

And Severus looked so smug about it!

Discreetly bringing her right arm down to her side, she took the end of the metal shard into her fingers.

Severus, still awash in the mix of terror and hate leaching into her eyes, leaned in and said in the most sympathetic voice, "This is *madness*, isn't it, Kara?"

"Just leave me alone!"

"Testify that Emir Kern killed Sigmund Pollux, and all this will end. I promise."

"You know I can't do that."

"He'll die anyway. I'll make his execution quick and painless. I'll risk Lord Galerius' disapproval for your sake—but only if you testify."

Kara, her eyes swimming in her tears, said nothing. When Severus urged her on with an assuring expression, she looked away and stared at nothing in particular.

"You're a fool, Kara."

Sipping the last of his tea, he waited until she looked at him. "That was your last chance. Trajan wanted you to implicate Emir Kern so that he could secure your release." His face waxed sad. "I'm sorry, this will end badly for you—just as I predicted. You see, I really *do* tell you the truth."

The old man gazed at her for some time, radiating something of sympathy for her. Yet she hated him all the more.

"And I told you the truth earlier. We *did* capture Emir Kern. I executed him myself."

Kara, her lips pursing, searched the smugness inhabiting his genteel gaze. "Don't say that."

"It's quite true." he grinned morbidly, sitting before her like a schoolboy eager to recount an adventure. "Emir Kern and I spent quality time together while he lay on that interrogation table ... *poor man.*" He let his words linger. "And the *screaming* ... my ears are still—"

"*You're lying again.*"

"We talked about you."

The hate welled within her, the strong emotion mixing with the dread readily apparent on her face. She clutched the shard behind her tighter, and her eyes welled up. "*You're a bastard.*"

"That's when everything went wrong. When I asked him what happened between you two at ambush site, Emir ..."—shrugging—"... *gave up.*"

"*You're lying!*"

"That's when he died."

"*Don't say that!*"

Her eyes swam in tears, and her face twisted.

"I never saw anything like it," Severus mused. Seeing the madness and the dread ripe in her painful gaze, he feigned sadness once more. "Your betrayal hurt him more than *anything* I could inflict. That makes you a lot like me—"

Kara, wielding the metal shard in her hand, lunged off the cot! Severus' eyes shot wide open just before she pummeled him! Both crashed onto the floor—the folding chair snapping apart and his teacup and saucer shattering upon impact with the floor. Though Severus struggled against her weakened condition, she twisted the old man around until he lay facedown on the cold floor with her on top of him. Locking him in a chokehold amidst her sobbing, she pressed the metal shard to his throat!

"I advise *ag—against* any sudden *mov—movements* on your part," the old man strained through halting breaths. "You'll rip *y—your* sutures."

"Shut up, *Malach!*"

"Don't do this, Kara! The *g—guards* will kill you."

She sobbed that much more. "Tell me you're lying about Emir!"

The old man, struggling to breathe, winced at the sharp blade against his throat. "What if I—I *can't t*—tell … you what you want to hear?"

"Tell me he's alive!"

Severus said nothing. She began trembling uncontrollably as she wept. When his defiance persisted, she pushed the makeshift knife against his throat harder.

"Ahhh!"

"Tell me!"

Severus hesitated. "What *i-if* … I can't give *you th—the* answer you want to hear? *Will you kill me?*"

"Just tell me he's alive!" she begged, her tears coming faster and her face twisting harder. "*That's all I want to hear.*"

"And if *I—I don't?*"

"*Please … just say it!*"

"No! You'll *k—kill* me!"

"Say he's alive! Promise me you'll protect him too—or yes, I will kill you."

Severus recoiled hard against her when she broke the skin with the blade. Blood seeped from the wound, though Kara had yet to sever the artery just a little deeper. Panicking, the old man pleaded with her out of the corner of his eye. "*Stop!* I have just one *ques-question—just one question!*" A pause as he tried to gather himself through labored breaths. "Will my *dea—death be ...* an accident too?"

Her thoughts flooded with images of Sigmund Pollux in the same chokehold, while she held a pistol to his head—and then the sudden flash: the deadly round shooting into Pollux' back just after she had let go of him.

Dread washed over her!

Panicking, she recoiled onto the floor away from him—and threw the shard across the cell. Bringing her hands to her head inconsolably, she screamed a primal scream and wept harder. Her whole body trembled. *"What do you want from me?"*

Severus, cautiously standing and recomposing himself, looked at the shard lying in the corner of the cell. Wiping the blood from his throat with a handkerchief, he took in her crushed state with much satisfaction. "I saw the denial in your eyes every time I mentioned Sigmund Pollux' murder." A cruel pause. "Now, you know better. *You're a cold-blooded killer, Kara Ricci.*"

She recoiled away in horror as he walked past her to the door. When he knocked, the door opened from the other side. Stepping into the entryway, he turned to her again. "I'm glad I could help you realize your full potential. Emir Kern's capture *is* imminent, and I no longer have to worry about his execution."

Kara sat frozen in fear and speechless, her face covered in tears.

"You see, Kara, *you* will execute Emir Kern."

Though she shot a defiant glare at the old man, a telling dread crept into her gaze nonetheless.

"And don't worry about surrendering the metal shard," he said. When she waxed quizzical, he smiled a relishing smile. "Who do you think planted that piece of metal under your cot? I knew your tormented mind would figure out what to do with it." He took in her dumbfounded stare for the longest time. A gleam appeared in his eyes. "*So keep it.* You and I both know who that shard is *really* for."

He left, and the door shut behind him.

CHAPTER ELEVEN

Palace Courtyard

The garden courtyard atop the Europan Royal Palace was opulent. A small Greek-style marble edifice rose up from the corner of the palace roof, serving as a gateway to the courtyard from below. An elaborately hewn stone wall spread out in both directions from the edifice. Just short of two meters in height, the wall trailed the roof's edge and enclosed within its perimeter a lush green lawn. A stone walkway looped around the courtyard just inside the wall, adorned with statues and meticulously groomed shrubs, gardens, and small trees. High atop the palace, the courtyard gave a bird's-eye view of the entire Europan settlement. It was quite the place to be, if one ignored the soldiers and guardbots posted throughout.

At the head of an elegant table in the center of a stone terrace near the edifice, Aurelian Galerius sat facing away.

The cruel dictator was at peace in his sanctuary, for the courtyard was his favorite place on the entire planet. The large, towering palace on which the courtyard sat stretched far and wide, creating a seclusion the ruler rarely enjoyed. The elevated courtyard also allowed him the pleasure of surveying the entire settlement. All the problems and worries of ruling a kingdom had fled from his mind. Therefore, he enjoyed the view of his kingdom while buttering a roll from a serving plate on the table.

However, the meal was just a distraction for him, for he eagerly awaited the arrival of his guest.

The grey-haired man's eyes lit up at the sound of the access door opening behind him. Footsteps approaching quickly followed. Tom Andrews appeared around one side, wearing his tattered *Endurance* mission uniform and boasting many bruises and cuts. Dark circles adorned his eyes from the lack of sleep, and he had lost some weight. Yet he offered the dictator a warm, reassuring smile.

"*Trajan*," Galerius smiled, patting the hand Tom had placed on his shoulder. "I didn't think you would ever arrive."

Tom reached down and kissed him on the forehead. "Hello, Father."

"Wake," Michael heard Raathe's deep voice calling through the fog of a sound sleep.

When the young man opened his tired eyes, he found himself face to face with the Dulos leader's sizeable head. Raathe's hulking form cast a broad shadow over both him and the makeshift bed in the Dulos home. "What time is it?"

"Too late for sleep. Gillen come now."

Michael nodded as Raathe stepped away from the bed. At once, the light of the mid-morning sun streaming in through the windows accosted his eyes. He quickly sat up and started dressing. "Where are we going?"

"Gillen need see. Come quick. Wear masters' cloths." Raathe, very much in a hurry, turned to leave. "Meet outside."

A few minutes later, Michael joined Raathe in the courtyard outside. Three other Dulos standing with him carried Europan rifles, which looked like toys in their massive hands. One of them carried a field pack over one shoulder. None of them paid mind to the stolen Europan corporals' uniform Michael wore.

Raathe wasted no time. He waved everyone to follow and set off around the back of the home. The small band negotiated down a narrow alley between the rows of adobe homes, with the Dulos looking around warily the whole time. Raathe led them through a labyrinth of alleys until reaching the village's perimeter. Giving a cautious look both ways, Raathe led them across the narrow clearing and onto the path leading into the woods. Following the path quite some distance into the woods, the small band reached a clearing.

"Where'd you get that?" Michael asked, taking in the modest Europan personnel carrier sitting in the middle of the clearing.

"Have ways. Masters not know it gone. Gillen fly us?"

"Sure, but how'd it get here if you can't fly it?"

"Jaunto fly!" one of the other Dulos proudly exclaimed.

However, Raathe flashed a skeptical gaze in the subordinate's direction. "Jaunto fly … make Raathe sick—almost kill Raathe. Jaunto watch Gillen. Jaunto *learn*." Having humbled the sizeable creature, Raathe motioned, and the three Dulos underlings squeezed through the open hatchway of the craft.

"Where are we going?" Michael asked as Raathe turned to follow them.

"Master's palace."

"You'll have to excuse me, Father," Tom Andrews—*Trajan Aurelius*—said while navigating around the other side of the table in the courtyard atop the Europan Royal Palace. The entire time, he labored over his many injuries. "I had some business with Malach Severus."

As he took in the young man's disheveled appearance and halting movements, Galerius' smile fell. "You look terrible, Trajan."

"You say that every time we visit, Father," Tom deflected. Wincing in pain, he sat down in the chair opposite Galerius and looked around the courtyard. "This is beautiful."

"I thought it would be a nice change of pace. You can see all of New Tyre from here. When you're finished with your little project, I'll take you out to see it."

Tom nodded and began fixing a small plate of food, taking barely enough to stave off his hunger.

"By the way," Galerius began, setting down the roll he had buttered, "The Coverts disappeared."

"What happened?"

"No one knows yet. The last report from the field indicated that our forces had surrounded the Coverts. The next thing …"—snapping his fingers together—"they vanished, leaving nothing but dead troops and destroyed equipment."

Tom shook his head. "That doesn't make sense. Even *Kern* couldn't have turned such a dire situation around like that." His eyes narrowed. "This is General Taun's fault. The Coverts eluded his troops for over a month. Emir Kern is making sport of our entire military, and Taun is letting him get away with it."

"There is speculation the Coverts had help from the Dulos."

"But you yourself told me that the Dulos befriend no human."

"I'm just telling you the speculation," Galerius replied. "It doesn't really matter. The Dulos are weak-minded creatures under our control, just as we designed them to be. They are unable to turn on my men. But if the Dulos are hiding them, they will be found."

"Good. The sooner we eliminate Emir Kern, the better."

The two men fell silent and enjoyed their lunch. As the old man watched his son, the wrinkles in his face grew prominent. "It pains me to see you this way."

"I look worse than I actually feel," Tom assured while picking at the food. "Although, I must admit that your guards are pretty good at roughing me up."

"That reminds me," Galerius lit up as he reached into his chest pocket. He pulled out a small vial of medication. "Here's a gift from your guards." He threw him the vial, and Tom caught it in mid-air. "The medication will produce bruising and lesions lasting several days. My men aren't too happy about having to rough up a member of the royal family."

"I haven't been too happy about it, myself." He opened the vial and quickly swallowed the medication.

Galerius busied himself with fixing his plate of food. "Well, Trajan, when this is all over, you can beat one of the guards senseless. That'll make you feel better; it always works for me." Galerius returned to his lunch to deflect the tension, though clearly distraught over his son's condition. "Couldn't you *at least* clean yourself up for our visits?"

"I don't want to risk ruining my plan."

They both began to eat their lunch. Tom noticed out of the corner of his eye his father's disapproving grimace.

"I know how much the woman means to you," Galerius mused while cutting off a slice of meat. "But I don't understand why you're doing all this right now."

"She's a widow now—the wife of my friend who died in the rockslide."

"Men of ambition don't wait for opportunity, Trajan. They seize it. Why didn't you win her affection from your friend while he was still alive?" When Tom fell silent, he pressed, "And why the charade? You're the son of an emperor; you have wealth and power. Women are attracted to those qualities. Just the thought of my potential attracted your mother to me." When a smile washed over his face, he added, "The rest came later."

"I know Kate too well. If she detects any hint that I deceived her all these years, she'll draw away."

"If that's true, she'll never accept the truth."

Tom looked at his father eye to eye. "I'll continue the deception my whole life, if that's what it takes to keep her. And right now, it's for her own good: She needs something to connect her to her old life. She needs *Tom Andrews*."

The old man offered a polite smile in surrender, picked up his glass, and raised it to him. "Then here's to my future daughter in-law—even if she never knows it."

The two shared a toast.

"I don't think that will be the case," Tom mused, setting down his glass. "With time and a little work on my part, I think I can get her to come around."

"And how do you intend to do that?"

"By giving her something Michael Gillen wouldn't: *children*."

The old man stopped eating. A gleam came to his eyes.

Relishing his father's reaction, Tom continued, "*I'll give her children.* She'll get her chance to be a wife and a mother—something she could never have done with my late friend. Once her mothering instincts take over, her concern for the welfare of her children will open her to persuasion. Eventually, she'll embrace her role as a future queen."

"Children," Galerius mused with such satisfaction. "—heirs to the throne."

"I thought you'd like that idea."

The old man lingered over the thought. His gaze steeled. "Regardless of her acceptance, her role in providing the next generation of rulers will be vital. The galaxy is growing smaller every day. As we expand our empire to other stars, we will need governors. What better place to find them than among our own children."

Tom smiled. "And when you and I are gone, one of them will take the throne."

"A whole galaxy of Europan systems led by my progeny," Galerius exclaimed, still basking in the thought. He lifted his glass once more—happier than the first time—and waited while Tom followed suit. "Here's to my grandchildren—and lots of them!"

Michael Gillen, looking through powerful binoculars at the Europan Royal Palace a couple kilometers away, stood in stunned silence at the edge of the high cliff. Raathe and the other Dulos stood near him, keeping vigil as powerful emotions overcame the young mission commander.

"Can we hear what they're saying?" Michael asked Raathe in a monotone voice, never taking his eyes off the sight the Dulos leader had directed him to view.

"No tools."

Michael wished he had never set foot outside the Dulos village. Nevertheless, his eyes remained haplessly transfixed on the dreadful scene in the distance: the courtyard atop the palace, Aurelian Galerius sitting there with Tom Andrews, the two men immersed in chitchat as they shared a meal.

His heart sank as the truth set into him; nausea overwhelmed him. His body trembled in anger, and he grew inconsolable. Sadly, everything made sense to him now: the tampering with the Slipstream drives, the sabotage of the *Endurance*, Galerius' double at the ambush site.

Unable to look any longer, he lowered the binoculars to his side.

"Name *Trajan*," Raathe said in deep tones, watching his new friend's mortified expression. "Arrive with Gillen, yes?"

Michael nodded his head, his expression withering.

"Master son. Gillen not *know* this?"

Michael nodded a resigning *no*. With his eyes transfixed on the palace far away, he stood there through an awkward silence. Finally, he turned to Raathe. "Let's get out of here."

With the luncheon and chitchat continuing on the courtyard atop the palace, Aurelian Galerius watched the uneasiness growing in his son's expression. Tom picked at his food nervously. The old man said nothing about Tom's changing demeanor. Instead, the frail man remained cordial while finishing the food on his plate. However, he bristled at the imminent conversation.

"How are my friends?" Tom predictably asked.

Galerius put down his utensils and let out a telling sigh. "Trajan, you know the two men, Marcotte and Tashjian, are well taken care of …"—looking him squarely in the eyes—"… so I assume you are *really* asking about the woman, correct?"

Tom offered a reluctant nod, causing Galerius to continue eating lunch as if they had never broached the awkward subject. When Tom's gaze persisted, the dictator paused from his meal. "I drew up Kara Ricci's execution orders yesterday."

"But what about Malach Severus' investigation? What if he concludes that Emir Kern was the one who killed your body double?"

"It's been weeks, Trajan. Even the woman has yet to refute her guilt. The only one who's convinced Emir Kern is the real murderer is you. No, time is running out. Her public execution will take place on my birthday—a gift to me of sorts."

"That's only a week away. Did you sign them?"

"No. the orders await your signature, Trajan. Can you do me this honor for my birthday?"

Tom fell silent, and his gaze waxed over in dread.

But the old man's eyes steeled. "Trajan, Kara Ricci murdered an Europan citizen *and* attempted to assassinate me. How long will we engage in this *endless* debate?"

"I never asked for anything else, Father—except sparing her life."

"Ask for anything else, and I will give it to you forthright. But the woman deserves to die." His growing impatience welled up through a tense pause. "I cannot understand your lack of agreement on this issue."

"She's my friend," Tom retorted. Upon seeing Galerius' indifference, he rather huffed. "What your interrogators are doing to her is inhumane!"

Galerius slammed his fist on the table. "Enough!"

Tom, falling silent, looked around self-consciously at the guards posted throughout the courtyard.

Galerius watched him through a long, awkward moment. Surprised at how easily he had cowed him, the dictator's face turned affable. He wiped his mouth with his napkin, pushed away from the table, and smiled. "I want to show you something."

Following his father's lead, Tom rose from the table and escorted him on a leisurely stroll through the courtyard gardens. Several gardenbots were busy manicuring the displays, though the two men paid them no attention.

"Here's the other medication you requested," the grey-haired man said after pulling out a vial and handing it to him. Tom, keeping a slow pace next to him, examined the transparent container's contents.

"Will it work the way I need it to?"

"It'll give you the near-death symptoms you're looking for."

"All of them? This needs to look real."

"That's what my medical advisors tell me. The pain inducers are much stronger than what you've taken before—no feigning this time. You *will* feel as if you're dying—the medicine may even kill you."

"I'll take my chances."

Though he began opening the vial, Galerius took it back from him.

"Here we are," the old man announced as they entered the inner courtyard.

Tom turned to look while coming to stand before an elaborate marble fountain, the centerpiece of the entire courtyard. Countless waterspouts inside the fountain created an effervescent, waist-high cloud of rolling water. At the center of the fountain, a statue of a beautiful woman rose into the air. Arrayed as an angel in flight, the marble image gazed down at him warmly from her lofty position. The name on the front of the fountain prominently read *Livia*.

Tom immediately fell under the power of the image.

"I guess the sculptor did his job," Aurelian Galerius smiled upon taking in his son's reaction. But the image captured his gaze too.

Tom never took his eyes off the woman's sculpted face. "It's been so long since I've seen her face."

"This is what makes this courtyard special. Some days, I'll just stand here and look at her for hours." He paused while staring at the sculpture. "When the main palace is finished, a much larger version of the statue and fountain will grace its entrance. Your mother made a tremendous sacrifice for the Europan people. It's only fitting that she is both re-membered and revered."

Tom nodded.

"Do you understand your mother's reasons for what she did the day she died?"

"You mean *the day I killed her.*"

"She chose her fate, Trajan. You simply obeyed her wishes. ... *but do you understand?*"

"To make me stronger ... to shock me out of my Terran perspectives, I guess."

"That was part of it. Your mother blamed herself for indulging your Terran side. She knew she would continue to influence you—because of the influence the Terrans had on her. When she realized she would never see you again, she remembered the Europan *Rite of Vengeance* reserved for the son of a noble, an old custom that most of our people had forgotten. Her infidelity against me by taking another husband—a Terran husband at that—gave you an ironclad ascension rite. No one can question an heir's right to the throne who executes his own mother for the sake of his father's honor—at age seven, nonetheless. And when you returned to Earth States as a teenager and killed your Terran father, you sealed that rite indisputably."

"That wasn't my intention," Tom looked down, his eyes churning with regret. "He found out Mother wasn't a Callistan—and whose son I really was. He threatened to expose me publicly and cut me off. My plan to infiltrate the Terrans' intelligence organizations was at risk. I'm still haunted by the images of killing him."

"It doesn't really matter. The results speak for themselves." Galerius paused intentionally. "Your mother made a tremendous sacrifice for you.

Now, her legacy begs you to fulfill everything for which she sacrificed herself. Executing Kara Ricci is the first decision in a long line of difficult decisions you must make."

However, Tom shrunk under his father's expectant gaze. "I think Mother made a terrible mistake about my potential."

Galerius remained quiet for the longest time, choosing to deflect the tense discussion by gazing up at the image of his deceased wife. "Have you ever heard the story about David and Solomon?"

"No."

"What kind of literature education did the Terrans provide?" the old man chided before turning back to the statue. "David lived thousands of years ago. He was a shepherd boy who rose to become a great king—a man of war and greatly feared by every kingdom who opposed him. But at the height of his reign, David despised his god: He slept with Bathsheba, the wife of another man. When he could no longer hide his indiscretion, David had the innocent man killed and took Bathsheba as his wife."

"What was so egregious about that? Such actions by nobles are not unheard of today."

"Times were very different, Trajan. Anyway, when Samuel—David's prophet—confronted him on the transgression, David immediately confessed and repented of his evil." He shook his head in a sad fashion. "But it didn't matter. Because of what David had done, Samuel prophesied that the sword would never depart from David's house. And that's exactly what happened: The illegitimate child died, and David spent the rest of his life fighting civil wars with the sons of his other wives."

"So his kingdom crumbled?"

"No, David was highly favored by his god. Samuel *also* prophesied that Bathsheba would give birth to Solomon, who became a great king and ruled during a time of peace. Solomon was so great and so wise, kings came from the ends of the earth to witness his wisdom."

Tom took in his father's contented gaze as the man stared at the sculpture before him. "I'm not sure I understand."

Galerius turned his head and looked at him with the most relishing glimmer in his eyes. "Trajan, do you believe in divine providence?"

Tom shrugged.

"I never did—at least not at your age," Galerius began, turning toward the statue once more. "No, everything I achieved I earned by unflinching resolve and ruthless means." An intentional pause followed. "But the moment I first saw you standing with your mother when you were seven, I saw a soft, spoiled, *Terran* child. Even as you grew to a young man, I could never expunge your Terran identity from you. Despite your attempts to go back to Earth States as a spy—in a desperate attempt to please me, no doubt—I always wondered whether you could really succeed me. And the stories your friends recounted to me about you ... they convinced me I could never reverse your Terran heritage. Even now, I see the conflict in your eyes."

Tom's face fell. "I'm sorry, Father."

But Galerius smiled. "I see things differently now, Trajan. You're *not me*—and that's a good thing. My ruthless tactics always came easy to me ... a simpler way to accomplish my objectives. And because of who I am ... this *sword* will never depart from me, so to speak. My legacy will always be one of imperialism and brutality."

"I don't think of you that way, Father."

"That's your mother's softer side within you speaking," Galerius assured. "Trajan, fate insulated you from my violent ways for a reason. Fate gave you your dual identity as Europan *and* Terran for this very moment in history: The Allies are languishing as we speak. They are vulnerable, and our chance to subdue them will soon be upon us. At that time, we will strike! In one fell swoop, we will take back everything we lost. We will subdue all of Solaris in the process!

"... But my time in history is quickly passing. I'm returning to Terrae Solaris to crush Earth States and the rest of the Inner Rim, just as destiny has called me to do. The Europan Empire will then rule all of Terrae Solaris—18 Scorpii too. The victory will usher in a glorious era of peace."

"It sounds wonderful."

"But a kingdom at peace needs a peaceful ruler, a ruler who can bridge the divide between Europan and Terran ways of life. That's why fate made you who you are, Trajan. The Empire will fall apart otherwise." He turned toward his son, who shrank under his confidence. "Yes, you will succeed me as ruler, even as I live. Then, you can take my place in history and bring my empire to a glory never achieved by mankind. History will credit me as the great architect of that legacy."

With Tom still silent before him, Galerius took his hand and placed the vial of medicine in Tom's fingers. "But even though you won't have to bear the burden of the conqueror, you must vigorously defend my kingdom against any threat.

"Trajan, Kara Ricci is guilty of capital offenses against your own father—the sovereign ruler of Europa—*and* the Europan people. A great ruler must sometimes make great sacrifices." He opened the vial in Tom's hand and gave him the medication. "Take this. Go and win the hand of the woman you seek. But while you're indulging your Terran desires, consider all the Europans waiting for you to embrace your *Europan* heritage."

Galerius' face waxed affable once more. "I won't sign Kara Ricci's execution orders against your wishes. When the time is right, *you* will sign the orders for me."

With much trepidation building in his return gaze, Tom took the medication into his mouth and swallowed.

Kate Gillen sat alone in the dank cell, waiting for time to pass. Never was her cell more of a prison than when Tom Andrews was gone for interrogation.

The wait grew more unbearable each passing minute. The guards had dragged him from the cell hours earlier. When he had left, he could barely walk. She feared that he had finally succumbed to the abuse and died. Every minute seemed to confirm her worst fears.

The groaning of iron hinges broke the silence, and Kate sighed in relief. When the thick metal door swung open, she shielded her eyes from the blinding light streaming in on her.

But her heart leapt into her throat!

Tom, slumped over between the two guards carrying him, appeared at the door. Disgusting bruises covered his arms and face, and he lapsed in and out of consciousness while groaning terribly. The soldiers held him so gingerly too. Rather than throwing him to the floor as usual, they carried him all the way to his cot and eased him down onto the mattress.

Though she kept back against the wall while the guards worked, she leapt off the cot the second the door slammed shut.

"Tom!" she cried, falling to her knees beside him and taking him into her grasped.

Moaning in pain, he barely acknowledged her presence.

"*Tom?*" she pleaded, taking him by the hand—desperate for him to look at her.

Yet he remained barely lucid and suffering terribly.

Kate pursed her lips while gazing at him. A dark coldness washed through her, and she fought the dreadful sensation. Nevertheless, the grim reality overcame her, causing her to tremble in fear.

Tom was dying.

CHAPTER TWELVE

Fireside Chat

Michael Gillen sat in quiet resignation against a large boulder in Raathe's courtyard, basking in the light and warmth of the fire before him. Night had fallen over the Dulos village, bringing with it a sharp chill. Yet the dancing flames kept the cold air at bay.

He wasn't alone. Several Dulos men also sat around the fire, their massive bodies blocking most of his view of the darkened village. Others mulled about in the shadows draping the immediate compound. Like him, his companions kept to themselves.

He yawned. The late hour had turned his thoughts into a jumbled mess. He wanted to drag himself into the adobe home and onto his makeshift bed. Yet the soft glow of lights against the night sky from the Europan settlement far over the horizon—and his longing for Katey somewhere in that settlement—kept him there.

So he would keep vigil as long as his strength allowed.

"As I live and breathe...," echoed a familiar voice from somewhere in the darkness ahead of him.

Michael perked up and scanned the night. Out of the shadows, a small group of Dulos labored in random fashion toward the fire. Right behind the arriving Dulos, an equally exhausted band of Coverts appeared. He noticed their disheveled appearance, thinned faces, and Brent Tasker limping from some sort of leg injury. Behind the Coverts, another wave of Dulos carried equipment from the abandoned base camp cavern.

"... *Michael Gillen* ... back from the dead...," Emir Kern quipped as he came into the firelight. "They told me you were alive, Gillen, but I had to see it for myself."

"Sorry to disappoint you."

Emir laughed.

The Dulos sitting around the fire stood and met the arrivals. When one of them bellowed an odd howl into the air, the surrounding village came to life. Dulos appeared from everywhere to greet the returning rescue party.

Raathe came out of the home, followed by his mate. Word spread that the rescue team had returned, and the courtyard filled with Dulos greeting each other and exchanging stories of the rescue. Raathe welcomed each of the Coverts personally. The Coverts, in turn, expressed thanks for their rescue.

Michael, never moving from his rock, watched Emir sit down near him at the fire. Thoughts of the standoff at the ambush long ago filled his mind, and he saw the same preoccupation in the Covert's gaze. When Emir said nothing, he exchanged awkward looks with him amidst the celebration filling the courtyard.

Though many from the rescue team soon left with their families toward their homes, the reunion continued. Eventually, Raathe called out to everyone, "Must hunger. Come, will feed." He motioned the entire group into the house.

"I'm starving," Brent Tasker said, waving the other Coverts to follow as he hobbled toward the adobe home.

"When *aren't* you starving," Eric Gunn quipped. Following his teammates toward the entrance, he looked to where Emir sat near Michael at the fire. "You getting something to eat?"

"You guys go ahead. The commander and I need to catch up."

The two *Endurance* leaders watched the courtyard empty, until only they remained outside. Michael, feeling the chill in the air that much more, cinched up his jacket.

"This is quite the vacation spot you've got here," Emir quipped.

"It's kept me out of harms way—gave me a place to recover from the rockslide."

"We took the scenic vacation package," Emir rather laughed. "Saw the whole planet—at least it felt like it." But his cynical grin quickly faded. "The goons were brutal. If your friends hadn't shown up, I'd be dead by now."

"Do the Europans know the Dulos rescued you?"

"I doubt it. The Dulos left no survivors—left no trace they were there either."

"I hope you're right."

Emir nodded.

The two men fell silent and traded contending gazes through the awkward moment.

"So did you know Tom Andrews' true identity?" Emir asked unexpectedly, studying Michael's strong reaction to the question.

"You know?"

"*Trajan*"—and the Covert said it with such cynicism—"left a message back at the base camp in case any of us escaped to the *Aurora*—which he sent into deep space so we couldn't leave, I should add."

"He sabotaged the *Endurance* too. And before that, he modified *Endurance*'s Slipstream drives so we arrived here early."

"I guess he couldn't wait to get back to *Daddy*." An awkward pause followed. "So did you know?"

Michael rather shrugged. "I thought all that tampering with the *Endurance* was you." When Emir half-nodded, he added, "No, I've known Tom Andrews since my first year at the university—never even a hint he wasn't who he claimed to be. I guess that's the idea with Europan infiltrators."

"At least he considered you a friend. In his message, he promised you Centauries safe haven."

"That's hard to believe, not after the welcome we received at the ambush."

"The soldiers came for us Coverts. I guess *Trajan* doesn't appreciate my vendetta against his father. Our part of his message wasn't as friendly."

"Maybe the sabotage and everything else was to play us against each other."

The two men fell silent and traded awkward looks.

Finally, Emir looked him straight in the eyes. "I won't apologize for what I did at the ambush. I did what I had to do, even if it meant disobeying a direct order."

"I won't apologize either."

Emir studied his face through a long moment. "So what do we do?"

Silence fell once more over the two men, who traded contending gazes amidst the crackling of the fire before them.

"Nothing," Michael replied, offering a rather intentional though innocuous nod. "I want to rescue my team and get off this forsaken rock as soon as is humanly possible. Rehashing our standoff won't help."

"On the way here, the Dulos told me you're planning some sort of grand rebellion."

Michael shrugged. "I don't know how *grand* it is ... but yes."

"What's that have to do with rescuing the Centauries?"

"It's the right thing to do. The Dulos deserve a fighting chance against the Europans. It also provides an opportunity to destroy those three thousand warships."

Emir rather huffed, and his gaze steeled. "The only thing that's going to happen is a Dulos slaughter."

"The Dulos are willing to take that chance—and a rebellion will create the distraction we need to rescue our people."

"We?"

"Yes, I need your help to do it. I need your help with the rebellion too. The Dulos were engineered to follow, not lead."

Emir's gaze steeled once more. "When my men are rested, we're doing what we came here to do: kill Aurelian Galerius. Nothing has changed. This rebellion idea will only complicate our objective."

"What about rescuing Kara? You want that, don't you?"

Emir hesitated, and his face waxed grave. "Kara's dead."

"You don't know that. The Dulos claim everyone taken to the settlement is still alive."

"Then they're lying to get whatever they need from you."

Silence fell over the tense exchange. Both men, bristling at each other, stared into the fire for the longest time.

Finally, Michael looked up at Emir. "What if I promise you your chance for revenge against Aurelian Galerius?" When Emir flashed him an incredulous look, he shrugged. "Of course, the Dulos want Galerius as much as you do, and I need to keep their allegiance." He quickly looked around to make sure they were still alone. "... *But* ... if something happens to Galerius during the rebellion, before the Dulos can get to him ..."—once more shrugging his shoulders—"... what can I do about it?"

"You'd give up your mission?" Emir asked, still looking him straight in the eyes with such incredulity. "—your chance to take Galerius back to the *Weightless* and clear your family name?"

Michael returned a sober look. "I want my wife back—the others too; nothing else matters."

Emir turned and gazed into the fire, his eyes churning with such a gleam—a dark, even lustful gleam. Then, he took in Michael's resolve as indifferently as he could muster. Yet his face betrayed such a subtle satisfaction, even a relishing of the words he had just heard. "Yeah, you never know what will happen when artillery rounds start flying."

"So you'll help?"

"I think you're crazy," Emir laughed a sardonic laugh while straining to stand. Fighting his own exhaustion, he sighed. "But since you're dead set on complicating my plans, I guess I have no choice." He glanced at the glow of lights from the Europan settlement against the darkened sky. "But the first chance I get after the rebellion starts ... I'm going after Galerius."

"Fine. I'll make sure you get first shot at him."

Emir flashed a satisfied look and turned toward the adobe home.

"Kern," Michael called out to him before the Covert had taken too many steps. "How can you be so sure Kara's dead?"

Emir stopped and returned Michael's concern. "Europans aren't known for amnesty." Though he tried to remain flint-like, his face nevertheless betrayed him. "And imagine what she going through if she's still alive."

A shadow had fallen over the dimly lit prison cell, pressing in on Kate Gillen cruelly. This hour was by far the darkest hour of her imprisonment and the low point of her three-day vigil.

Tom Andrews lay unconscious under a blanket on his cot. A cold sweat soaked his forehead. Although the cuts on his face had scarred over and the bruises on his cheeks had faded, he looked worse than ever.

She sat close to him on the cot, leaning over and searching his expressionless face. Keeping his closest hand tightly grasped in hers, she stroked his hair with her other hand.

She tended to him almost robotically. Lack of food and sleep had taken its toll. Her face had grown hollow, and she could barely see him through blurred eyes. Yet exhaustion did not diminish the expression of complete desperation that defined her. She *was* desperate, just as she had grown since Tom had returned from his last interrogation, beaten senseless.

The memories from that time on haunted her. The first day, Tom barely responded to her cues as he writhed in pain. The second day, he lapsed in and out of consciousness. A high fever came over him. He sometimes spoke unintelligibly, and he suffered fits of dementia. His breathing grew heavy and erratic too. At times, he lay drenched in perspiration; other times, he shook profusely as if cold—so much so that Katey would lie close to him to keep him warm. But her futile attempts to help did nothing to stave off the infection riddling his broken body.

However, this day had hit her the hardest day of all. Tom had lapsed into unconsciousness very early on, and his breathing grew shallow. Death seemed only a matter of time. She could do nothing except talk and encourage him—to encourage herself as well. But each moment grew more unbearable than the previous, and she found herself quickly coming to her wits end.

"Tom, you need to wake up. ... I'm running out of stories from the university."

He gave no response—again.

For whatever reason, the cold reality hit her like a sledgehammer. She pursed her lips and fought against the overwhelming sensation.

"... If you don't wake up soon,"—her voice shaking and her eyes welling up a little—"... I'll have to resort to telling all your bad jokes." Sobbing a laugh—unable to bear up under the growing anxiety that had tormented her through the eternity of her imprisonment— she surrendered. So lying down next to him on the cot, she laid her head on his chest and wrapped her arm around him.

Vacantly, Kate gazed at the stone wall beside the cot—but not really seeing it. No, everything faded into the shadows around her. The faint beating of his heart thumped weakly against her cheek, capturing all her attention and consoling her. As long as the steady rhythm persisted, she wouldn't feel the loss of another loved one—wouldn't lose herself once more. She hung on to every pulse. Yet how long would the rhythm last?

"You shouldn't have taken my interrogations," she sobbed, a single tear dropping from one eye down over the bridge of her nose. "I never asked you to."

Michael Gillen and Emir Kern struggled up the thick, overgrown embankment. Pulling themselves up by exposed roots and branches along the ground, the two men quickened their pace through the darkness.

Though the undergrowth made their journey difficult, they welcomed the cover. The thicket lay deep in the heart of the Europan settlement, far from the safety of the Dulos village. Despite the dangers of running into Europan patrols, the other side of the bluff provided an excellent view of the Europan settlement, thus allowing the two men to finalize their plans for the upcoming Dulos rebellion.

"I'm telling you," Kern exclaimed through his panting, "Those infernal cryogenic chambers have diminished my endurance. I've never been this much out of shape."

"Maybe you're just getting older."

"How *old* do you *think* I am?" Kern asked, not appreciating the humor.

Michael laughed.

"Keep it up, *funny boy!*"

After much laboring, the men arrived at the crest. The top of the hill ran flat a short distance before descending sharply down the other side. Lights from the settlement peaked through the tall trees crowding the skyline ahead.

"Can you believe all this?" Michael mused as they navigated through the thick underbrush. Wide-eyed, he took in the vegetation, the insects buzzing in the air, and the sounds of small animals rustling the undergrowth. "None of this was here when the Europans arrived."

Emir, who walked just ahead of him, looked back and grimaced. "It loses its appeal real quick when Europan thugs are chasing you through it. Just hope we don't run into any large carnivores—or a strikebot."

The two men set off through the thick undergrowth toward the northeast edge of the rise. Upon reaching the edge of the precipice, both men's jaws dropped in unison.

"Our reconnaissance didn't do it justice," Emir exclaimed while looking out across the horizon.

"Still think we don't need a rebellion?"

"Not for what I need to do—but this is one scary sight."

Down in the valley below, less than a half-kilometer away, the perimeter of the Europan fleet complex bordered the wilderness. From there, the base spread out in both directions all the way to the horizon. A million lights peeled back the darkness, and the sounds of industry broke the quiet. The massive, grey hulls of three thousand warships filled the entire field of view, and a partially constructed fueling tower spiraled into the night sky at the center of the fleet. The ships were so large and so close together, one could almost walk all the way to the horizon on the backs of the vessels without having to step foot on the ground.

"I never saw this many ships in one place," Michael gasped while Emir took out his binoculars and scanned the base. But his face waxed quizzical. "Even if you count every Europan and Dulos here on Sco-II, you still couldn't fill all those ships with enough foot soldiers for an Earth States invasion."

"They've got enough resources back in Terrae Solaris to compensate—and the Dulos are killing machines." Emir handed him the binoculars and pointed to the nearest ship. "You can see them loading all kinds of armaments, FW-190s, and landing vehicles into the ships' bays. These guys are armed to the teeth. Even a million Dulos can't compensate for hardened artillery. This rebellion idea of yours *will* turn into a slaughter."

Taking the binoculars, Michael watched the Europan support teams loading the formidable equipment into the destroyers. After a careful study, he handed the binoculars back and directed Emir's attention to them once again. "Maybe not. Look at the bay doors: They're overriding the locking and powering mechanisms. That means these ships' power plants are still cold. And that means the fueling tower isn't operational yet."

"That will merely delay them."

"More than that," Michael replied with a gleam in his eye. "Europan battleship designs are similar to Allied ships. Every outer hatch and bay door is designed to remain secured while in port—it takes an override by the computer and a functioning power plant to open the locking mechanisms. If we can catch them by surprise and destroy the fueling tower and control stations, they'll have a devil of a time trying to open them again."

Emir took in the sight of the warships before looking back at him. "That's assuming we actually surprise them."

Michael shrugged.

Calm permeated the gloomy prison cell deep beneath the Europan Royal Palace. Kate Gillen lay fast asleep against an unconscious Tom Andrews, her head still on his chest and one arm clutching him. Having kept a constant vigil over him, the young woman had finally succumbed to exhaustion during the night.

Something nudged her.

She resisted. The comforting emptiness of sleep enveloped her, its dissipation far too alluring to disregard. So she drifted back into the blackness.

But the force imposing itself upon her refused to be deterred. It nudged her arm once more—still gently, but this time with a little more emphasis and impatience.

"… *My arm's asleep…*," a very faint, very weak voice broke the silence.

With the fog of a sound sleep still heavy upon her, Kate lifted her head and looked around through bleary eyes. Tom remained lifeless and in her grasp. "… *What?*"

A moment passed in silence.

"… *You're on my arm,*" Tom barely eked out, tensing his arm as if trying to pull it out from under her. His movements were weak, and his eyes remained closed.

Instinctively, she labored to comply—*but quickly came to herself.*

"*Tom?*" she called to him, tapping his cheek to awaken him.

When he remained still, she felt his forehead. The fever had left him, and his face was full of color once more. Fighting her mounting hopes, she practically slapped him. "*Tom, you okay?*"

His eyes gradually opened, and he looked at her with a vacant expression. Another long moment passed until a familiar, quirky half-grin washed over him. "I will be when you get off my arm."

She smiled and sighed all at the same time, even laughing a bit as a wave of relief washed over her. Nothing else mattered. She didn't even notice him clearly enjoying her lying so close to him. After freeing his arm, she felt his forehead once more just to be certain: no fever—again. "How do you feel?"

"Do we have any food? I'm starving."

Kate cried a laugh as her eyes welled up at the encouraging news. "I was so worried about you."

Taking in the warmth radiating from her haunted brown eyes, he assured, "I told you I would take care of you." With his fingers, he combed a strand of hair hanging in her eyes behind her ear and smiled. "I keep my promises."

She kissed him—much to her surprise! Even more to her surprise, the kiss felt good. So she reveled in the gentle caress, falling under its power as Tom responded in kind. Feelings welled up deep inside her that she hadn't felt since—

"*I'm sorry,*" she panicked, abruptly sitting up and folding her arms in front of her. With Tom propping himself up on an elbow and looking at her rather awkwardly, she averted her eyes self-consciously. "I don't know why—"

The locking mechanism turning within the cell door broke the uncomfortable moment.

"Not again," Kate lamented, her heart leaping into her throat.

The cell door opened. Two Europan soldiers, their guns at the ready, appeared through the entryway.

"Come with us," the lead guard barked, motioning them toward the door with the end of his rifle. "Both of you."

With much trepidation, Kate helped Tom stand. Taking his weight upon her, the terrified, young woman helped him through the door and down the corridor. The whole time, her thoughts raced over the fate awaiting them.

Chapter Thirteen

Turning Point

Kara Ricci, her lips pursed and her eyes filled with a terrible fear, stood alone before the sterile metal exam table affixed in the center of the interrogation chamber. Long restraining chains hung from each wrist, while a thinner chain attached to the dagger in her hands ran under the table likewise. Her haunted, blue eyes remained fixed on the empty table, for the familiar sight of the gruesome tools and equipment throughout the room terrified her.

The door to the chamber slammed open!

Three Europan guards wrestled a very agitated Emir Kern through the door. The Covert, slinging a continuous round of obscenities at them, resisted as the soldiers wrenched him all the way to the table.

"*Kara!*" he cried out to her at first glance—stunned motionless at her deplorable condition. His captors, availing themselves the opportunity, pulled him up onto the table. "*What have they done to you?*"

Kara, the dagger in her hand, said nothing.

Malach Severus appeared through the door and came to stand at the exam table opposite her. Ignoring Emir's struggling against the soldiers restraining him to the table, the noble asked, "Where did you find him?"

"He was skulking around the settlement."

"Was he alone?"

"Another was with him—but that one got away."

Severus' expression steeled as he gazed down at the defiant Covert. "Don't worry, Lieutenant Kern, we'll find the rest of your men soon enough." He glanced at the guards. "Expose his chest."

As one of the soldiers ripped his filthy shirt top to bottom with a knife, Emir looked up at Kara and the dagger in her hand. His face filled with dread at her vacant gaze. "Kara, what have they done to you?"

"She's saving you from a terrible nightmare," Severus declared before turning to her. "Are you ready?"

"What'd you do to her?" the Covert seethed, fighting against his restraints. He looked up at her, his eyes pleading. "Kara, he's manipulating you! This isn't about me … *this is about you!"*

Kara, clutching the dagger, took in the sight of Emir helplessly strapped to the table with his shirt torn wide open. As she looked into his eyes, her own eyes churned all the more. Trembling, she barely eked out, *"I can't do this."*

"Good, Kara," Emir looked up at her from the exam table. *"Don't let him manipulate you."*

"We discussed this, Kara," Severus assured from the other side of the table. "You know the terror awaiting him if you don't help." The noble waited her out. Yet when she stood frozen in terror, Severus nodded to the lead soldier.

The soldier worked a control panel at the head of the table. A machine descended from a compartment in the ceiling, until the half-dome interface at the device's base shrouded the top of Emir's head.

"Don't!" she gasped at Severus.

However, the device continued its work. Mechanical fingers within the interface pressed sensors and probes to the Covert's scalp. Two other protrusions flipped down just above Emir's eyes, causing him to close them in defiance. However, tiny armatures reached down and peeled back his eyelids, exposing the eyes and the surrounding pinkish flesh. Emir, his head locked in place and in a fair amount of pain, fought the assault. Yet sensors within the protrusions descended and pressed hard against both eyes.

Her face only waxed graver. *"Please don't do this."*

"I'm okay, Kara," Emir assured—though his trembling voice betrayed his fear. *"Don't let them manipulate you."*

At Severus' commanding nod, the soldier at the head of the table activated the device—

Emir screamed in agony, and his whole body snapped rigid against his restraints!

"Please don't!" she cried out over Emir's screaming.

Severus fixed his gaze on her. "You can end this, Kara."

Emir fell limp on the table when the diabolical machine paused. But as the Covert struggled to catch his breath, the indicator lights on the interface flashed on again. Emir screamed once more—only worse!

"The longer you wait, Kara, the more he'll suffer."

The indicator lights on the interface fell dark once again.

Kara withered as Emir writhed in terrible pain on the table. Knowing the capabilities of the diabolical machine first-hand, she lifted the dagger up over the Covert's heart—only to recoil it to herself once more.

Emir paid the price for her hesitation. The indicator lights flashed on, and the whole room filled once again with his agonizing screams!

The longer she watched him suffer, the more her head began to spin, the more she pitied Emir—the more the desperation swelled within her. As if detaching from herself and her dreadful reality, she saw Severus urging her on, though his words never reached her ears. No, every sound fell victim to the surreal silence enveloping her and the madness tormenting her mind. The sight of Emir's face twisting harder against the pain filled her whole being; watching his humanity draining from his tortured gaze tormented her more than anything she had experienced.

This was simply the beginning of his suffering, a suffering she knew all too well.

So with her head spinning madly amidst all the confusion, she raised the dagger into the air over her beloved—and plunged it deep into his chest!

"Just go down and check in with the woman behind the desk," the guard said to a petrified Kate Gillen, taking her place in helping Tom Andrews walk down the corridor deep beneath the Europan Royal Palace. The other guard sidled up to Tom likewise on his other side, while the first waved her down the intersecting corridor. They paused at her hesitant stare.

"It's okay, Kate," Tom said, still holding on to the two soldiers.

Kate, watching Tom disappear with his escorts down the other corridor, proceeded in the intended direction until reaching a service counter. An older Europan woman garbed in military regs appeared from the small room behind the counter.

"Here you go," she smiled at Kate, who remained cautious. Pulling out a bin of women's clothing and personal effects from under her side of the counter, the woman set it before her. "These are yours now. You can use any of the showers down the hall to your right. The clothes will be a little loose until you get a few hot meals in you. Put your old clothes in the bin and bring it back when you're done. We'll return them to you cleaned and pressed. If I'm not here when you return, just leave the bin and go down the hall where they took your friend. Medical wants to make sure you're in the same condition as when you first arrived. Then, you and your friend can get something to eat in the guards' cafeteria. We're between shifts, so no one will disturb you. Any questions?"

"I don't understand."

"This is *Prisoner Out-Processing*. You're moving on."

"We're being released?"

"The orders say *progressive parole*." The old woman threw a towel set and toiletries into the bin. "Consider yourself lucky. Most prisoners processed through here leave feet-first on a gurney with the Dulos." When Kate flashed a quizzical look, she added, "You should thank your friend: I understand he had a lot to do with your release."

Kate, acknowledging with a bewildered nod, took the bin and turned to go.

"—Wait," the woman called, stopping her in mid-stride. She reached behind the counter once more, pulled out a container of food, and placed the container in the bin. "Take my lunch."

"I—I *can't* do that." Kate replied, waving her off sheepishly. However, her eyes lingered on the food too.

"Your friend will be a while in Medical"—flashing her a sympathetic smile—"... and you look like you *really* need it."

"Thanks," Kate surrendered.

Very much taken back by the unexpected hospitality, she proceeded down the hall to the first open door on her left. The lights came on as she entered the room, revealing very sterile, utilitarian shower and changing facilities. Setting the bin on the changing bench, she closed and locked the door, carrying out her actions in a nonchalant manner. But once alone—she ripped open the container and tore into the food!

Kate sat on the bench with her knees coiled up and her back against the wall, enjoying what remained of the food given to her by the Europan woman. She didn't care that, because she had eaten so quickly, her face was a mess—a quick swipe of the back of her hand would fix that. Instead, she slouched against the wall of the changing facility, reveling in the solitude and change of fortune

Still savoring the last bite of a simple sandwich, the young woman picked up the final item in the food container: a piece of fruit. She had saved it for last. Her eyes lingered on the sphere, its shiny, succulent exterior almost smiling upon her. Fruit—*real, unprocessed, unsynthesized fruit*—was a rarity in her world. She hadn't eaten such a delicacy since her time on Earth long ago. Yet the fruit sat in the lunch container as if it were commonplace on Sco-II. Perhaps it was. Despite being famished, she set the fruit back into the food container, determined to wait until she could enjoy it properly.

So she kept chewing the remnants of the sandwich as a distraction.

One other thought captivated her: *Tom kept his promise*—that crazy notion that he could secure their release. Somehow, he had turned a bleak future around. He had kept her safe too—and at a great cost to himself nonetheless.

The time for enjoying the unexpected meal quickly passed. Swallowing the food in her mouth, she stood up, walked over to the shower, and turned on the water. Streams of hot water hitting the floor broke the silence. Steam wafted into the air, and the cool room began to warm. So Kate busied herself, putting her towel, washcloth, and toiletries in place, and disrobing while the warm water made the air more comfortable.

When she stepped into the shower—Kate succumbed to the hot water washing over her. Her eyes closed, and she swooned under the pulsating stream pelting her face and shoulders. She even heard herself groaning in relief. The water washed away the dirt and the musty stench of that dreadful prison cell, while its warmth drove out the cold that had permanently set into her bones. Never had she relished the simple ritual more than she did at that moment. So the young woman melted into the water stream, unsure if she could bring herself to leave.

Kara Ricci, waking from unconsciousness, found herself lying on her side on the cot, facing the wall of her cell. She felt not herself. Though she wasn't cold, her whole frame trembled, while a terrible knot had tied in her stomach. Her head was terribly foggy too. She couldn't remember returning to her cell.

Her thoughts suddenly filled with the last images she remembered.

A singular tear fell from one eye. Almost catatonic, she looked down at the pieces of her tattered uniform. She cringed! Blood—Emir's blood—covered much of the fabric of her shirt.

She hadn't dreamed the nightmare.

"You passed out," an all too familiar voice said from just behind her.

Straining to turn over, Kara beheld Malach Severus sitting beside her on the cot. Yet she didn't recoil; neither did she adjust the torn pieces of fabric to cover herself. No, with a vacant gaze, she stared up at him.

"I'll send you an additional food ration to help you recover," the old man offered. When her empty expression didn't change, he hesitated. "Kara, I still need you to name Emir Kern as Sigmund Pollux' murderer. I can't get you released without it."

She took in his empathetic gaze for the longest time.

"This is almost over."

But she rolled onto her side away from him and put one arm over her head.

"Kara, *please* ... don't waste your sacrifice. None of this can end without your testimony." Though he waited her out, Kara never moved or spoke a word. So he stood up and headed for the open door. Pausing at the entryway, he turned back to her. "Rest up then. Everything continues tomorrow."

Tom Andrews, propped up in a bed at the medical station near the *Prisoner Out-Processing Center* deep within the Europan Royal palace, watched the team of medical personnel and medibots attending him. A single white linen sheet covered him up to his waist. His discarded *Endurance* mission uniform lay heaped in the garbage can nearby, while a clean set of clothes sat waiting on a table against the wall. An IV ran into his left arm. Yet he had already made a tremendous recovery from his medicine-induced brush with death.

Malach Severus appeared through the entryway. The small team immediately stopped and drew their attention to the noble.

"Leave us," Severus ordered. While medical personnel and medibots alike scrambled from the room and shut the door behind them, Severus came to stand next to the bed. "My Lord, I am glad to see you well."

"Did it work?"

Severus hesitated, his nervousness readily apparent. "Yes, the memory implant was successful. As far as Kara Ricci is concerned, Emir Kern is dead."

"Did she implicate Emir Kern as Sigmund Pollux's murderer?"

Another hesitation. "Not yet."

Tom's countenance fell, and he shook his head in frustration. "Then remove the memory implant immediately."

"Give it time, my Lord. Memory implants are tricky. The woman is wrestling with the emotions of murdering someone she loved."

"That was our mistake."

"If we implanted a memory of her watching us execute him," Severus said, mustering his courage, "She would never give us the confession you need to obtain her release. No, her defiance against us would have steeled. But this way, she can console herself with the rationalization of saving him from terrible suffering. I'll make sure the memory is removed after she testifies. She'll come around."

Tom looked at him, his face ripe with concern. "What if she doesn't?"

General Aulus Taun, garbed in his officers' uniform, stood waiting in the corridor outside the medical station near the *Prisoner Out-Processing Center* deep within the Europan Royal Palace.

The door to the medical station opened. Malach Severus appeared and started down the corridor. When Taun sidled up to him, Severus said, "I told you I'd let you know what happened."

"What'd he say?"

"When he found out Ricci didn't give us the confession he needed, he ordered me to remove the memory implant immediately."

"And?"

"I persuaded him not to do such a thing."

"He's so weak," Taun rather laughed.

"And yet he may very soon be our new Sovereign."

"Only because of the mistake we made long ago, Malach. We can't ever let that upstart ascend to the throne." Taun paused to let a medibot heading in the opposite direction pass by. When the machine hovered out of earshot, he continued, "At least you got what you wanted. I must commend your cunningness: persuading Trajan to implant the very memory that will undo Kara Ricci while letting him think it was his idea. But how will you explain it to him when she's dead?"

Severus steeled while walking several paces. "He shouldn't have forbidden me from executing her in the first place. He can blame himself."

"He'll blame you."

"That's a chance I must take. Just make sure you have discredited him by then."

"I still need to figure out how to do that."

"If he refuses to execute Kara Ricci—that will be his downfall with the Sovereign. Figure out how to force his refusal. I'm counting on you."

"Don't worry, I'll figure it out by the time I get back from my hunting trip."

"You're leaving?"

"Just as soon as I complete my last assignment from *Lord Trajan*."

"Your last assignment is to eliminate the Coverts—which I know you haven't done," Severus said. When Taun grimaced, his face sobered. "Watch out, Aulus, that upstart still has Galerius' ear. Imagine the irony of *him* ordering *your* execution."

"*Our executions*, Malach, *our executions*."

Kate Gillen stood before the built-in metal vanity of the shower and changing room in the *Prisoner Out-processing Center*, readying herself to leave. After running a comb through her long, brown hair one last time, she stepped back and gazed at her reflection in the mirror.

She particularly relished the attire given to her by the Europan woman. Aside from matching her complexion nicely and bringing out the color in her brown eyes, the soft, long-sleeve yellow shirt felt so comfortable against her skin; so did the slacks. The Europan woman had even thrown a makeup kit into the bin. Taking in her reflection in the mirror, Kate felt pretty for the first time in such a long time.

She gathered the toiletries, towels, and personal affects scattered about the small room, throwing them into the bin to leave. Then, she grabbed her filthy mission uniform and other discarded garments heaped beside the bin. She hated even touching the uniform, for the clothing smelled terrible. In disbelief that she had worn them in to the room earlier, she brought them over the bin to drop them onto the pile inside.

But she caught sight of the *Endurance* insignia sewn onto the collar of the shirt.

Bringing the garments back to herself, she gazed down at the insignia for the longest time. Every so often, she ran her thumb over the worn emblem, and her face glowed radiant despite her somberness. But the longer she looked down at the insignia, the more distant her gaze grew, and her face waxed over in the oddest way.

So Kate threw the mission uniform into the garbage.

Tucking the bin of personal affects under one arm, she grabbed the piece of fruit sitting in the open food container with her free hand and left.

With the thicket draped in darkness behind him, Michael Gillen stood once more beside Emir Kern at the edge of the remote precipice overlooking the Europan settlement. This time, however, the *Endurance* leaders had ventured to the western side of the bluff, which overlooked the New Tyre Capital Center construction zone's perimeter just a kilometer away. Powerful floodlights bathed the entire area in bright light, making the razed area easily discernable from such a distance.

Michael watched the Dulos night crews laboring under the cruel hand of the taskmasters there. The faint noises of their activities echoed in the night. Much farther in the distance, the top of the palace rose majestically over the steep bluffs behind the construction site.

The main palace was merely a temporary arrangement: The eventual New Tyre Capitol Center, the intended seat of government for New Europa, would boast a larger and far more opulent palace. He looked down at the settlement, pondering his chance to make Aurelian Galerius' rule over the planet just as temporary.

"You still have time to call this off, Gillen," Emir said while looking out over the darkened terrain. But Michael didn't respond. "Call off the rebellion, let me kill Galerius … and I promise to rescue your wife and the other Centauries."

But Michael, also gazing out onto the horizon, merely took in the words out of propriety. "The Dulos are more than eager for tomorrow. Who knows how they'd react if we didn't follow through. *No*, we've passed the point of no return."

"So you're still in denial that the Dulos won't get slaughtered tomorrow?"

Michael looked at Emir, shrugging off the man's obvious intent to unsettle him. "I figure we'll find out about thirty minutes into the rebellion—more or less, depending on your leadership skills."

"Yeah, I'm not too happy about that. *You* should lead the main assault. I'm better a sneaking around."

"That's what Tom Andrews—Trajan—would expect. He doesn't know I'm alive—doesn't know many other things either. Once the rebellion starts, he'll assume your involvement. The more we do unexpected things, the less Andrews can anticipate our plan." A pause followed. "Besides, while you're on your way to the palace, Raathe and company will be securing the troop and fleet bases to the east. If you're successful, you'll arrive at the palace first and get your chance to kill Galerius. You should be happy about that."

Emir flashed him a dismissive look before turning back to the view of the terrain. Silence fell over the two men for quite some time, and the Covert leader grew more unsettled.

"I can't help noting the irony of all this," Emir mused. "It's as if I'm watching history repeat itself—but under different circumstances, of course."

"The irony hasn't been lost on me."

"Do you think Jonathan Gillen knew what he was getting into so long ago? Do you think he realized his decision would result in a century of discord, political turmoil, prejudice … *genocide?*" When Michael flashed him a rather impatient look, he shrugged again. "Here we are once again: The Dulos, a race of genetically engineered humans, are in conflict with the Europans, a race of unaltered humans. And who is caught in the middle? *Another Gillen*. What happens tomorrow will go down in the history books. You may become as famous as your great grandfather—*good or bad.*" He hesitated. "And both you and I know that destroying that fleet isn't why you're doing all this."

Michael bristled, and his athletic frame stood tense. "Oh, really? So why *am* I doing all this?"

"I figured out something about you, Gillen," Emir rather boasted, kneeling but keeping on the balls of his feet. Setting his rifle across his legs, he pulled a weed from the ground and ran it between his fingers. "What you did back at the ambush site baffled me for the longest time. But I realized something: once you assumed I had stranded your team on Sco-II and sabotaged the *Endurance*, making sure I failed was the only thing that mattered to you." He let the statement linger in the air. "You're a trouble-maker, Gillen—just like me."

Michael laughed.

"The Centauries are the only family you have left. Yet you were willing to sacrifice them—*even your wife*—just to spite me. That's why I failed." Watching Michael bristle even more—and relishing his reaction—he pressed, "But this time, instead of railing against me, you're railing against the Europans: They have your wife … and your best friend betrayed you by being an Europan spy." A nod of satisfaction followed. "So you're making Tom Andrews and the Europans pay."

Michael fumed. "Did it ever occur to you that I was trying to accomplish our stated mission? Or trying to protect Earth States from three thousand warships?"

"No," Emir stated matter-of-factly. "But how convenient for you that you're always on the noble side of the equation. That's the difference between you and me: I'm the troublemaker always bucking the rules; you're the loyal soldier following orders and saving the day—but you showed who you really are at the ambush. And tomorrow … the Europans *will* slaughter the Dulos, who are all following *your* orders."

151

"You can be a real bastard sometimes!"

"And I figured out something I know you already know," Emir pressed. "The Europans created the Dulos from their *Weightless* victims back in Terrae Solaris—not a petri dish. Instead of eliminating the *Weightless*, the Europans genetically changed them into something they could control and use. The Dulos and the *Weightless* are the same people."

Michael said nothing. Instead, he fumed all the more. Regardless, his expression betrayed him.

"I knew it," Emir beamed with pride, looking up from where he knelt. A foreboding pause followed. "Another Gillen ... another genocide." He took in his stoic gaze through a long moment of silence. Finally, he turned and studied the darkened terrain before him. "I just hope your wife is worth it."

Kate Gillen, following the lead guard and still holding the piece of fruit in one hand, walked into the brightly decorated apartment in the Europan palace—her mouth dropping at the sight of the modest dwelling. Despite her surprise, she kept a close eye on Tom Andrews, who followed behind her at a modest pace. Just seeing him up and walking around sparked a glimmer in the young woman's eyes, a glimmer noticeably absent for quite some time.

Though the abode was still a prison cell, Kate marveled at the apartment's simple but enviable creature comforts. It was warmly decorated by orders of magnitude over the dismal cell they had left earlier. The dwelling even boasted simulated virtual windows, allowing the apartment to appear as if having outside windows. A nighttime scene of the New Tyre settlement filled the view.

"View change," she ordered, coming to stand before one of the windows. "Rolling countryside on Earth in the summer."

Immediately, the nighttime view changed, and bright sunlight streamed in through the windows. She took in with much satisfaction the sight of green, rolling hills surrounded by forest.

Tom took up residence on the couch, sighing in relief when finally off his feet. After all, despite the tremendous work of the Europan medics, he was still somewhat weak. Kate relished watching the soldiers doting over him, making sure he was comfortable, had all his medications, and the like. In fact, she almost laughed at the sight.

While the guards helped Tom settle in on the living room couch, Kate toured the dwelling, taking a quick sweep through the fully stocked kitchen, bathrooms, and two bedrooms. One of the bedrooms appeared to be hers, because a chest of drawers was full of women's clothes her size.

She returned to the living room—surprised to find a high-ranking Europan officer standing in the entrance to the apartment. He was an older, heavyset man with an intimidating presence about him. She had never seen the man before, and Tom's expression indicated his unfamiliarity with the man. Kate, uncertain of the Europan's intentions, moved close to Tom.

"I trust you find this place acceptable?" the grey haired officer asked.

"Yes," they replied one after the other.

"It's very nice," Tom added cautiously.

"Good. I'm General Taun. Responsibility for you has transferred to my command." He glanced at the orders displaying on the reader in his hand. "Because you cooperated with us, we have commuted your sentence."

Kate and Tom looked at each other in disbelief.

"That's correct: You've been pardoned, and you should consider yourselves lucky. For your protection, you will stay here until we are satisfied that you are willing to remain with us peaceably." General Taun's face waxed affable. "We have much work ahead of us to make this world livable. Your skills would contribute greatly to our cause. Perhaps the time will come when you can live among us as peers. But that will be up to you. Any questions?"

Tom and Kate, both of them dumbfounded, shook their heads.

"We'll take our leave of you now."

After nodding graciously, the man left the apartment, followed by the two soldiers. The door shut behind them and locked from the outside.

Kate sat down next to Tom, and both remained silent for the longest time.

"I can't believe it," Kate finally exclaimed, still dumbfounded.

"Me neither, Sunshine."

She sat there, taking in her new surroundings—but Tom's reassuring gaze most of all. Her thoughts filled with the many challenges that had brought her to this point, how Tom had sacrificed so much to keep her safe during her imprisonment, how she had lived on the edge of insanity for—well, she really didn't know. But all those bad times were finally over.

Tom grew awkward. "I'm sorry for what happened this morning. I shouldn't have taken advantage of you."

"You didn't. I shouldn't have kissed you."

"You were just relieved I didn't die. I saw how drawn your face was—how you must have spent so much time worrying about me. You were exhausted and not thinking clearly. I should have considered that when I kissed you back." A contrite pause followed. "Can you forgive me?"

She took in his gaze for the longest time—and stood. "I'll be right back."

Leaving Tom on the couch, Kate walked into her bedroom. After setting the piece of fruit on the dresser and opening the top drawer, she looked down at her left hand. With a pause, she slipped the wedding ring from her finger.

She stood there alone, delicately holding the tiny gold band in her fingers. Gazing down at the jewelry, she washed over in a sentimental smile. Through a long moment, her thoughts fled far away, and she cherished them. Part of her wanted to live in those memories forever—a fleeting wish. So she lifted the ring to her lips and gently kissed the small diamond setting.

"*Goodbye, Michael*," she whispered, welling up a bit. "*I'll never forget you.*"

After kissing the ring once more, she tucked it safely into the corner of the drawer. Shutting the drawer, she picked up the piece of fruit on top of the dresser. Admiring the delicacy and unsure of why she was still saving it, Kate took a bite. She savored its exquisite taste, letting its sweetness linger for the longest time.

Taking another bite, she returned to the living room.

CHAPTER FOURTEEN

A Birthday Celebration

Michael Gillen, smartly garbed in an Europan corporals' uniform, escorted his three Dulos prisoners down the narrow street at gunpoint. The mammoth beings weren't really his prisoners, nor was he really holding them at gunpoint. Rather, the intentional charade signaled the start of the Dulos rebellion.

As he made his way along, the late afternoon sun warmed his face, and the soothing, deep-blue pastel sky above imposed itself on him; the lilting sound of rustling leaves gently brushed his ears too. The mission-weary commander so wanted to lose himself in the splendor, and the laisser-faire attitude of the Europans he passed did nothing to dissuade him. Even the utilibots passing by seemed relaxed.

For that reason alone, he pushed forward. On the heels of a long, Europan holiday weekend celebrating Aurelian Galerius' birthday, commerce had halted throughout the settlement, leaving the streets mostly desolate. Much of the populace, abandoning their normal duties, chose instead to engross themselves in frivolities, especially among a military foreseeing no immediate threats. If he and the Dulos intended to strike the Europans, no other day would afford him such an opportunity.

Michael churned deep within under a torrent of emotions, just as he suffered before every battle. The knots in his stomach tightened over thoughts of another potential command failure like on the *Comanche*—or the failed ambush of Aurelian Galerius. Perhaps he would not survive the day. And what legacy would he leave the Gillen name if the Europans slaughtered the Dulos? But the anticipation of learning what had become of Katey sickened him most of all.

His thoughts labored so much over his precarious fate, Michael actually entertained the temptation to pray for good fortune. But to whom would he pray? No one. No, he was merely entertaining a passing thought—one he quickly put out of mind.

He and the small band of Dulos pressed deeper into the remote area. The thick canopy of trees on the right thinned, revealing a row of spiny shield towers behind them. Ten meters high, the towers lay spaced every fifty meters and ran parallel to the road. They stretched across the entire northern and northwest perimeter of the New Tyre construction zone. Producing an invisible but deadly energy field, the towers prevented the Dulos from crossing into the palace and military base areas.

The sight of the metal structures forced all other concerns from his mind.

"The access gate is about a kilometer ahead," he said to his team. "Anyone not clear on what to do?"

The three Dulos looked back, turning their sizeable heads in the negative. The Dulos in the center spoke up, "We know. Hope others do too."

The prison cell door swung open, the groan of its heavy iron hinges grazing the silence. As light streamed in from the outside corridor, two Europan guards entered, dragging between them an unconscious Kara Ricci from another interrogation session. Carrying her through the entryway until her feet dragged across the threshold, they suddenly let go. Kara fell hard onto the stone floor. The painful landing jolted her back to consciousness, and she immediately broke into tears—not from hitting the floor, but from the cruel treatment she had endured for so many hours.

Wrapping her arms over her head, she wept miserably. One guard, boasting a rather perplexed expression, glanced down at her before looking at his companion. But after trading mutual and indifferent shrugs, the two men stepped over her, slamming the iron door shut upon leaving.

She lay prostrate on the floor while the guards' footsteps outside faded away, her tears only coming faster and her face twisting in anguish. Shame washed over her too, and she chided herself for letting them see her brokenness.

She suffered under the terrible images and dreadful sensations of the previous hours. The memories ravaged her; remnants of the pain still coursed through her body, while humiliation inhabited her. Logic would not assuage the agony; shear determination no longer kept the indignity at bay. The mayhem of her thoughts drowned out Tom Andrews' reassuring words too, words she had rehearsed so often. Worse, the haunting voice speaking in her head right then—the one voice she had driven away so many times since her first interrogation session—spoke loudly and clearly. For the first time, the voice made perfect sense.

She realized the guards had not restrained her.

Malach Severus was on his way for another visit.

With the voice in her head urging her on, Kara lifted herself off the cold, damp floor until coming to lean against the metal frame of her cot. A labored sigh and sober pause followed. Gathering her strength, she inserted one arm between the frame and the mattress. She strained over the simple task. But her hand reappeared, holding the metal shard.

As she gazed down at the shard, the oddest, most relishing glimmer appeared in her eyes.

And the voice urged her on.

She studied her battered physiology through shredded clothing—clothing stained with Emir's blood. The voice in her head rehearsed the necessary sequence of actions, and her mind raced ahead of its own sensibilities. Feeling the same adrenaline surge she experienced before every surgery, Kara pulled her matted, auburn hair behind each ear and turned her free hand palm-side up. Determined to kill herself, she brought the blade to hover just over the artery in her wrist.

The young Europan ensign slouched over his monitoring console in the Terra-Tanker Controllers Complex, fighting the urge to catnap. The mesmerizing yellow glow from the display did nothing to help his disposition. Rather, the tiny lights flickering across the screen irritated him, and the tactical readings seemed pointless. His supervisor lay sprawled out behind him at a desk several meters away. Otherwise, the entire complex lay abandoned, save the utilibots hovering about as they performed janitorial work. Regrettably, he realized just how tedious his job could be, especially on the eve of a long, holiday weekend.

The silence unnerved the young man.

Abruptly, the console before him blared, and he shot to attention.

"*What is it?*" the supervisor, Lieutenant Junior Grade Tighe, urged as he shot up and made haste toward the console. Taking up position over his subordinate, Tighe looked wide-eyed at the graphic of Sco-II and the flashing indicator accenting one of the tankers' orbit paths.

"Tanker A141-7 just dropped its cargo," the ensign began, his voice cracking nervously. He studied the data spilling onto the open areas of the display. "But it's reporting a propulsion failure on re-ascent." After relishing the thrill of the surprising turn of events, his face sobered, and he gazed up vacantly at Tighe. "What do I do?"

Tighe walked him through executing his training. Despite sending several commands to the tanker, its status failed to change.

"This one's not staying up," Tighe sighed. "Plot the trajectory of the crash."

"Won't it just burn up?"

"Not unless there's a catastrophic failure. The navigation systems on these tankers are sophisticated. They'll navigate through to the very end."

Somewhat reluctantly, the ensign, a trainee of the more experienced Tighe, ran the calculations on the console. His eyebrows shot up when the answer came across the display. "Wow! That's close to the settlement."

"But I don't think the settlement's in danger. Looks as if it will crash just southeast of the industrial quadrant."

"At least there won't be any casualties."

"You're wrong," Tighe shook his head. "Our weekend just bit the dust. Prepare to answer every ranking officer in the settlement when this thing crashes."

The Europan guard stood in nervous deliberation in the corridor of the Europan Royal Palace, gawking at the closed door before him. Formerly in very much the hurry, he repeatedly lifted his hand to the security scanner—but abruptly pulled it away at the last moment. Knowing he was about to disobey a direct order from Lord Trajan, the man pondered all the dire consequences that may befall him.

Finally, the urgency of his task bested him, and he reluctantly passed his hand over the scanner. Taking a deep breath and another long pause, he punched in the access command, releasing the door's locking mechanism. He knocked and waited for a response from the other side.

None came.

The young man, dropping his head in frustration, wallowed in his misfortune. Left with no other recourse, he timidly entered the apartment.

He walked into complete darkness, which caught him very much by surprise. After all, the time was late afternoon. But he realized the occupants had spent the past month imprisoned deep beneath the palace, a windowless place whose constant artificial light easily played havoc with one's circadian rhythm. He reckoned they must be asleep.

So activating the living room lights barely enough to see, the man navigated the room and entered the first bedroom, which was also dark.

"*Sir*," the guard whispered.

Light from the hallway washed into the room, leaving lingering shadows throughout. A startled Tom Andrews lifted his head from his pillow, boasting a rather disoriented stare. He peered bleary-eyed at the guard, clearly confused by the man's presence. He also appeared very much annoyed.

At the slightest movement of the covers, Tom waxed affable. An equally surprised and disoriented Kate Gillen appeared out of his shadow, propping herself up on the bed by her elbow and gazing up bleary-eyed at the guard as well.

The guard's mouth dropped. Kate, quickly coming to herself and catching sight of her bare shoulder, discretely pulled up the fallen blanket to cover herself. But the guard noticed and grew more uncomfortable and embarrassed. She, in turn, saw his increasing awkwardness and blushed.

"What is it?" Tom asked, the impatience in his voice readily apparent.

"Sorry, Sir, but my commander requested an interview with you. Please come with me."

"In the middle of the night?"

"Sir, it's late afternoon."

"Oh—okay," Tom replied, looking at the clock and realizing his mistake. Straining to a sitting position, he rubbed his face with his hands. "I'll be right there."

Wasting no time to alleviate his discomfiture, the guard left in a haste and waited in the corridor outside the apartment.

"Do you think this is another interrogation?" Kate asked, her gaze ripe with concern. She sat up on the bed, keeping the sheet draped up over her with one hand.

As he reached for his shirt hanging over the chair beside the bed, Tom shook his head no. Quickly dressing, he sat down next to her and took in her anxiousness. "This is just an interview like they said—standard stuff. I'll be back before you know it."

He offered a reassuring smile, evoking an equally warm response in return.

But her gaze grew self-conscious, even awkward.

"You okay?"

Kate, taking in his concern while keeping the sheet draped up over her, collected herself while offering a reluctant nod. "Yeah … everything's just so new." Dismissing her thoughts, she locked him in a tight embrace with both arms and kissed him. When Tom caressed the curve of her back, her actions grew overtly amorous—as if assuaging his expectations. The two doted over each other for several long moments, until he reluctantly kissed her goodbye and left.

Making his way out into the corridor, Tom met up with the guard, who shut the apartment door and sidled up to him like a nervous pup.

"This had *better* be good," Tom whispered to the guard as he left with him.

"*What's this about?*" Tom Andrews barked, making his way into the security center of the palace.

"My apologies, Lord Trajan," the Europan commander in charge offered, bowing his head in obeisance. "But we have a situation needing your attention." The commander, entreating him to follow, led him to a security console in the far corner of the room. "We think the Coverts are attempting access to the palace."

"I'm not surprised. Given Kern's hatred of my father, they are long overdue for a palace raid. Perhaps now we can finally capture them."

"Our computers alerted us to several failed attempts to access a security console near the northwest gate. They are trying to penetrate the perimeter fence."

The display, changing over to video, showed the obscure image of four individuals, one human and three Dulos. They stood at a distance in the frame, so their faces remained indiscernible. The man, clearly garbed in an Europan corporals' uniform, led the Dulos at gunpoint. Another image of the same quickly overlaid the first. This time, the four acted as one team: The corporal stood by, his gun pointing away and covering the Dulos.

"That has to be Kern," Tom bristled at the distorted picture. "My father was right: The Dulos are helping them. Where's General Taun?"

"He left earlier today on holiday."

"He's *vacationing* while Kern is still a threat?"

"We dispatched troops to intercept the four in the video," the commander nervously offered to change the subject. "But the man here doesn't match your description of Kern or his men. We're hoping you can confirm his identity." He motioned to the lieutenant seated at the console, who executed a close-up and enhancement of the imposter corporal.

Tom eagerly watched Kern's blurred image grow prominently on the screen and morph into a more defined image—

His jaw dropped. "*I can't believe it.*"

"So this is a Covert?"

Tom, not answering, stared at the screen in dumbfounded amazement. He brushed his hair to the side to get a better look, even though his brownish-black bangs barely graced his eyebrows. His gaze waxed sentimental, even bittersweet.

The commander, taken back by the unusual reaction, traded curious glances with the lieutenant. Tom's reaction persisted, despite the commander's growing impatience. "Lord Trajan, what do you want us to do?"

"*Oh,*" Tom replied, coming back to himself. "Definitely fortify the area around the gate—just in case. Who knows how many Dulos are lurking out of sight of our surveillance cameras. But don't move in on the man. I'll take care of him myself. Bring me a lieutenants' uniform."

"So he's no threat?"

"No," Tom shook his head, taking one last look at a very much alive Michael Gillen. He smiled, and a sentimental laugh followed. "He's not raiding the palace. He's attempting a rescue."

"Hey! How 'bout some service!" Brent Tasker called out, pounding his fist on the service counter at the Europan armory complex.

A wary Eric Gunn, standing to his left, leaned in toward his taller companion. Acting as inconspicuously as possible, he whispered, "*Don't ham it up too much. They'll get suspicious.*"

"*No,*" Glen Volk countered in the same hushed tones. "*That's the way these guy act. Don't worry, Tasker. Go full ham!*"

They fell silent. A lance corporal even younger than Volk appeared at the service door. Visibly frazzled and glaring at the three Coverts dressed as Europan privates, he sidled up to the servicing side of the counter. "What's your problem?"

"Is this armory open or what?" Tasker demanded.

"What do you need?"

Tasker sighed, leaned against the counter, and turned his head in disgust. "Our weekend's been ruined! We're supposed to be on leave. But they ordered us to work one of the highway demolition teams. *Can you believe that?*" He beseeched the corporal, who returned an indifferent stare. "We need some blasting supplies. Here's the list."

Volk handed the corporal an electronic card containing the list of supplies.

The corporal, in turn, slipped the card into the console on the desk. The display came to life, showing falsified authorizations and order details. "Give me fifteen minutes."

"—*Oh*, and do you have some sort of cargo transport we can borrow? Our transport is too small."

"Yeah, we've got two transports in the docking bay that can carry just about anything. Just bring it back."

Four Dulos entered the armory just then, squeezing their massive frames through the normal-sized doorway. The corporal, his eyes shooting wide, stepped backward. His mouth dropped when Tasker waved the creatures over to the counter. "What are *they* doing here? This is against regulations."

Tasker, Volk, and Gunn offered dismissive looks.

"What?" Tasker shrugged. "Who do you think is going to carry all this stuff onto the cargo transport? *Us?*"

The corporal flashed a condescending look at the three lazy privates. Working the console, he said, "I wish *I* had some help. Everyone got passes for the long holiday weekend and left me here all alone. Worse, now that we've loaded the fleet with armaments, I have to inventory the remaining munitions and weapons. I'll never get it all done."

"So you're here all alone?"

"Didn't I just say that?"

"That's too bad," Tasker sympathized, his mouth twisting into a smug grin. He traded telling looks with his companions and the Dulos standing behind him. Then, he turned back to the corporal. "Maybe we can give you a hand with all those munitions."

Michael Gillen glanced into the sky, noting 18 Scorpii's progress toward the horizon. The brilliant yellow sphere's position heralded the imminent arrival of early evening. Realizing that time was fleeting, he once again turned his attention to the Dulos working the security terminal—

An indiscernible noise caught his ears.

He took a quick look around. However, the isolated area surrounded by forest remained silent and still. On the other side of the road, the pathway leading to the northwest gate lay abandoned too. Perhaps the breeze had dislodged a loose twig from a tree, or a small animal foraged nearby in the thicket.

"Gillen okay?" the Dulos standing next to him asked, looking down at him.

"Yeah, but next time, Kern gets to do the sneaking around."

They fell silent again and watched the third Dulos working the access panel. The terminal stood a meter tall, forcing the gargantuan to kneel almost into a lying position. The access panel was also quite narrow, even by normal human standards. Yet the Dulos worked his giant fingers inside the opening with much dexterity and nimbleness. Michael watched him in awe.

Each attempt to deactivate the shielding at the gate, which lay down the adjacent pathway, failed.

"Do you think they've detected us yet?" Michael asked, looking around once more.

"Know soon," the Dulos working the terminal quipped in low tones and returned to his work.

Michael watched the darkened green indicator light on the terminal. The indicator was the only way of knowing whether the shielding at the gate had deactivated: They couldn't see the gate from their location, given the dense thicket surrounding the area.

"Mike?" an all too familiar voice beckoned.

Michael's breath went cold in his chest, and his stomach twisted in knots. Though he longed for his imagination to have played another trick on him, he knew he had no such luck. He looked up and beheld the haunting form of Tom Andrews, garbed in an Europan lieutenants' uniform, standing at the mouth of the trail to the gate.

Immediately, the Dulos working the terminal stopped working and stood. All three Dulos fanned out protectively around him.

Michael said nothing at first. Instead, he stared haplessly at the specter; a thousand thoughts and emotions raced through his mind—particularly, the strong desire to draw his gun and kill the imposter. "Tom?"

The two stood at a distance, exchanging awkward glances. The meeting wasn't the heartfelt reunion they had shared on the *Tranquillus* long ago. No, everything was unnatural, uncomfortable.

"I'm relieved to see you alive, Mike. I can't believe you survived the high wall collapse."

Michael looked at the man, searching for some trace of the person he had known as Tom Andrews. Yet his normally disarming charm fell out of sorts. Instead, the man seemed veneered, and his words rang hollow. "It's good to see you too."

"You brought a lot of muscle with you. Good thing: This is a dangerous place to be alone."

It pained Michael to listen to him, but it pained him even more to feign a polite reciprocation. So he gestured at Tom's military garb. "What are you doing in an Europan uniform?"

The air grew thick with tension. The ten meters between him and Tom may as well have been ten kilometers.

"The same thing you are," Tom replied, gesturing toward Michael's Europan garb. "I'm on my way to rescue Kate."

"Is she safe?"

"She needs our help. Come with me."

CHAPTER FIFTEEN

Falling Star

The cargo transport lumbered through the dusty construction site, the uneven terrain jostling it about. Maneuvering around various obstacles, the sizable vehicle came upon a cluster of temporary construction warehouses. It turned and slipped into the narrow alley between the structures. Once safely hidden from spying eyes, the vehicle halted.

Brent Tasker and Eric Gunn, still dressed as Europan foot soldiers, bounded off the suspended drivers' cabin at the front, stirring up the dusty ground upon impact. As they hurried to the cargo bay doors at the rear of the transport, Raathe and a line of Dulos men appeared from the adjacent warehouse.

"Problems?" Raathe asked, greeting the two.

Tasker shook his head. "Everything went like clockwork."

"Build clock?"

Tasker ignored the quizzical look from the Dulos leader. Instead, he and Gunn swung open the weighty cargo bay doors, revealing weapons and armaments heaped into large storage containers crowding the cargo bay. "Guns and ammo! Compliments of Aurelian Galerius—and a very bewildered lance corporal. Volk and the others are coming with another transport filled just like this."

Raathe surveyed the containers for a moment. With a broad smile washing over his gigantic head, he motioned to the Dulos subordinates behind him, who began carrying the containers into the warehouse—and without the liftbot that Tasker had used to load the bay.

"The armory is still loaded with munitions," Tasker said to Raathe. "If your group doesn't take control of it soon after the fighting starts, no doubt the Europans will head there first. We wired the buildings with explosive charges, just in case."

"Dulos ready to fight."

Emir Kern, garbed in field gear, hurried out of the warehouse straight toward them. "Raathe, you need to arm the first wave of men. Tasker and Gunn, change into your field gear; make sure Volk does too. Zeidler just sent word that it's on its way."

"Damage!" Captain Michael Gillen called out to Engineering, as the ESS Comanche *suffered under another artillery strike.*

Commander Tom Andrews—Trajan Aurelius—sat in his position next to his good friend, watching the mayhem engulfing the Terran bridge. The Europan ambush of the Executive One *somewhere in Terrae Solaris' asteroid belt was in full swing. Having waited patiently since the time* Comanche *had joined the defense, Tom saw an opportunity.*

Lieutenant Herschel, Comanche's *engineering officer, struggled to his feet and analyzed the incoming data on his console. "Auxiliary power generator in Section-D has been hit, cascading into the"—again, the ship rocked violently under the power of several smaller explosions—"cascading into the navigation controls. Hull experienced some damage but is contained. Three crewmen are dead and one has been wounded. Section-D can't take another direct hit. Nor can its auxiliary shields be activated if the mains are lost."*

"Bypass navigation controls away from Section-D," Michael ordered, the concern in his eyes readily apparent. "Send containment crews. Don't let this get out of hand."

"Crews already on their way. Navigation is in the process of bypassing. We should be okay soon."

Tom, seizing his chance, interjected, *"Mike, I'll go see what I can do."* Upon receiving an approving nod from his friend, he jumped up from his chair and left the bridge like a shot.

Blissfully unaware of his destiny thirteen years into the future and forty-six light-years away, Tom navigated the labyrinth of corridors. But instead of veering down the passage toward Section-D, where the crew struggled against the crippling injuries to the ship, Tom hurried straightaway until arriving into his quarters.

With the same urgency, he locked the door, opened one of his storage drawers, and removed the false bottom with a tool he kept on his person. Reaching in, he retrieved from the hidden compartment a thin, rectangular device about the size of his palm: an Europan targeting beacon.

The sophisticated device sent rapid-pulse communications to Europan warships in range. Picking up a broadcast not easily detected by Earth States tracking systems, Europan warships could train their weapons on its location. Allied shielding, though normally strong, could stress if hit successively in the exact same spot and at the exact same modulation. Of course, accomplishing such a feat was impossible under normal circumstances—without inside help.

The intercom system announced the demise of another Europan cruiser.

Hurrying, Tom programmed the device to communicate *Comanche's* shielding parameters to the destroyer, hoping that Engineering hadn't already changed them. He thought little about the irony that he was most likely carrying out his own death sentence; Michael's too.

Instead, his mind filled with all the failures he had amassed during his time as an Europan spy: namely, his failure to infiltrate Earth States Intelligence when the war started—because Michael had conspired to obtain him as *Comanche's* first officer. Because of Michael, he had spent most of the war fighting against his own people.

But the chance to sabotage the defense of President James Mitchell aboard his transport: This was Tom's chance to make everything right.

Tom rushed out of his quarters and to Section-J, which housed the main gunneries on the starboard side. He had little time: He felt the ship already changing course to return to the Allied convoy. Worse, Michael, using his typical impulsive tactics, was quickly turning the conflict in favor of the Allies.

Despite his loyalty to his friend, he would not let Michael Gillen interfere with the welfare of the Europan people.

Tom arrived into Section-J Gunnery Bay. With the ship already turned and engaging the Europan destroyer, the crew working the guns barely noticed his arrival. He navigated between the three energy charge generators taking up most of the bay. Looking both ways and assuring no one was watching him, he affixed the targeting beacon to the side of the center cannon generator, activated the device, and hurried toward the door.

"What's this?" a voice called behind him.

Tom turned and beheld one of the gunnery crewmen, who had come around the other side of the third charge generator. The man pointed to the targeting beacon. The first incoming artillery round exploded against Comanche's shielding, rocking the ship but doing no harm. "Hershel gave it to me. The tactical computer lost contact with the guns."

"That's not what my readouts are saying."

Once more, the ship shuddered under another artillery round hitting the exact same place on the shielding. This time, the deck beneath his feet began vibrating.

Tom mustered a commanding tone. "All I know is what Hershel told me. We can't coordinate the offensive without the readings it's sending to the bridge. Make sure it keeps transmitting!"

While the crewman studied the device, Tom turned and hurried to the hatch—

He braced himself as a third incoming round assaulted the ship. The three concussions, so perfectly timed, caused the gunnery crewmen to look at each other wide-eyed. So disappearing through the door, Tom rushed down the corridor toward the center of the ship—

The blast from the fourth incoming round threw him against the bulkhead!

Fire from the explosion filled the far end of the corridor from the decimated gunnery bay. As the flames raced toward him, Tom put his hands up in front of his face—a futile effort to shield himself. The blast doors between him and the destroyed gunneries began closing. Yet the flames shot up the corridor even faster! He could already feel the intense heat pressing upon him! The heavy doors descended into place just in time, preventing the flames from burning him to a crisp.

He lay there through a sober moment, pondering his close call with death. But his mission had been successful. Comanche no longer had the luxury of having a complete weapons compliment for the battle. Pleased with his work, he hurried away, even as rescue teams going in the opposite direction passed him. Navigating the labyrinth of corridors and ascending several decks, he finally reached the bridge and fell into his seat.

"I almost bought it on that last explosion," he quipped to Michael, still catching his breath. "I came up the starboard side, thinking it was the safe side of the ship. Didn't know we had turned."

"Everything okay down there?" Michael asked, still rather preoccupied with his command.

"Yeah. Let's just hope we don't have too many hits like the last one."

"Mike, what's *wrong* with you?" Tom Andrews pleaded from the edge of the clearing, gesturing for Michael Gillen to follow him down the path toward the Europan palace. "Don't you want to help Kate?"

Michael didn't budge. Safely ensconced within the protection of the three Dulos surrounding him, he kept eye to eye with Tom. Giving the imposter the once over, he rather grimaced. "You look very convincing in that Europan uniform ... but should you have chosen such a low rank?"

"What are you talking about, Mike?" When Michael didn't respond, he gestured impatiently to the wooded area behind him. "Europan soldiers are on their way. *Let's go!*"

Michael rebuffed the man's insistence. As if caring not a whit about the urgency of the moment, he flashed an incredulous look in Tom's direction. "How did you survive since the ambush?"

Tom's affable gaze unraveled and waxed cold. "I'm not stupid, Mike. What's wrong?"

"I know who you are, Tom—or should I say *Trajan?* And if my understanding of Europan culture is correct, I assume it's Trajan ... *Aurelius?*"

Both men traded contending looks through a long silence.

"So you know."

Michael nodded. "You betrayed me, Tom."

"I had a job to do. But I'm the same person you've always known."

"Just another lie."

Tom fell silent under Michael's contempt. When his pleading gaze failed to change his friend's flint-like demeanor, his eyes narrowed. "You should feel pretty good about yourself. Instead of infiltrating your country's intelligence network as I was supposed to do, I spent two years with you on *Comanche* destroying my own warships. Do you know how many of my own people I killed for nothing?"

"One less than I would have killed—if I had known who you were."

"You don't mean that, Mike. I can tell by your expression."

The two men stared across the way at each other in silence.

Michael's gaze grew unsettled. "Prove there's one shred of Tom Andrews left in you: Bring Kate to me so I can take her away from this forsaken place."

"I can't."

"You can do anything you want—unless she's dead."

"Of course she's not dead," Tom rather scoffed. But composing himself once more, he added, "It's not that I can't bring her to you; I can't take *you* to *her*—not anymore. So come with me." When Michael stayed put, he rather sighed. "I was hoping this would be easier." Turning toward the woods, he shouted, "Commander!"

Dozens of Europan platoons spilled into the clearing from every direction of the adjacent thicket, until Michael and the three Dulos stood surrounded by too many armed soldiers to count.

"I'm sorry, Mike, you'll have to come with me now. But I promise your safety."

The captain of the guard motioned to his troops, and the soldiers moved toward the four captives—

A loud thunder crack broke the tense moment!

Everyone—Terran, Dulos, and Europan alike—stopped. All eyes turned skyward.

Several kilometers overhead, flames shot through a clear-blue sky, leaving in its wake a long plume of smoke. Racing over the settlement toward the southeast, the charred and distorted remains of a terra-tanker burned within the inferno. Chunks of debris separated from the cauldron, and the dying terra-tanker continued falling from the sky.

Everyone traded bewildered looks—except Michael Gillen.

Just as the terra-tanker passed directly overhead, a huge chunk of debris fell away from the twisted hull of the vessel—yet arcing gracefully in opposition to its inertia and clearing the inferno. The *ESS Endurance* sped away from the terra-tanker that had hidden its descent to the planet's surface.

Tom looked coldly at Michael.

Endurance circled high in the lazy evening sky, its black hull making it appear as if a bird of prey on the hunt. But the vessel turned northward and dove toward the surface. Quickly reaching the proximity of the military complex in the distance, the ship fired a hailstorm of artillery.

Both *Endurance* and its weapons fire disappeared below the tree line of the steep bluffs on the horizon. A powerful concussion—far more powerful than the sonic boom from the falling terra-tanker—broke the afternoon air from that direction. The security terminal behind Michael wailed in protest, and the shield indicator light turned green.

The Europan private, standing guard at the northern access gate a great distance from the standoff between Michael Gillen and Tom Andrews, fought his urge to doze off. His companion standing guard with him suffered the same. After all, the Dulos working the construction site in the distance provided little intrigue.

Loud thunder broke the tranquility of a perfect day.

He turned and spotted the plummeting terra-tanker engulfed in flames high above.

"What is it?" his companion asked, never taking his eyes off the spectacle.

"I don't know."

The two men watched the flaming debris follow its perilous course across the sky. When an odd piece of debris—a rather large piece—separated and changed course against its inertia, the private spoke up again, "That's got to be some kind of ship."

"Which one?"

"Both. Isn't the larger one a terra-tanker?"

"Looks like it. But what's the other ship?"

The Europans watched the smaller ship navigate toward the surface—in quite the hurry too! Artillery fire lit the sky, followed by a fireball rising into the air, followed by an ear-splitting concussion. Yet the events unfolded so quickly, both men traded dumbfounded looks.

But the faint hum that had always lingered in the air around the gate faded, and the two men looked slack-jawed at each other.

"The shield is down!" his friend gasped.

The young private withered at the clamor rising into the air from behind him, and the color drained from his face—just like his friend.

With a terrible fear welling within them, the two guards turned and beheld thousands of armed Dulos rushing straight toward them!

Michael Gillen and his three Dulos companions stood in a sea of heavily armed Europan soldiers, readily outnumbered and at gunpoint. Tom Andrews played the host of the capture at the northwest passage, accompanied by the captain of the guard to his right. Yet both Tom and his Europan subordinates gawked haplessly at the *Endurance* flying high in the sky overhead. The vessel, re-ascending from its first strike, quickly changed course and homed in on its next target.

Though having the opportunity to be smug about the *Endurance's* surprise attack, Michael steeped with impatience. To him, the ship couldn't maneuver through the sky fast enough. *Endurance* had mere minutes to take out all Europan strategic targets before becoming one itself.

Artillery fire erupted once more from its guns. This time, the topography and tree line didn't interfere with the view of the destruction: A massive ball of fire breached the tranquil sky, briefly turning back the clock to high noon. A violent concussion followed the brilliant flash, shaking the ground. Everyone cringed at the piercing noise.

Endurance raced overhead and away, leaving the settlement's power generator in ruins. Within seconds, the settlement came to a complete and vulnerable standstill.

"You had me fooled, Mike," Tom lamented, looking at him. "I thought you were attempting a rescue. I guess I don't know everything about you either."

"I guess not."

The communicators on the Europan soldiers' utility belts blared in chorus, catching their attention.

"Lord Trajan," the captain of the guards interjected, having examined the readout on his communicator, "You need to return to the palace—for your own protection. Take my transport. We'll stay here and take the prisoners into custody."

The soldiers moved in toward Michael, their guns trained on the three Dulos behemoths.

"No!" Tom exclaimed.

"But my Lord!"

"No one's arresting him! Haven't you figured it out? This was a ruse. Dispatch your troops back to the north gate. *Hurry!* Before the situation there gets out of hand!"

Hesitating through a defiant moment, the captain waved for his men to redeploy. The Europan platoons began dispatching from the area, though a small contingent remained to protect Tom.

"I don't know how you gained control of the Dulos," Tom rather sneered at Michael. "But whatever you're doing won't work. Instead, you've made things worse for yourself and Kate—and you've doomed the Dulos to annihilation."

"We'll see."

"I guess so. But to show that I mean you no harm, I'm saving your life once again." He bristled at him. "Leave! Leave and don't come back! After what you've done, I can't protect you if you return."

Trading one last contending gaze, Michael and Tom parted company.

Emir Kern, walking in Raathe's sizeable and long-drawn shadow on Sco-II, made his way through what had been the north gate. He and Raathe—named a general by Michael—followed the turbulent sea of the Dulos army spreading out into the plateau before him.

Beneath a clear-blue early evening sky, a dark and dreadful storm swelled against the densely populated plateau. Deadly energy blasts flashed like lightning around the edges of the fierce tempest, while artillery concussions thundered. Buildings, trees, and anything else in the path of the deadly munitions toppled in the distance, consumed by the raging maelstrom. The desperate cries of its victims rose hauntingly into the air. The Dulos would grant no reprieve, at least not to anyone resisting their advance. The exasperated slaves, tasting the chance for precious freedom, took their bounty of casualties, leaving in their wake the crushed and twisted bodies of the Europan dead.

The storm moved quickly northward, and that was exactly what bothered Emir Kern.

"Your men are moving too far ahead of us," Emir exclaimed, crooking his neck to look up at Raathe. But in doing so, he practically tripped over the mangled remains of an Europan foot soldier. He stumbled for a moment, quickly recovering himself.

"Just excited of battle," Raathe shook his head. "No concern. Still have control. Commanders with them; know plan."

"It won't take long for the Europans to fortify positions against us." Emir said. He pointed toward the *Endurance* flying well overhead and to the east. "When that happens, we'll need air cover. But our ship still needs to take out Europan air threats first. It's not ready to provide cover yet."

"Raathe agree."

Emir surveyed the area. The mass of Dulos soldiers far ahead began separating into two armies. One group pressed north around the bluff, while the other diverted eastward toward the armory and troop base. Emir would lead the assault on the palace quite a few kilometers to the west, while Raathe subdued any threat from the military strongholds in the east. So offering a casual salute to Raathe, he set himself northward as Raathe headed east. "I guess this is goodbye for now. Good luck!"

"Kern luck too!"

"Don't move your men outside air cover!"

Emir quickened his pace toward the fighting, the Dulos aides attending him easily keeping in lockstep. Still jogging, he activated his communicator's call function. "Zeidler, what's our status?"

The virtual morning sunlight of Ceres Beach streamed in through the master bedroom window, washing the bed in bright light. Emir and Maddison Kern lay haphazardly stretched across the bed, fast asleep under tousled covers. With a holiday upon them and their children at Bailey Armstrong's bungalow—and a night of romance behind them—this was the couple's chance to sleep in.

A series of low rumbling sounds broke the early morning silence.

"I hate when the fleet starts operations early in the morning," Maddison eked out, her eyes still closed as she readjusted herself on the bed. Finding a comfortable spot, she went limp once more.

More rumbling far in the distance soon followed.

"Must be a change in plans," Emir replied, stirring likewise. "Most of the fleet is still on holiday." The couple fell into a peaceful sleep once again. However, when the sporadic, low rumbling persisted, Emir opened his eyes and sat up in bed with a quizzical brow. "That's not equipment."

Watching him jump out of bed and hurry to his Covert gear sitting in the corner, Maddison pulled the covers around herself. When he picked up his communicator and gazed oddly at the device, she sat up. "What is it?"

However, the young man studied the device in silence. The occasional low rumbling continued.

"Emir, what's wrong?"

"I'm not registering a call to general quarters. ... *I'm not registering* anything.*"

Her face filled with dread. "What?"

But Emir, barely dressing himself, shot out of the bedroom. She wrapped the blankets around herself and followed, catching up to him on the front porch outside. Standing in his boxers in the grass next to the porch, he studied the air. The rumbling, coming from kilometers away in another bay of the settlement, was more evident than inside the bungalow. From the other bungalows on the long, common porch, the other Coverts appeared in random fashion with their wives. Everyone traded quizzical gazes while gathering in front of the Kern bungalow.

"What's going on?" Mark Armstrong asked Emir, who still had his ear to the air.

"Sounds like explosions in Bay-Two," Eric Gunn interjected. "Maybe some kind of accident?"

Curran Zeidler shook his head. "Whatever it is, it sounds farther away. I think the noise is coming from Main-Bay."

"But that's twenty kilometers away—and with a lot of solid rock between us."

"The rock is carrying the vibrations," Emir said, stepping onto the porch. "That's artillery we're hearing. The security network is down too; that's no accident. The fleet base is under attack—by the Europans, I assume."

Everyone traded anxious looks. Soldiers from surrounding residences were already leaving their homes, hurrying in the direction of the base.

"Guys, go get your gear and meet back here," Emir ordered his men over the uneasiness. "We'll leave together for Main-Bay to help."

"Do you want us to take the children to the emergency shelters in Bay-Two?" Bailey Armstrong spoke up for the wives.

"No." Upon receiving a round of dubious looks from the women, Emir added, "The shelters are for natural disasters. Bay-Two is a military habitat—and a military target. If the Europans are inside Ceres' core, any military target is vulnerable. But the beach is the deepest habitat bay in the settlement, save the environmental bay. The bungalows are self-supporting if environmental goes down too. So stay here." He looked to his men. "Get ready."

Everyone dispersed from the impromptu gathering. Without pause, Emir hurried back into the master bedroom of the bungalow. Maddison followed on his heels.

"I don't like this," she shook her head while watching him dress into his Covert gear.

"Everything will be fine."

"Can you guarantee that?"

"No, but it has to be a fighter attack: Those goons can't get their warships into the ports with our warships already inside. The most they can do is block the access tunnels to the surface. Once we drive out the fighters, we'll have to wait out a blockade until Earth States and the Martians can send ships to counter."

"We're supposed to be safe here. Something strange is going on."

"I know."

He finished dressing and stood. Taking the picture of Maddison, Nicholas, and Anna from the chest pocket of his discarded suit, he tucked it into his uniform's chest pocket—for luck. "Just get the children.

Stay inside and lock yourself in. You'll be safe here." He turned toward the door to leave—

She grasped his forearm, forcing him to turn around. A grave expression covered her face, and she searched his eyes while clutching him. "Don't be a hero, Emir. Come home to me when this is done, okay?"

He took in her pleading gaze for the longest time. "I promise."

The young couple shared a long kiss, until Emir pushed himself away. With much reluctance, he smiled at her one last time and left.

He didn't know the journey he started then would end sixteen years later on a far-away planet called Sco-II.

The young Europan major made haste out of the New Europa Imperial Strategic Command building. Hurrying down the lengthy walkway, he arrived at the sidewalk's edge barely in time to meet the arriving transport. Before the nervous soldier could collect himself, a furious Tom Andrews—Trajan Aurelius—appeared from the vehicle and headed toward the building's entrance.

"*Lord Trajan*," the officer stammered, matching Andrews' pace to follow, "I'm glad to see—"

"Enough!" Tom fumed, turning his ear to the artillery concussions in the distance. "Where's General Taun?"

"He's on his way in. He was vacationing in the—"

"This is ridiculous! Is *anyone* in charge here?"

"General Taun didn't realize that—"

"General Taun is stupid! I made it clear that as long as the Coverts were on the run, they were still a threat." He took a few steps in indignant silence. "What's our status?"

The young subordinate swallowed hard. "The Dulos are making significant progress against us. They took out most of our tactical fortifications and weapons—anything readily available for defense. With the central generator disabled, the whole settlement is at a standstill."

"We need heavily armed ground troops."

"We're having trouble organizing troops," the major replied after hesitating. "Everyone's scattered for the holiday, and the Dulos and that ship in the air are shooting down the transports."

"This is terrible. My father doesn't deserve this on the heels of his seventieth birthday."

"Admiral Fowler is at the fleet base fueling a number of destroyers. Once they're in the air, we can end this."

Tom stopped in mid-stride, his cold stare incredulous. Directing the subordinate's attention to the *Endurance* executing a strafing run in the eastern sky, he said, "As long as that ship is in the sky, I doubt he'll get a paper airplane off the ground."

"But my Lord, Admiral Fowler assured me."

Tom let the comment go and set off again. The subordinate followed.

When they reached the entrance to the building—a violent shockwave jolted them! The concussion from the blast rumbled in the distance. They looked east just in time to see another billowing fireball on the horizon—where the fueling depot at the fleet base lay.

With much disdain, Tom stared down the slack-jawed subordinate. "I'll bet they took out the mooring override systems too! So much for Admiral Fowler." Grimacing, he disappeared into the opulent structure.

CHAPTER SIXTEEN

Forward Assault

Michael Gillen, accompanied by his three Dulos companions, hastened down the abandoned roadway, bathed in the long shadows of the buildings and trees surrounding him. Only a half-hour into the Dulos assault—the 18 Scorpii sun quickly setting—he listened with an attentive ear to the rumbling artillery in the distance: how would nightfall influence the rebellion?

Eventually, the small band came upon an innocuous-looking cargo transport sitting off the deserted road. Stealing a quick look around, he waved his companions out of sight and entered the bay.

"*Gillen*," Curran Zeidler, sitting alone at a console inside, quipped. Bringing his hand up to shield his eyes, he squinted at the bright light flooding into the bay, "You made it back alive. *That's* a surprise."

"Today's full of surprises."

Letting the door shut—the bay darkening so that only the consoles lit the hold once again—Michael grabbed a backpack from the corner, pulled out his combat uniform, and started changing into it. "At least I got away. Let everyone know I'll make it to the rendezvous point."

Zeidler nodded and continued his work.

As Michael changed, he watched Zeidler controlling the *Endurance* using the console in front of him. The Covert also oversaw the communications network and monitoring of Europan forces. "How are we doing?"

"Okay, so far. *Endurance* just took out the fleet fueling depot and the mooring controls. The destroyers and FW-190s in their holds aren't going anywhere soon."

"I heard the explosion. Good job."

Michael finished changing and came to stand behind the Covert.

Zeidler pointed to the tactical scanner in front of him. "Kern's forces have advanced well into the northern passage toward the palace." He pointed to the blue blips on the screen, which represented Europans positioned just above the bluff formation. "We pushed them back significantly here. But look at the Europan reinforcements coming from the west." Gesturing to another set of blue blips navigating around and below the bluff, he added, "These are the forces that intercepted you at the northwest gate. They're moving in on him. Kern will have to fight on two fronts soon."

"He'll need air cover. Can you can handle it?"

Nodding, Zeidler directed his attention to the depiction of the armory and troop base to the east. "Raathe has secured the armory complex, and his forces are pushing well into the troop base. But he'll need air cover soon too."

Michael studied the busy screen, absorbing the entire battle zone. Most of the Europan fortifications lay obliterated, and other Dulos fronts had pushed into the industrial and civilian areas of the settlement.

A quick nod of satisfaction followed.

However, he also saw hundreds of other blue dots representing Europan transports that the *Endurance* needed to shoot down. Random blue dots scattered throughout the display—more Europan forces—also began coalescing around the conflict. "You'll need to direct *Endurance* over two fronts simultaneously. I'm also sure the Europans will try to launch some FW-190s. It won't take many fighters to do some real damage."

"I'll do everything I can. The rest is up to fate."

"*You can do it*," Michael said. Powering up his communicator, he offered him a quick, encouraging nod. "I'm off to the rendezvous point. Good luck."

Michael exited the cargo bay, leaving Zeidler alone.

"Tell them to send more men up to that ridge!" Emir Kern shouted above the din of artillery fire. When the Dulos behemoth standing next to him relayed the order, Emir returned his worried attention to the violent conflict before him. Too many unbearable moments passed without any change in the Dulos assault far ahead. His eyes filled with trepidation, and he whispered under his breath in a gruff voice, "*Come on!*"

Far ahead at the front of the assault, the Dulos overwhelmed Europan troops in close order combat. Energy rounds flashed within the churning struggle, felling the occasional Dulos soldier. Yet with Europans and Dulos interspersed within the mayhem, weapons provided the Europan troops little hope. The Dulos' colossal size, surprising speed and dexterity—and a newfound rage toward their diminutive assailants—provided Emir some of the most grotesque images he would ever see. The Dulos, so docile otherwise, carried out the assault with such malice and cruelty.

But the sight of Europan troops dying en masse far ahead brought him little consolation. An hour had passed since he and Raathe had parted company, and all Dulos forward progress under his command had halted. Europan reinforcements coalescing behind their main front were quickly organizing, and their sheer numbers and weapons posed a significant threat. Setting up gunneries on the main ridge away from the Dulos front, these new forces would soon pummel the mass of Dulos coming in behind the main front.

And the 18 Scorpii sun was setting fast.

Emir fixed his eyes on the ridge far ahead. Dulos foot soldiers, maneuvering up a small gully, began ascending the side of the ridge, just as he had ordered. They moved cautiously, keeping behind cover whenever possible. However, Europan gunners set atop the ridge spotted them.

Energy blasts flashed from those guns, strafing the Dulos. Amidst the mayhem, more Dulos came from behind, replacing those who had fallen and continuing the assault.

"Zeidler!" Emir called into his communicator. "We need air cover at the ridge! Where are you?"

Several long moments—too long for the impatient Covert—passed before the communicator crackled.

"Hold on," Zeidler's voice emerged from the crackling. "I've got *Endurance* over the fleet base now. The goons are hitting me with FW-190 launch attempts. I can't let them get airborne."

"*Hurry.*" Emir fell silent through a sober pause, and he watched the Europan gunners on the ridge strafing the Dulos. "The Dulos won't last long without—"

A violent concussion slammed him to the ground! His mouth filled with the taste of dirt, and disorientation lingered from the unexpected blast. He winced! Fighting against the passing sensation, he strained to one knee and patted himself in search of injuries. Aside from a few bruises and scrapes, he was okay. The Dulos aide beside him, also knocked to the ground and boasting minor scrapes and languid eyes, struggled to stand while shaking his massive head. But much closer to the impact crater a short distance away, several Dulos lay dead. Others, suffering severe and sometimes grotesque injuries, lay crying out for help.

Emir quickly came to himself and followed the trajectory of the round. The incoming artillery had arrived from his left, just south of the western bluff. Looking, he beheld a regiment of Europan troops advancing from that direction. Though still in the distance, the forces were pressing toward his position. The Europans had flanked him!

In a panic, he once more activated his communicator. "Zeidler!"

Raathe stood command over the assault on the troop base in the distance, overwhelmed at his first military challenge. He kept the fears and doubts plaguing him well concealed from his Dulos subordinates and the three Coverts—Brent Tasker, Glen Volk, and Eric Gunn—standing close by. Yet while taking in the sight of his men pummeling the Europan troops far ahead, one thought consumed him: The conflict was growing increasingly more difficult. His army's forward progress had stalled, a sharp contrast to the previous hour. The Europans, having regrouped to the northeast, had successfully formed a buffer zone away from the Dulos, preventing hand-to-hand combat. With reinforcements arriving in the distance and powerful weapons coming online, the Europan defenses were coalescing into a formidable threat. Dulos casualties were multiplying. If he stood any chance at pulling out a victory, he needed air cover. He looked down at Brent Tasker. "Call friend. Need ship."

Nodding, Tasker lifted his communicator to his mouth. "Hey, Zeidler, things are getting ugly without air cover. We need *Endurance*—now! "

Yet even as Tasker spoke, Raathe perked up when catching sight of the distant buildings to the southeast. Poking Tasker's shoulder with a large forefinger, the Dulos leader gestured in that direction. "Look!"

Tasker, catching sight of Raathe's concern, nodded again. "Got it."

"Hey, guys," came Zeidler's frazzled voice over the communicator, "I can't help—"

"Zeidler, new request," Tasker broke in over the incoming message. "Some kind of formation is approaching from the southeast around the main complex. Can you confirm?"

A few long moments passed with no response.

"I see it," Zeidler's voice returned. "A whole contingent of Europan soldiers is moving in: armored transports, tanks, and heavy artillery."

"How could you let them sneak up on us? You're supposed to take out the hardened targets—not us. We need air cover more than ever!"

"Off my case!" Zeidler shouted, his voice distorting the communicator speaker. "I've got one ship that needs to be in three places at once. The goons are throwing FW-190 launches at me left and right. Kern got flanked—it's a real mess over there. Now, you guys!" A telling pause. "*Endurance* is having its own problems. So hold tight."

Tasker, Raathe, and the two other Coverts traded sober looks. Finally, Tasker shrugged at his audience and spoke into the communicator once more, "Got it." Muting the device, he turned to Volk and Gunn. "This doesn't look good."

Tom Andrews—Trajan Aurelius—presided over the frantic activities in the War Room of the New Europa Imperial Strategic Command center, well aware of the incredible tension his presence engendered. Keeping vigil with General Taun and several other high commanders around a large, three-dimensional tactical display sitting in the middle of the room—and all of them standing away from him—the heir to the Europan throne noticed them trading nervous looks. He kept flint-like while studying the battle representation before him, a sign of his continued dissatisfaction with their performance, General Taun in particular.

Yet despite the high commanders appearing as unnerved as if Aurelian Galerius himself were present, Tom fought his own trepidation. Presiding over the Dulos' unexpected uprising provided his first test of leadership. He bristled over the attention and feared making a terrible mistake.

"The conflict is finally turning in our favor," one of the high commanders said. He gestured toward the large display, which showed the two fronts of the battle. The status indicators hovering over those positions changed from red to yellow, while other indicators showed the Dulos forces halted in place. At the same time, Europan forces had not only coalesced and organized, but had also flanked both Dulos assaults, which were weakening in intensity. The palace graphical stood in the far corner away from the conflict, well protected from any threat. "If we can push the two Dulos fronts back together, we can surround them and cut off their escape routes."

"There's no *if* to be considered here," Taun steeled. "The Dulos are only effective military assets when taking orders from *us*. That's why their surprise offensive is crumbling." He traded confident nods with the other high commanders.

Tom never looked up from the display, nor did he nod in agreement. Instead, the young man studied the display in silence, his expression waxing heavy with concern.

"What is it, my Lord?" Taun beckoned from his side of the display.

"Something's not right."

"Our flanks are working. Give them time."

"The Dulos have responded to our tactical shifts quite effectively—particularly in regard to air cover."

"The Dulos have gotten lucky, that's all. One ship in the air won't give them the advantage they need. The turn in the battle proves that. Now, it's just a matter of time with these beasts."

Tom shook his head dismissively. "I suspect the Coverts are orchestrating the battle—not the Dulos."

Taun unsuccessfully fought the grimace washing over his face. The other commanders traded odd looks, more than familiar with Taun's tiring of hearing about the Coverts. After taking in Tom's insistent gaze, he replied, "Even if that is true, how much help can they really provide?"

Andrews' irritated expression returned. "They are smart and know our weaknesses. And I'm sure they're controlling the *Endurance* from the ground. We need to neutralize them."

Taun surrendered with a sigh. "What do you suggest?"

Tom studied the broad display as if taking in the entire region all at once. "I suspect the Coverts have a command center just outside the perimeter of the battle. That's where they're controlling the *Endurance*." Another pause as he remained in thought. "They would also keep communications limited to avoid exposing the location—but they need to communicate nonetheless. So jam all known Terran frequencies and dispatch a contingent to destroy the command center. *Endurance* will return to AutoNavs. If we put enough pressure on the ship, its AutoNavs will retreat."

Taun, trading looks with the other high commanders, nodded and turned to the subordinate behind him. "Relay Lord Trajan's orders."

Michael Gillen sat on a large rock at the edge of the lush, green forest just south of the northwest access gate, watching for any sign of a threat. However, the isolated thicket lay far from the heated conflict kilometers away. The air was rather still. Even the faint sound of birdsong sang out over the soft rumble of artillery in the distance.

The 18 Scorpii sun hovered languidly just above the horizon, casting a reddish glow across the western sky. Soon, night would fall over the settlement; the air had already turned crisp. So the young commander cinched up his coat in anticipation of a long wait.

He looked to the northeast where Raathe and Kern fought the Europans. The faint rumbling caught him in the pit of his stomach, for his appointment to face such peril drew nearer each moment. As with any imminent conflict, he began questioning himself.

The tranquility of the woods also unnerved him.

He looked down at the communicator nestled snugly in his hand. Kern had ordered limited communications to prevent the Europans from deciphering the Dulos signals, so the lack of transmissions didn't faze him. However, Michael quickly realized that the last transmission had occurred quite some time before. In fact, the wireless receiver in his ear didn't even crackle anymore, despite the communicator reading *monitoring*. A little hesitant, he brought the device to his mouth.

"Kern, you copy?"

Nothing came back, not even a crackle.

"Tasker?"

Nothing. He fiddled with the frequency settings. Still nothing.

"Zeidler?"

Nothing again.

He gazed down at the tiny device, shook his head, and sighed uncomfortably. Somehow, the Europans had cut him off from the Covert network. Perhaps the entire Covert network was down. Regardless, he and his team were isolated and in the middle of nowhere. That thought unnerved him even more—

The low hum of a small engine broke the silence!

Michael retreated under the cover of the tree canopy, waving his companions to do the same. All eyes trained skyward.

A small Europan transport appeared low in the not-so-distant sky, hovering just over the tree line at the edge of the perimeter fence towers. Two Europan gunners, their oversized guns at the ready, protruded from the transport's hatches, thoroughly searching the area.

He examined the life sign dampening field generator sitting next to his field pack, wondering if he had set the device correctly. The instrument masked heat signatures and other means of detection.

If he had set the signal too low, the Europans might spot him. If too high, the scanners on the transport might detect the masking signal itself, bringing a torrent of laser fire upon him. One thing was certain: He would know soon enough.

Artillery fire broke the air!

He froze stiff, waiting for all the sensations of an energy round cutting through him. But when the moment passed without harm, he scanned the area. A column of smoke rose into the air near where the transport hovered in the sky. The tree line prevented him from seeing the destroyed target, though he knew nothing of tactical value to the rebellion lay where the gunners had fired.

He studied the transport quizzically.

After hovering over the smoking debris a moment, the transport navigated toward the northeast, following the spindly perimeter fence towers. Going just a little farther, it came to hover once more in the sky. Once more, the gunners fired at the ground. Black smoke rising into the air followed. Just as the previous time, Michael could not see the target. The transport, still following the perimeter fence, moved toward the northeast and repeated the same actions.

His eyes shot wide open!

"Zeidler!" he called into his communicator. "Come in!"

No response followed.

"Come on!" he yelled at the device. "Work!"—pressing the call button once more—"Zeidler!"

Nothing.

The young commander looked around in a panic. Perhaps he could chase after the transport and shoot it down—no, it was too far away, and such a move would compromise his mission.

"Zeidler! If you can hear this, get out of there! Gunners are coming your way! They're looking for the command center! Get out of there!"

No response.

"Zeidler!"

Once more, deadly artillery rounds echoed against the evening sky. Another column of black smoke appeared in line with the others—but this time from the place where Curran Zeidler had been.

Watching artillery pounding the sea of Dulos soldiers in front of him, Emir Kern sickened with grief.

The entire rebel army under his command was pulling back—a futile effort to regroup away from the swelling Europan forces. Nothing changed the results: Powerful Europan forces pushed against the Dulos from three separate flanks, forcibly squeezing the Dulos out of the valley between the two bluffs. Many Dulos on the front lines were succumbing to the carnage.

What do I do? he thought, his face slack-jawed.

The Covert gazed down haplessly at the communicator holstered in his belt. *Nothing.* The Europans were still jamming communications, and Zeidler had not yet countered the tactic. Neither could he call Zeidler to chew him out for the lack of air cover. No, he would have to wait until the network cleared. The army had reverted to using a series of bullhorns to communicate.

As he moved backward in response to the Dulos forces executing the slow retreat, the *Endurance* suddenly streamed overhead and away from him. The deafening roar of its engines shook the ground.

Finally! he thought, impatient to see the heavy Europan artillery in the distance destroyed.

But *Endurance* raced toward the horizon like a shot—moving far too fast to provide air cover. The vessel darted about erratically in the sky too! Just then, two Europan FW-190 fighters passed overhead, chasing the *Endurance* while firing a torrent of artillery in its direction.

Emir's countenance fell.

The FW-190s quickly caught up with the fleeing vessel. They swarmed around the unmanned ship, strafing its hull with artillery fire. The *Endurance* returned fire with its only aft gun while zigzagging through the sky to escape—but then veered upward and ascended into open space away from the battle.

"What wrong?" the Dulos aide beside him asked, never taking its eyes off the fleeing ship.

Emir simply shook his head in reluctant surrender. "Zeidler's lost control of the ship. The AutoNavs are programmed to flee circumstances with doubtful odds."

"Masters jam *Endurance?*"

"No, the ship has a complex communications system. There's no way they could know how to jam—"

His eyes shot wide, and a terrible dread washed over him!

Panicking, Emir spun around and scanned the broad valley. Nauseous with grief, he watched black smoke billowing into the sky from the place where Curran Zeidler had been.

"Tell *pull back more!*" a visibly frustrated Raathe ordered the Dulos aide standing nearby.

The Dulos sent the communication to another Dulos standing in the distance using a bullhorn (for communications were still jammed). That Dulos, in turn, acknowledged and signaled ahead to another Dulos even farther away likewise.

Raathe, ignoring the makeshift communications relay, watched as heavy artillery arriving from the southeast pummeled his Dulos soldiers. Europan troops from the northeast pressed in, forcing the Dulos contingent out of the troop base.

Things were turning grim.

A loud rumbling echoed from behind the leviathan. Raathe turned in time to see *Endurance* fleeing two FW-190s chasing it across the sky. He heard the three Coverts beside him talking amongst themselves, their voices hushed and their faces full of dread. Raathe, however, kept fixed on the vessel, for he needed *Endurance*'s air cover. When the vessel suddenly turned skyward and headed for deep space, he turned to the Coverts. "*Call Zeidler now?*"

The three Coverts, who stared haplessly at the black smoke rising into the darkening sky behind him, didn't say anything.

"Call Zeidler?"

"No," Tasker finally replied, shaking his head and the communicator too.

"Bad," Raathe shook his head. "Need—"

The ear curdling sound of another FW-190 rushing just overhead pierced their ears. The fighter flew directly over them before turning toward the main Dulos front, its guns spitting forth deadly energy charges. The rounds pummeled the sea of Dulos, slicing the army in two. Dulos scattered in a panic to flee the unexpected assault.

Raathe once again turned to the Dulos aide nearby. "Tell *Retreat!*" Then he turned to the three Coverts. "Bad turn. Must regroup to Kern."

"We'll take care of the armory," Tasker replied, waving Volk and Gunn to follow. "We won't let it fall under Europan control."

Brent Tasker, Glen Volk, and Eric Gunn huddled behind a cropping of trees, looking out onto the campus-like armory complex across the way, its fortified buildings wired with enough explosives to set off the armaments inside them. Between the safety of the trees and the armory in the distance, hundreds of Dulos foots soldiers rushed by in full retreat from oncoming Europan ground forces, while an FW-190 racing overhead strafed the fleeing Dulos. Dulos after Dulos succumbed to the deadly artillery. Their sizeable corpses lay scattered throughout the entire area.

"You sure it's safe to detonate the armory?" Eric Gunn asked, watching the Dulos rushing by in front of them. "We might take out a bunch of Dulos."

"We don't have a choice," Tasker shook his head while fiddling with the remote detonator in his hand. "Imagine how many Dulos the Europans will kill if we don't." Finishing programming the device, he looked at his companions. "You guys ready?"

When Volk and Gunn braced themselves for the imminent concussion, Tasker unlatched the safety on the remote detonator and entered the activation code. Flashing one last sober look at his two companions, he cringed and pressed the trigger.

Nothing.

A quizzical look washed over Tasker's face. He pressed the trigger once more.

Nothing. The fortified buildings standing before the Coverts remained intact.

"*What's wrong with this?*" Tasker huffed, shaking the detonator and wearing the most indignant gaze.

"Did you program it right?" Glen Volk offered in a rather chiding tone.

"*Of course I did.*"

Tasker impatiently and repeatedly pressed the trigger with no results, while Gunn tried examining the detonator as Tasker fiddled with it.

Eventually, Volk shook his head. "Forget it: The goons must be jamming everything, not just the communicator frequencies."

Tasker, furious by then, threw the detonator into his pack sitting at his feet. "We'll detonate it manually."

Both Volk and Gunn looked slack-jawed at him.

"You're crazy!" Gunn declared with Volk nodding in agreement.

"I promised Raathe. I'm not letting those goons gain control of the armory. We'll lose for sure, and that means Zeidler died in vain— Armstrong too."

"Don't compound their misfortune with your own."

"But I promised Raathe."

"Tasker, think about it: You can only detonate one building. That won't help—and neither Glen nor I will help you do such an absurd thing."

"Then what do we do?"

The three Coverts fell silent.

Volk, boasting a rather pensive gaze, looked out onto the carnage before him. Eventually, he shook his head in resignation. "Let's get out of here." Flashing a sober look at his two friends, the young man stood, slung his pack over his shoulder, picked up his rifle, and turned toward the thicket to leave.

"Where you going?" Tasker demanded, stopping the Covert.

"This isn't our battle … this *isn't* what we do." Volk paused and took in the dreadful scene of the Dulos retreating, how they dodged the corpses of their fellow Dulos while fleeing. "We're *Coverts*." Looking at Tasker and Gunn soberly once more, he turned and headed deep into the woods away from the conflict.

When Gunn began gathering his gear to leave, Tasker grimaced. "Where are *you* going?"

"Wherever Glen's going. He's right: this isn't what we came here to do."

Watching Gunn jump up and hurry after Volk, Tasker huffed. He looked at the armory one last time—and then to his teammates heading into the woods. Reluctantly, he gathered his gear in surrender and followed them. Quickly catching up to Gunn, who walked about ten paces behind Volk, Tasker huffed once more. "Since when did *Volk* become the leader?"

Tom Andrews stood over the broad, three-dimensional tactical display at the center of the War Room in the New Europa Imperial Strategic Command center, watching the conflict in relief. His troops pressed in upon the Dulos rebels from five different flanks, ready to crush them. The Dulos fronts were collapsing and retreating under the surge, even coalescing into one mass near the Capital Center construction site, the place the uprising had started. Soon, his forces would surround the Dulos horde.

His satisfaction was readily apparent, for General Taun and the other high commanders stood closer to him. Of course, the upturn in the Europan defense would not assuage his indignation over them allowing the Dulos uprising in the first place. No, they would answer for their lack of vigilance.

"Congratulations, my Lord," Taun offered, looking at Andrews. "Your observations and recommendations earlier were right. And clearly, it has made the difference. My apologies for disagreeing with you."

Tom returned an indifferent nod, less than impressed at Taun's ingratiating remarks. He turned to a subordinate standing nearby. "Let my father know of our good progress."

"What shall we do with the Dulos?" another commander standing nearby inquired.

"Just what you'd do with any beast that turns on its master: Annihilate them all and start over again—fix whatever went wrong. Send that command along."

The officer nodded and directed his subordinate to pass along the command—

But Tom stopped him. "If our troops find any humans among the rebels, make sure they are captured and not killed. I'll take care of the Coverts *myself*. … And by all means, Michael Gillen is *not* to be harmed."

Mayhem engulfed Habitat Bay F-2 of Ceres Fleet Base. Earth States warships sat helplessly in their dry docks, while hundreds of Europan FW-190s swarmed around them. Artillery fire spewed forth from the fighters' guns, reeking havoc on the docked ships. Explosions erupting from the hulls were commonplace, and many of the ships sat in their docks ablaze. Choking smoke hung in the air. But the enemy fighters did not save their fury for the warships alone. No, many of the fighters strafed operations and administrative sections on the perimeter of the habitat, sending Earth States crewman and soldiers scrambling in every direction.

Emir Kern and his team of Coverts rushed across the open plain toward the protection of the operations buildings, dodging artillery fire from an Europan FW-190 fighter racing overhead. Though the fighter sped off toward the dry docks, another FW-190 rushed in from behind to replace it. The Coverts ducked behind the burning remains of a service vehicle, just as artillery rained down around them.

"Let's go!" Kern waved his men on when the fighter sped away and turned for another pass. He led them at full speed toward a protected passage built underneath the operations complexes. The small band raced ahead of the artillery fire raining down around them from behind. Each second, the strafing closed in as the fighter neared. With artillery nipping at their heels, the men ran even faster until reaching the safety of the passage.

Relieved at the narrow escape, the Coverts navigated down the passage and into the command center of the bay, which was awash in chaos. General Boyce Derringer stood with several subordinates around a tactical display at the center of the room, shouting orders while watching the battle unfold. Other technicians and officers staffed the many consoles throughout the room.

"Kern, I'm glad you're here," Derringer greeted the Covert, waving him over to the tactical display. "I wasn't sure if you received my coded message."

"We got here as soon as we could," Emir replied through panting, leading his men to the tactical display. "We were on our way to Main-Bay to help with the defensive."

"Forget Main-Bay. There's nothing left to defend."

Emir, surrounded by his men, looked down at the grim story playing out on the Tactical. F-1 Bay, Main-Bay, and F-2 Bay—the forward bays of Ceres Fleet Base's eleven total habitat bays—suffered under the Europan onslaught. Europan fighters swarmed everywhere, and many Earth States warships registered as crippled or severely injured. Access tunnels between the forward and mid-section bays all read secured, which meant the attack could not proceed any deeper into the base. However, all access tunnels to Ceres' surface were under Europan control. Emir looked up. "Where's the Europan fleet?"

"Not anywhere in the region," Derringer replied. "These FW-190s came a long way—to hide the attack, no doubt. When they waltzed through our defensive shields and poured into Main-Bay, the officers manning the tunnel's observation posts couldn't sound the alarms: everything went dead. Most communications channels went down too."

"So the Europans sabotaged us."

"Right," Derringer said in a sober voice. "A team of Europan Coverts is loose in the settlement. The other surface tunnels fell first, followed by the access tunnels connecting F-1 and F-2 to Main Bay. They keep overriding our security too. Their next targets are the access passages to the mid-section bays."

"Now I know why you called us," Emir said, looking around at his men. "We'll intercept them before the access tunnels fall."

However, Derringer shook his head. "Forget the mid-section bays, Emir. I need you to head for B-2 to intercept and kill the Europan Coverts." An awkward pause followed. "They're heading to A-Bay—the environmental and life support plants. We think they're trying to poison the base's air handling systems; they'll kill tens of thousands of soldier in the open-air bays."

"That doesn't make sense," one of the Coverts interjected.

"The Europans just don't want to destroy our fleets," Derringer replied. "They want Ceres for themselves, and they'll kill every military personnel to do it. Between the fighter attack and the sabotage—only the beach habitat will survive."

"Because it has its own life support systems," Emir added. "And the Europans will need the civilian areas when they take control." When Derringer nodded, Emir gazed down at the tactical display. Soberly, he took in the realization that most of the settlement would fall. With concerns over Maddison, Anna, and Nicholas running through his head, he turned toward the door, waving his team to follow. "Let's get to B-2 and take out these goons."

Pure Mayhem!

Those were the only words Emir Kern could use to describe what he was seeing.

Night had fallen over the entire Europan settlement on Sco-II. The full wrath of the Europan military on Sco-II had descended on the Dulos, whose two fronts had collapsed into one disorganized mess. Rather than gaining their freedom, the noble creatures instead had become as if prey to ravenous dogs.

Emir stood alone at what remained of his command contingent, desperately trying to regain order over his troops. But it was too late. The constant strafing by Europan FW-190s from the darkness overhead, incoming artillery from heavy armaments in the distance, and the ever-shifting firepower of the Europan soldiers had thrown the Dulos into confusion. The frustrated leader dared not try intimidating the massive creatures into obedience, for he didn't know how they would react in such a frenzied state. Even the Dulos aides had abandoned him.

As Dulos after Dulos rushed by him in retreat, Emir looked toward the west. In the distance and towering high into the night sky, Aurelian Galerius' palace stood. Its grandeur stood in stark contrast to the chaos of the battlefield.

The sight captivated him.

He stared at the structure for the longest time, his face waxing pensive. The sounds of the battle and the flashes of artillery faded into obscurity. With such a heavy expression, he pulled the tattered photograph from his chest pocket. Immediately, the image of his family, his wife Maddison, his son Nicholas, and his baby daughter Anna—gone for so long—captivated him. For a brief moment, the man even smiled.

But the longer he stared at the picture, the more his bittersweet gaze grew dark and disturbing. Memories the picture conjured fell victim to the dread of finding their charred corpses, the sleepless nights he had spent since then vowing to avenge them, the cries of anguish he heard every night in his dreams.

Emir grabbed his field pack. Opening the main compartment, he double-checked that his Covert gear was intact. Then, he picked up the incendiaries he had carried since the first failed ambush—since that fateful day at Ceres. After a long look at the cluster of firebombs, Emir Kern threw the incendiaries back into his pack, threw the pack over his shoulder, and quickly disappeared away from the battlefield into the darkness.

CHAPTER SEVENTEEN

Change of Plans

Kara Ricci, her back against the frame of her cot, sat on the cold floor of the dimly lit prison cell. As she stared at the metal shard she held over her wrist, her blue eyes welled up with angst. The sequence of arteries needing sliced open to ensure death rehearsed in her mind. From her peripheral vision, she took in the sight of herself: her mission uniform tattered and torn beyond repair, the many bruises and welts covering her, her filthy appearance—but how her outward appearance merely hinted at the desolation inhabiting her broken spirit.

And of course, bloodstains from Emir's death covered the front of her battered uniform.

Yet she had held the shard at the ready far too long.

Certainly, the urgency of the moment had passed since determining to kill herself. Malach Severus had yet to arrive, leaving her to wonder why the guards had left her out of her chains. The grim satisfaction of Severus finding her corpse lying in a pool of blood had faded. Instead, one horrifying question remained.

Why can't I do this? she thought.

With her face twisting in travail and her eyes welling up, Kara mustered her resolve once more. She plunged the shard downward toward her wrist—but abruptly recoiled again.

"*Please … just let me do this,*" she cried out in a whisper to no one in particular, the tears streaming down her face. "*… just let me die.*" Wiping the tears from her face with the back of her hand, she brought the shard over her wrist once more and waited for an answer.

None came—at least no answer she could discern. No, her reluctance to kill herself persisted.

Instead, her eyes focused on the hand holding the metal shard, how her forefinger stretched across the blunt top-edge to balance the cutting blade below. Memories of holding a pistol in the same hand suddenly filled her thoughts, how that same forefinger had pulled the trigger to kill Sigmund Pollux. Images of the dead man lingered among conjured images of her corpse lying in a pool of blood—and the shard lying in the blood near her hand. Malach Severus' voice mocked her. "*So much for your altruistic views on the value of life,*" his voice echoed in her mind. A fear of something larger than herself or her dire circumstances—what she didn't really know—swelled in her conscience.

Kara, still weeping and staring down at the shard, fought the conflict raging in her thoughts. The dread of not killing herself fought her newfound dread of what would become of her if she *did*, and she trembled uncontrollably.

Finally—*huffing!*—she threw the shard across the cell! The *pinging* of metal hitting the rock floor rang out several times, until the makeshift weapon came to rest in the corner of the cell.

She wept even harder.

With tears streaming down her face, Kara rolled up onto the musty cot behind her, melted facedown into the mattress, and buried her head in her pillow.

Michael Gillen sat on a rock at the edge of the forest near the northwest gate, which lay draped in darkness. The serene canopy of night did nothing to soothe him, nor did gazing up at the stars bring him his typical fanciful musings.

He churned with anxiety on so many levels as his chronometer counted down the night. Images of black smoke rising into the air earlier—marking Curran Zeidler's untimely death—lingered in his mind. The eerie sight forced him to wonder what would become of him that evening, what he would learn about Kate's fate, and the like. The jammed communications, leaving him unaware of the rebellion's progress, only made him doubt himself that much more.

But then, the chronometer finally heralded the appointed time.

Looking down at the defunct communicator in his hand, the young man let out a heavy sigh, stood up, and threw his field pack over his shoulder.

"Okay, let's move!" he shouted into the air.

The dark forest moved as if coming to life. The shadowy forms of thousands of Dulos soldiers waiting with him moved about in the darkness. Following him, the scattered Dulos coalesced into a highly organized mass of companies, platoons, and squads. Within minutes, legions of Dulos foot soldiers hurried as if rushing waters through the forest toward the northwest access.

And eventually the palace.

The mood in the Europan War Room took a quick turn from its previous elation.

"What do you mean *they just appeared?*" an indignant Tom Andrews huffed.

The subordinate working the tactical display swallowed nervously. "I'm sorry, my Lord. I can only tell you what the scanning equipment is detecting."

With his face waxing like flint, Tom studied the broad, three-dimensional tactical display before him. Disgust washed over him as he took in the formidable Dulos army that had appeared on the display. Kilometers away from the main conflict in an area having little defensive capabilities, the new threat had an unobstructed path to the palace.

"Lord Trajan," General Taun interjected, "We didn't start observing the settlement until after the uprising began. These Dulos are probably workers for the evening shift construction. We thought they had folded into the assault to the north. Apparently, that was not the case."

"It was a fateful assumption!" Tom shot back. Looking down at the display once more and pausing in thought, he added, "We can't let them encroach on the palace."

General Taun turned toward one of the subordinates working the communications console. "Dispatch two FW-190s to intercept. That will slow them down."

"That's not enough," Tom countered. "There are as many Dulos coming from the northwest as there are in the north—look how close they are to the palace!"

"Okay," Taun conceded, turning to the subordinate once again. "Have the commander in the north redeploy half his troops to the palace. Redeploy our troops on the construction perimeter to the northwest access too. We'll flank them from both sides. Then, redeploy half the heavy land artillery to the palace—just in case." He turned back to Andrews and the other generals. "With so much redeployment, we will lose superiority over the Dulos. The remaining troops will have a tough time keeping them at bay."

Raathe stood in the midst of the violent conflict, all hopes for a new life for his people evaporating before his eyes.

The Europans were merciless. FW-190s raced overhead in the darkness, spewing artillery into the sea of Dulos soldiers and scattering them in all directions. Heavy ground artillery from the east pounded the troops, while Europan foot soldiers formed a deadly semicircle perimeter, pushing the Dulos back toward the south.

Yet the south would provide no haven for the Dulos slaves. Raathe knew the Europans were not just forcing a retreat. No, the Master's wrath remained at full force, while heavy artillery from the east slowly laced its way around the Dulos' rear flank. Once the Europans surrounded the Dulos army, they would annihilate the Dulos rebels and move on to the Dulos village to complete the massacre.

Once again, an FW-190 roared over his head and streamed away in front of him—

He tilted his large head curiously at the sight. FW-190s were flying in pairs, yet the fighter streaming away flew alone. Raathe searched the sky with his brooding eyes in search of the other fighter. To his surprise, the glow of a single fighter's engines trailed away from the battlefield, heading west.

Raathe, looking around at the conflict, realized the wayward fighter wasn't the only noticeable anomaly. Europan troops were redeploying to the west in a hurry. Europan heavy artillery moving westward in the northern hills caught his ears too.

"What's going on?" the Dulos aide to his right asked in the Dulos native tongue, looking in the same direction as Raathe.

"Gillen's army is finally on the move," Raathe replied in the same language. "They are redeploying to intercept him, and he won't survive unless we make ourselves a threat here. Signal the troops to push north!"

Tom Andrews, General Taun, and the other Europan high commanders, debating the defense against the new Dulos threat at the northwest passage, stood watch over the large tactical display in the War Room of the New Europa Imperial Strategic Command complex.

"Excuse me, Lord Trajan," a sub-commander beckoned, interrupting the discussion. "You need to see something."

"Put it up on the display."

"This doesn't concern the uprising—but it is most urgent." the sub-commander gestured to a security console in the corner of the room.

Nodding in acknowledgement, Tom followed the underling across the room and sidled up behind the lieutenant operating the unit.

The sub-commander, standing to his left, continued, "Fifteen minutes ago, surveillance caught this activity behind an administrative building a kilometer away from the palace."

He motioned to the lieutenant, who displayed a video clip on the console's display. The obscure picture, enhanced to account for night, showed a man in military garb skulking behind the structure. When the ten-second scene ended, the lieutenant ran the clip on a loop. The video zoomed in until the intruder's face filled the entire display.

"Kern!"

Upon hearing the exchange, Taun sidled up next to Tom. As the other generals followed him to the security console, he asked, "Has this man been caught?"

"No, Sir," the sub-commander replied. "We dispatched an entire platoon of troops to the area. But the man just disappeared."

"Dispatch more troops to the area."

"You won't find him," Tom shook his head. "But we know he's heading for the palace."

"He'll die before he gets past the first checkpoint."

Tom grimaced. "Don't be so sure. He eluded your troops for over a month before disappearing." An intentional pause followed. "He wants revenge on my father, and he'll gladly sacrifice his own life to accomplish it. He *will* get through."

"I'll increase security around Lord Galerius."

"Good," Tom nodded, a look of concern covering his face. "But until Kern is killed, my father is vulnerable; the Dulos uprising only makes things more precarious. We must divert Kern away from the palace until this conflict is over." He paused in thought. His eyes sparked as if an idea had come to him—but then his whole face fell tellingly. After deliberating with himself in silence, he looked around at his generals. "Does anyone have an idea?"

The entire contingent before him fell silent and traded telling looks. General Taun took in Tom's odd, crestfallen gaze through a calculating pause. His eyes lit up, and boldness washed over him. "Lord Trajan, since your arrival, you have demonstrated that you are much more adept in understanding Emir Kern, his skills, and motives. Do you know of *anything* that could divert his attention away from the palace?"

Tom, his face betraying the heaviness churning within him, studied Emir Kern's face still-framed on the security display.

"You look like you have an idea," Taun pressed. "What else does this man value—other than revenge against Lord Galerius?"

Tom offered a nervous laugh, and he looked around at the other generals. "Do you mean with all the combat experience in this room, no one has an idea?"

The other commanders remained anxious and silent while watching the exchange between the two men.

"*Kara Ricci*," Taun exclaimed. "Kern was romantically involved with her. Isn't that true, Lord Trajan?"

"He won't relent—not even for her."

"I'm willing to try, my Lord. We have nothing to lose except a murderer already condemned to die."

"*It won't work.*"

"We should try General Taun's suggestion," another general heaped on.

Tom, falling silent before the other officers, fought to suppress his unsettled thoughts. But they remained fixed on him with expectant gazes.

Taun, his face brimming at Tom's hesitation, looked him in the eyes. "Lord Trajan, your father is at risk of another assassination attempt. Whose welfare will you choose this time? Your father's—or Kara Ricci's?" A calculating pause. "I can give the order if you can't."

Tom took in the round of imploring expressions, overwhelmed and unsure of himself.

Two Europan soldiers, one a lieutenant and the other a lowly guard, hurried down the prison corridor deep beneath the New Europa Imperial Strategic Command military complex. Turning the corner down an adjacent passage, the lieutenant studied the numbers on the cell doors the two men passed.

The guard, a rather young Europan male with a boyish face, studied the holograph projecting into the air above the reader in his hand. Though the mechanism steadied the projection against his jostled movements, the guard struggled to read the screen while keeping pacing with his superior. "Are we supposed to carry out *everything* on this order? Some of these items aren't signed ... and what's written here isn't what we were told to do."

"We do what the nobles tell us," the lieutenant stated matter-of-factly, counting down the cell numbers. "I've seen hundreds of these. We stick to everything written *and* what they told us. Now give that back to me."

Reluctantly, the young Europan handed the reader to the lieutenant. Powering down the device—the holograph dissipating—the man tucked the reader into a side pocket. He drew his pistol from the holster at his side, gesturing to the cell door just three paces away and to the left. "We're here."

The two men stopped at the door. The lieutenant worked the security panel, causing the locking mechanism inside the metal door to turn; the indicator on the jam flashed green. Bringing his pistol to the ready, the lieutenant pulled the door open as the guard readied himself.

When the door opened all the way, bright light from the corridor streamed into the dimly lit cell. The two men looked in. Gazing back at them bleary-eyed from her cot was Kara Ricci.

The grassy hillside at the edge of the thick forest was quite serene. Brent Tasker, Glen Volk, and Eric Gunn lay flat on the ground at the crest of the hill, looking down at the darkened fleet base below. Tasker, holding binoculars to his eyes, scanned the entire complex: the buildings, the perimeter fence, access roads between the lifeless warships, and the like.

"Sure is quiet down there," Gunn rather whispered.

"It should be," Volk nodded. "Zeidler took out most of the base with the *Endurance*."

The three Coverts continued watching this base, which was a contrast of varying activities. Most of the complex lay subdued in a forced blackout. Yet other places boasted a frenzy of rescue and containment activities. At the center of the base, the burning fueling tower cast a menacing yellow glow against the night. Emergency vehicles and personnel surrounded the inferno, desperately working to extinguish the flames.

"The fuel depot's transfer conduits are destroyed," Tasker announced, his eyes still fast to the binoculars in his hand. "That'll keep 'em busy for a while." He fell silent while studying the close-up view of the base.

"Of course, lots of soldiers are scattered about, just lookin' for a fight."

"Just a precaution," Glen Volk assured. "As long as the main conflict keeps well to the west, they won't expect any trouble—and we've gotten into more secure places."

Tasker lowered his binoculars and looked at his companions. "But can we really pull this off without Zeidler?"

Silence fell over the three, and they traded sober gazes. Both Gunn and Tasker looked expectantly at Volk, who had led them there.

"*It's your idea,*" Tasker pressed.

"Yeah, Glen, you sure you can do this?"

Volk took in their incredulous looks before shrugging. "We don't have a choice. If we're not successful, then Curran died in vain—Mark too."

Another awkward moment followed.

"Okay then," Tasker sighed, lifting his binoculars to his eyes again. "Let's find a way in."

The young guard walked his post outside the Europan Royal Palace, his eyes wide as he surveyed the night. With the opulent structure towering high over him, he paced the stone foundation of a modest, elevated courtyard just above him. As he walked, his feet disturbed the thick fog lingering close to the ground. The courtyard, built against the back of the main building, lay quite isolated from the frenzied activities elsewhere on the grounds.

Walking past a cluster of shrubbery and trees adorning the courtyard foundation—

The intruder lunged out of the shadows, grabbing the Europan from behind!

The Europan, his eyes filling with terror as he struggled, tried yelling for help! But the assailant bludgeoned him from behind with a forearm, muffling the panicked shrieking. With the assailant's other arm contorting his neck, the soldier fell under the power of his attacker, who wrenched him into the vegetation. The gruesome sound of bones cracking sounded out; the Europan ceased his defiant twisting about, and he slumped lifeless onto the ground.

With his eyes aglow in the madness plaguing him, Emir Kern dragged the dead man farther into the protective shadows of the shrubbery. Thick fog rolled over the corpse, and the Covert knelt and searched the corpse for anything useful to his crusade. Finding the dead man's security transponder, Emir gazed up at the palace towering into the night sky. The anticipation of seizing his chance for revenge welled within him.

"Communicator on," a computer voice sounded in his earpiece.

Taken off guard, the Covert brought his communicator to his eyes, boasting such a quizzical gawk. The small device indicated that the Covert network was still down. Instead, the small display read *point-to-point transmission*. Cautiously, he activated the communicator.

"Kern?" came an unfamiliar voice from his earpiece.

Emir hesitated. "Who is this?"

"Your good friend Tom Andrews."

Emir's eyes shot wide, and he surveyed the palace grounds from within the shrubbery concealing him. However, the darkened terrain remained still. A sneer washed over him. "Lord *Trajan*, to what do I owe this honor?"

"My men tell me you're in the area. I'm asking you to stay away from the palace."

"And why would I do that?" Emir rather laughed.

An awkward pause followed.

"A luxury of my position is that I have so much information at my access," Tom boasted. "I'm looking at your intelligence file. Why are you so set on seeking revenge against my father, when you know someone else is to blame for your family's deaths?"

Emir fumed.

Brent Tasker, holding his rifle at the ready, charged into the security substation somewhere in M-2 Bay in Ceres Fleet Base. Though Mark Armstrong, Eric Gunn, and Glen Volk followed closely behind, he waved them back. Flashes of artillery rounds from both directions erupted at the entrance.

But the weapons exchange abruptly ceased.

"All clear!" Tasker yelled from just inside the room.

The remaining Coverts spilled into the room from the adjoining corridor and looked around. The corpses of Earth States security personnel, all killed some time earlier by the Europan Covert team, lay scattered throughout the room full of equipment. But taking in the sight of two Europan Coverts lying dead on the floor, they looked around with crumpled brows.

"Where are the rest of them?" Glen Volk asked.

While Emir Kern paced the room in search of clues, Curran Zeidler rushed over to the security monitor at the center of the room. After looking at the display, he took in the charred controller units sitting nearby. "The goons overrode security to M-1 and M-2 Bays' access tunnels. I can't reset them either." He looked at Emir. "FW-190s are already flooding into the bays. That's five bays already."

Emir took in the troubling news. Looking once more at the two dead Europan Coverts, he shook his head. "This can't be all of them." Studying the dead men a little longer, he looked at his team. "Zeidler, stay with me here. The rest of you, pair into two's and search the immediate area. Find out which way the rest of them went."

As Tasker, Armstrong, Volk, and Gunn hurried from the substation and disappeared, Emir knelt where Zeidler was examining one of the dead Europans. "Can you find out anything from them?"

"I doubt it," Zeidler replied as he searched the dead man's person. "Those goons have been notoriously discreet about—"

His hand reappeared from one of the pockets with a familiar device.

The two men traded telling glances while staring at the equipment.

"Why would they leave these two with their transponders?" Zeidler asked quizzically. "That's a rookie mistake. They had to know someone would show up here."

Emir's face sobered. "Maybe they wanted someone to find it."

A tense silence followed, and the two men traded telling looks.

"Hurry," Emir urged.

With Emir following him, Zeidler stood and rushed over to the security monitor—the only equipment left undamaged in the room—and inserted the transponder. Both men watched the computer overlay the settlement map with the transponder's information. A map of the Europan Coverts' movements throughout the settlement appeared, starting from the access tunnels earlier that morning and snaking through the habitat bays ahead of the fighter assault.

But in Habitat Bay B-1, the singular path split in two: One path predictably followed in the direction of the environmental plants in A-Bay, while the other path veered off toward a secured access tunnel leading to Ceres Beach Habitat Bay—where Maddison, Anna, Nicholas, and the rest of the Covert families waited out the assault. With an indicator flashing at the end of each path to signify the location of the Europan Coverts, both teams were still far from their targets.

Dread washed over the two men—but Emir more than Zeidler.

"They knew we were following them," Zeidler said, looking at him tellingly.

"They want us to make a choice: save the base or the civilians the base defends."

Zeidler, glancing once more at the settlement map and the moving indicators, slung his rifle over his back and turned toward the door. "I'll go get the team and let them know we're heading back to the bungalows."

"No," Emir commanded, grabbing his forearm to stop him. When the subordinate glared at him in stunned disbelief, Emir almost pleaded with him—his eyes already haunted. "We still have a base to defend. Tens of thousands of people are in danger. Nothing we see here changes that."

"But they're going to attack the beach habitat. Ceres Beach has no defenses. *We can get back in time to stop those goons from getting to A-Bay."*

"No we can't, Curran—and they know it. That's why they split up."

"But our families are in danger"—his face turning bitter—"because you *told them to stay in the bungalows instead of going to the emergency shelters in B-2." Zeidler steeled his gaze at his superior. "I'm not letting Vicky and little Evan die. And I know what the others are going to decide, once I tell them what's going on." Glaring at him once more, Zeidler turned in defiance toward the door—*

But Emir slammed him hard against wall!

"You're not telling them!" Emir exclaimed. "They can't know about this! That's an order!"

"Look at B-2, Emir! It's secured! See the emergency shelters? They're safe! We can take our families there and go back to A-Bay!"

Emir traded posturing looks with Zeidler, forcing his own dread deep down inside him. "You have your orders, Curran." Another pause. "Gather the team so we can head off to A-Bay. That's all they need to know."

Zeidler said nothing. Instead, he looked at him bitterly.

"That's an order!"

Zeidler pushed him away and flashed a defiant stare at him through a long silence. Turning toward the door in surrender, he gestured with his eyes at the settlement map once more before looking Emir straight in the eyes. "If anything happens to our families ... just remember you had your chance to save them."

Then he left.

Alone in the substation, Emir's unflinching gaze withered, replaced by a terrible dread and mounting ambivalence as he stared haplessly at the indicator moving ever closer to Ceres Beach's access tunnel.

The foreboding display mesmerized him, making him helpless. So pulling the glistening photo from his chest pocket, he stared at the images of Maddison, Nicholas, and Anna. He looked into Maddison's eyes, wishing she could look back at him, wishing for her assurance—wishing he could go back and tell her to go to the emergency shelters.

He could save his family—but only at the price of tens of thousands of soldiers depending on him.

A terrible war sparked deep within him, and his face twisted painfully. He put both fists to his brow and trembled uncontrollably, writhing about as if in physical pain. The conflicting images fought one another in his mind, as did thoughts of what would become of him if he chose wrong.

Suffering under his ambivalence, he took a deep breath and looked down once more at the foreboding display. Then, with just the slightest hesitation, he pulled the Europan transponder from the console's interface. The Europan Coverts' map disappeared from the display. Recomposing his unflinching expression—burying his dread deep down inside himself—he hurried out of the substation in the direction of A-Bay.

"My father may have ordered the attack on Ceres Fleet Base," Tom Andrews' voice sounded from Emir Kern's communicator earpiece, as Emir Kern crouched in the dark behind the Europan palace on Sco-II, "But you had the chance to save your family—and you let them die." He let his words linger through a tense silence. "It's time you faced the truth."

Emir fumed. Images of the dream that had haunted him of late filled his thoughts. But Emir steeled. "I'm coming to wish your father a happy birthday." He looked down at his field pack holding the incendiaries. "I'm bringing candles for his cake, but I'll save some for you too."

The communicator fell silent for a long moment.

"Then I must return your kindness," Andrews began, his voice resonating with a false hospitality. "In honor of my father's seventieth birthday tomorrow, Kara Ricci will be executed at *exactly* one minute past twelve tonight. Her execution will commence the entire day's celebration."

"Kara's dead ... and you know it!"

"I can assure you that she's very much alive—for now."

"What do you want?"

"I know I can't stop you from taking revenge on my father—or me, for that matter. But know that while you're *here* satisfying your lust for revenge, Kara will be paying the price for your failed assassination attempt." He paused intentionally once more. "It pains me to think about what will become of her ... *there are so many painful ways to die.* Don't you agree?"

"You *bastard!*"

The earpiece fell silent, causing Emir to fume that much more.

But Andrews' voice—serious and emphatic this time—returned. "You still have time, Kern. My men left on foot with her a half-hour ago. They're taking her to the execution site. We downloaded a homing locator into your scanner during this transmission. The signal will lead you right to them."

Pausing, Emir surveyed the landscape once more for hostiles. Nothing. Yet he looked around again, and he paused as if unsure of himself—trying to contain his rage as well. "Why should I believe you?"

"I'm giving you a chance to save Kara. Don't let me down."

Emir cut the transmission—to prevent the Europans from tracking him as much as in anger. Bringing his scanner to his eyes, he studied the screen. A blip had appeared on the scanner's display, moving at a walking pace toward the southeast. His shoulders fell: On foot, the blip traveled a good half hour ahead of him.

With his face waxing ambivalent, he gazed up at the palace towering before him. Thoughts of how close he was to exacting his long-sought revenge mocked him, as did very real doubts concerning Tom Andrews' sincerity. After all, Andrews wanted him dead; the blip on his scanner was probably a trap. Worse, chasing the ghostly blip would be difficult, for the rebellion was converging in the quadrant. Europans would be everywhere.

Yet what if the blip really was Kara?

Pulling the tattered photo from his chest pocket, he stared at the images of Maddison, Nicholas, and Anna. Not that he could see the picture in the sparse light. No, but he knew every pixel by heart. A smile washed over his face, and he lost himself once again in the memories flooding his thoughts: memories of a happier time when he was a different person. He reveled in the moment caught in time. If only he could return to that day.

He looked into his Maddison's eyes, wishing she could look back at him, wishing for her assurance. He missed her terribly; he wished he had died with her—perhaps he had.

But his face twisted bitterly as he gazed back at the palace and everything it represented. Images of his family's charred corpses filled his mind, and the madness possessing him returned to his eyes.

Yet what if the blip really was Kara?

Images of her dying a horrifying death accosted him.

As if a terrible war sparked deep within him, his face twisted painfully, and he put both fists to his brow; his whole upper torso trembled, and he writhed about as if in physical pain. The conflicting images fought one another in his mind, as did thoughts of what would become of him if he chose wrong.

Suffering under his ambivalence, he took a deep breath and looked up once more at the palace before him. Then, with just the slightest hesitation, he threw his field pack over his shoulder and took off, heading away from the palace into the darkness.

Emir's quick departure into the night, aided by a brief, swirling breeze, disturbed the thick fog covering the ground. The fog rose, still swirling in the air, steeping high upon the place where the Covert had stood. The thick haze, continuing to eddy, formed into the unmistakable image of a man, a contorted and hideous man at that. Had the dead Europan soldier lying nearby been alive, he certainly would have shot it in defense.

The fog-born image churned in place, defiantly facing the palace with arms raised in anger and its fists clenched. Its distorted face swirled with pain, never relenting from its indignation.

But another breeze tore the image asunder. The churning fog wafted downward and came to rest once more upon the ground.

Chapter Eighteen

End of Many Roads

A single, Europan artillery round struck the ground far ahead of the advancing Dulos army, erupting into a violent fireball and sending an ominous warning. Nevertheless, the army marched on, undeterred.

From his command position within the churning Dulos horde, Michael Gillen watched the fireball far ahead dissipate as he hurried along, convinced that his next hour of command would not go as easily as his first hour. No, that first hour had afforded him the element of surprise. His Dulos army, realizing little resistance from Europan defenses, had moved at a quick and furious pace through the northwest passage. The broken, contorted bodies of dead Europan soldiers littered the wake of the charging Dulos. They had even shot down one of the FW-190s that appeared in the sky and disabled the other.

His second-in-command, a young Dulos male, directed his attention toward the northeast. Far off in the darkness, the advancing Europan army marched toward them—and in a hurry to put themselves between the Dulos and the palace. The rumbling of heavy equipment sounded in the distance behind the troops, and the flash of incoming artillery rising into the air lit up the night sky.

"What do?" the Dulos subordinate inquired.

"Send the signal to spread out," Michael replied. "That should protect us from the immediate heavy artillery. Then order a full charge. Let's make this a man-to-man assault before the Europans establish a front. With our men interspersed with theirs, the heavy artillery and air cover will be meaningless."

Michael watched as the signal went out. Within mere moments, the entire Dulos army rushed toward the Europans, letting out an unnerving battle cry.

"Hold the Line!" Raathe yelled in his native Dulos tongue. The Dulos subordinate, repeating the orders with a bullhorn to the next Dulos in the line of communication (for communications were still jammed) proceeded to communicate the command to the front of the conflict.

Raathe watched his forces dug in at the captured Europan armory far ahead, lamenting that he was fighting a war in two different directions. Though his army had pushed north with a vengeance against a thinning Europan defense (half of the Europan army redeployed against Michael Gillen's forces to the west), his success had come at a price: The eastern Dulos front assaulting the troop base and armory complex was collapsing. He didn't regret the decision to redeploy some of those forces to the northern front. No, he knew Michael Gillen needed as much help as he could get. Raathe just hoped he could maintain control of the armory.

A single FW-190, high in the night sky and shrouded by darkness, rocketed down toward the Dulos forces to the east. Energy rounds spewed forth from its guns, and the Dulos soldiers caught in the line of fire succumbed to the barrage. Energy rounds from Dulos guns shot into the night sky at the speeding enemy fighter, which easily dodged the return fire and sped away.

Europan artillery suddenly fell from the sky like rain onto the Dulos army!

Both Raathe and his subordinate looked far in the distance toward the east.

"Masters have more artillery coming online," the subordinate lamented.

The explosions lit up the darkened battlefield, sometimes as if daylight had arrived again. Cries of agony from the Dulos injured in the thick of the battle rose into the air, and smoke filled the valley. When the artillery strikes ceased, Europan troops poured into the crack in the Dulos defense.

Raathe watched his battered eastern forces pulling back in response. A mass of Europan soldiers rushed the armory complex almost unopposed.

"If the Masters take the armory," Raathe's subordinate began, his deep voice heavy with concern, "Things will get bad quickly."

Raathe shook his head in resignation. "We have no choice. Order the men to hold their positions at all cost." He pointed to the northern front. "Tell our northern forces to push hard! We must help Michael Gillen."

The door to the isolated substation in the Europan fleet base opened, letting in Brent Tasker, Eric Gunn, and Glen Volk, who were dressed as Europan ensigns. When the three Coverts cleared the entry—shaking off the cold night air—Gunn secured the door to ensure they remained alone. Volk hurried over to a control console at the far end of the dimly lit room.

Tasker, sighing in relief, tugged at his loosely fitting uniform. "The next time I jump one of those goons, remind me to pick someone more my size."

"It looks good on you," Gunn replied with a sarcastic gleam in his eye. "You look better in the Europan fleet service than in their army."

"Yeah, I *do* like these uniforms. Europan admirals have such good taste."

Glen Volk, already seated and ignoring the banter, began working the console in front of him. "Turn up the lights."

Gunn studied the small panel adjacent to the doorway. A shrug followed. "How?"

"If we can't figure out the lights," Tasker rather wagged his head at Volk, "How are we going to accomplish this *big idea* of yours?"

Volk, irritated, ignored the comment.

"We've skulked around this fleet base for an hour," Gunn heaped on. "This is the third substation we've broken into. You sure we're in the right place?"

Tasker's face sobered. "We can't do this without Zeidler."

"Just use the security tag we stole off of the Europan," Volk replied, pointing at the security panel on the wall and ignoring the comments. "It will give you access to the room controller."

Gunn lifted the security tag in his hand to the panel, and the panel indicator light turned from red to green. With a press of a button, the lighting in the room brightened considerably. The substation, filled with many consoles and utility panels, lay cluttered with construction gear and materials.

"I hope that guy had the right security access," Tasker cautioned. "Otherwise, we may have just let them know where we are." He shook his head. "*This isn't going to work.*"

Volk shrugged. "You didn't think we'd make it this far either."

"I know you helped Zeidler do this once, but you haven't pulled it off yet."

"And you need to do it fast," Gunn added. "Remember those FW-190s we saw powering up? If we don't do something soon, our Dulos friends won't stand a chance."

"What's taking Fowler so long?" General Aulus Taun asked, looking into the large, three-dimensional tactical display at the center of the War Room in the New Europa Imperial Strategic Command center. His impatience was readily apparent.

"Your lax security measures caused this uprising," Tom Andrews shot back, "—that has lasted four and a half hours already. Be more patient with someone who may end up saving your dignity."

Taun fell silent.

"If Admiral Fowler is successful," one of the other generals looked around, "It shouldn't take long to end this. We've been weak on air cover the entire battle."

"But what about *this?*" Taun asked, pointing at the tactical display where Dulos forces occupied the northwest passage to the palace. "Our troops are scattered among the Dulos. Air cover can't help them."

"Nothing can help them," another general spoke up. "We can't let the Dulos gain a foothold so close to the palace. We have no choice but to bombard those positions."

"Fire on our *own troops?*"

"They're dead anyway."

Tom shook his head in agreement. "This whole uprising is an insult to everything my father has accomplished. As far as I'm concerned, we can't end this soon enough." He turned to the sub-commander behind Taun. "Order the bombardment."

"Word just came in from Admiral Fowler, my Lord," another subordinate interjected, approaching the leaders. "The FW-190s are launching right now."

"Good," Taun replied. The tactical display showed a squadron of FW-190 fighters ascending from the fleet base. A collective sigh of relief came over the room. Taun, humbled, looked at Andrews and then back to the subordinate. "Give my congratulations to Admiral Fowler."

"Order our troops to increase forward pressure," Michael Gillen commanded from his place at the northwest passage. "We're getting bogged down in close-order fighting." He waited patiently, watching the intense conflict while the order relayed to the front of the assault by bullhorns.

In time, the convulsing mass of the two interspersed armies began an indiscernible creep toward the palace, which still lay a great distance away.

"Going well," the gargantuan subordinate standing beside him said in deep tones. "Masters can't pull away. Crush many!"

"So far"—pointing for him to look toward the horizon—"but we still have Europan forces moving in."

"Long night."

Michael nodded in sober resignation and returned his eyes to the conflict.

In the churning mayhem before him, he couldn't distinguish Europan positions from the Dulos positions, except by matter of stature. Fighting in such close proximity to one another, the two armies appeared as one indiscernible mass, essentially nullifying the power of heavy Europan artillery in the distance. The nebulous of men sparring took on the most gruesome realities of warfare. In that twisting, convulsing mass of confusion, the threat of rifle fire had vanished; hand-to-hand combat ruled the day. The shear size, strength, and speed of the Dulos soldiers prevailed.

Michael winced at the carnage transpiring before him. The sight had turned too gruesome to watch. As docile as the Dulos had acted in the village, they went about the battlefield possessed, as if brute beasts to their prey. They seethed with vengeance against their Europan tormentors, even indulging in the pleasures of torture and making sport of them. The Dulos soldiers, picking up one Europan after the other, twisted them into something unrecognizable; they pulled arms and legs from their sockets, they twisted the soldiers' heads from their bodies; they ripped men open, causing their victims' innards to spill onto the ground. Men were left turned inside out. The cries of terror from the Europans only spurred the Dulos on that much more. The ground was littered with contorted corpses, which the Dulos trampled under their massive feet.

The Dulos forces pressed Europan positions well away from the center of the conflict, slowly engulfing their army. However, Michael remained painfully aware that the Europans still had much resistance to offer. Europans forces not on the periphery of the Dulos assault still held defensive positions. Dulos within the mass were much larger targets, and snipers easily distinguished them from the much smaller Europans. The Europans had also resisted the Dulos' push to the north, keeping the Dulos from moving on to the palace. Moreover, more Europan forces were arriving every minute.

Watching the battle unfold in the darkness before him, Michael felt a few drops of rain hitting his shoulders. He looked skyward and beheld the unexpected cloud cover congealing overhead. As raindrops pelted his face, he looked up at the Dulos subordinate beside him. "We never checked the weather."

A heavy downpour commenced.

The Dulos subordinate looked up at the sky indifferently, though becoming wetter each moment. "Good sign: Dulos rugged, masters weak. Dulos *rain* on masters!"

Michael nodded and looked toward the main front. Barely able to see through the deluge, he brought his binoculars up to his eyes, availing himself of the device's image enhancement functions.

The battlefield was quickly turning into a muddy pit.

Michael transformed into a drenched rat while standing his command. The infrequent flashing of lightning, the low rumbling of thunder, and the sound of a steady breeze joined the harried cadence of the battle, bringing a new level of confusion to the scene—

An artillery round exploded fifty meters to his right!

Michael ducked. The massive Dulos subordinate, also to his right, mostly shielded him from the concussion. When the sound of debris flying overhead dissipated, he returned to his feet. Fortunately, the round had been a small one.

However, the Dulos soldier strained to stand again.

Michael leaned over the Dulos, whose height lying down was half of Michael's standing height. Through the darkness and the rain, he saw the telltale marks of shrapnel that had scoured the Dulos' right side. Blood issued in varying degrees from each of the puncture wounds. "You okay?"

The Dulos shook his large head in an attempt to regain his bearings. Eventually, he nodded and strained to stand again. Michael reached out to help the injured soldier. Of course, the offer was a polite gesture, for he couldn't even lift the Dulos' massive arm if his life depended on it.

"No worry," the Dulos waved off his offer, "Dulos strong."

Suddenly, the ominous sound of fighter engines in the distance rose above the clamor. Michael, his eyes wide and his face filling with dread, searched the night sky for approaching Europan FW-190s. The engine sounds grew louder and rolled like the thunder over the storm, except constant and unyielding. The sound signified the arrival of more than just a few fighters—many more this time!

At once, the pouring rain morphed into deadly energy rounds! Explosions at the heart of the battlefield repelled the darkness.

Flames erupted, engulfing Dulos and Europan alike in the infernos. Every soldier not consumed by the flames scattered in all directions.

Michael looked at his Dulos subordinate, who came to stand on unsteady legs by then—both cringed as FW-190s thundered over them. He looked up and counted ten, maybe fifteen fighters speeding away. Though racing off into the distance, the fighters would clearly return for another strike.

The Dulos, watching the fighters with him, gawked in disbelief. "Killing own too!"

Michael remained fixed on the desolation before him. His shoulders fell in surrender. As abrupt as the strike had been, it had also been surgical. The fighters had targeted as many of the Dulos as possible. The two opposing armies were stratifying back into two distinct units. The Europans were already forming a front in order to keep the Dulos at a distance. Soon, heavy artillery would resume against the Dulos. Soon, the fighters would stagger their runs, keeping the sky constantly lit up with artillery and preventing the Dulos from regrouping.

The battle had taken a horrifying turn.

"Order our men to push forward!" Michael shouted, trying to conceal his panic.

But the Dulos subordinate shook his head in defiance. "No. Dulos die! Flyers strong!"

Michael fell silent, studying the Dulos standing twice as tall in opposition with every muscle tense. With much hesitation, he feigned the most unrelenting stance he could muster. "We'll die anyway. And we'll die faster if we let them push us back. Let's take a few of them with us!"

The Dulos huffed. He looked at his dying comrades in the distance and then back at him. With a heavy sigh that moved the surrounding air as much as any breeze, he turned and relayed the fateful order to the front line.

However, both of them knew the rebellion was doomed.

The isolated Europan fleet base substation brimmed with tension. Glen Volk, working the console in front of him, suppressed his increasing frustration with Brent Tasker and Eric Gunn, who both paced the floor. Wishing they would monitor the access door rather than aimlessly hovering over him, he sensed their frustration over his lack of progress. He was frustrated too, for his work was taking far too long to complete.

Upon failing a third time to gain access to a particular Europan security algorithm, Volk huffed. The gesture was clearly an overreaction on his part. But he cringed: His comrades had noticed. Out of the corner of his eye, he saw them rolling their eyes at each other. Tasker even threw one hand into the air in resignation.

"What is it now?" Tasker barked.

"I'm just having a little trouble getting past the security grid, that's all."

"That's *all?* You said that forty-five minutes ago when you started."

"Don't chide me if you can't do any better," Volk exclaimed, turning back to his work at the console. "Besides, I *am* making progress. Just be patient. You're driving me crazy."

Tasker huffed and turned away to let his indignation pass—much to Volk's relief.

A couple moments later, a smile came to Volk's face. "I'm in. I told you I could do it."

"*Finally*," Tasker quipped sarcastically, ignoring Volk's prodding gaze.

The tactical console to Volk's left came to life. Lighting up, the display showed a holograph of the conflict to the west in miniature. Volk barely noted the unit's activation and continued working. However, his companions looked slack-jawed at him.

"*What are you doing?*" a mortified Eric Gunn asked while looking for the switch that turned off the console. "You can't just tap into the security grid. They'll detect us."

Volk shook his head. "This is *exactly* what Zeidler did. I can't accomplish the reprogramming without having the AutoNavs initiate the Tacticals: That's standard Europan procedure. Besides, no one will detect us." Ignoring his companions' incredulous gazes, he returned to his programming.

Tasker and Gunn turned and took in the information presented on the tactical display—and traded anxious looks.

"How soon until you're done?" Gunn asked Volk, this time kinder—but emphatic too.

"Why?"

"Look at the display," Tasker urged. "If you don't hurry, there will be nothing left to save."

Volk glanced at the tactical display, and his eyes lingered when he realized the grim picture the holograph portrayed: Europan FW-190s, long-range artillery, and troops were pummeling the Dulos armies. "Got it!"

He worked the console that much faster. Tasker and Gunn kept silent in order to let him concentrate, while they watched the Tactical tell its dismal story.

A noise from the other side of the locked entryway broke the silence!

Everyone stopped and looked toward the door. Volk, more anxious than ever, turned back and worked feverishly, while Tasker and Gunn stood up and stared at the door.

The sounds from the other side of the metal door persisted. The panel beside the door flashed an override command from the other side, though the door remained locked.

"*They're not going away,*" Gunn whispered.

"*I thought you said we wouldn't be detected?*" Tasker whispered at Volk. Waving Gunn with him, both men brought their rifles to the ready and moved toward the door. Gunn suddenly veered off and grabbed a piece of scrap piping lying with the other construction materials. Watching his teammate jam the pipe into the access door's manual override, Tasker nodded. "*Good thinking.*"

The manual override turned against the pipe from the outside until jamming against the door's structure. The override jiggled back and forth, loosening the pipe—that Tasker and Gunn immediately secured. They looked up expectantly at Volk.

Glen Volk, working the console in a rush, whispered, "*Give me more time. I'm not ready.*"

A dejected Kara Ricci made her way through the dark, rain-drenched forest, her heart pounding in her chest. With her arms bound behind her, she strained at every step through the isolated woods and pouring rain. However, the Europan guard walking behind her, his rifle squarely aimed at her back, more than compensated for her own will. So she submissively kept pace with the lieutenant ahead of her, following the narrow, unsteady beam emanating from his flashlight.

She looked down at herself, mortified over what she had become—lamenting not killing herself earlier that day. The two-hour journey on foot had been a nightmare, just as the Europans had cruelly intended. She was completely undressed, having been forcibly stripped at gunpoint back in her cell. Her locket and medal had been ripped from her too. The words from the guard, *just part of your sentence*, still echoed madly in her head. Memories of them parading her through the military complex as a spectacle lingered fresh in her mind. She sensed them ogling her behind veiled glances even then. Indeed, she had become something less than human, something to be thrown away.

Only one thought consoled her: She no longer carried Emir's blood on her anymore.

Her captors refused to tell her where they were taking her, leaving her imagination to conjure what malicious torments awaited her.

But she already knew.

She was a waif, orphaned by whatever forces were carrying her to her untimely end. All of nature had disowned her. With each step, mud oozed into open cuts and broken blisters on her bare feet. Scratches from thorns and low-hanging branches covered her head to toe, while bruises from mistreatment adorned her gaudily. As if to add insult, the freezing rain drenched her bitterly, and the cold night air scoured her skin. She trembled at the agonizing cold, and her extremities ached. The sensations made her conscious of every part of herself—a dreadful reminder of her humiliation.

And that was how she knew they were taking her to her execution: An Europan execution was nothing if not dehumanizing.

Kara lifted her head, letting the downpour wash away the tears covering her face. Hers was a silent cry, discretely hidden from her unsympathetic captors; she would not give them the pleasure of watching her succumb to their treatment. But in reality, she was drenched in her own tears.

"Watch your step," the lieutenant warned, stopping where the path descended a steep, tree-covered bluff in front of them. He turned and waved the flashlight right at the edge of the drop-off. When she nodded in acknowledgement, the man turned back—though letting his eyes linger upon her for a moment—and started descending the hillside.

Kara followed, as did the guard behind her. Unable to balance or steady herself with her arms, she clumsily made her way down the rugged slope, tripping and stumbling several times. By the time the trio finished the long descent, the rain had tapered off to a slight drizzle. Soon, the rain would stop altogether, and so Kara forced back the tears once more. This was a time for bravery, if only an illusion.

Just a few meters from the bottom of the bluff, the thick forest gave way to an all too familiar roadway. The pristine highway, stretching out in both directions, lay oddly abandoned.

A terrible shiver raced up her spine at the sight!

Kara, her face filling with dread, stopped mid-stride. Predictably, the guard behind her shoved his rifle barrel into the small of her back, knocking her forward. So she continued following the Europan officer down the middle of the curving road.

"Do you know where you are?" the lieutenant inquired, turning the flashlight on her. He slowed down just long enough to walk beside her.

Kara reluctantly nodded, recoiling self-consciously at the flashlight trained upon her—though this time, her self-consciousness grew from something stronger than her modesty.

"It's rather ironic," the officer rather sneered. "The name of this road is the *King's Highway*." He panned the flashlight out over the road in front of them. "Can you show us where you executed Lord Galerius' body double?"

With the memories of that terrible day accosting her, Kara fought back the tears welling up inside her and the lump forming in her throat. Nor did she answer right away. Instead, the young woman stared off in the distance at nothing in particular, which irritated the Europan. So choking against the lump in her throat, she replied, "Sigmund Pollux."

"*What?*"

"The man I killed ... his name was *Sigmund Pollux*."

The lieutenant took in the heaviness of her gaze with much indifference. "Just tell us where you killed him."

Kara surveyed the dark landscape before her in search of the ambush point. Much had changed since that day. Rather than a dusty construction site, grassy sidings bordered by manicured trees adorned the roadway on both sides. Towering floodlights lined the highway too, though all of them were dark for some reason. Nevertheless, the basic layout of the roadway and terrain remained the same. With her arms restrained behind her, she pointed down the road with the blunt end of one shoulder. "Over there."

"You'll have to show us."

Receiving a consenting gesture from the lieutenant to move in that direction, Kara reluctantly started down the road. The two Europans followed, the officer keeping the flashlight ahead of her and the guard with his rifle at the ready. After walking quite a distance, she stopped in the center of the road. She looked down at where her bare feet touched the ice-cold road, and she trembled uncontrollably—but not just from the cold anymore. Gathering her courage, she turned around and faced them. "Right here."

"You sure?"

"Yes."

Bathed in the pale illumination of the flashlight with her arms bound behind her, Kara trembled before her captors. The end of the guard's rifle barrel peeked out at her from the shadows behind the flashlight. Her eyes filled with dread, and her whole body grew rigid against her trembling. She couldn't breathe. No, she could only wait for the deadly round that would end her life.

Yet the night air stayed hauntingly tranquil.

Instead, the lieutenant, pausing in thought, carefully studied the place where she stood. Eventually grimacing, he panned the flashlight around the area, studying the terrain, until coming upon a rock wall chiseled out of the adjacent hillside. Tapping his subordinate's shoulder with one hand, he pointed to the wall with the other. "We'll set up over there."

When the two men knelt, set their packs on the ground, and began working and talking amongst themselves, Kara's stomach tied in knots. A flood of emotions washed over her. The fact that she wasn't already dead brought her little consolation. No, her execution was imminent, just a matter of implementation and of standard protocol. Watching them carrying out her sentence—standing before them naked and bound in chains—she began to see the procedure as morbidly surgical in nature. It was a cold, dreadful feeling.

The lieutenant turned the flashlight toward the ground, and the soldiers began unpacking items from their field packs. A mobile floodlight appeared first from the lieutenant's pack. Then, the guard pulled out a restraining spike and a hammer, which she considered odd. After all, she saw little need for such a restraint for an execution at gunpoint. But when the lieutenant's hand reappeared from his pack the second time—Kara's heart leapt into her throat!

The man was holding a bundle of incendiaries!

"So you know what these are," the Europan rather smiled at her petrified gaze.

Kara said nothing—she couldn't! No, all words fled from her. She could barely breathe! She was to be burned to death—vaporized! Just as the Coverts had intended for Aurelian Galerius. She longed to kill herself quickly, and the fear welling up inside her was almost enough to accomplish the task.

However, she would receive no such reprieve. While she stared in terror at the incendiaries, the guard took her by the thick of one arm and dragged her toward the wall—the place where she would soon be set on fire.

CHAPTER NINETEEN

A Most Desperate Time

"**H**urry up, Volk!" Brent Tasker pleaded across the obscure substation, straining with Eric Gunn to hold the scrap metal pipe jammed into the access door's manual override. The two men, every muscle in their bodies taut and their faces beet-red, pushed with all their might against the Europan soldiers fighting to open the door from the outside. The manual release mechanism turned back and forth precariously. "We can't hold it much longer!"

"I'm almost done," Volk assured, working the console feverishly. "Just need another minute."

"I don't think we—"

The Europans on the other side of the door clearly let go. The scrap pipe jerked forward, turning the door's manual override closed. The two Coverts fell forward into a heap against the door. Gunn, his hand crushed between the pipe and the doorframe, screamed out in pain! Panicking, Tasker pulled the pipe toward him, freeing the crushed appendage. The injured Covert retracted the limb to himself like a hurt puppy.

"It's broken!" Gunn choked out over the pain, nursing the injured hand in his other and fighting back the tears welling up in his eyes.

"Help me secure the door!" Tasker barked at him, still taut against the scrap pipe holding the access shut. But upon hearing some obscure mumbling from outside—his eyes shot wide! "Get down!" He dove behind a heavy piece of equipment sitting away from the door, pulling Gunn down behind cover with him. Volk, still working the console, ducked as well.

The access door exploded!

Shards of metal flew everywhere, and choking black smoke filled the entire substation. Grabbing a grenade from his vest, Tasker threw it through the charred, gaping hole where the door had been. The short-fused grenade met the charging Europans in mid-air at the entry, slicing them into pieces upon detonation. The first Europan through died instantly, and shrieking cries from the wounded rang out.

Tasker and Gunn, putting themselves between the door and Volk, jumped up with their rifles at the ready. They fired a continual stream of energy rounds through the doorway. A similar torrent of artillery streamed haphazardly into the substation from Europan troops, who remained out of view and behind cover outside.

With the protection his two companions afforded him, Glen Volk jumped up into his seat at the console and resumed his programming work—but keeping his peripheral vision keenly trained on the deadly gunfire streaming around him too. With each stroke on the keyboard, the young Covert wondered if it would be his last.

Mayhem and confusion raged through several unbearable moments.

Volk held his breath while typing out the last commands needed to complete the job. Just as his fingers entered the last several keystrokes—

A grenade flew through the doorway from the other side!

Tasker and Gunn dove for cover amidst the firestorm!

Volk's heart leapt into his throat at the ominous sign: He couldn't duck for cover *and* finish typing the last command! So he typed faster—

A violent explosion rocked the substation!

As his finger descended toward the last key—the shockwave cut through him!

The rock wall stood bathed in the pale, yellow glow of a floodlight directed from the middle of the abandoned road.

Kara Ricci, both arms still bound behind her and still completely exposed to the male guard working her execution, stared at her distorted shadow adorning the lonely wall, her face drawn and her gaze distant. Her delicate frame, emaciated and battered from the harsh treatment imposed upon her by her jailers, shivered uncontrollably against the cold night air, which felt like a thousand knives cutting into her. However, the pain barely registered, and all modesty had fled into the shadows. No, all these sensations paled in comparison to the dread of what lay ahead of her. Instead, Kara's thoughts raced over just one concern: the incendiary charges in the hands of the Europan lieutenant kneeling behind the spotlight.

The guard attending her started walking the base of the wall, pacing from one end of the illuminated section to the other. With a restraining spike in his grip, he carefully studied the ground beneath his feet. In reality, the wall was a very steep grade cut out of the hillside. A concrete drainage ditch ran the base of the wall in both directions.

Kara looked at the restraining spike in the soldier's hand, its chain and cuffs dangling about as he walked. At once, images of her charred corpse hanging in those chains from the wall haunted her—and she shuddered at the thought.

After pacing the ditch for a while, the guard stopped dead center and studied the place on which he stood. Quickly determining that the spot was as good as any, he kicked away the rocks and other debris lying there.

Then, he looked up at her.

"Kneel down here"—pointing down the ditch toward the direction they had come—"and face this way."

Swallowing hard through a sober pause, Kara reluctantly stepped forward into the ditch. Her self-consciousness returned. Every muscle in her body, suffering from hypothermia and the long journey, moved like rubber. So, in trying to negotiate into a kneeling position, she rather fell into place—and cringed in pain at the jagged gravel cutting into her knees and shins.

The guard grabbed her by the thick of her arm to steady her. "You okay?"

Kara nodded, biting her lip against the pain. So the young man moved on to the next task.

She stared far ahead into the darkness, afraid to watch him working behind her. Self-consciousness welled within her, as did her increasing sense of vulnerability. At the simplest sound from behind, her mind raced. Chills ran up her spine at the clanging of the metal restraints.

The soldier took hold of her ankles from behind—Kara gasping at his touch—and swiveled her legs closer to the wall. Though he had finished moving her, his fingers remained straddled across both ankles—a dreadful sensation.

Then, she felt the cold, metal restraining spike slide between the heels of her bare feet.

The hammer striking the metal spike broke the night air!

She cringed against the force resonating through her whole body. Every successive strike brought the same discomfort, and she felt the cold metal slipping deeper into the ground. When the ground finally muffled all resonance from the spike, a brief silence returned, followed by the sound of the chains moving around near her feet.

Click-click. Click-click. And the cold metal cuffs hugged her ankles, effectively restraining her to the ditch.

She fought the tears welling up in her eyes.

The guard came around her, lifted her to a standing position, and turned her face-forward against the cold rock wall. Once again, self-consciousness and her sense of vulnerability welled within her. With the side of her face flush against the rock and her arms still bound behind her, she watched him moving in close to her from the very corner of her eye. But the guard simply unlocked her wrist restraints, allowing her stiff arms to fall to her side.

She sighed in relief at the unexpected reprieve.

"Don't move," he warned, leaving her.

Kara labored through an anxious moment pressed against the wall.

Upon returning, the young man spun her around until she faced him, and then he leaned her back against the rock wall. Another restraining spike and cuff set dangled from his utility belt. Restraining her wrists, the guard lifted the cuffs dangling from the spike chain to shackle her wrists once more. She hated facing him at such a close distance while exposed, especially backed against the cold rock wall as she was.

More self-conscious than ever, Kara couldn't look at him, nor did she want to suffer under his offhanded, ogling glances. So she gazed down at the restraints he was placing over her wrists.

The cuffs were unusual. Built to withstand much abuse, they had a single metal clasp that, when closed, form-fitted around both wrists at once. A single locking mechanism with an old-fashion keyhole secured the cuffs.

After placing her left wrist palm-side-down into the bottom holder, the guard crossed her right wrist over top of the left—again, palm side down—so that her hands and forearms formed a cross. With a quick flip of the open side of the cuffs, the restraint clicked shut.

"*I have to drive this spike into the rock well over your head,*" the young guard whispered, glancing to the side to make sure the lieutenant was still out of earshot, "*I have to lean against you to do it. Sorry.*"

Kara—taken back at his gracious tone—forgot to nod.

Pulling his hammer and the spike end of the restraint from his utility belt, the guard stretched upward to place the spike, pulling her arms with him and leaning against her, just as he had warned. With much straining on his part, he began pounding the spike into the hard surface above her.

With her arms raised well over her head, Kara suffered through the awkward experience. Despite his body shielding her from the cold, biting air, she longed for him to finish the task. Because his face was close to hers, she looked away. But glancing at him just briefly—she caught the nervous expression hiding behind his forced, flint-like gaze. When he realized she was watching him, his face waxed self-conscious. For the first time, she noticed his baby face. In fact, the young man was barely over the age of conscription.

Kara saw an opportunity.

"*I'll bet this is your first execution,*" she whispered after ensuring the lieutenant remained out of earshot.

"*Don't talk.*"

She watched him pound the spike into the wall. His eyes kept to his work, though he watched her from his peripheral vision. Increasing anxiousness crept into his expression. So she whispered, "*Do you know how I know?*" a deliberate pause. "*Because you look more nervous than I. ... You're young too.*" When he glanced at her tellingly, she gestured with her eyes to where his rifle sat in the grass. *"I'll bet you never even fired that gun before."* Mustering her courage, she took a deep, reluctant breath. *"You don't want to really do this, do you?"*

Though remaining silent while striking the spike above her with the hammer, he strained to remain indifferent.

"Do you even know what I did?"

"Something deserving a death sentence."

"I killed a man who was about to be burned to death."

Yet the young soldier remained awkwardly silent.

"No one should have to die such a terrible death."

"I have my orders."

Kara fell silent, trying to maintain her composure. But her eyes welled up. *"Please ... take your gun and kill me!"* When he looked around nervously, she pressed, *"You can tell your lieutenant I insulted Aurelian Galerius—or whatever's believable. Then, you and your lieutenant can burn my corpse afterwards so you don't get in trouble. Just don't let me die like this! I'm begging you!"*

With the restraining spike driven deep into the rock, the young man stepped back and breathed an intentional sigh of relief—to cover his interaction with Kara from the lieutenant working behind the floodlight. Yet his eyes betrayed his anxiousness. He returned her pleading gaze through an awkward silence. *"I'm sorry."*

He turned and walked away.

Kara watched the young man pick up his rifle from the grass—and return to his superior's side. She gazed up at the unrelenting chains restraining her arms above her, still conscious of the cuffs restraining her ankles to the ditch.

She was chained to the wall like an animal.

The Europan lieutenant, his pistol at the ready, followed his troops rushing the obscure substation somewhere on the Europan fleet base. After making his way through the charred entrance—stepping over his dead subordinates caught in the grenade detonation earlier—he paused to let the soldiers secure the room. The men fanned out into the smoke-filled station, constantly training their rifles on potential targets as they searched the rubble.

Two soldiers immediately trained their rifles on the motionless, contorted bodies lying face-down near the entrance. Another soldier, kicking away the guns lying on the floor near the intruders, knelt and examined them. "They're dead." He rolled the corpses onto their backs.

Brent Tasker and Eric Gunn's lifeless faces, bloodied and mangled from the blast, stared up at them. The lieutenant studied the two dead men, while the subordinate started to stand—

"Don't move!" came a shout from another soldier at the far end of the room. "And remove your hand from that console!"

The lieutenant spun around toward the ruckus, where an ensign and three other guards pointed their weapons down at some unseen target behind the console there. Rushing to the back of the room and around the console, he finally caught sight of the injured intruder.

Glen Volk lay on the floor with his back against the control console, facing his captors. His twisted legs stretched out in front of him like that of a rag doll. Blood ran down his face from a gash in his head, and his shrapnel-torn shirt was drenched in blood. His head tilting to one side tellingly, he stared up at his captors with doleful eyes amidst labored breaths. Every now and then, he gnashed his teeth in pain.

Oddly, his left arm hung suspended over his head onto the console behind him; one finger hovered over a particular key on the console's controls.

"Remove your hand!" the Europan lieutenant cautioned, pointing his pistol at Volk's face. "Whatever you were attempting to do is over." When Volk persisted by keeping his finger over the key in defiance, the officer steeled his frame. "I don't want to kill you, but I will if you leave me no choice."

The standoff continued. The Europans kept their guns trained on him, while Volk's uniform grew bloodier each moment. As his breathing waxed into abrupt gasps, he shook uncontrollably.

"Don't make me kill you!" the lieutenant repeated.

"I'm *already* ... already dead," Volk seethed through shallow breaths. "You *can't* ... can't prevent it." Upon seeing a hint of pity in the officer's face, Glen gestured with his eyes at the man's communicator.

He strained a singular laugh. "I suggest *you* ... you turn *that* ... *off.* ... Do you know *how* ... how deadly a reprogrammed *life* ... *life pod* ... *can* ... *can be?*" Straining to make his face like flint against their quizzical gazes—

Glen pushed the key beneath his finger!

The four Europans opened fire on him! Round upon deadly round pummeled the Covert's body, until Glen Volk slumped over dead.

The lieutenant, re-holstering his pistol while sighing in frustration, gazed down at his corpse. "Find out what they were trying to do."

The console above Volk came to life.

Knocking Volk's corpse out of the way with his boot, the officer moved in and studied the display.

Hundreds of indicators and elaborate icons filled the screen. The console was running some sort of program, which quickly sequenced through its intended steps. Graphics of the warships docked outside appeared. The screen continuously changed over, graphically showing the program working its way through the labyrinth of the warships' designs, until their emergency life pods displayed on the screen.

The officer, his eyes wide, worked the controls in a desperate attempt to shut down the rogue program. "He locked out our security overrides!"

The life pod design settings displaying on the screen changed each moment. Original programming disappeared in favor of new commands—but the changes abruptly stopped. A beeping sound broke the tense quiet, and the words *Status: Launch* prominently appeared on the screen.

Loud thunder—continuously rolling thunder—roared from outside the substation, causing the startled officer to rush outside into the cold night air ahead of his subordinates.

Three thousand lifeless warships sat in place all the way to the horizon, still marooned and dry-docked from the earlier *Endurance* attack. Yet erupting from the darkened hulls, their emergency life pods streamed into the night sky in waves.

"What's going on?" one of the soldiers asked, looking as slack-jawed as his peers also gazing into the crowded sky.

"Three thousand warships," the lieutenant said, deactivating his communicator and turning toward him with a sober grimace. "—one hundred life pods per warship, all containing AutoNavs, sufficient fuel reserves, and Europan communications protocols." He shook his head. "Turn off your communicators if you want to live."

The subordinates quickly complied. All eyes trained on the three hundred thousand makeshift missiles launching into the pitch-black sky.

"*What are they?*" Tom Andrews demanded, looking down in stunned disbelief at the broad, three-dimensional tactical display in the center of the War Room of the New Europa Imperial Strategic Command.

Thousands of tiny dots had appeared on the tactical display before him, ending the room's previous elation. The tiny blips of light ascended from the fleet base and raced toward the main battle zones. When no one answered him, Tom looked up. "What are they?"

However, General Taun and the other high commanders looked just as dumbfounded, save the fear leaching out from behind their grave expressions.

The sub-commanders and terminal operators to the side worked that much faster to identify the rogue apparitions, while Tom and the high commanders watched the blips of light speeding toward Europan positions.

"My Lord," a sub-commander called from his place beside one of the command consoles to the side, "The projectiles are life pods launching from our warships."

"It has to be some sort of malfunction," Taun said.

The man received incredulous looks from Tom and the other commanders.

"That is doubtful!" Tom chided. "Their trajectories are intentional— and they're heading straight for our forces."

Just then on the tactical display, some of the blips veered toward and collided with Europan positions closest to the fleet base, causing both indicators to disappear upon impact.

"Recall them!" Taun pleaded.

"We can't, Sir," the sub-commander shook his head, "The life pods are denying us access to their AutoNavs—and our guns won't target them, since they register as friendly." He swallowed hard. "It will take a while to reprogram the guns."

"We don't have a while!" Tom exclaimed.

On the tactical display, the hundreds of thousands of speeding blips descended from high in the sky toward Europan armies, military complexes, and the palace.

"Eliminate their targeting protocol," Taun pressed with much desperation, turning toward the sub-commander. "How are they targeting our positions?"

The sub-commander and his aide studied the console before them, ignoring the generals' impatience. "They're using their status as Europan ships to gain access to the military network. They are randomly targeting anything transmitting on the network. Our positions don't even know they are being acquired."

"Then shut down the network!"

The sub-commander shook his head. "The network is seamlessly integrated into every function. If we shut it down, our defenses shut down as well. Until we can reprogram our systems, anything on the network is vulnerable."

One of the other generals looked at the barrage of incoming projectiles on the display. His face drained of all color. "*We're* on the network!"

Michael Gillen, standing crestfallen at his command post in the northwest passage, watched his Dulos army taking a terrible beating. Europan FW-190s fighters racing through the sky pummeled the Dulos from above, while troops and heavy artillery added insult to injury. The mounting Europan assault gained strength each minute, and the Dulos would soon meet their demise. His mind raced with a thousand thoughts, as he searched for some way to help them. However, he had run out of options.

Something caught his eye.

He glanced away from the battlefield toward the eastern horizon. Thousands upon thousands of tiny specks of light rose into the night sky. They seemed to hover low in the sky for quite a while, as if swarming in the distance. But he quickly realized the specks of light were actually racing westward toward him, though moving rather randomly through the sky.

Michael watched the horizon quizzically. The lights resembled flares, which didn't make sense to him. But as the projectiles neared, he realized they were much larger than flares. His shoulders sank. *What new weapons are the Europans inflicting upon us?* he thought. *Aren't they beating the Dulos bad enough already?*

The projectiles approached the battle zone, moving faster and with ever-increasing accuracy. Many of them dove toward the planet's surface and disappeared behind the bluffs in the distance—where Raathe commanded his army. Lights flashed in the night sky from behind the bluffs, followed by the rumble of explosions. The rest of the projectiles raced through the sky toward the northwest passage.

Another swarm of lights appeared on the eastern horizon. The armaments were coming in waves.

Michael looked up at his Dulos subordinate. "Warn everyone to prepare for incoming."

The leviathan, still bleeding from his previous injuries, sent the communication through the line of bullhorns. Both of them cringed at the imminent barrage.

The screaming engines of the new arrivals overwhelmed the thundering sound of Europan FW-190s swarming over the battlefield.

The projectiles moved fast and with deadly resolve.

Suddenly, one of the projectiles turned and struck an FW-190! The Europan fighter burst into flames in mid-air, lighting up the night sky before its debris fell to the ground. Other projectiles struck Europan gunneries in the distance, while still others crashed into unsuspecting Europan ground troops.

Michael looked at his Dulos aide in disbelief.

Mayhem enveloped the battlefield!

While Dulos soldiers fled out of harms way, Europan soldiers died by the hundreds as life pods dropped from the sky onto them and exploded. Other life pods pummeled the remaining FW-190's, which fell from the sky—sometimes the debris falling onto the very troops they were defending. Gunneries in the distance, meeting a similar demise, turned to smoking heaps of rubble. Life pods struck the palace and military complexes in the distance. The whole Europan military fell under the siege.

Michael looked toward the eastern horizon, where the life pods had originated. He fell silent for a long moment, pondering the unexpected turn of events. Then, turning back toward the battlefield and watching the Europan defenses collapsing, he smiled at the Dulos. "Tell our troops to push ahead to the palace."

A stunned Raathe surveyed the mayhem engulfing the battlefield before him—filled with awe and wonderment of the divine fortune that had befallen him.

Having moved his troops safely out of harms way, Raathe stood his command with such satisfaction. He relished watching Europan troops scattering from their positions, all the while deadly projectiles rained down on them mercilessly. The Europan army was collapsing in on itself. The debris of its largest weapons littered the battlefield, along with their dead and dying soldiers. Those soldiers not consumed by the fury of the projectiles fled into the hills.

For the first time in the battle, Raathe's troops had an unabated path to the palace and military complexes to the west. More than pleased with the wondrous turn of events, Raathe gave the signal to charge the palace.

The three rooms insulating the Europan War Room from the outside lay destroyed by a maniacal life pod. Rather than three separate rooms, the place was one large heap of twisted metal, cables, smashed equipment, and dead bodies. Thick smoke wafted out through the gaping hole in the side of the New Europa Strategic Command building.

The War Room fared no better. A charred, gaping hole existed where the life pod had breached the room's thick wall. Every subordinate in the path of the deadly projectile lay dead under smashed equipment. Debris lay scattered throughout the room, and all of the room's occupants were injured to some extent.

Tom Andrews, scraped and bruised but fortunate to escape serious injury, strained out from under the debris covering him. Laboring to stand, he surveyed the rubble. Most of the high commanders scattered throughout the immediate area suffered various injuries.

However, General Aulus Taun was dead.

Tom looked down at the dead man, taking in his mortal wounds with such indifference. "Good riddens."

He looked down at the tactical display in remorse. The explosion had damaged the unit, and the three-dimensional images flickered sporadically, sometimes phasing out completely. Through the interference, Tom saw the same dire circumstances: The Europan defenses had crumbled. The Dulos were quickly advancing toward the palace.

He could neither avert nor delay the impending fall of New Europa.

Pounding from the other side of the blocked entryway broke the dirge of moaning. Several more emphatic blows upon the door followed, until the door flew open. The room filled with rescue personnel.

"Lord Trajan," one of the officers in charge of the rescue implored, approaching him, "We need to get you out of here."

"I'm all right."

"My Lord, the sky is full of maniacal life pods. Another strike on this place could be fatal."

"Concentrate on taking my father out of the settlement instead—before the Dulos arrive."

The officer hesitated. "If we move you or your father now, we'll put you in even more danger." He hesitated. "Besides, your father refuses to leave—but we can hide you until it is safe."

Tom, looking at the dire graphics flickering on the tactical display, shook his head. "It's too late for that now." His face waxed pensive. "No, the rule of Aurelian Galerius is sadly over. But we still have work to do. Come with me."

CHAPTER TWENTY

King's Decree

Michael Gillen made his way on foot through the darkness, following the fast moving Dulos army closing in on the Europan Royal Palace well ahead.

The atmosphere buzzed with electricity—but not from the storm that had moved through the region earlier. No, that storm had passed, and the crisp night sky hung draped with the haze of a myriad of stars.

Instead, the palpable force was anticipation, rising from within thousands upon thousands of reinvigorated Dulos soldiers. Having escaped annihilation, they pressed on toward the palace with abandon, no longer fighting just for existence, but for the chance to grasp hold of precious freedom.

Michael was optimistic too. After watching the mighty Europan war machine pounded into confusion—by something as seemingly innocuous as a rogue fleet of life pods—he had witnessed the emboldened Dulos coalesce into a formidable threat. Rather effortlessly, they had pushed toward the palace.

However, the battle was far from over.

"Order our troops in front to slow down, group with the squads behind them, and fan out into a wider flank," he said to his Dulos subordinate keeping pace with him. Gesturing to where the remaining Europan forces had established a perimeter around the palace, he added, "Despite the beating they took, the Europans won't surrender the palace so easily."

"Move Dulos guns to front? Crush Master house?"

"No, In fact, order them to target *only* the Europan fortifications protecting the palace—not the palace itself." When the Dulos flashed a quizzical look, he added, "Now that victory is imminent, we must retain as much of the settlement's infrastructure as is possible. We need to remove the rest of Europan control over the planet surgically."

As the Dulos sent the message along, Michael trained his gaze on the palace before him. His forces rushed to engage the remnants of the Europan resistance, and the knots returned to his stomach. His mind raced with all the possibilities over what had become of Katey—Phil Marcotte and David Tashjian too. But Katey more than anyone.

Soon—maybe too soon—he would learn her fate.

And another reunion with Tom Andrews lay ahead of him too.

But he suppressed the confusing thoughts: The very front of the Dulos army far ahead of him had reached the perimeter of the palace.

Tom Andrews led a group of subordinates up the stairwell to the garden courtyard atop the Europan Royal Palace. Reaching the top of the stairwell, he pushed open the access door and stepped onto the garden courtyard. Darkness draped the secluded haven, save the occasional decorative light scattered about. The air hung hauntingly still too. Immediately, his eyes trained on the table sitting on the stone terrace in front of him.

He paused at the door.

Aurelian Galerius, facing away from the access door and alone in the courtyard, sat at the head of the table, which boasted a lavish spread of food. A pistol lay on the table near his left hand. Upon hearing the access door opening, the old man reached for the pistol.

Waving off the Europan subordinates following him, Tom started toward Galerius. "Father?"

Immediately, Galerius' hand recoiled from the pistol.

Tom approached him, noticing the false sense of serenity hanging in the air. Upon navigating around the old man, he saw a small piece of cake sitting on a plate in front of him. Ironically, Galerius' chefs had prepared the elegant desert for his birthday celebration—which, of course, would no longer happen. Taking in the strange expression covering his father's face—how the old man's eyes shone hollow and his gaze distant—he forced a smile. "I thought I would find you here."

"Trajan," he smiled, his eyes warming. "Sit down. Have some cake."

Tom complied, taking his seat across the table. Cutting a piece of cake, he ceremonially set it on a plate in front of him. Of course, he had taken the dessert out of respect for his father, for hunger was the last thing on his mind.

"No matter how old I get," Galerius relished, taking a bite of the desert and off in a world of his own, "I never get over how good chocolate cake can be."

Studying his father's odd enthusiasm, Tom nodded out of deference and took a bite of his own desert. "Yes, it's very good."

"This is a very special day for me, Trajan. I never thought I'd make it to seventy."

"Your birthday has come too soon for me, Father. Time is moving too fast."

"That's because of the ten years you spent in cryogenic suspension, Trajan. It must have been terrible seeing me age so abruptly. But that is the way of things." Galerius' face waxed sentimental. "I must admit that I've seen a lot. When I was twenty, I dropped out of school and took a job as a lowly transport pilot. I barely made a living—but I had so many ideas. I was full of pride and empty of pocket. If someone had told me then that I would someday rule Europa, turn it into one of the most powerful nations ever, and stir up a hornets' nest of trouble across all of Terrae Solaris—I would have thought them crazy."

"I'm sorry I let you down today."

"You did your best," the old man dismissed with a subtle wave of the hand. "Our commanders grew complacent on this planet." He took another bite of his desert before shaking his head in disbelief. "We came *so close*, Trajan ... so close to achieving something never before accomplished: the first family to rule two solar systems. It would have been marvelous."

"There's still time," Tom added, his voice hollow.

"If only there were."

An awkward silence fell over the table. Tom, attempting to reflect an encouraging gaze, watched his father stare at nothing in particular.

"No, it wasn't meant to be," the old man sighed and wiped his mouth with the napkin on his lap. "I wanted to come up here one last time before I"—his face waxing grave and his eyes falling spellbound at the pistol—"... well ... *you know.*" He let out an unsettled chuckle. "I didn't have the courage to do it."

Tom, taking in his disturbing expression, remained silent.

"It's just as well," Galerius assured, as if gathering his resolve. "History is full of leaders too cowardly to face their enemies—leaders who took the easy way out. Not me. No, I'll face the Dulos with my head held high." Setting his napkin over the empty plate before him, he looked at Tom. "Let's take one last walk around the courtyard before I order the surrender."

At Galerius' lead, the two stood up from the table. When the old man took hold of his son's arm, Tom escorted him at a slow pace around the courtyard. Taking in the sight of the beautiful gardens lining the walkway, the old man wore a pensive smile.

Finally, the two came to stand before the elaborate marble fountain entitled *Livi*a. Lighting from underneath the water illuminated the effervescent, waist-high cloud of rolling water. At the center, the statue of Livia arrayed as an angel looked down upon them. However, the shadows created by the night had voided the statue of all warmth. Instead, the woman's face churned uneasily.

Both men fell under the power of the familiar image.

"Promise me something," Galerius said, still looking at the statue. "Let my men take you into hiding. My capture will satisfy the Dulos, allowing you to escape. Promise me you'll redeem my legacy and take back New Europa someday."

Tom looked at him through a long silence. "I promise."

Galerius smiled and turned his gaze back to the image of his deceased wife. A long moment passed, until he offered a telling sigh. "Okay, Trajan, accompany me down to the communications center so I can issue the surrender."

Galerius, sadness filling his face, turned toward the exit—

A bright flash lit the immediate area, and the sound of gunfire broke the silence! Galerius' face contorted under intense pain, and his whole body snapped rigid. Clutching at Tom—who looked on in dismay while steadying his father with one hand—the old man slumped to the ground.

Tom, overwhelmed with grief, knelt over the old man and watched him suffering in agony beside the fountain. With his face twisting in despair, Tom re-holstered his pistol and took him by the hand. "I'm sorry, Father. I won't let you fall into the Dulos' hands."

Galerius lay there, holding his son's hand while suffering through the work of dying. The strength to talk had fled from him. However, his eyes turned warm once again, and he gazed with much affection at his son, even managing a faint smile.

Still kneeling over his dying father, Tom watched the old man's life ebb from him. The sound of the soldiers' footsteps nearing came to his ears. Tom paid no attention. No, he merely took in his father's approving expression and clutched his hand even tighter. "Father, you were right about Kara Ricci. I had her executed tonight ... my *gift* to you."

Galerius smiled once more. But the expression drained away, and his eyes waxed glassy.

Aurelian Galerius was dead.

Tom Andrews—Trajan Aurelius—held vigil over his father's corpse, fighting back the strong emotions washing over him. His eyes welled up, and he looked up at the unforgiving face of his mother's statue looking down on him.

The soldiers arrived.

"Take my father's body and have it incinerated," Tom exclaimed, gathering himself. "Scatter the ashes in an undisclosed location. Don't give the Dulos the satisfaction of a public display. And *never* disclose what happened. As far as you're concerned, Aurelian Galerius escaped alive and well."

"Yes, my Lord," the commanding officer replied. "But let us take you away before it's too late."

Tom shook his head. "Unless you have an interstellar ship waiting somewhere, I doubt it will matter. Here's what I want you to do: Transmit all the *Endurance* crew's locations on the Covert network, just as we did with Ricci—Kate Gillen, Phil Marcotte, and David Tashjian. But this time, label the identifiers. It will be a goodwill offering to Michael Gillen. Once he sees his wife on his scanner, he'll infiltrate the palace. Give him resistance, but make sure that he—and he only—gets through."

"What about you, Lord Aurelius?"

Tom smarted at the address. As indicated by Europan custom, he became *Lord Aurelius* only after Aurelian Galerius had died. "Just make sure Michael Gillen gets into the palace."

"Locator beacon identified," a computerized voice sounded from Michael Gillen's communicator earpiece.

Michael, preoccupied with his troops engaging the final remnants of the Europan army near the palace, looked around upon hearing the unexpected voice. But quickly realizing the source, he lifted his scanner attached to his utility belt.

The device's display cycled through identifying every Europan and Dulos positions throughout the battle zone. Unsatisfied and working feverishly to identify the target piquing its electronic brain, the screen changed to a regional view of the immediate area. Several blips appeared with labels above them: Phil Marcotte, David Tashjian, and—*Kate Gillen!*

Michael, looking up wide-eyed in the direction indicated by Katey's locator beacon, took in the Europan Royal Palace towering into the night sky.

"Kate!" Tom Andrews called out, barreling through the door of his apartment cell somewhere in the Europan Royal palace. Emergency lighting barely lit the apartment, allowing heavy shadows to drape the immediate room. Tom wore the same clothes as when he had left the apartment seven hours earlier.

Kate rushed toward him from the bedroom hallway. "Tom!" She locked him in a tight embrace and held on to him with abandon. "I was *so worried* about you!"

"I'm okay."

"I heard all these noises outside the palace—*terrible noises!* And the building shook like it was being bombarded!"

While she kept him in her grasp, alighting an occasional kiss of relief upon his cheek, her eyes wandered toward the open door. The corridor outside lay oddly abandoned—and she remembered catching sight of a pistol in his hand. She recoiled and searched his troubled gaze—the fresh bruises and scrapes covering him too. "What's going on?"

"We need to get out of here."

"Why?"

"The Dulos are on a rampage." When she tilted her head quizzically, he gently shook her out of her stupor. "*Remember the creatures the Coverts talked about?*" Her expression fell tellingly grim. "They're killing everyone! The whole settlement is in confusion—that's how I got away. We need to leave *now!*"

Kate took in his concern. However, sadness washed over her. "I'm staying here."

"Don't do this, Kate. Come with me."

"It never ends, Tom. ... *It never ends!*"

He took in her unsettled gaze for the longest time. An anxious gulp followed. "What if I told you that it all ends tonight? That tomorrow, you'll have put all this behind you once and for all?"

With her eyes searching him out, her face twisted quizzically—but in a morbid, even fear-struck way. "What are you talking about?"

"You'll have to trust me. Do you trust me, Kate?"

An awkward silence fell over the room. The young couple traded contending looks. When her eyes softened, Tom said, "Now get dressed for travel—*quickly.*"

She stood there looking at him for a moment longer. Offering a reluctant and rather subtle nod, Kate turned toward the bedroom to comply—

But Tom grabbed her hand and pulled her back to him again. As he took her by the thick of her arms, his gaze steeled with resolve. "But make me a promise."

"What?"

"Whatever happens—*whatever you see*—you'll do *exactly* what I say. Okay?"

She fell under his imploring gaze, her mind racing at his unspoken concern. "I trust you implicitly. Why even ask?"

"Because our biggest trial is still ahead of us. We won't survive if you don't do exactly what I say. So promise."

Another long silence.

"Okay, I promise."

"Good," Tom barely smiled, releasing her. "Now hurry so we can leave."

Kara Ricci, chained to the rock wall on the abandoned highway and bathed in the pale yellow glow of a floodlight, churned within over her imminent execution. Knots tied in her stomach as she imagined the horror of her execution. Her experience as a front-line doctor in the war did her no service. No, she had seen far too many burn victims not to dread what was about to happen.

She whispered a prayer for deliverance under her breath, though not to anyone or any god in particular. No, Kara was not a religious person. And she expected no deliverance. After all, the young, Europan guard standing before her earlier remained unmoved by her pleas for a mercy killing. Why would the unseen forces delivering her up for death be any more sympathetic? Nevertheless, she whispered the prayer. The more she prayed for deliverance, the more her thoughts filled with the memories of killing Sigmund Pollux long ago.

The Europan lieutenant appeared from behind the floodlight, followed by the guard. Both made their way toward her. Kara immediately spotted the incendiaries in the guard's hands. He looked at her awkwardly while approaching.

Kara stared at the deadly firebombs. Eight incendiary charge packs, each boasting a single, red indicator light on its front, hung affixed to a carrying band. The red lights flashed simultaneously, indicating they were active and awaiting the command to detonate. Kara's heart sank when she caught sight of the insignia on the charges. She wanted to die that very moment. Rather than vaporizing her in a single blast, the incendiaries would burn slowly. They were a crude form of firebomb, constructed to inflict terrible pain and injury long before death.

"Where do these go?" the guard asked the lieutenant, just as both of them came to stand in front of her.

The lieutenant, holding the remote detonator in his hand, studied her top to bottom and rather scratched his head. "I don't know exactly. The incendiaries are designed for ground combat." He paused in thought. "We could lay them on the ground."

"What about affixing them to the rock wall around her? The instructions on the side say the back of the charges will stick to anything."

"No, the charges are already active. I don't want to risk detonation while we're pulling them off the carrying band."

"If you strap them over my shoulders the way they carry them in the field," Kara interjected, her face full of trepidation and her eyes welling up. "You'll have much better success." When they gazed upon her chained to the wall, she fought hard to keep her wits about her. She refused to let them see weakness.

Nevertheless, the lieutenant rather sneered. "And how do you know that?"

"I'm a doctor. I worked the front lines of the war—saw a lot of casualties from incendiaries."

The officer looked at her and then to his subordinate. He shrugged. "If that's what she wants...." He motioned to the guard, who unclasped the ends of incendiaries' carrying band and moved in toward her.

Kara watched the young guard dress her in the deadly charges. She hated him touching her; she hated the officer's offhanded remarks about her finally having something to wear. But her suggestion was intentional: She knew she would die quicker if the fiery gases penetrated all the way into her lungs. The charges had to be close to her nose and mouth to accomplish a quick death. She shuddered at the very thought of suffering one second longer than necessary—but such a gruesome thought nonetheless!

When the subordinate finished, the two men stepped back and examined their work. Sighing, the lieutenant patted the guard on the shoulder while turning back toward the road. "Let's get this over. It's almost time anyway."

Emir Kern raced with abandon through the thick forest, his mind transfixed on one singular thought—Kara!

Nothing else mattered. He cared not a wit about his haphazard pace across the dark, dangerous terrain; tripping or falling wasn't an option. He could afford no delays, nor did he care that he was soaking wet, cold, and exhausted from his long journey. He couldn't entertain the threat of a possible ambush by Europan troops either.

No, his time to rescue Kara had run out!

He glanced down at the small scanning device in his hand, trying to keep it steady while running. He didn't need the scanner to show him her location—he already knew. He had known since happening upon the specter of the woman being marched through the darkened woods long ago—and the foreboding flash of incendiaries just before the specter disappeared.

He shuddered at the thought.

But the scanner showed the same dire reading as the previous time he had looked at it. Kara's location—still so far away—was constant; she had arrived at the place of her execution. His chronometer was quickly counting down to midnight too: the time Tom Andrews had given him for her execution.

Panic washed over him, and his breathing grew all the more labored. Fear of him arriving too late to save her engulfed him, and images of her imminent execution tortured his mind. He was on the verge of losing her forever.

So he pushed even harder through the remote forest—

Suddenly, bright light flooded all around him! The sound of soldiers training their rifles on him broke the night!

Emir stopped and threw his hands in the air. The powerful light accosted his eyes, and he strained to see four drenched Europan foot soldiers behind the light. Oddly, they appeared equally startled to have happened upon him. Nevertheless, Emir found himself at gunpoint.

"Move and you're dead!" one of them shouted.

CHAPTER TWENTY ONE

At the Palace

The remnants of the harassed Europan armies, positioned on the perimeter of the palace, had dug themselves in against the advancing Dulos army. The violent exchange of hostilities engulfed the area, which lay draped in darkness. Dulos troops, buffeted by heavy outgoing artillery, pressed in against Europan strongholds. Yet the Europans, having the advantage of well-designed fortifications, kept the Dulos at bay.

A battle-weary Michael Gillen stood watching his troops assault the palace. The Europans stood as strong in their final resistance as he had foreseen. However, he took satisfaction that defeating the Europans was just a matter of time. Eventually, the Dulos would breach the Europan lines, and gruesome hand-to-hand combat would commence. The Europan defenses would collapse under the assault, allowing the Dulos to storm the palace. The offensive simply needed enough Dulos soldiers to overwhelm the Europan defenses. His army was moving into position, even as Raathe's army trickled in from the east.

He also kept a close eye on Kate's location shown on the scanner in his hand. She remained deep inside the palace. Holding on to the hope that she was safe, he waited for the right time to mount a rescue.

"Gillen!" Raathe's deep, booming voice called from behind him.

Michael turned just as Raathe sidled up to him. The Dulos' aides followed closely behind. The two leaders exchanged greeting and quips about the imminent victory, all the while watching Raathe's army spilling into the area.

But then, Raathe looked at him quizzically. "Where Kern? Found Kern army abandoned."

Michael shrugged. "So you have command of both armies?" When the Dulos nodded his sizeable head, he said, "Good, take command of my forces too." He held up the scanner to him. "My wife is in the palace. When we have a way in, I want to rescue her."

"Raathe understand."

Commotion erupting somewhere behind him made Michael turn around.

Out of the mass of Dulos soldiers coming in from behind, five Dulos pushed along a badly beaten and bloodied Europan man. The Europan, his face ripe with terror, repeatedly attempted to flee from his assailants, who prevented his escape each time.

"Who's that?" Michael asked, directing Raathe's attention to the spectacle.

Raathe turned and looked at the man. His face fell dour and unsympathetic. "Taskmaster!"

Standing a good distance from the ruckus, Michael realized he was watching the beginnings of an impromptu death sentence.

He cringed at the sight.

The mammoth Dulos made sport of their diminutive prisoner, swarming around him and striking him repeatedly—just hard enough to taunt him. A crowd of ranting Dulos formed around the spectacle. But as the taunting continued, the five Dulos tired of holding back.

Showing no mercy, they pulled the Europan's fingers one by one from his hands; then his hands from his wrists, working each piece of bone and sinew up the arms. They waved the torn pieces of flesh before him as he screamed in agony, mocking him before throwing the bloody appendages to the ground. One of the five took hold of him from behind, and the other Dulos did the same with his legs, painfully disassembling him piece by bloody piece. Each Dulos took a turn, while those Dulos watching spurred on the tormenters with unnerving howls.

The Europan cried out his pleas for mercy—to no avail.

Michael suddenly remembered seeing the man three weeks earlier, the day Raathe had taken him to the construction site. The taskmaster was the man who had beaten a Dulos senseless, until another Europan shot the defenseless Dulos at point-blank range. Watching the Europan pay the terrible price for his deeds against the Dulos, the young commander pitied him: it was a terrible way to die.

"Disturb Gillen?" Raathe asked, seeing Michael's remorse.

Michael, unable to avert his eyes from the dreadful sight, shook his head. "Yes, but I know what this man did."

Raathe nodded.

The execution played out to its miserable end. The five Dulos taunted and struck what was left of the taskmaster, who grew bloodier each moment. When their victim's eyes waxed over in shock, the five Dulos took hold of him and ripped his torso to pieces. Innards spilled out onto the ground, and sounds of bones cracking filled the air. They threw the dismembered man to the ground. One of the Dulos crushed the Europan's head with his massive foot, marking the end of the gruesome execution. After a moment's pause, the Dulos band departed, leaving bloody appendages and entrails scattered across the ground.

Raathe once more turned to Michael, whose face betrayed his horror. "Nothing compare to what Dulos do to Master Galerius."

With one final look at the sobering scene, Michael turned back toward the siege.

Michael watched the Dulos push hard against the western flank of the Europan defensive at the Europan Royal Palace. The flank had not yet breached the line, though the Dulos pressed in mercilessly. Soon, grisly hand-to-hand combat would begin.

He glanced down at his scanner—his eyes shot wide!

Kate was moving inside the palace toward his location. He followed the blip's movements on the screen, the anticipation welling within him as she approached the porticos adjacent to the palace's west wing.

Michael brought his binoculars to his eyes and scanned the porticos and western wing behind them. The wing boasted large, opulent windows. He hoped to see her appear in one of those windows—if only briefly.

He continuously scanned the windows with his binoculars. Eventually, one of the doors on the second story portico opened. Kate stepped out onto the portico, her face betraying her concern—and Michael's jaw dropped!

Tom Andrews was leading her by the hand.

Just then, the Europan flank collapsed, and the Dulos fronts moved in on the breach. The distance between the two sides collapsed, and the Dulos began their gruesome assault on the Europan troops. Mayhem ensued.

From where she stood hand-in-hand with Tom on the west wing portico, Kate surveyed the whole palace grounds. Her heart leapt into her throat! Thousands of massive, ugly Dulos beasts crowded the courtyard, killing the Europans defending the palace—and in such hideous ways at that! Nothing Tom had said prepared her for what she saw.

For the first time, she feared for her life.

Back at the Dulos command post, Michael seethed with anger; he could barely hold his binoculars steady. Tom wasn't dragging Kate away. No, somehow, she had fallen under the man's spell, even appearing as if following his lead.

When Kate turned and followed Tom away from the courtyard—still clutching his hand—Michael panicked. He grabbed a discarded bullhorn from the command equipment stashed nearby.

"Kate! Kate Gillen!" he yelled into the microphone, repeating himself several times. However, the amplifier barely penetrated the din of battle noises.

On the portico, Kate hurried to keep pace with Tom. She grasped his hand as if holding a lifeline, and fear of falling under the Dulos' wrath spurred her on. Yet while racing by the windows of the west wing, she slowed down—though Tom pulled her along. Above the roar of noise, a familiar voice barely emerged from the clamor.

Kate shook her head, thinking she had imagined the voice. However, the voice echoed again, and then once more, calling her name ever so faintly. She didn't recognize the distorted voice itself, for noises around it cowed its prominence. No, it was *how* the voice called her name.

Coming upon a side entrance into the main palace, Kate halted, breaking Tom's grip. When he stopped and turned around in concern, he noticed her nervous expression. "What is it?"

"It's ... *Michael*. He's alive ... isn't he?"

He looked at her, mustering his best attempt at a dumbfounded gaze.

"Tom, I know his voice." Searching his face, her expression turned. "You already know he's alive, don't you?"

His expression withered. "I just found out this evening ... *honest*. That's why I asked you to trust me."

"Is he safe?"

"As much as any of us are. This escape is part of our plan to get you to safety." He garnered the most sympathetic gaze. "Come with me, Kate. Once we're safe, I'll take you to him."

But she recoiled away, and she looked at him with such dread. Her eyes welled up too. "I *can't* see him—not after what we've done!"

Tom's shoulders sank a bit, and his expression fell. Nonetheless, he kept eye to eye with her. "You've got to go to him, Kate."

She didn't move, and her face brimmed with doubts.

"You can't stay here. It's too dangerous."

Taking in his encouraging nod as he took her hand once more, the young woman looked around at the dangerous conflict and the exchange of artillery. Though hesitating through an awkward silence, Kate reluctantly disappeared with him through the doorway.

Michael Gillen stood at a distance, watching Kate disappear from sight. Looking down at his scanner, he watched her locator beacon moving on the display.

He turned to Raathe standing beside him. "I need your help getting into the palace."

Kara Ricci hung limp from her chains against the rock wall beside the abandoned highway, her shivering form bathed in the pale yellow glow of the floodlight and mounted there like some sort of trophy. She wore nothing but the small band of incendiaries draped over one shoulder, though sadness and fear covered her face.

The two Europan soldiers stood at a safe distance—ironically, on the very spot where she had killed Sigmund Pollux.

Even more ironic, she had grown impatient with them. Though she feared the terror of burning to death, the dread of knowing the imminence of that terror devoured her from within. She obsessed over the remote detonator sitting snugly in the Europan lieutenant's right hand. With his thumb dangling over the trigger, a thousand thoughts raced through her mind. Her heart sat in her throat, and her stomach tied into knots. She couldn't breathe!

When will this be over? she thought.

The lieutenant pulled a small reader from his side pocket and activated it, causing a half-meter square holograph to appear in the air over the device. Then, he recited rather formally:

> *"Kara Ricci, having been found guilty of high treason in the attempted assassination of Aurelian Galerius, sovereign ruler of the Europan Empire, and having also*

*been found guilty of the murder of Sigmund Pollux,
a loyal Europan citizen in good standing..."'*

Though the Europan continued citing the execution decree, Kara couldn't bear listening to the condemnation. She could barely concentrate anyway. Her senses were already afire with the terrible reality of what was happening to her. Feeling the ice-cold rock draining the remaining warmth and strength from her feeble frame, she turned her gaze to a hillside in the distance.

Though the night hid all but the outline of the terrain from her eyes, she didn't need the light. No, Emir Kern stood at the crest in brilliant sunlight, just as he had done the day of the ambush. She stood close enough to touch him. A smile came to her face, and she lost herself in the illusion. His eyes searched her out, just as they always did, while warm memories of him washed over her. Michael came to mind too, as did Kate and the other Centauries. And for the briefest moment, she was playing games once again with eight-year-old Mia at her sister's home, relishing her daughter's laughter and uncontainable energy. The conjured images drove away the unrelenting cold. She gloried in their presence—even in the person she had known as Tom Andrews.

—But images of a pistol flash and then Sigmund Pollux's corpse felled the sky black again. Memories of plunging a dagger into Emir's chest flashed before her eyes, causing his face to turn bitter just before he disappeared into the ether. Every other precious memory affording her refuge faded away, and everything turned dark. Kara once again hung from her chains against the cold rock, listening to the officer spouting the mindless execution decree:

"'... Signed on this day, Trajan Aurelius.'"

Kara choked out a singular, despairing laugh, and her face grew all the more hollow. Tom's reassuring words promising her eventual release rang in her ears, and her forehead stung where he had kissed her. With a single tear trailing down one cheek, she laughed once more.

It was all too cruel!

"Where are we going?" A frazzled Kate Gillen asked Tom Andrews, as Tom hurried her by the arm across the enclosed walkway.

"We need to hurry."

Kate, rather unsettled over Tom's abrupt change of demeanor minutes earlier, took in the sight of the palace grounds far below and the darkened tower at the other end of the suspended walkway. With Tom urging her on, she complied and hurried along. Coming to the end of the walkway, he almost pushed her through the entry.

Hearing the sound of Tom closing the access door closing behind her, Kate took in the sight of the large, darkened dome. The transparent ceiling of the dome allowed starlight to shine through, giving her glimpses of the shadows of trees and other flora crowded throughout the enclosure. But the only entrance was the access she had just used. Though barely able to see him in the dark, she turned to Tom. "This is a dead end. Why are we here?"

"Because someone is following us. I think the Europans know we escaped—and I'm not going back to that cell again." He looked around in thought through a brief silence. "Kate, I'm going to need your help."

The Europan lieutenant stood with his young subordinate in the center of the road at the abandoned highway. Glancing at Kara chained against the rock wall with the incendiaries slung over her shoulders, he tucked the deactivated reader back into his chest pocket. "Stand back," he warned his companion. Lifting the hand holding the detonator, he brought his thumb to the trigger.

A blinding yellow flash peeled back the night!

Both men, wincing at the concussion, immediately shielded their faces with their forearms against the surge of intense heat! The raging fireball devoured everything caught within the turmoil of its flames! Even after withdrawing a few steps, both Europans bristled against the heat pressing against them—but they also looked slack-jawed at each other.

The fireball had erupted twenty meters to the east, consuming a cluster of trees.

Ignoring a panic-stricken but perfectly intact Kara Ricci still chained to the wall, the two Europans watched the inferno uneasily.

"Stray artillery from the rebellion?" the guard mused.

The lieutenant lingered on the sight before shrugging. "Anything's *possible* ... but—"

The flash and sound of gunfire from behind broke the night!

The young guard, his eyes wide and his whole body snapping rigid in anguish, looked at his superior in morbid desperation. His weapon fell from his hands, and his eyes waxed lifeless where he stood.

Watching the young man's corpse slump to the ground, the stunned officer drew his pistol and turned—

Emir Kern shot forth from the darkness, waylaying him with a forceful blow! The remote detonator in the Europan's hand flew into the air!

From where she hung taut against her chains at the rock wall, a petrified Kara Ricci watched the detonator fly into the shadows. *Plink-plink, plink-plink* rang out when the device landed in the concrete ditch on the opposite side of the road. She cringed in terrible anticipation! However, when flames from an accidental detonation didn't immediately consume her, her whole body slumped in relief— but Kara rose up once more and strained against her chains to see into the shadows.

Someone—who, she could not discern in the darkness—had come to rescue her!

The newcomer toppled the larger man over the floodlight—but accidentally dropped his pistol too. When the smashed floodlight fell dark, heavy shadows fell over the road. The dancing light of the distant flames did little to light the conflict. The Europan grasped at his assailant in defense, and the two thrashed about violently on the ground.

Kara, still taut against her chains and her increasing weakness, watched the deadly struggle draped in shadows. Both men, exchanging blow after blow, bloodied each other! The strained sounds of the conflict accosted her ears. The stranger attacking the Europan—his movements grew awkward. In fact, she realized how much he had labored from his first appearance, as if arriving there already injured. Watching him struggle to subdue the stronger man, Kara's face twisted, and her shoulders fell tellingly.

Emir Kern, already battered from killing the four Europan soldiers earlier, strained to subdue the determined Europan. Gaining the advantage briefly, he reached for his pistol lying on the ground, hoping for a quick end to the fight. However, the Europan volleyed a crushing uppercut with his foot, bloodying Emir's nose and sending him toppling headlong over the dead guard. The pistol once more shot out of his hand. He strained against his pain to recoil from his vulnerable position. But the Europan pounced too quickly, bounding over the dead guard onto him and beating him violently.

Suffering under one blow after the other by the Europan, Emir slumped lifeless onto the cold ground.

"No!" came Kara's voice from the darkness.

Kneeling over his victim—panting and wiping blood from his mouth—the Europan looked down at his fallen antagonist. A bloodied Emir Kern lay on his back, lapsing in and out of consciousness. Satisfied over subduing him, the Europan confiscated the Covert's pistol and every other potential weapon on his person. When Emir came to and resisted, the Europan pounded his face, sending Emir's head crashing into the hard ground again. Then, the Europan picked up the dead guard's rifle and destroyed the cache.

"I *will* kill you," the Europan declared to a moaning and disoriented Emir Kern. Though he surveyed the grounds in the direction his own pistol had shot out of his hand, the weapon was nowhere in sight. So wiping blood from his mouth again, he stood, slung the rifle over his back, and steeled his gaze at Emir. "But first, you'll watch her die."

Michael Gillen cautiously made his way down the deserted palace corridor, his pistol at the ready and all his senses on edge. More than anything, he was amazed at how far he had infiltrated the Europan complex.

He glanced down at the scanner in his other hand, taking in Kate's locator beacon shown prominently on the display. The small blip had led him through a labyrinth of corridors, up many floors, and high into the tower near the rear of the palace. Should the Europans detect him, he was *very* vulnerable.

Upon reaching the outer wall of the palace, he looked out onto an enclosed walkway extending toward another tower across the chasm. The main structure of the tower, circular in shape with a transparent dome roof, sat atop three massive curving legs rising up from the ground far below. The inside of the dome lay shrouded in darkness, and the access door on the other side of the walkway was closed.

Mustering his courage with a deep breath, he stepped onto the walkway. The ceiling and walls of the enclosed bridge were transparent, giving an unenviable view of the darkened settlement and the palace grounds far below. He rather cringed at the extreme height.

Reaching the closed access door at end of the walkway, he looked down at Kate's locator on the scanner. She was inside the dome but far across by the opposite wall. Though no other blips displayed on the screen, his stomach tied into knots: Certainly, Tom Andrews had led her to the remote place. He sensed a trap.

However, time was of the essence.

Throwing caution to the wind, Michael triggered the door release and raced headlong into the darkness. Before his eyes could adjust to the starlight—someone pummeled him! His pistol shot out of his hand, and he struggled against the assailant!

From where she stood in the dark beside the far wall of the dome, Kate heard the agitated sounds of a scuffle. Just as Tom had instructed her, she activated the switches on the utility panel affixed to the wall there.

Faint light washed over the dome, pushing back the starlight from above and giving view to the enclosed arboretum. Immaculately manicured trees, shrubs, and gardens crowded the central walkways made of stone. Light poles and other fixtures decorated the paths, giving the arboretum the ambiance of an elaborate park or garden.

However, Kate did not have the luxury of taking in the unexpected sanctuary. No, she stood there, aghast at the sight of Tom and Michael at each other's throats at the entryway! The two men, locked in each other's clutches, beat each other and struggled for control of Tom's pistol.

"No!" she yelled, hoping they would stop long enough to realize their mistake. However, the conflict only grew worse.

Kate rushed across the stone walkway, yelling for them to cease. When neither relented, she threw herself into the brawl, grabbing for the gun and pushing at them to relent. Tom's gun rose up into the air over their heads, as if floating on the churning mass of the six hands grasping at it.

"Don't, Kate!" Tom yelled for her to stop, straining against Michael.

"What are you doing?" Michael heaped on at her from within the brawl.

Kate took hold of the gun—but Tom and Michael (fighting each other for it) wrested it from her fingers, pushing the gun up and out of her reach. She clutched and pushed at both of them to stop. Unexpectedly, Michael slammed Tom backward against the arboretum wall. Kate, caught up in the clash and off balance, helplessly followed and crashed against him.

The pistol turned randomly above them as the two men twisted each other's grip; fingers fought precariously near the trigger—

Two bright flashes erupted, and the sound of gunfire pierced the air!

The unexpected shots forced the trio apart. Tom and Michael, both wide-eyed upon realizing the rounds had struck Kate, watched her slump to the ground!

CHAPTER TWENTY TWO

Two Friends

David Tashjian and Phil Marcotte sat in the living room of their apartment cell, looking out onto the dimly lit room draped in heavy shadows. The elegant suite somewhere within the Europan Royal Palace, intended to lavish its occupant in a warm and comfortable ambiance, took on a more foreboding atmosphere under the glow of emergency lighting. With the door to the apartment locked from the outside and their captors not answering courtesy calls for hours, the two men felt trapped—and they were.

"How long do you think they'll let us rot in here?" David Tashjian inquired from his place on the couch, lifting his eyes from the reader holograph screen in front of him. In an attempt to pass the time, he had engrossed himself in a novel, a boring Europan morality play.

Phil Marcotte, sitting in the adjacent chair, shrugged. "I wish I knew." He gestured to the cold plate of food on his lap. "Too bad the power hasn't come back on so I could heat up my dinner. This stuff is terrible cold."

Tashjian returned his eyes to his novel, and Marcotte set in to finishing his meal. Silence fell over the room, though their minds raced with the distant rumblings coming from outside the palace. Tashjian looked up again. "Should we try to escape?"

"They'll kill us for sure."

"I don't think anyone's out there. And if the Europans are gone ... we should go too."

Marcotte, shaking his head, drew his friend's attention to the formidable door across the room. "Just forget it. That door can withstand a small bomb blast. Unless you have something stronger, I suggest—"

The heavy door suddenly exploded off its hinges!

The two men recoiled with arms up in front of their faces, protecting themselves from pieces of doorframe flying through the air—

Two of the most hideous beasts appeared through the gaping hole!

The two centauries had never seen a Dulos—let alone two. But they recounted the ominous stories the Coverts had told them and recoiled back against their seats. Frozen in place, they stared up in fear at the beasts' brooding eyes and prominent foreheads, intimidated by the creatures' overwhelming size and muscles layering down their arms and legs. When the beasts approached, Marcotte and Tashjian fell into their shadows.

"Gillen send," the creature closest to them said in deep tones.

Marcotte and Tashjian looked slack-jawed at each other. After all, they had seen Michael Gillen crushed by a rockslide long ago, and they had heard the gunfire that had ended Kate Gillen's life—or so they assumed.

"*Gillen send*," the creature repeated, a little impatient. "Want rescue or not?"

Shadows shrouded the remote, abandoned highway. Even the burning cluster of trees twenty meters from the conflict, set aflame by Emir Kern's incendiaries, failed to push back the darkness.

The Europan lieutenant, carrying the dead guard's rifle slung over his back, looked down at a barely lucid Emir Kern lying on the ground.

Still panting from his struggle with the Covert, he glanced once more through the darkness to where Kara Ricci hung from chains against the rock wall. Then, turning to retrieve the remote detonator from where it lay in the far ditch, he looked at Emir once more. "Wake up so you can watch her die."

Not more than a few meters away, the Europan suddenly stopped wide-eyed! A burning pain shot through his chest! With the oddest sensation washing over him, he looked down. A sharp metal rod pushed out through the front of his blood-drenched uniform! Cuffs dangling on a heavy chain struck his left calf muscle. With surreal matter-of-factness, the Europan realized he had forgotten about the restraining spikes in the dead guard's pack. Once more, he took in the spike impaling his chest!

Immediately, the dying officer panicked.

He strained to turn around. Emir knelt before the dead guard's open field pack, struggling to stand with his gaze steeled in contempt.

The Europan, realizing his short time to live, pulled at the rifle slung over his shoulder to defend himself—more agonizing pain shuddered through him. However, the spike had also impaled the rifle—fusing his spine from rotating too! So the dying man turned awkwardly and stumbled toward where the detonator lay in the far ditch.

Emir, his strength and resolve returning, reached into the dead guard's pack for another spike—none! And the Europan officer was moving faster!

Looking around in a panic, Emir caught sight of the hammer on the dead guard's utility belt. The tool was a hammer on one side with a small axe on the other. Grabbing the tool and straining against his pain, he threw it axe-side-first at the Europan's head.

He missed!

The hammer side of the axe hit the dying soldier square in the back, knocking him to the ground. The Europan, crying out in agony, flailed about in an attempt to stand again—but was stymied by his fused spine and intense pain. Terrified but not giving up, he began dragging himself along the ground toward the detonator.

Rage filled Emir Kern.

The Covert strained to his feet and staggered toward the Europan. The Europan, looking back and seeing Emir approaching, pulled himself along the ground even faster.

Emir stumbled to where the hammer had fallen. Picking it up, he spun the blunt side around so that the axe faced outward, and staggered in the dark toward his dying combatant.

He was too late! The Europan, lying covered in blood and laboring to breathe, held the detonator in his hand.

"*She dies!*" the Europan choked out, bringing his thumb to the trigger!

Emir, his heart leaping into his throat, swung the axe with all his might—cleanly severing the man's forearm from the rest of him! The Europan screamed in agony!

But then, silence fell over the entire area when the man fell limp.

Emir knelt over the dying Europan, who stared blankly at his severed arm. Blood pooled at the separation, the small puddle expanding rapidly. The Europan's breathing grew heavier and more labored, though he just stared at the lifeless limb—and the untriggered detonator lying harmlessly in its palm.

Emir took the detonator and carefully deactivated it.

The Europan shot him a hollow look and moved his lips—though his voice was absent. Even dying, the man mustered such contempt.

"I feel sorry for you," Emir said.

With one last breath, the Europan's eyes waxed lifeless, and the man died.

For the longest time, Emir knelt over the dead man with the detonator in his hand. He gazed soberly at the device, forcing from his mind the terrible images of what had almost happened.

But from where Kara looked on helplessly at the rock wall, she strained at the end of her chains, anxiously searching the darkness. Her heart swelled in her chest at the dead calm that had fallen over entire area, for both men had disappeared into the shadows moments earlier. The voice of the Europan shouting out, "*she dies!*" from somewhere in the darkness still rang in her ears.

A silhouette of a man rose from the ground in the distance and turned toward her. Kara's heart leapt into her throat when the silhouette hurried toward her in the darkness. Her whole body trembled with the last of its remaining strength, for the shadowy form looked so much like the Europan lieutenant.

But then, Emir appeared from the shadows into the firelight!

"*Emir?*" she barely breathed out his name, taking in the apparition's reassuring but ghost-like appearance. A thousand thoughts—and the memory of her plunging a dagger deep into his chest—raced through her mind. Catching sight of herself undressed before him and chained to the wall like an animal amidst the confusion of her mind, she felt all her strength withering away. Everything turned surreal.

So Kara fainted.

Commander Tom Andrews leaned against the shoulder-high console affixed to the wall, his arms folded atop the fixture and his chin resting comfortably on his hands. He was alone in the room—all alone in the crowded Europan medivac hospital station somewhere in the asteroid belt of Terrae Solaris too.

Garbed in his Earth States military commanders' uniform, he gazed up at the security monitor before him. In the video feed from another room in the hospital, an injured Michael Gillen lay in a recovery bed with both wrists restrained to the bed's metal frame. While medical personnel attended him, Michael repeated his demand to know what had happened to his crew: the Comanche *crew.*

Watching his friend's defiance amidst his predicament, Tom let out a sentimental chuckle. But his gaze fell pensive once again, and his thoughts returned to everything that had happened since the Comanche *destruction the previous week. The conflict that had always raged within returned, and an unchanneled longing grew in the young man's eyes.*

"Excuse me, my Lord," a voice beckoned from behind.

Turning, Tom beheld a younger, thinner General Aulus Taun standing at the doorway. "Yes?"

But the officer paused abruptly, awkwardly too. "What are you doing in your Terran military uniform?" Though he waited for a reply while entering the room, Tom said nothing. The man cleared his throat rather nervously.

"I just received word from your father. He wants you to return with him to Tyre."

"But I just saw him. Did he say why?"

"No. A transport is waiting as we speak."

Tom took in the words through a long silence. *"I'm not returning to Europa. I'm returning to Earth States. Tell him I already left."*

"You're putting me in a difficult situation, my Lord," Taun rather bristled, yet maintaining his respectful demeanor too. *"He'll execute me if he finds out I'm lying."*

Tom's eyes narrowed. *"My father will not always be around, General Taun. I suggest you remember that."* He looked back up at the security monitor and watched Michael Gillen. His face sobered. *"I failed to infiltrate the Terran intelligence network, as I was sent to do.* Everything *that defines who I am has ended in failure."* A pensive pause followed. *"I* will not *return to my father until I have accomplished what I promised him. Otherwise, how could I succeed him in good conscience?"* He looked back at Taun. *"Can you understand that?"*

The general's gaze waxed empathetic. *"Yes, my Lord. But you should leave immediately. I'll have my men extract a life pod from the* Comanche *remains. You can use it for the trip back to Earth States. I'll make sure you have a clear path to Allied territory."*

"Very well. I need you to ensure Michael Gillen's safety while I'm gone."

Taun paused, and his anxiousness returned. Glancing up at the security feed of Michael Gillen now and then, he took in Tom's insistence. With much hesitation, he eventually eked out, *"My Lord, it would be much better for you if you let his fate play out to its natural conclusion."*

"That is not *going to happen."*

"Captain Michael Gillen has killed thousands of Europans—that many in the defense of his president alone."

"Yes. Imagine if he were fighting for Europa. Perhaps someday, I can persuade him."

Disgust crept into Taun's face. *"He is a Terran.* Terrans are weak. *Europan justice demands his death."* Taun fell silent, though he maintained his resolve. Upon seeing Tom's unwavering expression, he let the indignation drain from his face. *"My Lord, I know you are struggling over your destiny. Such sympathy for a Terran—any Terran—only weakens you in the eyes of the Europan people. Don't compound one failure with another."*

Tom turned away from the general. Leaning against the console again with arms folded atop the fixture and his chin on his hands, he watched Michael's image on the security monitor with the most pensive gaze. Eventually, he turned his head side to side on his hands. "Michael Gillen is my best friend. … He will always be my friend, *no matter who he is—or who I am."* *Another long, pensive pause.* "No, Michael Gillen's death will mean your own, General Taun. When he is well enough to leave this hospital, take him as far away from this war as is humanly possible."

Taun, taking advantage of Andrews facing away from him, rather bristled. "You're not expecting me to treat him like royalty, are you?"

"No. Everything must be logical. Take him to one of our prison camps on Charon. Don't let him receive any special treatment that might cause him to grow suspicious; just make sure he stays alive and well protected."

Taun hesitated, still bristling at the conversation. Finally, he sighed— almost huffed—in surrender. "You have my word."

"Kate!" Michael gasped, watching his bride doubled over in pain on the floor of the arboretum. Paying no attention to whatever Tom was doing behind him, he fell to his knees beside her, his eyes nervously fixed on her injuries. "How bad are you hurt?"

"Help me sit up."

Placing a hand under each of her arms, he gingerly lifted her into a sitting position against the wall. Kate, tears running down her face and her teeth gnashing against the pain, clutched her left knee just below the burn mark there. Yet her whole body stiffened in anguish. The other burn mark adorned her shirt on the left side of her abdomen.

Gingerly, Michael lifted up the bottom of her shirt and examined her stomach. The skin on her left side, scoured beet red but unbroken, felt firm and swollen—and she winced at his touch. However, though he lacked the proper expertise, his instincts told him the injury was mostly a surface injury. So he looked up. Another burn mark grazed the wall above her, indicating some sort of deflection. He hoped so. Otherwise, the injury could be fatal.

"You okay?" Tom asked her, standing over them with his pistol in his hand.

—Michael caught sight of his own pistol tucked into Andrews' belt.

Kate didn't answer. Wincing at the pain for the longest time, she finally glared at both of them. *"What's wrong with you two? Didn't you hear me yelling for you to stop?"*

Trading a quick, reproving glance with Tom while still kneeling over her, Michael turned a sympathetic gaze on her. She paid little attention to him. In fact, any acknowledgement of his presence seemed distant and awkward, even uncomfortable. So he kissed her on the forehead. "Okay, Katey, just stay still."

"Just let me be, Michael!"

Michael relented and stood back from her, garnering the most reassuring gaze in her direction. "Okay, Katey, whatever you need."

"Stop calling me that!"

He rather shrank back. Self-consciousness crept into his encouraging gaze. "I'm sorry, Kate." But when he looked at Tom once more, his eyes burned with hate. "This is your fault!" Michael charged at him—

However, Tom stopped him mid-stride with a wave of the pistol in his hand. Yet Andrews wore the same shaken expression as when the pistol had fired. "It was an accident, Mike ... *I swear!*"

"Right."

"You know I'd never intentionally hurt her."

"Maybe not ..."—his eyes steeling—"... but you weren't aiming for *her.*"

"The gun was set on low. I only jumped you to get your pistol so we could talk."

Michael replied with a cynical laugh.

Silence fell over the arboretum. Michael began pacing back and forth, his eyes trained on the pistol in Tom's hand that followed his every movement.

"There's a first aid station on the fifth floor of the main building," Tom finally offered. "When this insurgence is over, we'll take her there for help."

"We should take her there now."

"Too dangerous with the insurgence going on. We'll be safer here."

"*I'm all right*," Kate assured, looking up at them a little more composed. "I think my leg is broken … but my stomach's feeling better."

Once more, silence fell over the arboretum. Michael and Tom traded contending looks, while Kate kept to herself. After several long moments, a low rumble from a distant concussion shook the floor beneath their feet.

"The Dulos are coming for you," Michael relished, still pacing around Tom and the pistol constantly pointed at him. Looking at his own pistol holstered at Andrews' side, he rather sneered. "Those weapons won't do you any good though—neither will a lot of fast talking."

Kate looked up at them, her face twisting quizzically at the unspoken tension between the two men. "We should get out of here then."

"We can't. But you're safe, Kate. The Dulos aren't out for revenge against us." He looked Tom squarely in the eyes. "I can't say the same for you. I hope I'm not here when they rip you to shreds."

"Help me to a communications console," Kate beckoned with her arms out to them and straining to stand. "I'll recall the *Endurance*. Maybe it can arrive in time to escape."

"Don't," Michael knelt, gently imposing himself on her so that she remained leaning against the wall.

"He's right," Tom added, just as concerned as Michael. "Stay still. The *Endurance* has already come and gone—it won't help me anyway." He turned to Michael. "By the way, Mike, kudos for faking the *Endurance*'s demise. I never realized how devious you actually were: faking the ship's destruction with your crew unaware that none of it was real."

"Kate knew."

Tom looked wide-eyed at her. "You knew?"

An awkward silence fell over them, and Tom and Kate traded uneasy looks.

"I *couldn't* tell you the ship was okay," she finally pleaded. "I was afraid the interrogators would beat it out of you."

Michael, standing up again, watched the odd the exchange between Kate and Tom. His mouth twisted into a smug grin. "*Beatings … by the interrogators?*" A sardonic chuckle followed. "Now I've heard everything."

"What's wrong with you two?" Kate chided them, her face betraying her loss over their mutual hostility. Her eyes steeled at Michael.

"Don't act like this, Michael. Tom protected me from the interrogators. Doesn't that mean *anything* to you?"

Michael, bristling under her reproving gaze—and taken back by her defense of Tom—winced. But then his eyes lit up, and he looked at Tom with another smug half-grin. "She doesn't know, does she?"

Tom squirmed uncomfortably, and he fell speechless.

"What are you talking about?" Kate demanded, even more irritated at Michael.

Michael relished Tom's anxiousness for a long moment. "This is too good." With the most amused smirk turning the corner of his mouth, he extended his arm toward Tom and feigned a proper introduction. "Kate, have you met *Trajan Aurelius*, the son of Aurelian Galerius?" Watching her face fall slack-jawed, he let his introduction hang awkwardly in the air. But his expression grew bitter. "He's Europan, Kate. *He* reprogrammed our Slipstream drives; *he* tried to sabotage the *Endurance*—not Kern."

Kate, still leaning against the wall and grasping her injured leg, watched the awkward exchange of expressions between the two men. "*Tom, is this true?*" When Andrews remained silent, she pleaded with him with her eyes. His gaze turned tellingly, causing her face to fill with angst. "Michael's right, isn't he?"

Tom stood there, his face betraying his thoughts.

"*But why?*"

As she took in Tom's culpable gaze, her face churned with so many conflicting emotions. Though her unspoken concern remained just that, her strong reaction unnerved Michael—even more as Tom's expression grew increasingly guilty. Suddenly, Kate's gaze filled with dread. Flashing Michael such a self-conscious look, she dropped her head and brought her hand over her eyes.

"Kate, it's not like you think," Tom pleaded. "There's more to what transpired than either of you can see right now. I'm still the same person you always knew."

Michael, paying more attention to Tom's cowering than Kate's odd reaction—completely missing the guilt washing over her—shook his head. "And yet you're holding us at gunpoint."

"I took care of Kate and the rest of the Centauries," Tom pleaded, ignoring Kate glaring bitterly at him. "They're alive because of me.

I saved *your* life once—twice counting the incident back at the northwest gate. Doesn't that count at all?"

"Not when you're holding us at gunpoint."

Tom fell silent under their rebuke. But upon hearing the noises of the Dulos siege in the distance, he huffed. "Fine." Pulling Michael's pistol from his side, he threw it to him, lifted his arms in surrender, and pointed the pistol in his hand harmlessly toward the transparent ceiling. "Then take your shot."

Michael drew the pistol at Tom, while Kate looked up from where she sat against the wall. Indeed, he wanted to kill the imposter. Yet his resolve to pull the trigger evaporated. Tom's familiarity, even if just superficial, kept interfering with the indignation he felt toward him. Moreover, Tom radiated an honest, completely confounding sincerity. With his indignation succumbing to his own sense of justice, he lowered the pistol to his side—but keeping it readily in his hand.

Tom sighed in relief and lowered his arms to his sides.

An uneasy truce fell over the arboretum.

However, nothing settled the churning thoughts in Michael's mind. Shaking his head, the young man turned and beheld the garden spot that was quickly becoming his prison. Neither the beauty of the flora nor the starry night sky penetrating the transparent ceiling offered him any comfort. No, the arboretum was an isolated, dead-end. He turned once again to Tom. "Why are we here?"

"You deserve to hear the truth." An intentional pause followed. "And I came here to turn myself in to you."

"How do you know I won't kill you? Or hand you over to the Dulos?"

"You always do the right thing, Mike." Another intentional pause. "And the truth you need to hear has little to do with me—something far worse."

Michael kept eye to eye with him, rebuffing his old friend's sincerity. Tom seemed so sure of himself, and that bugged him. Kate looked oddly at him too—and he found himself at a loss to know why. The whole time the trio traded such looks, the sounds of the Dulos siege rumbled from somewhere in the palace.

The Dulos were nearing.

CHAPTER TWENTY THREE

In the Arboretum

Michael Gillen stood in the arboretum high atop the palace tower, facing down Tom Andrews—Trajan Aurelius. With the reunion between him and the man he had once thought of as his best friend turning bitter, he wished the long night would quickly end.

Occasionally, he glanced down at Kate leaning against the arboretum wall. She still suffered under the pain of her injuries, though she appeared more self-conscious than anything. He wanted to carry her to a medical station. Yet as long as the Europans occupied the main palace complex, venturing out of the tower was far too dangerous. Fortunately, her condition had stabilized.

Tom stood before him, his offer to turn himself in to Michael still hanging awkwardly in the air—his offer to confess some *truth* too. His expression pleaded for mercy.

Michael sighed and looked away, astonished at the thoughts racing through his head. Tom was actually growing on him again—

after everything the man had done. Hoping that Tom remained unaware of his change in attitude, he turned back to him, his gaze incredulous. "Why now?"

"What do you mean?"

"Why tell me the truth *now*?" Michael scoffed. "Why not before you sabotaged the *Endurance*? Or before you tampered with the Slipstream drives?" A cynical gaze washed over him. "If you wanted reunited with your father sooner, why didn't you just tell me?"

Tom hesitated, even huffing a bit. "Mike, you've been lied to so much, you'll *never* believe the truth."

"Oh really? So you didn't tamper with the Slipstream drives to arrive here early?"

"No—and you should know that." He mounted his resolve against Michael's mocking skepticism. "You know I always struggled with the finer points of Propulsion and Systems. How could I tamper with the *Endurance* in such a sophisticated way—that not even David Tashjian could figure it out?"

Michael, taken back while remembering Tom's time at the university and NSEA, glanced at Kate, who returned a similar look. Nevertheless, he grimaced. "You had help from other infiltrators—and don't try convincing me that you didn't try sabotaging the *Endurance*."

"That was definitely me. I wanted you, Kate, and the other Centauries to stay here with me. Despite what you think, I'm still your friend."

Michael rebuffed him and started pacing back and forth to assuage his anxiousness.

Tom watched him pace an invisible line for a long moment. "And you're wrong about infiltrators tampering with *Endurance*'s Slipstream engines. In fact, the whole Slipstream technology explanation is a lie."

Michael stopped in mid-stride. "What are you talking about?"

"How Earth States acquired the technology from Europa ..."—upon receiving another, dubious look from his friend—"... *'The prototypes found at the abandoned Europan dry dock'* story Cyril told you?" Tom paused, letting his sarcasm linger. "Europan scientists didn't discover Slipstream technology, Earth States did. *Ben Morris* discovered it."

"That's absurd."

"No it isn't. Remember Ben's obsession with the theory? Well, the war gave him his chance. He discovered how to make it work while he was at Research during the war."

"*So Cyril lied to me?*"

"No, the secrecy is much higher up than Cyril Davidson."

"I don't believe you."

Silence fell over the arboretum. While Michael brooded over the allegations, he resumed pacing. His pacing only grew more anxious as he remembered Ben Morris and his speculations about Slipstream propulsion theories from long ago. Kate's face betrayed her increasing ambivalence, which only unsettled Michael that much more. So he glared at Tom. "You have everything to gain from telling me such nonsense." He fell silent again, letting his indignation linger before shaking his head. "No, Tom, you've done nothing but prevent me from capturing Aurelian Galerius. I'm not falling for it this time. This time, I'm finding your father and returning him to the *Weightless* for trial. I won't let President Mitchell down."

Tom took in his defiance—but then he rather laughed. "Why would President James Mitchell want you to do that? James Mitchell is the one who exiled him here."

Michael stopped dead in his tracks and flashed Tom a chiding look. "That's the most absurd thing I ever heard. If Earth States had Slipstream technology, then why wouldn't President Mitchell use it against the Axis forces? Such an advantage would have brought the Outer Rim to its knees in no time."

"Because parts of the Slipstream technology lie are true," Tom replied, unflinching. "When Ben first developed the technology, the engines were far too big for even the largest destroyers. It would take him years to shrink them down to the right size and power requirements—about the time Mitchell rescued you from the POW camp on Charon." He paused, letting Michael take in the statement. "But initially, the engines were just the right size for a generation ship."

"And you want me to believe that exiling your father was President Mitchell's idea?"

"My father didn't know about the Slipstream limitations. When Mitchell showed my father proof of the Slipstream technology— *remember that mysterious trip your President took to the Outer Rim?*—

Europan forces were already taking heavy losses. Mitchell threatened to pound the Axis territories into oblivion with it, unless my father agreed to exile. The generation ship was a joint effort between Earth States and Europa. *Funny, huh?*" When Michael looked at him indifferently, he added, "My father accepted exile to save his people. Our Slipstream technology enhancements and my father's invasion plans came after his arrival here."

Michael, still pacing the invisible line on the floor, kept shaking his head. However, his defiant gaze had withered some. "Why would President Mitchell trouble himself with building a generation ship—with an enemy—during a war?"

Tom hesitated. "Because he had *other* plans."

Michael struggled against Tom's resolve. Taking in Tom's words with the most unsettled gaze, he finally shook his head and offered a cynical laugh. "You're going to so much trouble to make me believe this nonsense." His gaze steeled. "But nothing will prevent me from completing my mission this time."

"Your *mission?*"

"Yes ... *my mission.*"

Tom shook his head in disbelief at him. "As smart as you are, Mike, I'm surprised you didn't figure everything out when you found out who I was." When Michael's expression didn't change, he exclaimed, "I was the mission. I was *always* the mission."

Tom Andrews struggled through the darkened thicket with abandon, stumbling over every rock and fallen branch lying hidden in the heavy undergrowth. Every breath came haltingly, for the young man pushed against his exhaustion. A muddy blend of dirt, blood, and sweat covered his face, and his brownish-black hair lay drenched in a similar fashion. His Earth States commanders' uniform he had worn since his capture was just as dirty; it was torn here and there too—from the abuse he had received from his captors. His whole body ached from their mistreatment.

As he stumbled through the dark, his eyes fixed on the dim lights far in the distance. Though he had been running for quite some time through the cavernous habitat deep within the alien moon, the lights in the distance remained almost as far off as when he had started. Those barbarian soldiers pursuing him were closer than ever too.

Barely dodging a concealed access connecting to the artificial gravity generators and life support systems buried beneath the habitat—

The butt of a rifle pummeled the side of his head!

The stolen detection dampener flew from his hand, and Tom crashed to the ground just in time for a blow to the stomach! As he writhed in pain, the soldier over him flipped his rifle around and pressed the barrel's end to his head.

"Don't move!" the soldier warned, though the look in his eyes begged Tom to defy him. Searching the terrain, the soldier shouted out, "Over here! I've got him!"

Tom, panting and rather disoriented, kept frozen on the ground and stared up at the soldier. A minute later, another soldier appeared from the thicket and headed straight for him.

"You think you can get away from me?" the new arrival seethed, throwing his rifle to the side and kicking Andrews in the stomach. Though Tom doubled into a fetal position, the arriving soldier wrenched him off the ground and beat him. The other soldier joined in on the thrashing. At the end of the brawl, Tom fell into a bloody heap before them.

"Now who looks bad?" the second soldier gloated at Tom with a cold stare.

Tom, his face covered in as much fear as blood, fell speechless.

The second soldier picked up his rifle, and the two men looked around in all directions. The sounds of the other soldiers searching for Tom echoed from far off, growing farther away each moment.

The first soldier glanced at Tom before turning to his companion. "What do you want to do with him now?"

"I'm going to kill him."

"But they want to question him."

"I'm already in trouble for letting him get away ... "—glaring at Tom—"... and after everything he's done, he doesn't deserve to live."

"We'll say he jumped me ... that you had no choice but to kill him."

Tom, frozen in terror on the ground, cringed as the second guard lifted the end of his rifle barrel to the side of his head.

"Say goodnight!" the soldier mocked as he brought his finger to the trigger.

Two shots broke the silence—and Tom watched both soldiers slump dead onto the ground. Panicking, he grabbed for the dead man's rifle, just as a group of armed men emerged from the thicket.

"Tom, I wouldn't do that, if I were you," a well-dressed, middle-aged man standing center warned, training his pistol on him and radiating a no-nonsense intent.

Tom froze in place. Taking in the many guns aimed at him, he cautiously set the rifle on the ground and strained to stand. He lifted his hands into the air in surrender.

"That's the first thing you've done right," the man at the center of the soldiers said, lowering his pistol and approaching him. When sounds of soldiers from other search teams nearing broke the night air, he waved two of his soldiers in that direction. "Send the search parties back. Don't let anyone get through."

As the soldiers set off into the woods, Tom looked down at the two dead Earth States soldiers lying on the ground. "You killed your own men."

"Yes, so you know I'm not above killing you right where you stand." The nicely dressed man paced around the two dead men, sizing up Tom. "You should have never returned to Earth States after the Comanche *destruction, Trajan Aurelius. You were a better first officer than a spy."*

"What do you want?"

"I'm General Boyce Derringer. I work directly for President Mitchell." A pause followed. "I'm here to ask you one question. If you answer it right, everything will be okay. If you lie to me … I'll kill you myself."

"You'll kill me anyway."

"It's an easy question: Where is Michael Gillen?"

Tom returned an incredulous gaze. "That's what you want to know?"— but when Derringer trained the pistol in his hand on him—"He's at a prison camp on Charon."

"And you can assure that he's still alive?"

"He is my friend. I put him there myself for his protection. If you know who I am, then you know I have the power to keep him alive." Tom fell silent and took in Derringer's omniscient gaze. "But you already knew everything I just told you, didn't you?" When the man's face waxed tellingly, Tom's brow crumpled once more. "Why are you here?"

"President Mitchell dispatched me to find you. This is your lucky day, Trajan. Instead of facing an execution squad, you're going to be reunited with your father."

Tom offered a dismissive turn of the head. "*That's a lie. He already left for 18 Scorpii. Doesn't your president tell you anything?*"

"*I know about the exile agreement and the generation ship—I'm the one who made sure it happened. And if we had found you before the ship's departure, you would have left with Galerius: President Mitchell keeps his promises.*" He paused just long enough to holster his pistol inside his coat. "*We have one last ship scheduled to leave for 18 Scorpii. I'm here to make sure you're on it.*"

"*And why would President Mitchell do that?*"

"*Because he needs something, of course. That's why I needed to confirm our intelligence on Michael Gillen's whereabouts. Gillen is going to command the mission that takes you home.*"

This time, Tom rather laughed. "*Michael Gillen doesn't know my true identity. And if he found out, he would* never *agree to such a mission.*"

"*That's why he can't find out—no one can. In fact, we're taking you back to the Outer Rim so it appears that you have been a POW since the* Comanche *destruction.*"

"*Why?*"

"*Because knowledge of your return to Earth States from so deep in the Outer Rim will raise too many questions.*" He gestured with his eyes down at the two dead Earth States soldiers before him. "*Your presence in Earth States has already caused too much trouble. Have you been in contact with anyone close to the exploration teams?*"

"*Just one person—but I know how to cover my leaving again.*"

"*Good. Then we're all set. The stated mission objective will be to bring back Aurelian Galerius for war crime trials. Once you get to 18 Scorpii, you're on your own. But at least President Mitchell will have kept his promise.*"

Tom, brimming with anxiousness, looked down at the two dead Earth States soldiers—and then back to Derringer. "*Why is Mitchell going to such trouble for me?*"

"*He's not—you're just a benefactor. We don't care about Galerius or Mitchell's promise to him either. Hopefully, Galerius is already dead.*"

"*So why do all this?*"

"*Because this mission is really about a blow-hard* Weightless *and the incredible fortune he controls.*"

"*Mos Thieren.*"

"His funding will be the key to post-war rebuilding efforts,"
Derringer nodded. "He needs a reason to loosen the purse strings. I'm only
telling you because you have a vested interest in going to 18 Scorpii."
The man let his words linger through a brief silence. "I need to know if you
will cooperate with me—help make the official story work."

Tom reluctantly nodded.

"Good. I hope you're comfortable being the foil in this plan."

Tom kept silent for the longest time. But then he turned his head side
to side. "No, Michael Gillen is the real foil."

"That's when everything started," Tom continued to explain to both
Michael and Kate. "Mitchell had Cyril dispatch the Charon invasion
fleet to find you, while they sent me to Triton. We reunited, and the
rest is history."

Neither Michael nor Kate, both stunned but boasting incredulous
gazes, said anything.

"The mission to kidnap Aurelian Galerius was just a cover," Tom pressed.
"Just as much as delivering me here was a cover. President Mitchell
needed access to Mos Thieren's wealth, so he contrived a mission Mos
Thieren would believe." Though he waited them out, neither said a word.
"That's why the mission oversight committee—all ranking officers of
the Mitchell administration—rushed our launch schedule: All the prep
work had been done, and the Covert part of the mission was pointless."

"Michael," Kate began, the concern ripe in her voice, "If what he
said is true, they're not even expecting us to return home."

"We're going back, Kate," Michael said, shaking his head in defiance.
"History has to know what happened here. And when we find Galerius,
we can finally clear my family's name." A sardonic sneer at Tom followed.
"Besides, we can't take his word for it. No, we *have* to go back."

"You don't want to go home, Mike," Tom warned. "You won't
like what you find. Mitchell has gone to great lengths to cover up the
truth. Ben Morris knew; that's why he's dead. Mitchell's men killed him
when he was on his way to tell you the truth." Taking in their unsettled
expressions, he pressed, "And Mitchell's done far worse things since

we left. Because of him, Terrae Solaris is in chaos. I won't even try convincing you; you'll have to see the evidence yourself." An intentional pause. "The bad guys are winning, Mike. They just aren't the same bad guys you expected."

"And I should just take your word for it?"

Tom pulled a small reader from his chest pocket and handed it to him. "This is a dump of the Europan intelligence on James Mitchell. It's the only copy left: I purged it from the settlement's computer system after downloading it into the reader. All the evidence is inside: the exile agreement with my father, Earth State's secret contributions to the generation ship, documents proving Mitchell's intent to deceive Mos Thieren and the Allied leadership, Ben Morris' execution orders." Tom hesitated. "And of course, everything he's done since we left—things you'll have to see the evidence to believe."

Michael held the reader in his hand through a long silence. After shooting Tom a skeptical glance, he activated the device and read the holographic screen hovering before him. Not long into scanning the records, his face fell tellingly. Kate saw his visible consternation and immediately knew the dreadful truth.

Their mission was over.

"What did you think?" Tom asked as Michael stared down at the irrefutable evidence, his voice full of empathy. "I just happened to be in the right place, at the right time, to go on a once in a lifetime mission—that reunited me with my father forty-six light-years away?"

Michael didn't say anything. No, he was too numb. His world turned upside down that very moment. Even Tom no longer seemed to be the real enemy, as he had thought. No, the real enemy was President James Mitchell—who had played him for a fool.

And how could he forget that he stood in the middle of another human conflict forty-six light years away from Earth? The human race was its own worst enemy. Perhaps the human race *was* the enemy. He looked up at the stars gleaming down through the arboretum's transparent dome. The universe spread out above him: trillions of star systems ripe for exploration. He mourned for it, for Man was spreading throughout the universe like a parasite.

"President Mitchell is a megalomaniac," Tom said, more emboldened than ever. "And you know that now too. It's a shame to think that *Comanche* and its crew were lost trying to save him."

The rumbling of artillery broke the tense quiet. Tom turned toward the arboretum entrance in response. The sounds of the siege were growing louder. Knowing that the Dulos had reached the same floor in the main palace, he turned back again. "I know all this news is troubling, but there *is* a way to make things right."

Michael said nothing.

Filled with urgency, Tom put his hand on Michael's shoulder. "The Allies are weak. Mitchell is vulnerable. Once this uprising is over, we have access to three thousand warships, soldiers, and all the weapons my father's armies couldn't deploy during the Dulos rebellion. Combined with the Europan armies waiting for us back in Terra Solaris, we have more than enough to subdue Mitchell's threat."

Michael remained silent and kept looking away.

"I'm not my father. I'm not the mass murderer he was. I can help you: I have the favor of the Europan people. Earth States—all of Terrae Solaris—needs a champion. Who better to come to its rescue than a Gillen?" An emphatic pause. "You and I can make things right *together*."

Michael, keeping silent and looking away with such a grave expression, turned and searched Tom's face for signs of sincerity. Finally, he shrugged in resignation, and his head dropped. "I don't know."

Five Dulos appeared in the palace corridor across the walkway bridge. Michael recognized Raathe immediately, while the other four were tribal leaders he had met during his stay in the village. Upon spotting the arboretum and the gathering there, the creatures started for the walkway.

"I told you the truth, Mike," Tom urged, "just like I promised." He paused, briefly glancing at the approaching Dulos. His face waxed even more anxious. "If you want to take me back to Earth States on espionage charges ... *fine.* Just don't hand me over to those beasts!"

The Dulos arrived a few moments later, squeezing their massive frames through the arboretum access one at a time. At first sight, Kate recoiled against the wall in fear.

"It's okay, Kate," Michael assured.

Raathe led the Dulos in taking up a wide circle around Tom and Michael. The towering creatures, very much on the prowl, circled while fixing their brooding, intentional stares upon Tom. Tom, his face filling with an insuppressible fear, crept into Michael's shadow and brought his hand close to the pistol at his side.

Raathe glanced at Michael while circling. "Master Galerius no found."

"He escaped the planet," Tom offered rather nervously. "No one knows where he went, including me."

Raathe, still circling the two men with the other Dulos, took in the comment through a long, menacing silence. Trading looks between Tom and Michael, he said, "Trajan. Master son. Dulos deserve justice. Son *pay* for father."

Tom's eyes shot wide, and his insides turned to jelly before the menacing creatures. With a rather nervous laugh, he clumsily un-holstered his pistol and handed it to Michael. "I'm already in his custody … *right, Mike?*"

Watching an awkward exchange between the two men, Raathe glanced at his companions to warn them off. Everyone waited for a response. Yet Michael, still stunned and gazing at the reader and pistol in his hands, said nothing. Neither Tom nor Raathe's prompting shook him from his stupor.

So Tom put his hand on Michael's shoulder once more. In a hushed tone, he said, "I know I deceived you the whole time we were friends. Whatever truth I told you here doesn't nullify that fact. But I *am* sorry."

However, Michael said nothing, and his silence only emboldened the Dulos.

"… And I have no excuse for deceiving Kate after you were gone. My intentions were honorable, I assure you: both of us thought you were dead." A nervous pause followed. "And I'm sorry for what happened between Kate and me. … *I really am.*"

Michael stood even straighter, and all warmth drained from his expression. With such a piercing but quizzical gaze, he looked Tom straight in the eyes. "What … *happened?*"

Tom withered before him.

So Michael looked down at Kate, who gazed up from where she nursed her injuries with such an uncomfortable, self-conscious expression. She fell speechless too. Suffering under his probing stare, she discreetly moved her right hand over her left—but he saw through her veiled attempt to hide the absence of her wedding ring.

His face waxed bitter.

"I'm sorry, Michael!" she pleaded. "We thought—"

"Don't say it, Kate!"

287

"*No! I thought you were dead!*" Tears welled up in her eyes when he turned away from her. "I saw the rock slide … *I wanted to die too!* But I couldn't! I had to go on living without you—on a planet that didn't want me. You've got to understand that." When he continued gazing up at the stars in defiance, she pleaded, "Michael? Can't you understand?"

His brooding persisted.

So with tears streaming down her cheeks, Kate dropped her head, put her hand over her face, and wept.

"Mike," Tom rather choked out, placing his hand on his friend's shoulder once more. "Please understand. If I—"

But Michael swatted the hand and turned away from him again.

"Mike, please!"

Michael Gillen, facing away from everyone, felt a terrible dread wash over him. He was alone in the universe. His heart waxed within his chest, and his insides churned sickeningly. As if drowning in his thoughts, he grasped for any notion that offered reason to the insanity engulfing him. Nothing assuaged his torment. No, instead, he felt himself swallowed up by a *terrible* darkness.

He looked once again toward the man he had known as Tom Andrews. Conflicting emotions raged within him. Tom's countenance—the face of the only loyal friend he had ever known—pleaded for mercy. He wondered how much of Tom Andrews really inhabited the man. He couldn't trust his own instincts, for Tom's existence held the last strand to his own fleeting existence. And handing him over to the Dulos to pay for Aurelian Galerius' crimes? What sense did that make? Tom had transgressed against the people of Earth States, not the Dulos.

But taking in the familiar face, Michael only saw *Katey* lying in Tom's arms in an intimate moment, pouring her heart out to him—giving herself to him freely. And for that one reason alone, he burned with anger! Everything that had gone wrong incarnated itself upon the man.

Michael looked down at the pistol and then back at Tom. Turning to leave, he threw the pistol to Raathe and tucked the reader into his pocket. He glanced at Tom with such contempt. "I don't know this man."

Tom's jaw dropped in shear terror, and his face drained of all color. He grasped at Michael's arm, desperate to keep his friend between him and the Dulos—but Michael broke through and pushed his way out of the circle.

"Mike! Please don't do this!" Tom pleaded from inside the circle of angry Dulos.

Michael knelt, took Kate into his arms, and picked her up. Despite Michael's intentional indifference, Tom kept his wide-eyed gaze on him the whole time to plead—but in fear of the Dulos encircling him too. With one last, telling glance to Raathe, Michael turned toward the door and carried Kate from the arboretum.

Finally alone with Tom Andrews, the Dulos tightened their circle around him. In a panic, Tom shrank back from them—though he had nowhere to go.

Michael made his way onto the suspended walkway with Kate in his arms. He listened to Tom crying out to him from behind, each plea growing more desperate. The sounds of the Dulos striking Tom—a small taste of the terrible things to come—reached his ears. The dreadful scene earlier that evening of the taskmaster's execution flooded his mind; Michael knew the Dulos would not be as gracious with the son of Aurelian Galerius. He wanted to stop up his ears, for the tormented sounds grew too painful to listen.

Yet he did not look back.

The sounds of torture grew more harried. Not even halfway across the walkway, the Dulos began making sport of Tom.

From where she hid cradled in Michael's arms with her legs out to one side, Kate held on to him with abandon. She watched the morbid spectacle over his shoulder—thankful for the increasing distance between her and the arboretum. Her face churned with so many conflicting emotions, though pity for Tom abounded most of all: The execution was inhumane. The blows inflicted upon him grew more brutal, until Tom's clothing became drenched in his own blood; she could no longer bear to watch. So Kate buried her face in the crook of Michael's neck, stopping up her ears with her hands against the gruesome sounds of Tom's screaming.

Tears filled her eyes. *"I'm sorry, Michael ... I'm so sorry."*

Carrying her across the bridge, Michael strained to flee the dreadful screams clawing at him from behind. The Dulos' laughter intermingled morbidly with Tom's tortured cries for mercy. Tom Andrews was dying a violent death, and Michael shuddered at the many emotions washing over him. Kate still had her face buried in the crook of his neck; her hands remained over her ears. So he surrendered to the strong emotions, letting the tears well up in his eyes while struggling to cross the enclosed walkway.

Eventually, he carried Kate across the threshold into the main palace. However, the tortured cries in the distance persisted. So without breaking stride, Michael disappeared with Kate in his arms down the adjacent corridor.

The deserted palace area near the arboretum echoed with the ear curdling sounds of Tom Andrews dying. The morbid cries would persist for quite some time. No one, save the Dulos carrying out the execution, would hear them. The execution would be brutal, a death far more grotesque and painful that of a simple taskmaster. Whether intended or not, Tom Andrews—*Trajan Aurelius*—had taken his father's place in history.

CHAPTER TWENTY FOUR

Reunions

Kara Ricci, her eyes closed, awoke from unconsciousness into a surreal calm. A sea of blackness enveloped her—as did incredible and indescribable warmth. She lay in space as if floating, her frail body free of the chains that had bound her for so long. The incendiaries intended to accomplish her death were gone too. Nothing existed outside the warmth soaking into her frame.

She savored the unexpected sensation—until her mouth suddenly filled with cold water. Though instinctively swallowing, she choked a bit, causing some of the water to run down the side of her face.

Kara opened her eyes and beheld a myriad of stars draping the cold night sky. Branches overhead and the undergrowth rising up over her obscured much of the view—but Emir Kern knelt over her, holding a canteen to her mouth and lifting her head up with his other hand.

"Welcome back," he greeted with much concern.

With her mind still in a fog, she looked around. The indescribable warmth surrounding her was really Emir's field sleeping bag cocooning her shivering frame. The device, inflated for comfort and its heating element set on maximum, reflected the surrounding vegetation for camouflage. Also, she was dressed in his Covert uniform, which boasted several bloodstains. Emir wore an Europan lieutenants' uniform—also stained with blood and one sleeve cut off at the forearm. "Am I dead?"

"I hope not," Emir quipped, busying himself with tending to her. "This place sure isn't heaven."

"Then where am I?"

"In the woods just west of where I found you. The burning incendiaries will attract attention. We need to leave as soon as I know you're okay."

She noticed the faint traces of flickering firelight against his face.

At his insistence, she received another mouthful of water from the canteen—and then several more when her eyes pleaded for more. She stared up at the ghostly apparition, whose face betrayed his worry over her condition. When she started to sit up—

"Stay down."

However, Kara waved off his hand trying to ease her down. "I'm okay." After propping herself up against a small tree behind her—her head rather spinning at the effort—she took the canteen. "Why am I wearing your uniform?"

"Did you want the Europan's?"

"Absolutely not."

"I didn't think so. I need the Europan uniform anyway. There are goons in these woods. If we happen upon any, I want them to think you're my prisoner." He continued securing his pack as she drank from the canteen. "I've got food and more medicine. You can have whatever you need once we're away from this place." When he looked up at her sitting against the tree, he ignored her unsettled gaze. "What's your medical diagnosis?"

"*How are you alive?*"

"Kara, I need a medical diagnosis here." When she just stared at him with that troubled look, he pressed, "Remember? I'm on the *other side* of the equation."

Her eyes welled up, and her face rather twisted. "*I saw you die.*"

"You saw *me* killing the *Europan lieu*—"

"*No … I killed you with a dagger. … They made me do it.*"

Emir paused in stunned silence and searched her tormented face. Suppressing his dread over whatever the Europans had done to her, he took her by the thick of her arms and looked into her eyes. "Kara, you're here with me now. I won't let anything bad happen to you."

She took in his reassurance for the longest time, but her eyes welled up. "You *left* me at the ambush site—because you thought I stole your chance to kill Galerius. *You left me.*"

"I'm sorry."

"You left me, Emir."

Taking in her wounded gaze, he bowed his head. But then he looked up at her and took her face in his hands. Looking into her churning eyes, he radiated a grave contrition. "I'm sorry for what I did—I was sorry when I did it. I won't ever leave you again, I promise." When her eyes softened, he pressed, "I love you, Kara, and I'll walk through fire to make sure nothing ever happens to you again."

Kara basked in the sentiment. She took in with a deep fondness how he moved about haltingly against his many injuries. Ugly bruises adorned his face, and his lower lip and nose still bled. The bloodstains on his uniform that she wore came to mind—the blood he had shed to secure her rescue. He was a mess, yet his face was the most beautiful sight she had ever seen. Her eyes welled up once more. "I love you too."

Still holding her face in his hands, Emir smiled and kissed her.

The grassy clearing near the former Europan Royal Palace lay bathed in shimmering firelight. With the hostilities of the rebellion at an end, peace had once again returned to Sco-II.

A number of Dulos not securing the settlement had gathered throughout the clearing, deeply subdued by the late hour. Sitting on the cold ground in small groups, they conversed quietly amongst themselves around a central fire. Tales of the harrowing events of the previous hours rose into the air, while everyone took a turn feeding wood to the fire.

Michael Gillen, holding the reader Tom Andrews had given him and lost in thought, reclined against a tree near the blaze. The chilly night air had set into him, and the cold, rocky ground underneath the tree pressed at his aching muscles. Yet just like the Dulos, he relished the serenity of the remote spot.

Despite his exhaustion, he couldn't sleep. He had experienced the worst night of his entire life: In a single day, he had lost everything that defined his purpose. Instead, the night had swallowed him up, and he was no more than a cold, empty shell.

Kate Gillen sat on the ground much closer to the fire—and at an intentional distance. With her knees drawn in and her arms folded around her legs, she nestled her chin between her kneecaps and stared into the fire. A medical brace adorned her left leg, while white bandages peeked through the hole burnt into the lower part of her shirt.

The entire time, she kept Michael in her peripheral vision.

The young couple had sat at a distance since arriving in the clearing much earlier. The reunion had turned awkward and bitter, far from the reunion Michael had longed for. Neither had spoken a word to the other since leaving the palace.

Despite his subdued demeanor, Michael was beside himself. The terrible darkness that had overshadowed him in the arboretum persisted. Images of Tom Andrews seducing Kate tormented him. Though he tried expelling the dreadful thoughts from his mind, the images lingered. He dared not even look at her, lest the imagery grow stronger. And he wondered if he could ever look at her the same way again.

More than ever, he filled with regret over everything that had happened at the failed ambush long ago. Had he not lost his wits, Kate would have never fallen prey to Tom Andrews' seduction. Perhaps none of those other bad things would have happened either. Yes, her indiscretion was a bitter reminder of his failure as mission commander.

And yet, what mission? He laughed a cynical laugh at himself. No, the mission to capture Aurelian Galerius was just one in a string of lies fabricated by President James Mitchell.

Shifting himself against the tree in a vain attempt to soothe his aching back, Michael stared at the reader in his hand. Though the device was deactivated, he rehearsed the information it had conveyed to him earlier.

Tom had spoken truthfully: He would have never believed such terrible things without seeing the evidence. Yet the reader contained everything: records of Ben Morris developing Slipstream technology, records of the secret agreement James Mitchell had crafted with Aurelian

Galerius over his exile, correspondence proving James Mitchell's intent to deceive Mos Thieren, the *Weightless*, and the other Allied leaders; James Mitchell's illegal activities to cover up the real intentions for the mission—including Ben Morris' assassination orders.

And worse, the reader also contained evidence implicating the President in all the other terrible things that had happened to Terrae Solaris after the *Endurance*'s departure ten years earlier—things Michael dared not even ponder.

He looked around the darkened grounds, wondering if he could ever regard Sco-II as his home. He had nowhere to go—not with what he knew. No, the only home he had ever known was gone.

But Sco-II wasn't his home either.

So the distraught, young man sat there, ill at ease and unsure of which misfortune to wallow in.

Thoughts of the coming day washed over him. He had much work to do, work that would take him completely out of his element: ensuring the security of the settlement from hostilities by Europan factions, overseeing the clean-up of the devastation left from the rebellion, destroying the fleet of three thousand warships so they never threatened Terrae Solaris again, granting the Dulos sovereignty while keeping them from killing or enslaving the Europans, and establishing a provisional government between the Dulos and Europans.

Somehow, fate had appointed him de facto ruler over the planet—albeit a very fleeting responsibility. Michael bristled at the chaos such an upcoming challenge presented, and he wondered how anyone could thrive under such difficult circumstances.

Suddenly, a grand idea flooded his mind.

At first, the notion appeared in his thoughts as merely wishful thinking. Yet it grew within him—faster than he could restrain it. The more he pondered the crazy idea, the more all the intricacies of such a complex plan fell into place, as if some force were dictating his thoughts.

Yet that terrible darkness that had latched on to him in the arboretum fed off the notion—and swelled within him all the more. Emir Kern's *troublemaker* accusations mocked him too—or affirmed what he already knew. Perhaps he *was* a troublemaker. Whatever the notion sparked within him only grew more powerful the more he thought about it. What a possibility! What an opportunity! What danger—but more than worth the risk.

He wanted to pick up his communicator and call Emir Kern right then. But the more the wondrous thoughts race through his mind like untamed electricity, the more Michael realized that his new purpose in life could wait until daylight.